You can escap[e]
With a drink.
But no one can escape Shiva.

It travels relentlessly toward Earth, a great column hundreds of kilometers tall, an incandescent shaft, rainbowed and haloed, lighting the entire ocean floor from shore to shore, vaporizing the Pacific Ocean. Anyone closer than three thousand miles will turn to pulverized bone. It will last the space of two heartbeats.

In the largest space operation in history, two teams are launched into orbit: the Alpha Team, armed with a 400-megaton bomb, and the Omega Team, armed with 20-megaton bombs. Each team member is one of the world's finest astronauts or cosmonauts. American, Russian, Mexican, Japanese, Italian. White and black. Men and women. But there has been a critical slip-up.

One of them is a madman.

Gregory Benford, a Professor of Physics at the University of California, Irvine, is the author of four science fiction novels, and a Nebula Award winner.

William Rotsler, photographer, filmmaker, sculptor, and winner of two Hugo awards for his drawings, is the author of several novels.

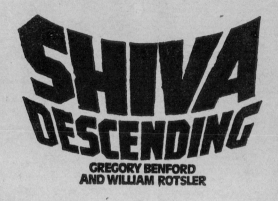

SHIVA DESCENDING

GREGORY BENFORD
AND WILLIAM ROTSLER

AVON
PUBLISHERS OF BARD, CAMELOT AND DISCUS BOOKS

SHIVA DESCENDING is an original publication of
Avon Books.
This work has never before appeared in book form.

AVON BOOKS
A division of
The Hearst Corporation
959 Eighth Avenue
New York, New York 10019

First Avon Printing, March, 1980

AVON TRADEMARK REG. U.S. PAT. OFF. AND IN
OTHER COUNTRIES, MARCA REGISTRADA, HECHO EN
U.S.A.

Printed in the U.S.A.

It had traveled through the silent void for countless millennia, since the formation of the solar system. A gray and black lump, it was well in advance and to the side of the rest of the hurtling swarm, a forerunner of what was to come. The irregular mass of iron and rock entered the outer atmosphere somewhere over eastern Iran, quickly heating up to become a flaming streak across the tranquil summer evening.

It had companions—specks and chunks that briefly lit up in long fiery trails before they burned out, or were deflected by the thickening blanket of air, spinning back out into space to begin a new path. But the big one flamed on, deeper and deeper, angling downward.

The air slowed it, but it was still traveling at a tremendous velocity when it struck the earth at Biskra, near the Tunisian border. In an instant the meteor obliterated the rambling Arabian town. Where forty-six thousand people had lived moments before there was only smoke, a steaming crater whose bottom was a bubbling pool of sand and rock turned into lava, and death. In the suburbs, along the roads and trails, lay blackened bodies, children and animals and twisted burned things. Every building was leveled. Sand dunes were fused to molten glass or blown away to the bedrock. Brick, flesh, machines, dolls, the mosque, animals, everything: molten, vaporized, burned.

The immense ball of orange flame that was the death knell of Biskra was seen by a crop analyzer on Space Station Three. She stared, blinked, then reached for the

1

emergency microphone. Earth had been struck by the largest meteor in modern times.

Zakir Shastri was normally calm, even placid, as befitted an astronomer, whose chief asset was patience. But now he bit nervously on his full lower lip, his dark eyes intent upon the words and numbers building in glowing lines upon the screen before him. He took a deep breath and exhaled it in a sigh. He glanced away from the phosphor dots, out the side port. Earth swung into view. Across the nightside, dotted with smudges of light, something suddenly scratched a long streak of orange light. Then it vanished. Soon, another. Then two dimmer ones. He sighed, closed his eyes to blank out the sight, and chewed nervously on his lip.

The Indian astronomer sat strapped into a chair bolted to the platform. He was at the sighting focus of the main telescope, where he could "eyeball" the precise fix he wanted. This was the place where he felt most at peace in the entire Orbital Astronomical Observatory. It was not vastly different from the famous cage at Palomar, where generations of astronomers had labored through the years in the biting cold of the California mountains. Now, pollution of the seeing conditions by the billion lights of the megalopolis below made Palomar a risky site for some kinds of observations, particularly for taking spectra of dim objects. And, of course, Palomar was the prime example of the basic limitation of all Earth-based telescopes: precision of resolution. Visitors to Palomar and other great observatories always thought the point of building such a giant telescope was to see more detail. In fact, Palomar couldn't "see" any better than a twenty-centimeter backyard telescope. The rippling air above any telescope scrambled light waves coming in, erasing any detail smaller than about a half-second of arc. Telescopes bigger than twenty centimeters were just buckets for catching more light; they couldn't make out any more detail than their smaller brethren. Only by putting telescopes in orbit could astronomers see any better. So the eighty-centimeter tube directly in front of Shastri represented a new dimension in peering at the universe. Without the obscuring blanket of air, this telescope could see fine features in the optical, ultraviolet, and infrared ranges. It would, in time, open a universe in a way the great Hubble could never have dreamed.

The lean astronomer bent over the eyepiece. Despite all the machinery and computers, sighting on a distant fleck of light was best done by the human eye and hand. He peered intently through the prime eyepiece, his long dark fingers on the knobs.

There: a muzzy patch of light. Dust and gas and pebbles. It was noticeably dimmer than the last time he looked. Soon the image would fade into the background. At the center of the pale white cloud was a pinpoint of light. The source of all the debris around it. An ancient rock, chipped over the aeons by small collisions. Shastri watched it drift sideways in the focus, declination increasing.

He estimated the arc width and did the numbers in his head. His face contorted in a brief, bitter grimace.

Then he caught the dim dot, calibrated it, and set the exposure time electronically. A deep plate this time, to resolve as much structure as possible in the cloud. He thumbed the proper button and sat back. He had only to wait.

Later he could measure the plate, for precision. But for the moment the computer programs would reduce the data from them, on on-line tracking. He switched on the display again and watched the figures building on the screen in long luminous lines. He wiped his palms on the thighs of his gray jumper. Once again he checked the computations, laboring through each step to be certain, the greenish screen light and the dim red bulbs making his face strange.

Shastri sat back, his face grave. Much of the life had gone out of his expression.

After a little while, he unshielded the side port and gazed out. The telescope's spherical housing was attached to one end of the three-hundred-meter-long Orbital Astronomical Observatory, commonly called Station Three. The sphere containing the telescope counterrotated against the gravity spin of the station itself. Around Shastri was the tubular bulk of the main optical telescope, dimly lit in red, and on the platform was the computer support system that controlled it.

Shastri shifted beneath the white strap that held him to the aluminum chair, glanced again at the figures building on the screen in long luminous lines, and wiped his palms on the thighs of his gray jumper. Impatiently Shastri turned and studied the readout screen from Station Six.

A third away around the same Earth orbit was Six, with its immense five-kilometer radio telescope. Radio astronomy, he thought, was where all the action was these days. But he knew if he really needed it, one call would enlist that giant ear/eye.

Both Stations were in Band Five, the outer Terran orbit. Both were awkward, bulbous objects, with spheres on protruding columns, radio discs, telemetry masts and landing docks sticking out at what seemed like random angles. Station Three had accreted over the years, growing, adding, but rarely subtracting. Shastri recalled his surprise at finding, deep within the complex, the Apollo tank which had been the foundation rock upon which the entire complex had been constructed. It was now used only for luggage storage.

Shastri shifted his hooded eyes at the dull boom of an airlock opening. He heard the clatter of someone moving awkwardly into the weightless environment of the observatory sphere. In a few moments Fakhruddin Radhakrishnan, Shastri's lean and bearded young assistant, came wriggling through the tube passage. His eyes were wide and concerned, dark with dread. His white turban was hastily wrapped, its loose end floating in the air. He scrambled onto the platform and secured the wandering cloth absently as he asked, "Is . . . is it true?"

Shastri indicated the large screen which was still printing out figures. "Starsearch is comparing the photographs now, and eliminating all the known and logged asteroids." Radhakrishnan pulled himself hand over hand to the console, twisted into a seat, and fastened the restraining strap. Then he peered anxiously at the screen.

"You backtracked on the trajectory?"

Shastri nodded. "Luckily it showed on a plate here, and at the Planetary Studies' scope at Six. It's an Apollo object. What it's doing in this area is . . ." He stopped talking when the printing ceased coming on the screen. He leaned forward, muttering as he read the information.

"Ah, elliptical orbit . . . the long axis—the semimajor axis—of um, only zero point eighty-eight . . . um . . . nearest approach to the sun is zero point three astronomical

4

units." Shastri sat back with a grunt, his eyes staring moodily at the screen.

Radhakrishnan pointed with a thin brown finger. "The orbit is tilted to the ecliptic plane." He looked at Shastri. "Most of the Apollo asteroids stay efficiently away from the orbits of the inner planes, don't they?"

Shastri nodded, his face shadowed. "Yes. Any other orbit and . . . well, most of them would have hit Mars and Venus—or Earth—long ago. And probably did."

Radhakrishnan frowned, staring at the screen. "The Apollo asteroids we know cross the ecliptic plane only at some intermediate point between the Earth and the sun, don't they?"

Shastri nodded, his lips drawn down. "Then . . ." Radhakrishnan swallowed hard, his eyes blinking as they stared at Shastri. "Then the swarm has been flattening its orbit, bit by bit . . . drawing closer to Earth as it . . . as it turns on its outer orbit, before . . . before returning toward the sun?"

Shastri did not answer. His fingers shifted the information on the screen into storage and then pecked out another set of instructions. The screen lit up with a computer simulation of the sun, the orbit of Earth, the moon, and the known Apollo objects. Then he added the orbits of the eccentric asteroids: Hildalgo, Adonis, Amor, Eros, Ceres, and Apollo. Then Hermes, Pallas, Juno, and Vesta.

"Just to be safe," Shastri murmured, adding tiny Hygeia, Eunomia, Psyche, Davida, Hebe, and Iris. Then other, still smaller "tagged" asteroids were put into the mix. The screen was a mass of elliptical ovals. Shastri hesitated, sighed. Then he took what was known of the orbit of the asteroid that had extinguished the Tunisian town and put it into the system. The glowing line, red against the white of the earlier computations, built up into the orbit of the meteor that had struck Earth. Quite plainly they saw the orbit flattening, tilting down into the ecliptic, coming closer and closer to the orbit of Earth.

Neither man said anything. Shastri punched out more information, to freshen his memory of the Apollo objects. The words and figures rippled quickly across the screen.

The first asteroid found with a semimajor axis and period less than Earth was 1976AA. Such objects are difficult to find because they are relatively faint, fast-moving objects. The standard search plan by Earth observatories had been to compare a series of standard sky shots, distributed along the plane of the ecliptic and extending to moderate longitudes north of the ecliptic. Planet-crossing objects can be recognized because they leave streaks on the twenty-minute exposures. Shorter exposure pinpointed the object precisely. The space observatories used a very similar method, but with clearer, brighter photos and with computerized comparisons. But in either case they had to be fast, as the objects quickly became lost in the star field.

"Why haven't we seen this swarm before?" Radhakrishnan blinked nervously, his hands crabbing fitfully across the control deck.

Shastri shrugged. "Most of the observation time has been directed outward, toward the outer planets, toward the stars. That's where we all thought the big payoff would be." He shrugged again and inhaled deeply. "We played percentages. Besides, a great deal of the time this asteroid has been near the sun, from our angle, or on the other side. We *did* see it before, only we didn't know what it was."

The youth's head snapped up. "Of course! Eleven months ago! That summer, all those meteorites!" He blinked rapidly, wet his lips. "And twenty-two months ago, when we first activated this station, all those—" He stopped abruptly, and the two men stared at each other.

"Elliptical orbit," Shastri said. "No telling how long it has taken to get here again."

"Again?"

Shastri nodded. "The Arizona crater, many of the bays in Canada—all could have been the result of earlier passes by this swarm."

Radhakrishnan licked his lips, his eyes flicking toward the slit of sky. "But . . . but there's so much territory, such a vast volume . . . a few asteroids . . ."

"It's definitely a swarm," Shastri said. "With a diameter twice that of Earth." The young astronomer stared brightly at his superior, his mouth working soundlessly.

"I'll double- and triple-check," Shastri sighed, "but . . ." His eyes went to those of the younger man. There was a terrible sadness in them. "There is an asteroid in the center. A big one. More than two kilometers across.

It's . . ." His mouth moved for a moment, but he seemed to have lost the connection.

After a moment his hand reached out. He recalled the orbit projections to the screen before them. He punched in instructions and the long ellipse stretched out, away from Earth. "The fixes on position and velocity I've gotten enable us to make a prediction. Watch while I run it forward in time."

The asteroid's ellipse arced around the sun and then back out. Meanwhile, Earth moved serenely through its nearly circular orbit, a yellow bead on a string. The dot swept most of the way around the circle while the asteroid's ellipse cut swiftly out from the sun's vicinity. Earth curved to meet it. The two points met.

"Collision," Radhakrishnan murmured.

"We will have to check this," Shastri said heavily. "But the closeness of the pass this time . . ." He shrugged.

In the silence Radhakrishnan studied his superior. He looked tired, so changed from the energetic man he knew. He changed the subject. "What do you intend to name it?"

"Name?" Shastri frowned. "Ah, yes." To the discoverer was given that honor. "I see." He stared at the screen, frozen at that moment of time when the two beads of light met.

Shastri nodded. "I name it . . . Shiva. Shiva, the Destroyer."

They all rose when the President of the United States came in.

"Sit, sit," he said brusquely, waving them down. He strode to the center of the lozenge-shaped table without any of the hand-shaking or camaraderie that was usually a part of John Caleb Knowles' public entrances. Several politicians exchanged glances, but none of them gave much away with their faces.

Knowles sat down, a tall, gray-haired man with a seamed, honest face. Myron Murray, his Special Assistant, took a chair behind him, a special bulky one with a computer terminal. Knowles's dark blue eyes swept around the table, gathering attention but not specifically acknowledging any of the generals, admirals, Secretaries, or other officials. He looked down at the closed folio on the table before him, resting under his hand, with the bright red diagonal markings of secrecy printed across its manila cover.

The President looked up and swung his head toward Charles Bradshaw, the operational head of NASA. Bradshaw, a thickset blondish man with his hair trimmed unstylishly short, sat somewhat nervously at the far end of the table, plainly uncertain and a little fearful at to why he had been so suddenly rushed to this Cabinet-level meeting.

Knowles assessed him in one swift look, his mind going over the dossier he had scanned just before leaving the Oval Office. It was a Top Secret Clearance dossier, Bradshaw's complete record from birth to yesterday, but John Caleb Knowles knew that what appeared on paper was never the whole man. A lot would depend on this one man, perhaps everything. Knowles could not afford a mistake in judgment, nor could mankind.

"Mister Bradshaw, I'm glad you could join us," the President said. Bradshaw nodded and muttered something inaudible. Being singled out made him even more nervous. Launchpads and control rooms didn't make him nervous. He was at home in computer complexes and welding shops. Engineering and personnel problems didn't bother him, but politicians like this did. He was awkwardly aware that more than one pair of eyes were assessing him in quick, penetrating glances.

"Ladies and gentlemen," the President said in his all-too-well-known voice, "we have a problem of some magnitude. Unless we solve it, it may be our *last* problem. I do not believe I am exaggerating." The chief executive looked back at Myron Murray. "Ready?"

"Yes, sir." Murray's fingers stabbed at a stud of his terminal. A stylized American eagle mural at one end of the room slid up, revealing a screen, and the room lights automatically dimmed.

The picture that appeared was static—a space shot, with a sprinkling of stars. A white circle appeared, enclosing a few tiny dots. "This is the problem," Murray said. "A meteor swarm, code-named Shiva. It is moving away now, but the disasters we have felt were from the periphery of the group." There was a murmur, but it died quickly. "It will return in eleven months, approximately, and this time—"

He covered a momentary pause by replacing the opti-

cal shot with a radar-generated computer mosaic, which was clearer. He followed this with computer animation, showing the elliptical path of the swarm and the orbit of Earth. They met. No one said anything.

"Thank you, Myron," the President said. The lights came up and the American eagle slid soundlessly back into position.

Knowles gathered the eyes again. "I don't need to tell you this is a bastard. Either we fix it the first time or we're dead." He gestured around vaguely. "Oh, maybe *we're* alive . . . maybe . . . in some silo or Air Force underground hard base. But for how long? And what shall we govern? Who will we lead?" He shook his head, which was lowered, bull-like and fierce. "No, we *must* destroy this . . . this Shiva, this space rock."

"More than a rock, Mister President," Myron Murray reminded him quietly. "It's a mountain."

"Yes, of course. But first I must determine in my own mind whether this is hokum or not. Doctor Kinney, is there any possibility that this is all a scare?" President Knowles slapped his hand down atop the papers before him.

The balding, heavy man down the table leaned forward. "There is *always* the chance that, at this range, there is some miscalculation, but . . ." He spread his hands. "At this point I do not think so. Shiva will miss us on *this* pass . . . we are only getting the outer meteors in the swarm. But it will certainly strike us on the *next* orbit. Which, um, is approximately eleven months from now."

There was a murmur and heads bent to confer. The President rapped with his knuckles on the table. "Gentlemen. Ladies. Doctor, you are saying that a collision is inevitable."

"Unless something is done to deflect or destroy the asteroid, yes. Even then . . . well, Cal Tech, MIT, the Thales Center in Boston, several independent . . . well . . . they all agree, sir. Within about ten percent, that is. The *swarm* will strike Earth and inflict severe damage . . . but if this central asteroid, this Shiva, hits . . ." He blew out his breath and made a gesture of fatalistic acceptance.

Caleb Knowles turned his head toward Chuck Bradshaw. "Mister Bradshaw, as head of the National Aeronautics and Space Administration it would seem to me that whatever we do will fall within your venue. Therefore, Chuck, I am naming you head of an emergency team." Knowles looked over his shoulder at Myron Murray. "Myron, find the right terminology, laws, presidential powers, and so on. I want it understood by *everyone* . . ." He looked around the table again, his voice firm, with that edge of danger that had terrified many an opponent, "By *everyone*, that Chuck Bradshaw gets whatever he wants." Knowles looked at Senator Oren Mathison, the majority leader, and then at Congressman Powell Hopkins, Speaker of the House. "I want action on this. No debates, no partisan crap, just action. Get the money, get things moving, and *do it!*"

"Yes, Mister President," the two politicians said together, then looked at each other questioningly.

"Chuck . . ."

"Yes, sir?"

"Pick your team and pick it fast. Whoever you want. Anywhere in the world. We'll arrange it. British, Russian, Chinese, anyone. If you need a Bulgarian midget with green hair, we'll find you one." His gaze moved around to Willard Woods, Director of the Central Intelligence Agency. "Full cooperation, Will. And fast cooperation."

"Yes, sir, of course."

"Carte banche and top speed, people," Caleb Knowles said. There were nods and murmurs all around. "And no interservice squabbles, either," he said, glaring at the uniformed men. "We have one shot at this. No more. No time for anything else. No foot dragging, no but-they're-Russians-so-we-can't-cooperate nonsense. If you don't realize that, I'll get people who do."

Gordon Brown, the Director of the FBI, spoke up in his dry, gravelly voice. "How public will this be allowed to be, Mister President?"

John Caleb Knowles grimaced. "I know, Gordy, I know. Panic, riots, the works. Then charges of cover-up if we do keep it quiet." He shrugged, then grimaced again, but this time from the terrible burning in his stomach and the involuntary cramping of his bowels. This was getting to him worse than election night nerves, he thought. "Well, keep it under wraps as long as possible, then I'll go on the tube and give 'em a straight-from-the-shoulder talk. But I'll need something definite to give them. A progress report. What we're doing about it and so on."

"What if the Russians spill it first?" a general muttered aloud.

The President swung around in his chair and looked at Gilbert McNellis, the Secretary of State. "When do I talk to Kalinin?"

The diplomat glanced at his watch. "In about fifteen minutes, sir. He was unavailable until—"

"Bull waste, Gil. He wanted to check everything out. Call up the Russian team at the Observatory and so on. What about Chairman Wu?"

"Right after, sir."

Knowles nodded and stood up. There was scraping of chairs and clearing of throats. The President looked at the table top for a moment, his face softening from the hard facade of moments before, then he raised his head, snapping back. "Gentlemen. Ladies. I am certain you will do your best. But if you don't . . . heads will roll. Be right the *first* time and don't take forever to decide. Forget all that bureaucratic bull waste you've grown to know and love . . . and use. This is the sudden-death play-off."

He left the room in silence and those standing around felt weak and uncertain. Then a four-star Air Force general looked down the table at Chuck Bradshaw.

"Mister Bradshaw, would you appreciate suggestions from us for personnel or action . . . or will you handle this yourself?"

All eyes went to Bradshaw, who had to force his clenched hands apart. "I . . . I will name the basic team this afternoon. I would appreciate Air Force transportation for everyone, to Houston, as soon as possible."

The Secretary of Defense said in his high-pitched Vermont accent, "Ayuh, and you'll need quarters, supply, logistical backup . . ."

Suddenly there were a dozen voices, each adding to the din, each making suggestions. After a few dazed moments Chuck Bradshaw stood up. "Gentlemen! Ladies!" The voices died down and Chuck heaved a sigh of relief. "Thank you all, but . . . I'll call upon you and your services as we need them. I'd appreciate a few minutes with the Joint Chiefs, then with Secretary Rogers." He raised his hands as more people started to speak. His voice grew harder and colder.

"I'll decide . . . and I will let each of you know. General McGahan, I will appreciate full global Signal Corps cooperation and open access to the satellites." The officer nodded briskly.

"Thank you, everyone, I'll get back to you," Chuck said.

President Knowles was thinking about his dead wife, Catherine. For the first time he was glad she was not here to see this global trauma. Or what is happening to me, he thought. I feel as though I'm crumbling from the inside out, like some termite-infested house. I put up a good front, but all politicians do that automatically. But *inside*, where I really live, it's getting to be hollow.

"Ready, sir?" Myron Murray gestured to Giorgi Sviatopolk, sitting nervously at one side of the dark Lincoln desk. He wore earphones and his broad fingers touched a blank pad before him.

Knowles nodded slowly. He looked around the room as if it were his first time there. It was an important room; anyone in it was an important person. History had been made here.

"Sir?"

Knowles looked at Murray. "You know, Myron, you're a good man. The perfect Number Two."

"Sir, the Vice-President is number two."

Knowles permitted himself a faint smile. "On paper, Myron, only on paper. *You're* Number Two, and damn good at it."

"Thank you, sir, but the premier . . ."

Knowles waved his hand to indicate a wait. "How long has it been, Myron?"

"Sir?"

"Since we got together? Sixteen, eighteen years?"

"Almost nineteen, Mister President. Since your second campaign for Congress."

"You happy here, Myron? Doing this job? Ever want to sit here yourself?"

A look of distaste and surprise appeared on Murray's well-trained face. "No, sir." The idea appalled him. He knew what he was good at, and had no fatal ambitions. He pitied those he saw every day who ate their hearts out

12

because they were not closer to the sun god . . . or weren't the sun god themselves. That was mental cancer. He took great pride in what he did and how well he did it, but it was a secret pride. He didn't think it showed. "Sir, the premier?"

"Oh, yes, of course." He turned to the interpreter with a soft smile. "Been reading up on this Kalinin, have you?"

"Yes, sir. The full CIA file."

Knowles smiled wryly. "*No* one reads the *full* CIA file on *anyone.* Maybe not even me. Tough bastard, is he?"

Sviatropolk nodded, his face gloomy. "Yes, sir. Survived the sweep after Stalin's death in '53. Tagged along with Khrushchev and survived his rise and fall. Really got going under Brezhnev, rose to First General Assistant of the Central Committee in the last days, then under—"

"Yes, yes," the President said impatiently, "I've read the file, too. Yaroslav Kalinin is a survivor. I'm counting on that. He'll see it is to his country's interest that they cooperate, if only to prevent us from getting all the credit if we succeed."

The dark-haired interpreter paled. "*If,* sir—?"

"When, *when.* He'll cooperate just as soon as we lay it all out for him. That Lenin Institute of theirs must know everything we know by now."

Myron Murray held up the red handset, his fingers holding down the disconnect. Caleb Knowles walked over, sat down, ran his tongue over his teeth, then grinned at Giorgi Sviatopolk. "Do you know your opposite number, too?"

Sviatopolk managed a weak smile. "Yes, sir. Not personally, but well enough through the uh, you know, the reports."

Knowles sank back. "And he knows you. They know me. I know them . . . and together we know nothing. Um, give me that." He took the handset and barked into the line, "The President of the United States here!"

In Moscow Yaroslav Kalinin handed the handset to Nikolai Menshikov, who cradled it carefully. The heavy-bodied premier looked at his interpreter with a fierce, searching stare. "Well, Comrade Petlyura?"

The young woman cleared her throat and put her fingers nervously to her chin. "Comrade Kalinin . . . I believe him."

Yaroslav waved his thick-fingered hand, the rough fabric of his severely plain uniform rasping in the quiet room. "The engineers will decide that when they have analyzed his voice stress, and when they are able to work on the data they are sending. Any other reasons?"

Petlyura thought a moment, her eyes on the pad before her, covered with neatly printed notes and more hastily scrawled lines shown to Kalinin during the conversation. "He is *aware* that we will think so. He is *aware* that there is a propaganda victory of incredible magnitude to be obtained. Even big enough to be shared. But . . ."

"But I think he is genuinely, realistically concerned." The young woman inclined her head toward the blue-covered report at the other end of the table. "If the Institute report is correct . . . we *must* cooperate." She raised her eyes and looked steadily into the harsh, eagle-like glare of the General Secretary.

After a moment Kalinin nodded and the interpreter breathed out. "I think so, too. But we must always be aware that there are ways to turn certain events to our advantage." His dark eyes moved to Nikolai Menshikov. "I want stepped-up intelligence reports. I want predictions on *their* plans and I want plans of our *own*." As Menshikov nodded, Kalinin added, "And I want two sets of basic approaches to *after*."

"After, sir?"

"After they—or we—stop this Shiva and after . . . if they don't."

Menshikov sighed. "Is there any point . . . if they don't?"

Kalinin glared at him and the younger man looked distressed. "There is *always* a point, comrade. You must look beyond the obvious . . . and beyond what is beyond."

United Airlines flight 235 arrived in the Cleveland vicinity slightly early, helped by a tailwind out of the prairie states. The big jet was in its assigned flight path and the pilot was taking it easy, thinking about a steak and a stewardess on an American Airline flight that was almost certain to arrive at about the same time.

The pilot banked slightly toward the distant glow that was Cleveland, his flying sense on automatic, with regular scans of the control panels. She was a leggy blonde who didn't mind his being married at all. The cloud cover was slight. He saw a line out of the corner of his eye and turned his head.

The thin orange line high in the sky suddenly grew a ball of yellow flame at its tip. Then he could see nothing more; a white glare filled the cabin.

The copilot, who had been looking down at a clipboard checklist, looked up, startled. He missed the flash of light. Through the windscreen he saw a luminous yellow egg sitting on the distant dark horizon. A growing egg. Billowing upward. Opening . . .

The blast threw their heads back into the neck braces. Their ears roared. The engineer screamed. The huge jet veered as though slapped by a giant hand. The pilot struggled to right the plane, swearing, muscles tense. A quick glance showed him they had lost four hundred meters of altitude.

Ahead, the egg faded to orange.

The pilot shook his head, trying to clear it. The copilot plucked at his arm, his lips moving, gesturing at the spreading reddish haze before them. The pilot's mouth sagged open. He was deaf.

Caleb Knowles left his hand resting on the red phone. He stared at the liver spots that mottled his hand and sighed, shortly, almost sharply. He listened to a question-and-answer session between Murray and Sviatopolk with only a part of his attention.

It had been a long time, he was thinking. A very long time. Even before Catherine died, it had been a long time. He'd been faithful, even though he'd often been tempted. Politicians had groupies just like pop musicians, and Caleb Knowles had been an unusually attractive candidate and president. He knew this, and had exploited it with cheerful, if ruthless, single-mindedness.

Everyone uses whatever they have to get whatever they want, he thought. Everyone. There are no rules for this. There cannot be. People are people. They want to be loved for themselves, without anyone thinking of their money, their power, their sexual attractiveness, who they know, what they do. Everyone wants a pure love, one on one, without qualification, without ulterior motives.

And none of us ever gets it.

"Mister President?"

"Oh? Eh?"

Murray was looking anxiously at him and Knowles realized that Brigadier General Sandra Cohen was standing there, looking pale. Knowles' face tightened with annoyance; he hadn't been aware that his military aide had entered the Oval Office, or that the interpreter had quietly left.

"Yes, Sandy?"

"Sir, uh . . ." The brigadier glanced down at the paper in her hand. Raggedly torn from a wire service machine. News.

"What is it now?"

"Cleveland, sir."

"What do you mean, Cleveland?"

"Wiped out, Mister President. Twenty minutes ago." She raised the paper, her eyes sad. "Verification from Station One, and from an overflight from—"

"*Cleveland?* The entire city?"

The officer nodded, her face pale and grim. "Total. Apparently the meteor came in over Pennsylvania. There were reports, but there are so many shooting stars right now, that—"

"Yes, yes."

"It, uh, this meteor . . . we have no idea how large . . . it, uh . . . it hit, uh, Cleveland Heights, uh, plowed right through almost to Lakewood."

"Jesus Christ," the President said softly. "Anderson Petrie, Darrell Ellison . . . they were there . . . and Fielder Elliot . . ."

"There's more, sir," the general said uncomfortably. "*More?*"

"Strikes are reported in the northern Quebec province . . . but in a pretty much uninhabited area. Forest fires, though. Some minor damage in western Kansas. And, uh . . ."

Knowles glared at her. "Go *on.*"

"The moon, sir. It didn't hit anything directly, but the seismic quakes knocked out the Russian station on Farside. Split the domes, twisted the mass accelerator."

The President sighed deeply. He seemed to age, his clothes to deflate. He rubbed his freckled hand across his face, sighing.

"The Vice-President?" Murray asked.

"Safe. He's in transit to Station One with the Secretary of Space."

The President spoke in a weary voice. "Any idea how many more hits we're going to get?"

"No, sir, but they think we're just being brushed by the outer fringes of the swarm as it moves on past. It's on turnaround, and, uh . . ." She swallowed rather noisily. "We've almost eleven months, Mister President, to—"

"I know how much time we have. It's pitifully little. You can't mount an operation like this overnight." Abruptly he looked up at Myron Murray. "Is Mrs. Carr still in the building?"

"I don't know, sir, I'll check." He reached for a phone.

"Ask her to come in. Thank you, Sandy. Keep me posted."

He stared at the empty desk top for a few moments, then Murray hung up the handset. "She's coming, sir."

"Thank you, Myron. Go shake up the lead-asses, will you? I don't want any foot-dragging. I told them, but I know damned well I'm going to have to tell them again."

"Yes, sir." He started for the door, looking back over his shoulder as Knowles spoke again.

"Ask Grace to send her right in, will you?"

"Of course, Mister President." He gave General Cohen a look.

"Will that be all, sir?" the officer asked and Knowles nodded. The general followed Murray out and closed the door behind her.

Knowles swung around in his chair and looked out at the darkening sky. He saw a shooting star. *Twinkle, twinkle, little star,* he thought, *How I wonder where you'll scar.* He felt sick again, the way he had in the service, before action. Helpless, vomiting into the weeds, into swamps, in the corner of the helicopter. But he'd always been all right after. Or almost always.

This is one of those "almosts," he thought sadly.

There was a discreet knock and Barbara Carr came in, her face worried and attentive. "Mister President?"

He forced a smile. It felt stitched on. "Hello, Barbara. Come in." He watched her close the door behind her and move across the thick carpet, passing through a corner of the great gold and blue seal woven into the fabric. He liked looking at her. She was in her early thirties, a handsome rather than beautiful woman, and he knew her to be efficient. "That's a lovely dress," he said.

"Thank you, sir," she replied, but her face held a questioning, alert look.

"You have excellent taste."

"Thank you, Mister President."

John Caleb Knowles sighed. "You know, I don't think I'll ever get used to being called that. It always reminds me of when a young woman first called me 'sir.'"

She smiled but said nothing. They both felt stilted and awkward. Knowles straightened up. "Well. I want to see Steve Banning the minute he gets in from the coast."

"Excuse me, sir, but I . . . well, there are rumors, and with all these meteor strikes . . ." She raised her eyebrows in a question and the President nodded.

"Tell Myron to brief you. It's true. We're on a collision orbit with a meteor swarm. A *big* meteor swarm. What we've been getting is just the fringe stuff." Her eyes went wide, but she retained her composure, then suddenly smiled, which surprised Knowles.

"Excuse me, sir, I . . . um . . . I can't help wondering how this is going to affect the election."

His face grew grave. "If . . . if we don't stop this thing, there won't *be* any election . . . or an electorate."

She attempted a cheerful disguise. "You've got my vote, Mister President."

"I had your husband's, too, when he was alive." Her smile lost a millimeter of its power. "Did a fine job for me on that farm bill. The space industries hassle, too."

She let her smile run down. "Yes, he was an effective congressman."

Caleb Knowles warmed up his smile and waved his hand. "Well, don't let me keep you, running on like that. It's just . . ." He sat back, his smile becoming a rather rueful grin. "Oh, I hate that stuff. You know, 'it's lonely at the top.' But it *is*, damnit."

Barbara raised her eyebrows. "And you no longer

have your wife to talk to . . . ?" She swallowed noisily, and covered her nervousness by changing her position in the chair.

He looked at her sharply. "Yes. Yes, you're right. I don't mind admitting that. Damned smart woman, Catherine. She had great antennae. Picked up the vibes on people and she was rarely wrong, and not by much when she was. Well . . ." He seemed unusually nervous, and Barbara started backing away. "No, wait," he said. "Uh . . . you've met Chuck Bradshaw, haven't you?" She nodded. "What do you think of him?"

She touched her tongue to her upper lip, paused, then spoke out. "Efficient. Not as confident of his own ability as his record might indicate. Smart. Inhibited. Careful, but willing to take a calculated risk. Good administrator. Gets along better with people who speak his language than those who don't, but don't we all?"

Caleb Knowles nodded, a faint smile on his lips. "Thank you, Barbara. Someday remind me to ask about the uninhibited part."

Outside, in the white corridors with the curving vault ceilings, she stopped at a water fountain. Did I do the right thing? she wondered. That's my inhibition, all right: never quite certain.

She smiled automatically at one of the aides as she passed, then walked briskly toward her office. She felt strange, and masked it with a slight frown.

Was the President of the United States *really* interested in me? *That* way?

She didn't quite know how to feel about that.

But she did know there was a stirring in her loins. A response. That kind of response she had not truly felt for some time.

It was very, very enjoyable, and made her feel guilty.

It was very quiet in the cabin of the shuttle. Earth had ceased to be a curved surface and California stretched out, green and brown beneath the scattered clouds. There were just the standard cabin sounds: the blip of the landing radar, the faint click of relays, and the buzz-blip of the special landing grid screen. They were into their final approach, the Pacific directly below them and

Point Arguello a protruding point of land to the south. Vandenberg Air Force Base was directly ahead.

Colonel Diego Calderon flipped the landing-gear systems switch and waited for the answering *thunk.* Nothing happened. He shot Lisa Bander a quick look but his co-pilot was already checking. Their eyes ran quickly over the array of lights.

Rear landing gear was down, check. Forward gear showed nothing. "Malfunction," he said softly, and simultaneously reset the landing gear subsystems. He flipped the switches again. Nothing. *"Madre de Dios."*

In the right-hand seat Major Lisa Bander leaned forward and automatically hit her manual override controls, her dark eyes frowning beneath her level brows. Nothing on the control panel before them changed.

"Vandenberg, we have a Mayday Able Baker," Diego said rapidly and clearly into his suit mike. "Repeat. Mayday Able Baker. Our nose wheel fails to deploy."

Diego glanced out the forward window. Cirrus clouds drifted lazily by and below a sandy brown scruff of California met the ocean. The shuttle craft was running smoothly down its glide pattern, coming in swiftly and almost silently to land. He saw Lisa point with her thumb toward her spherical glassite helmet in its clip. He shook his head. They wouldn't need them, not yet. They were almost down into breathable air.

"Shuttle Seven, *we read you Mayday Able Baker. Give us a diagnostic squirt."*

Lisa was already tapping out a systems inventory. She filed it into the transceiver processor with a nudge of her thumb. The screen before her rippled with a cascade of information. She tapped a blue button and a high-pitched squeal filled the cabin.

"Squirt received, Shuttle Seven."

Diego again scanned the airspace ahead. All air traffic had been rerouted, as was standard practice, since the shuttle came in as a glider and had relatively little control. But there was always the chance some civilian with a faulty radio could wander into the flight path.

"It's the hydraulics," Lisa said quickly. Her voice deepened. "I'll bet it's that damned turbo-pump shaft and housing." She looked at Diego over the metal rim of her spacesuit. "There was an amber hold on that in our preflight checkout, remember? But the board cleared before we had time to check it out further."

Diego nodded. "Seventeen minutes to touchdown."

A tinny voice spoke into his ear. "Shuttle Seven, *we have repped and verified your inhouse diagnostics. Apparent component failure in the pump subassembly of the forward Juno housing. That is Code Able Baker Four Eight Six.*"

"Recovery chances?" Diego asked.

"*None. Housing has separated.*"

"*Mierda,*" Diego muttered angrily. "Then foam the field," he said firmly. He glanced over at Lisa. Her eyes were bigger than usual, and brighter, but he was proud of her. Nothing else showed. No sweat, no fear, only alertness. Trouble was no stranger to any astronaut, not even on the milk-run shuttle flights. But when it happened, it usually happened fast. It was always bad, coming down from space, catching your emotions unaware. You do what you have to do and you don't feel much until it's over. That was what training meant. But beyond training, it was in the basic choice of the people selected as astronauts. They may get scared—they were *often* scared—but they rarely panicked, and that made the difference.

"Shuttle Seven, *we will not follow standard procedures on this. NASA Houston has taken charge.*"

Lisa and Diego exchanged quick looks. "What?" she broke in. "Get that foam out there or we won't have anything to slide in on! This is no time to fart around."

Diego grinned at her. Her way of reacting to things was one of the reasons he loved her. She gave him a faintly embarrassed look, then her lips grew firm again.

"*Ah, ah, stand by,* Shuttle Seven."

Lisa was automatically cycling through the hydraulics switches, trying to let the system redeem itself. She looked up and said, "This would happen when we're rusty as hell."

Diego formed a thin smile. He was watching their progress along the glide path on the screen before him. One good thing about the shuttle was that there was no fuel in the bird. When they came in at around one hundred thirty kilometers an hour, and slammed into the lake of foam, there would be no fuel to catch fire, even if the hull ruptured. He tried to remember the percentages on this particular malfunction. Hale and Zenowski had come through one much like this perfectly. But Mort Smith and Julie Short had pranged themselves good, split the fuselage open, and dumped their cargo all over the field. He hoped to hell that didn't happen this time, and not only because his lover sat in the copilot's couch. They were piloting down over eight million dollars' worth of products. There were steel bearings, perfectly round; forming them in orbit, with no gravity, made them spherical to the limits of measurability.

Farther back in the cargo hold, well secured, were high-Q silicon crystals. This was the first big shipment to come down. There had already been numerous news stories about the long, dark bars of silicon, and a special team from the National Science Foundation was meeting the shuttle to take possession of them. The bars were the crucial element in the gravitational wave detector being built at the University of Maryland, in the old lab where Weber had started it all. Tap one of the crystals and it would hum for over a million years. It was an absolutely perfect lattice. When a gravitational wave from some distant supernova passed by, even as weak a force as gravity would touch off a loud and clear vibration in the crystal. With signal strengths that high, astronomers would at last be able to study the ancient black hole at the center of our galaxy.

Diego sighed to himself. This cargo was damned valuable—more in potential even than in money—and they had to bring it in. What was Vandenberg stalling about?

"Shuttle Seven, *this is Chuck Bradshaw.*"

Diego and Lisa looked at each other with raised eyebrows. What was the head of NASA doing, getting into this?

"*I am ordering you to chute out. Read me,* Shuttle Seven? *Chute out. Jump.*"

"Bradshaw, that's crazy," Diego said quickly. "We've lost the nose wheel. The aft gear is deployed. Coming in on a tricycle gear with the two back wheels holding isn't that dangerous."

"*I am ordering you to eject.*"

"And *I'm* countermanding your order. You know Maydays are strictly an Operations matter. What in hell is going on with you people down there?"

"Diego . . ." The anger in Bradshaw's voice changed. He became more reasonable. *"Look, I had the regular crew bumped off this flight for a reason, believe me. You two are first-line astronauts, not just shuttle jockeys. There's something big brewing and . . . and NASA can't risk people like you."*

"What is it?" Diego asked. The Pacific beach was passing under them. There was not much time left. "What's more important that these high-Q crystals?"

"It's classified, Diego. Lisa, can't you do something with him?"

"He's in command, Chuck." She gave Diego a quick smile. "Besides, I think he's right. On the basis of the information we have."

"Look," Bradshaw argued. *"I know you're technically on contract with Space Techtronics, but that's just a formality. You're both still Air Force officers and—"*

"Come on, Chuck," Diego broke in, "you've got to do better than that."

There was a brief pause before Bradshaw spoke again. *"It's classified. I brought you two down three weeks early because I want you in on it."*

"I remain unconvinced," Diego answered, watching the flight path monitor. "This is an important cargo, Chuck." The noise of passing air was building up, whistling past.

"Damnit, I'm ordering you! Jump! We need astronauts now, not crystals."

Diego looked at Lisa. "What do you think, babe?"

She grimaced, her eyes on the dials and lights. "It's not easy to risk your life for a bunch of hardware. But that's what we're paid for." She looked over at him. "I don't want to be the first shuttle crew to bail out and lose one."

A pause. They looked at each other soberly.

"Me, either."

He glanced out at the clouds. Between them it was clear and bright. Glide path good. It looked as good as it would ever be.

"Get that foam out, Chuck," he said slowly.

"Mister Bradshaw?" the Vandenberg flight director asked.

A pause. Then: *"Foam it."*

* * *

The shuttle appeared awkward and slow, high in the air, shimmering in the heat waves reflecting up from the field. As it approached the field it seemed to gather speed. The white spacecraft came down flat and straight. The vertical stabilizer split along its length, opening about thirty degrees on a side, to act as a speed brake. The ship struck the dazzling white foam, sending it flying in a bow wave. The rear wheels bit in and flared orange and two centimeters of polyrubber burned away smokily. Diego kept the nose up as long as possible. An under-eddy built up at once, slowing them.

Within a few seconds the risk of destabilizing the craft became too great. He brought the nose down slowly. It was like descending into a white lake. They hit, skipped, hit again with a screeching of metal. The forward hull manifold came away with a wrenching crash, bumped against the fuselage, and clattered to pieces behind them. Vibration rattled them in their harnesses. Something crunched, howled, broke off with an explosive sound.

Diego felt the craft slew to starboard and corrected instantly, keeping the fire trucks in the corner of his eye for orientation. The howling noise battered at them, rose in pitch; a low growl began. The hull was groaning with strain, metal was popping, minor seams giving way.

But it held. It held. Shuttle Seven skidded on its belly across the foam, splashing up a sluggish bow wave, spewing blobs and streamers right and left. The big space-craft slewed awkwardly to the left, touched one stubby wing to the earth, and stopped.

Lisa popped the emergency exit and went out. Diego hesitated only a moment, checking on the integrity of the cargo hold. It was still intact. The silicon bars, ears to listen to the whisper of the stars, were undamaged. Then he followed Lisa out of the hatch. The ground crew snatched at him and wrapped him immediately in a protective blanket to keep off scorching metal fragments. He was smiling broadly as he trotted away from the ship, wading through neck-deep foam.

Captain Carl Jagens, the United States Navy's top-ranking astronaut, was very popular with the media people. Blond, good-looking in a harsh way, tall for an astronaut, he was always good for a story or a quote, with an uncanny ability to predict the direction and force of current thinking within the political and scientific community, and unafraid to try to sway that thinking. He was holding court for a carefully selected group of newspeople when he saw Lisa Bander and Diego Calderon enter the NASA briefing hall.

Carl frowned as two of the newspeople broke away to intercept the newcomers, but he went quickly back to his subject, the same subject he so expertly propounded all over the world: space exploration. But he remained aware of his two chief rivals for the attention of the popular press.

"Hey, Lisa, wait up," Py Rudd said. He looked over his shoulder and caught the attention of his cameraman, who swung his shoulder-mounted video camera at them. "Heard you two pulled a stunt out at Vandenberg. Care to comment?"

Lisa smiled. "Don't quote me as saying 'no comment,' Py. We just wanted to save the taxpayers a few bob."

CBS's Nancy Darrin joined them, deserting Carl Jagens. "There's a rumor you disobeyed orders, Colonel Calderon."

Diego just looked at her, his face expressionless. "Really, Colonel," Nancy said, her smile icy, "sometimes your reputation for nonverbal behavior gets in the way of the public's right to know."

He shrugged and looked away. "When I have something to say, I'll say it." His rebuff did not stop the aggressive reporter, who opened her mouth to speak, but NBC's Rudd spoke first.

"Major Bander, what is going on here today, do you know? There are so many rumors—"

The female astronaut smiled politely. "I'm just a hired hand, Py. I come when they call."

"This *is* about the meteor strikes, isn't it?" he asked. Lisa shrugged, aware of Rudd's open admiration of her as a woman, as well as an accomplished astronaut. Blonde and tanned with a trim, sturdy figure, Lisa always stood erect, with a kind of coiled tension. She was not a fragile flower, nor was she the archly glamorous "astronette" and champion of women's rights as the media so often portrayed her. She was simply Major Lisa Araminta Bander, United States Air Force officer and American astronaut.

"Diego," Nancy Darrin said crisply in her no-nonsense,

25

don't-lie-to-me-or-I'll-have-your-hide voice. "Do *you* have anything?"

The dark-haired astronaut shrugged. "No more than you, Ms. Darrin. Excuse us, will you?" He smiled, his white teeth flashing in his olive face, and he included the camera lens. He took Lisa's elbow and started to guide her away.

"Still lovers?" Nancy asked. Py Rudd made a sound in his throat and swallowed a smile. Diego's hardened gaze swung back to her, cool and dangerous. "Off the record," she said, her smile icy.

"Off the record—and on—it's nobody's business."

"Astronauts are everybody's business," Nancy Darrin replied, her professional shark's smile bright and predatory. "Especially since you are no longer all cut from the same goody-goody mold." She sighed dramatically, but her eyes were calculating. Diego saw the CBS camera pointing at them. Some European news agency swung another one toward them. "You space types used to be cookie-cut, all Wasps and neat. Look-alikes, even the wives."

"Uh-huh," Diego said, looking away, resisting the impulse to rise to her bait.

"They used to think the wives were all manufactured in some secret laboratory somewhere," Nancy persisted. "Maybe clones from some Miss America."

"Yeah, right, they were," Diego muttered. His dark eyes slid sideways to the reporter. "Came from the same place writers get their ideas."

Nancy's cool smile stayed on and she tipped her head to the side as though to acknowledge Diego's point. Then she made a large show of "discovering" Senator Howar and moved away, as if to more important matters. Py Rudd grinned at them and waggled his fingers as he moved off toward another important figure.

Lisa looked at Diego, a smile hidden but dancing in her eyes. "Touchy wetback," she muttered.

"None of her business," Diego said tightly, but he, too broke into a grin. It had happened before, this invasion into their private lives, and they both knew it would happen again.

A short, wide man came sauntering up to Lisa and Diego, grinning and doing a little mock dance before them. "Lisa! Amigo! Beauty and the beastie. You look just as beautiful as ever," he said to Lisa, then slapped Diego on the arm. "How the hell are you, Zorro?"

Lisa smiled. "Ah, Dink—off duty?"

"You betcha, starlady. Ol' Dink Lowell has fallen heir to a plush job." His face shifted expressions for a brief moment, then the smile was confidently restored. "Grounded, my ill-starred couple, grounded. Tied to a desk and a terminal."

"Why?" Diego frowned, holding the man's upper arm.

"Entropy," Dink sighed. "Age, m'man. Slowing down." He winked at Lisa. "My finger just isn't as quick on the button as it used to be."

"That's nonsense," Diego said over the increasing noise. "How much strength does it take to run a computer or sit still for six months? It's judgment and experience, not . . ." He looked briefly at Lisa. "If it took brute strength, we'd not be co-ed."

Dink sighed dramatically and pulled away. "Aw, what the hey, Zorro. Law of averages. Only so many boosts to orbit in a man, huh? So now I get kicked upstairs and I get to tell you fumble-fingered dolts what to do. How about that, huh?" He turned jerkily toward Lisa and grinned widely. "See ya around, Beauty. You, too, Lisa," he said as he turned into the crowd.

There were murmurs as someone entered. The people began moving toward the folding chairs and Lisa could see Chuck Bradshaw mounting the dais. He bent to speak to Lyle Orr, NASA's publicity chief, then moved to the podium and flicked his finger at the microphone. There was a soft metallic boom and relative quiet descended. Bradshaw started to speak, then was interrupted by the twitchy screech of a chair being pulled across the floor. No one laughed.

Bradshaw cleared his throat, then looked around the room, his face bland, but those who knew him well read the tenseness under the calm exterior. "Well," he began, then cleared his throat again. "You've heard about the Algerian strike, of course . . . and Cleveland." There were nods and grim faces. "There's more." As he pulled a paper from his jacket there was a wave of whispers, but they quieted down as Bradshaw spread the paper on the lectern. "Uh . . . some minor strikes in the Quebec area. Not much damage." He glanced up, and a kind of rictus smile twitched across his face. "By the standards that have been set recently, that is. Then uh . . . this morning, about 5:10 our time, there was a strike on Farside. No damage to any facility but it registered eight point two on the Lunar Richter Scale."

Bradshaw rubbed at his chin, his eyes shadowed as his head hung down, bull-like. "There's, uh, there's more. Another strike. We don't know all the details yet, but it was in the Arctic Ocean at 11:17 our time. We just got it in from Station Three. It . . . it sent a tidal wave over Murmansk and . . . it's gone. Erased."

"*Another* meteor?" someone asked in a disbelieving voice. "My God, what's coming at us?"

"A swarm," Bradshaw said in a flat voice. There were more murmurs and Bradshaw waited it out, breathing slowly and deeply. Then: "It is going to strike the Earth." He quickly held up his hand as people began talking. "Wait a minute! Wait a minute!" The noise died down. "There are an unknown number of *small* asteroids in the swarm, as well as dust and pebbles and so on, most of which will burn up in the atmosphere. Now by *small*, I mean like those that have been impacting Earth—"

"*Small?*" several people said at once in startled voices.

"Yes, small . . . compared to Shiva."

It was the first time most of them had heard the name. It sent a cold chill through Lisa and she sought out Diego's hand and grasped it tightly.

"Shiva is approximately two kilometers in diameter," Bradshaw said, raising his voice over the tumult, "and it *will* hit the Earth. Our mission is to destroy or deflect it."

He stopped for a moment, ignoring the questions, looking rather blindly down at the floor before the dais. Then the questioners and the speculators ran down and he raised his head.

"We'll be giving you more definite details as they come in. But . . ." He hesitated, then plunged on. "We . . . NASA . . . your government, that is, we *request* that you play *down* what's happening here."

"Censorship, Chuck?" someone said genially, but there was steel in the anonymous voice as well.

"No, responsibility. Things are bad enough without a lot of wild stories." He waved his hand in the air. "End-of-the-world kind of thing."

"Is it?" asked the Reuters man.

"No, no, of course not, but it *is* very serious."

28

"You didn't say this was off the record," the *Yomiuri Shimbun* representative said testily.

"That's right, I didn't," Chuck said with obvious nervousness. "But I am counting on you, as responsible members of the—"

"Cut it out, Chuck," the *London Daily Express* stringer snapped. "We know our job—the public has the right to know!"

Chuck nodded several times as others made similar comments. He held up his hand and after a moment got silence. "Yes, the public does have that right . . . but remember the adage about shouting 'Fire!' in a crowded theater. This is a crowded planet—and we have no place to go. At least no place that Shiva can't . . . that . . . where there might not be a strike. What would happen if you told them the *whole* truth *now?* Where will they go? We just don't have enough data as yet. We do *not* know the strike zone . . . or zones. They might run right into it. Don't you think it is better not to let this out until we have more definite information and some kind of suggestions to offer?" There was some muttering, but no one spoke up.

"Look, people," Bradshaw said, "I'm just asking you to cool it, to report it, yes, but don't write inflammatory reports."

Nancy Darrin spoke up, her voice dripping with sarcasm. "You mean, 'End of the World, story on page six'?" There was some laughter, but Chuck Bradshaw spoke through it.

"In a way, yes. This is just too important. We might easily have more deaths from panic than from any strike."

"But hundreds of thousands—a couple of *million!*—have died already!" cried out the PBS reporter.

"I know. But why add to that toll?"

There was an uncomfortable silence, then Hughes Michaels of ABC spoke up. "It's *that* serious?"

Bradshaw nodded. "It's that serious. I'm talking about *millions* dead, about, yes, the end of the world, in a way." His next words were drowned out in sudden turmoil, but he calmed them down and continued. "I'm asking for your cooperation for a few days, then we'll have a presentation for you, something that will show the magnitude of this whole thing. Then you can decide what to trumpet and what not." He rubbed at his chin, then put his arms straight out at the podium and lowered his head, looking at them from under his eyebrows.

"There's a lot more out there than we ever guessed," he said in a low voice. "Every day the observatories log more . . . more things. More asteroids, more stars, more galaxies. The radio telescopes are turning up all sorts of strange things. There are more interstellar molecules floating around out there that we ever thought, more dust and rocks, more whole *galaxies* than we ever dreamed!"

He paused, his voice almost a whisper, and they listened attentively. "And some of that space debris is too big to burn up in the atmosphere. Some of it . . . some of it will get through. Some of it has." He raised his head. "Ladies and gentlemen, we have eleven months. Maybe a little less. I ask your cooperation. Panic can kill millions, and we may be able to avert the whole thing."

"*May?*" Nancy Darrin asked.

There was no answer to that, and everyone knew it.

It was a small meteor, a mere metric ton of space debris. Mostly iron and rock, it was white hot when it came down to Earth. Small enough to be deflected by the atmosphere, it took an erratic course and was one of the few meteors to strike in the southern hemisphere.

John Fitch was having a pipe, sitting on a park bench facing south, near the modest monument to the first settlers of Adelaide, South Australia. There was a searing blue-white streak in the crisp, cold air and a thundering crack that brought shopkeepers and customers out of the hotel and shops around the square.

Fitch tugged his sheepskin coat tighter about his bony frame and sauntered toward the beach. He stopped at the edge of the sand, the biting wind coming up from the polar cap tingling his face, making it blotched and red. He squinted at the horizon, the pipe clenched between his teeth, his ears still ringing.

"Oh, my God," he muttered. The overcast had parted and a distant gray-white column rose, growing fast, that shocked him. Coming in across the Spencer Gulf from the southwest was a tidal wave.

"Goddamn bloody meteor," he said without much passion. He turned and walked quickly back toward the square.

"What is it?" a butcher asked, his hands white and wet.

"One of those space rocks," Fitch said. "Better get inside, Sean."

The butcher looked past him. "Don't think it would do much good, John, but thank you. Better . . . better find the wife."

Fitch walked on, warning others. A woman grabbed his arm. "A tidal wave, y'say? Why, in the name of God, why?"

Fitch shrugged and pulled his arm free. "Not for me to say, mum." He crossed the street, nimbly avoiding the trolley tracks buried in the tar, and went into the hotel bar. He caught the eye of the bartender. "Wave coming," he said softly. "Bloody damned Shiva, anyway."

"Big?"

Fitch nodded, taking the offered whiskey without answering. He swallowed it in a gulp and set down the glass with exaggerated care. "Thanking you, Carey," he said soberly, but the bartender was gone.

Fitch went into the hotel lobby and turned left into the dining room. "Missus Bray?"

"Yes, Mister Fitch?" The middle-aged woman looked up with a twinkle.

"It has been nice knowing you, Margaret."

She raised her eyebrows and a sudden comprehension crossed her face. "The sonic boom, John?" He nodded and she rose from the table where she had been having tea with friends and excused herself. Without haste she walked into the lobby, preceded by John Fitch. They embraced awkwardly, but with affection. He was still patting her shoulder when they heard the roar.

The water crushed all the seashore buildings and carried the debris up toward the hills. Much of the city was saved. The long beaches had a new configuration along the southern shore.

10 July: Collision minus 10 months, 16 days

Chuck Bradshaw stepped up to the podium, which was set to one side of the stage. Behind him was a screen. About half the seats in the little theater were filled. There were military uniforms, some in police garb. Most wore summer-weight suits, with pens and pocket calculators sticking out of their pockets, radiolink phones clipped to their belts. Both sexes were represented, mostly middle-aged, but many in their twenties and thirties. All appeared serious.

Lisa came in, saw Diego, who was watching for her, and waved. She slipped into the seat next to him. Most of the astronauts were sitting together, at one side, toward the back. Carl Jagens was in the front row.

"All right, let's get the picture," Bradshaw said. He cleared his throat. "Doctor Canfield?"

A tall, thin man with a mane of graying hair stood up and walked to the side of the dais, nodded at Bradshaw, and started to speak. People jerked their heads as he spoke too loudly and too close to the mike. Bradshaw whispered to him and Canfield nodded impatiently. "Yes, yes," he said. He peered out at them. "The object designated as Shiva will intersect the orbit of this planet in, um, ten months, twenty days, and . . ." He peered at his wristwatch, "um, eight hours, twelve minutes. Plus or minus forty-two hours, four minutes."

"Yes, Doctor," someone said from the front, "but what will be the effect?"

"Ah, the effect. Well, um, if it hits land—and there is a one-out-of-four chance it will—this is approximately what the result will be." He took an electropad from his pocket and turned it on. He peered at it, his lips moving silently. "Ah. From the readings at the site of the Cleveland strike we assume a nickel-iron composition. Shiva itself is estimated to be thirty billion tons."

There was a murmur from the audience and Canfield stopped, peering curiously at them. "Yes, that much. Now the energy of a moving body equals half its mass times the square of its velocity. Or, in other words, E equals one-half M times V to the second. When a moving body is involved in a collision, as you know, the energy of movement degrades into heat."

Dr. Canfield's voice was swift, as if he were hurrying through obvious facts and impatient to get past that point. "Now whatever the angle of collision, a meteorite's impact is violently explosive. Its speed—and thus the speed of the explosion of super-hot gases which will result —is *vastly* greater than those of chemical reactions." He smiled, peering at the crowd with a pleased expression.

"To illustrate. The Barringer strike in Arizona is estimated to be about two and a half *megatons* of TNT, and it created a crater about four thousand feet across." Again he peered, but seemed dissatisfied by the reaction.

"The material forming the crater floor is broken. The blast will result in pieces as large as boulders . . . and as fine as rock flour. There will also be minute spherules of iron, um, oh, point one millimeters or so across. They will condense from vapors produced by the impact flare, and will be distributed in the area. There will also be some unusual minerals—coesite and stishkovite—which are found only at these sites and which are produced by the pressure of the explosion."

"Uh, excuse me, Doctor," Chuck Bradshaw said, stepping forward, "but about Shiva—?"

Canfield gave him a glare. "I'm getting to that. I am establishing the foundation." He looked out at the audience. "Where was I? Ah. Rocks surrounding the crater are likely to be shattered in a unique fashion. Compression waves originating from the strike point diffract on small irregularities within the rock, which break into shatter cones pointing to the center of impact."

The audience stirred restlessly and Dr. Canfield glared at them. "The Barringer crater, to use that as an example, again, is not the largest known on Earth. But it could have been caused by an asteroid weighing ten thousand tons, striking at forty kilometers per second."

There was another stirring as the members of the audience compared that weight with Shiva's estimated weight. "The meteor which created the Vredevoort Ring in South Africa," Canfield continued, "was much bigger. Approximately the size of Shiva, in fact. Its volume has been estimated at a cubic mile. It blasted out all the sedimentary strata and exposed the naked magma at the base of a pit scores of miles wide." He peered closely at the audience. "So big, in fact, it was only discovered when we got far enough into space. It approximates the cratering of the moon." He shrugged. "Then the pit was filled with magma from the depths. That was very long ago, of course, and—"

"Excuse me, Doctor." Chuck Bradshaw stepped forward again. "Doctor Donnelly, didn't you have a comment at this time?"

A chubby, redheaded man stood up. "Aye, but it is only a theory and has little to do with our problem."

"But it might help give perspective," Chuck said.

"Aye, well . . . the Vredevoort strike may have caused man to spread out over the Earth. We don't know, of course, but it would be natural for primitive man to move away from—"

"As you say, Doctor," Canfield interrupted impatiently, "this has nothing to do with Shiva." He looked grumpily at Donnelly until the plump scientist sat down. "Um. Well. There is considerable evidence for *many* other strikes. Hudson's Bay, for example, the Sea of Japan, Carswell Lake in Canada . . . the twin strikes of Clearwater, which are craters thirty-two kilometers across, and Manicouagan, which is sixty kilometers."

The scientist paused, looking from under his bushy brows at the audience. "We are talking here, ladies and gentlemen, of *complete* conversion to energy of a million tons of matter, or the explosion of a hundred thousand million *million* tons . . . of TNT."

He waited while the audience murmured on. "If as little as one percent of the energy of such a meteor strike were to be transferred as heat to the atmosphere, the air temperature *everywhere* would rise by about two hundred degrees Centigrade."

There was less reaction from the audience than Canfield expected. He smiled at them. It was a cold, almost wolfish smile. "Too much for you to digest all at once?" He nodded, then made a deprecating gesture. "This is approximate, of course, as the expanding atmosphere would also add heat. And my one percent figure is *quite* conservative, I assure you." He raised a bony finger. "However, it has been estimated that the Vredevoort blast yielded more than a million *megatons* of TNT."

Lisa blinked. The figures were becoming astronomical. She felt the urge to reject it all, to ignore it, but she grimly narrowed her concentration.

"Meteorites as heavy as a thousand tons and up are all but unchecked by the atmosphere," Dr. Canfield continued. "They strike the ground with most of their original speed. This ranges from about twenty to seventy kilometers per second, though there have been some tracked as fast as over one hundred fifty kilometers per second."

Lisa stared at the podium, but in her mind's eye she saw the great asteroid entering the atmosphere, creating a pressure wave that would precede it. At Mach numbers sixty to two hundred the sonic boom would be truly awesome. Yet she knew moments later the blast rising from the surface impact would make the sonic boom unimportant. The impact flare would convert a quarter of the total energy into *immediate* heat. Vaguely she heard Canfield speak of the 1908 Siberian meteor, a relatively small one, that flattened the trees of Tiaga for a thirty-mile radius.

But the impact of Shiva would be staggering. Roughly equivalent to a two hundred fifty thousand megaton fusion bomb, the fireball would reach a diameter of three hundred kilometers. It would be greater than the total depth of the atmosphere and stratosphere together, billowing out in a fiery sphere until there was no more air. It would squat upon the impact area, doming up into space, and the site would glow for weeks, months, perhaps years.

There would be earthquakes, even damage to the crust. Everything from huge blocks to microscopic powder would be ejected far beyond the searing crater's edge.

In those first few moments of impact, she knew, there would be shatteringly intense light, a flood of X-rays and neutrons, for the pressure would cause a nuclear reaction in the heart of the immense flare.

Lisa's mouth was dry, her breath short as the full realization struck her. With three-quarters of the Earth's surface water, the odds were three-to-one in favor of an ocean strike—and that would be far worse. She dimly heard Canfield speak of over forty known land craters, so there should be over one hundred and twenty strikes at sea. The conservative estimate was that Earth had suffered over a thousand *sizable* strikes —which meant seven hundred and fifty were marine hits.

Impacts in water were even more lethal than the devastating effect of land hits. Lisa made some quick mental calculations. Shiva's volume was about one cubic mile. If Shiva *was* nickel-iron, it would have eight times the density of water. A mid-ocean impact, at fifty kilometers per second, would be a thirty billion ton punch. She gulped and wet her lips, thinking.

The moment of impact: a tremendous glare of sheer violet radiance—a color few had witnessed outside a high-energy lab—would light the ocean for four or five hundred miles around the target area. It would last perhaps two heartbeats, but people three or four thousand miles away would be dazzled. The air would become incandescent. Compressed by Shiva's sudden passage, it would glow into the violet and beyond. Anyone closer than three thousand miles stood a good chance of being turned into pulverized bone and homogenized tissue by the sonic blast.

A jet of plasma would rocket into space, too hot to watch, brighter and hotter than the surface of the Sun. Lisa's hand clenched Diego's. Naked energy, verging on the nuclear reaction range. They'd see only the visible spectrum before their eyes were burned out. The jet of stripped atoms would travel high and fast, a great column hundreds of kilometers tall, an incandescent shaft, rainbowed and haloed, lighting the entire ocean from shore to shore, even the great Pacific.

Lisa's throat seemed filled with tacks as she swallowed, fascinated and horrified by the fantastic event she pictured. The fireball below the jet expanding from a blue-hot blob to a sun-white dome . . . incandescent chaos . . . planet death.

A mile or two of the ocean would be vaporized, deep down through the ocean floor, deep into the very crust of the earth, blowing out slabs of the surrounding ocean bed. Beyond the radius where the mantle was laid bare, rifts would spit hot magma. A wound scores of miles wide, right to the bedrock . . .

Lisa struggled for breath, her mind filled with the demonic vision of the ringed waterfall, as high as a mountain range, rushing in to quench the fire. An area as big as Rhode Island, white-hot. The oceans would rush in . . . and change at once to pure steam. The vaporized water would stream up . . . a gush of super-heated vapor . . . enough to cloud the atmosphere. Crustal rifts would extrude lava, convulsions and seisms would rack the planet, surpassing the power of any earthquake.

All the waters of *all* the oceans would be set in oscillation. Waves would circle the earth a dozen times or more. Every unit weight of the meteor would cause the evaporation of six hundred unit weights of the ocean. There would be enough energy to free the molecules from the binding forces in the liquid state—to *vaporize* eight thousand cubic kilometers of ocean.

There would be enough water vapor put into the air to provide one and a quarter inches of average rainfall over the *entire* planet. She knew it would not be evenly distributed, but the deluge, the earthquakes, the great waves . . . Lisa licked again at her dry lips. When the water vapor turned into rain the calories which were used to evaporate it would be released to go to work elsewhere. It was the same energy cycle that kept the hurricanes spinning, that lifted thunderheads higher than Everest. For a while, the latent heat of the evaporation would be employed in moving air. In wind-making. They would not be gentle winds. They would shriek around the entire planet.

Lisa took Diego's hand in both of hers. Canfield's voice droned on, but the pictures in her mind continued with relentless cruelty, adding image upon image. In the end the heat from Shiva's impact would radiate back into space. But the effect would create a long-range weather prediction: very windy, very wet, very cloudy. For an indefinite period. Years, perhaps decades.

She heard Canfield using the 1883 explosion of Krakatoa as an example. The detonation pulverized several cubic *miles* of the volcanic cone. Where the volcano peaked originally at three thousand feet, the ocean now covered part of the base. He compared it to two or three megatons of TNT. A merely volcanic incident.

The volcanic cone was shattered so finely that it hung twenty miles high in the stratosphere for the next decade. Sunsets and dawns were quite gaudy all over the world in the late eighties and nineties of the last century. And the temperatures were slightly lower than average. Some of Krakatoa's dust was undoubtedly still up there.

And the estimated impact of Shiva would release six million times the energy released by Krakatoa.

But, depending upon the strike zone, perhaps only five or six thousand times as much material would be thrown up as the pulverized cone of Krakatoa. What counted

was the fineness, the minuteness, with which the material
—earth, rock, water—was divided.

The jet stream rising into the atmosphere would scavenge all powder from the crater, all ocean-bed ooze for miles around. Salt would be carried up and would float as fine crystals quite high up, creating a persistent and effective dust cloud over the Earth. And it would last longer—much longer—than the decade-long Krakatoa dust.

The ability of Earth to reflect light would increase, which meant a perceptible decrease in the solar heat reaching the surface. The weather of the world was delicately balanced on the solar constant, the solar radiation received on the surface in clear weather. There would be radical changes.

Lisa's hands were clammy with sweat. She knew the weather had changed in the past, and there were numerous theories why. But the Shiva-generated dust was going to make Earth colder for at least ten years and probably much longer. That was enough time for the polar ice caps to grow considerably. Even decades later, when the cloud cover had dispersed, and the dust settled out, the ice growth would leave the planetary albedo seriously increased. More of the sun's heat would be reflected back into space. A long cold spell would be certain. A *very* long cold spell.

Lisa gave Diego a quick look, and saw his look of concern. He, too, was imagining the effects, and their hands tightened on each other's. They looked again at the podium as Dr. Canfield cleared his throat and continued.

"A few points. The tidal wave we have discussed is actually a tsunami. Tsunamis are caused by tremors in the ocean bed . . . actually only rises or drops for a few inches . . . or by jerks along a fault or a movement in the tectonic plates. These long wavelength tsunamis move very fast indeed. In the Krakatoa explosion ocean-going ships were stranded miles from the beach. Hundred-foot-plus tsunamis hit the Indonesian coasts. It was visible as far away as the Cape of Good Hope and detectable in the English Channel." He nodded vigorously, and smiled his wolfish grin. "Yes, these tsunamis are very efficient vehicles for transferring energy over long distances. Thus giving Shiva, wherever it hits in water, the capability of causing disaster on a global scale. At the very least, coastal belts all over the world—which is a sizable area—will be in serious peril."

"But there *is* a chance of a land strike, isn't there?" someone asked from the audience.

Canfield nodded. "Yes. Most of the heat will be radiated back into space, but . . ." He shrugged and bared his teeth. "The percentages say an ocean strike. The radiation of the fireball will be quenched by the steam. Its heat will be sent far and wide by the huge steam geyser. Rain will follow rain, tsunamis recur, typhoons, hurricanes, tornadoes . . ." He grinned at them. "All that grows or moves will be destroyed. The power of the Shiva incident will harm—perhaps destroy—the biosphere itself. Certainly in human terms it will."

Canfield took a deep breath, quite audible over the microphones in the quiet auditorium. "After the storms have died and the last of the immense heat radiated out or transferred . . . dust and cloud-cover will veil the planet. And the long winter will set in."

He looked out at the audience with an almost gleeful expression and Lisa could not help but shiver. His voice continued. "The estimate is something like one-megaton bombs detonated at five-mile intervals over the entire surface of the world."

The audience sat in silence, numbed by the constant barrage. Canfield sniffed and walked off the stage with what Lisa thought was almost a strut. Chuck Bradshaw stepped to the microphone. "Doctor Lang?"

A bearded man with longish hair, old-fashioned glasses, and a stooped back rose from the aisle and shuffled up to the stage. "Mister Bradshaw. Doctors. We must remember that what has been depicted here today by my colleagues has happened many times before."

He let the words stand a moment, allowing them to sink in. People stirred, frowns on their faces, and Lisa exchanged a look with Diego.

"The craters of the Canadian Shield are probably a reliable guide to our meteorite past. It is a record in stone; it has been ground clean by glaciers, and reveals more than two gigayears—two billion years of meteoritic history. The Canadian Shield is about a million square miles, approximately one half of one percent of the planet's surface. There are craters of moderate size —and upward—scattered all across it. Manicouagan, for example, is in the range of the Vredevoort crater. From this we have determined a moderate strike every half-million years, somewhere on the Earth."

Dr. Lang raised his eyebrows at the murmurs. "Seems too spread out? Um, perhaps. But I am speaking here of rather fair-size impacts, which leave craters dozens or scores, even hundreds of miles across." The scientist looked from right to left. "Any questions?" There were none, though everyone was looking very thoughtful.

"Thank you, Doctor Lang," Bradshaw said as he stepped to the podium and the other man left. "All right," Chuck said to the assemblage. "There's the problem. Now we must look for—and find—a solution." Two hands went up, but the NASA executive shook his head. "No, not now. Think it through. Check with whoever or whatever you need. You have unlimited computer time and unlimited access. There is nothing that is not open to you. Even things marked *Secret*, though you'll have to clear inquiries like that through me and I'll have to go through the President. But I'll get it if it can conceivably be useful. People, information, comptime, whatever." Another hand went up, waving frantically.

"No," Bradshaw said firmly. "Submit all ideas in writing, in as simple a form as you can. As soon as you can, but not without some thinking. That will be all, except that I would like the NASA flight teams to report to me in briefing room four right after this. If any of you have any complaints about housing, transportation, or anything else, please call my office. I have a staff there to handle this. The same for special equipment, clearances, and so on. Thank you all." He shut off the microphone and started off the stage.

Lisa looked at Diego, who smiled back reassuringly. "Well," he said, "we've been warned."

They got up and went through the antiseptic white corridors to the briefing room. Carl Jagens stood at the lectern, checking everyone in with his eyes. Lisa was annoyed at his assumption of command, but sat down without comment.

Chuck Bradshaw entered, tossed his coat over a chair, and went to the lectern, where he was buttonholed by Jagens, who whispered to him in a proprietary way. Bradshaw shook his head and pulled away, waiting with a frown until Jagens surrendered the lectern.

"Everyone here?" he said, looking around.

"Perhaps you've wondered why we called you here," Dink Lowell said. There was a sprinkling of nervous laughter. Bradshaw twitched a small smile and nodded impatiently.

"We've got a job to do, one hell of a job," the NASA head stated. "There is only us to do it. We know the goal, but not how to do it."

"They should have built those space colonies," Dink Lowell called out. "Some place where mankind *could* survive a catastrophe like this one."

"The disaster hasn't happened yet, Dink," Chuck said. "And it is our job to see that it doesn't. A life and death job."

"Yeah, but what *can* we do?" George Palmer asked. He ran his hand over his closely cropped red hair and grumbled. "And even if they think of something, are they going to give us enough time?"

"We have eleven months, more or less," Chuck said. Lisa looked out of the window. They were on the third floor of the Armstrong building. The grass was green, the trees in bloom, but there was a tinge of mid-summer brown coming around the edges. In mid-summer next year where shall we be, she wondered.

"Hell, eleven months is nothing," someone complained. "We take years to plan missions."

"This time," Chuck Bradshaw said strongly, *"this* time, there are no other distractions, no other priorities. That's why all but basic station and base functions are cut back. Nothing fancy, no new projects. Just Shiva."

Shiva the Destroyer, Lisa thought.

"*Now* they need us," griped Dink Howell. "Where were they when we wanted to fund a manned program?" He waved his hand around at the two dozen astronauts. "There should be five times as many, probes out to Jupiter, a Mars base . . ."

"Yes, yes," Chuck Bradshaw interrupted. "We know all that, Dink. It's spilt milk now. But we do have several space stations and they are sending out a steady supply of information about the biosphere and—"

"Aw, come on, Chuck," Dink said. "That's the official

line. It's just us here, man. All that weather stuff and crop info, they've come to expect that. What have we done for them lately? My God, remember back in '69 and the seventies? They turned the *rest* of the Apollo landings into film clips on the late news. Same with Skylab, after they got over watching guys do exercises in zero gravity. Same with the space shuttle, same with *Luna One,* same with the space stations. Overnight delights. Lots of publicity . . . for a week or so. Then what? Congress votes a funding cut. The President vetoes the Space Exploration Bill. Congress puts more money into fighters and bombers that go obsolete at the speed of sound than they *ever* put into space. Americans spend more on *pizza* than NASA gets!"

"Oh, come on, Dink, it's not that bad," Carl Jagens said in the kind of voice one uses to a sulky child.

"Bug off, Carl, you company fink."

Chuck Bradshaw peered at Dink. "You drunk?"

"Bet your boosters I'm drunk. You heard that stuff. Hundred-foot tidal waves in Kansas. Greenhouses and icebergs. The Ice Age cometh. The big blast, man. The big, final blast."

"Dink . . ." Lisa said softly.

"Lemme alone! You know why there are no space colonies yet. The public's so fucking afraid of technology it's been sitting on its hands for thirty, forty *years.* They knew in the *seventies* that O'Neill colonies could be built, that the lousy investment would have been paid off in thirty years or so, even if it *was* a couple hundred billion." He shook his head angrily. "Goddamn, goddamn. So we got one stinking lousy dome on Luna, one mass-driver that sends us moon rocks, one dinky little station that just growed, that wasn't planned to be a manufacturing colony like it should have."

"Dink . . ." Lisa said.

"Oh, don't Dink me, damnit." He glared around moodily. "All the money going into welfare and the fucking arms race *still* and into wasteful programs. Into guarding the fucking nuclear *wastes.* How much we spend last year on making satellite power stations, huh? Bestest, freest fucking energy in the world, damnit. *Solar* power, beamed down, enough for everyone in the fucking *world,* half-cent a kilowatt, for Christ's sake, if they could put enough up there, but *do* they? No.

Fucking lobbies, fucking special interests. Our moon base—hah! We keep it going for propaganda reasons, because the Russians can't seem to keep one going. So we 'explore' for ice and minerals on a temporary basis and launch a fraction of what we could."

Dink looked around again, suspicious and belligerent. "We didn't discover anything dramatic, that's our trouble." He stood up and moved into the aisle. "Drama! That's what the mouth-breathers want! Like the fucking teevee! Find an alien colony of supermen in cryogenic suspension in a space bubble. Or some mysterious weirdo in a moon grotto. Drama! No drama, no money for the Jupiter project, for space colonies, for power satellites, or . . ." He swayed and Diego jumped out to grab him, but Dink pulled away. "Lemme *alone*, Zorro!" He pointed a finger at Bradshaw. "You know it's true. You make do, that's what you do, right? You quibble over cuts and fudge on the budgets and . . . aw, shit, you know what you do—just to keep us alive, to be around, like now, when we're needed."

"Come on, Dink," Bradshaw began placatingly.

"No, no," he said, moving away, holding on to a seat. "If America had half the brains of a goat, it would have been building colonies *years* ago. Mankind wouldn't be wiped out—*ever*—by some fucking rock, or anything else. But did they get their head out of their ass in time? No. No, they said the money was needed here on Earth. Shit. Oh, they were happy for the observation satellites, for teflon and silicon solar cells and all that." He waved his hand at the sky. "Only the fucking beginning, only the *beginning!* Why don't they realize that?"

"Lieutenant Colonel Lowell," Bradshaw said with soft determination.

"What the hell was the matter with NASA, anyway? They fumbled the fucking ball. They had the world by the *balls* in 1969. Everyone was watching. Did they tell the people the benefits in a way they'd understand? No. They were too snooty or too busy or too stupid. All the public saw was guys on the moon, bring back a shopping bag full of rocks. For this we spent *billions?* Don't blame 'em, don't blame 'em for being pissed. Hell, no one *explained* it to them in a way they'd *understand*, for Christ's sake."

Dink coughed and looked around again, his eyes

misted and weary. The others present didn't look at him or each other. "Well?" he asked, "Am I right? They fumbled the ball, right? They didn't get *popular* support. They were too fucking fancy to talk to the common fucker in the street, huh?" Dink made a rude sound and staggered several steps away. "Now they're paying for it and *we're* paying for it." He lurched into a seat and slumped, his face puffed and sullen.

Chuck started to speak but a woman came in, her face white. "Doctor Bradshaw?"

"Yes, what is it?" Chuck turned to her but kept his eyes on Dink Lowell.

"It's Miami Beach, sir."

"What about it?"

Diego was talking to the sulking Dink Lowell in low, intense words.

"A meteor, sir. Offshore, but close enough. The . . . the city is gone."

An astronaut stood up, spilling a cup of coffee. "Miami Beach or Miami?"

The woman looked at him. "Miami Beach."

The astronaut fell back in his seat with a groan. Several of his friends bent over him. The woman who had brought the news stared at him. "I'm sorry, I'm sorry," she said.

"Tommy's family is there," someone said. There was a silence. Even Dink subsided.

Chuck Bradshaw spoke into the gloom. "All right, that's all for today. But starting at oh eight hundred tomorrow I want a complete readiness check. An updating on anything and everything that will be needed to put every bird into orbit. My office will have a duty roster ready. Tom, you have leave . . . if you want it. The rest of you—get some sleep. You aren't going to get much for the next eleven months."

Dink put his face in his hands. Lisa thought he was crying. Diego knew he was.

In the following days the astronaut schedule became relentless. Meetings, systems inventories, contingency planning, backups, training of all kinds, integrated minimax analysis, medical examinations, personnel shifts—all took up the waking hours of thousands of people. Lisa was handed an order to report to a certain building after her last class. She found someone had moved everything she owned from her condominium in River Oaks to a hastily constructed astronauts' quarters in a former office building. Screaming at the Astronaut Office did no good: security was the reason, and everyone had been moved, lock, stock, and wastebasket contents.

Diego was five buildings away; in the bachelor officer's quarters, but they made a deal with Blaine Brennan, who had sent his wife into "safety" in Wisconsin, and traded him for his married officer's quarters. The Astronaut Office shrugged and had their gear moved.

Somewhere, somehow, the hologram of her dead parents was lost, but she had always liked the small album of old-fashioned flat prints better, anyway. That they hadn't managed to lose.

Lisa and Diego had similar schedules, but often they were out of synch, and saw each other in stolen moments. They met for lunch, spilling over with news, asking questions, exchanging rumors, discussing speculations. Then they wouldn't see each other for days, except as hurriedly dressing figures in the morning, silent and grumpy. The security arrangements more or less masked their living together from the press, but the rumors did spread. Anything and anyone connected with the Shiva mission was news.

Lyle Orr, the NASA publicity chief, pleaded with them to "get respectable" and either marry or apply for a cohabitation certificate. But neither Lisa nor Diego had the time. Or made the time. And both were aware this was one subject they were still a little uncomfortable with. They said it was because the whole world was unsettled and they both knew that was not the reason. Yet they wanted to marry, and the stress continued to grow.

1 August: Collision minus 9 months, 25 days

Dr. Canfield's arrow drifted erratically around the image projected on the big screen. "As you can see, the Shiva swarm is moving slowest nearest the Earth. That is, obviously, because it is climbing up out of the gravitational well from the sun. This is to our advantage, as it will take the least energy to divert it."

Chuck Bradshaw spoke up. "The orbit worked out?"

45

Canfield nodded and the light arrow bobbled on the chart. "Back for thousands of years. We are almost certain which of the Canadian strikes were on what intersections. Naturally, there were many thousands of years when Shiva was nowhere near us. In previous encounters—and we estimate over fifteen at the moment, all peripheral—we only brushed against it, as it were. We anticipate no more strikes on *this* orbit, but can expect the leaders of the swarm to be encountered in approximately ten months."

Chuck Bradshaw thanked Canfield, who returned to his seat. "Now here are the four major plans we have worked out." He touched a button on the podium console and words appeared on the screen, which Chuck read aloud.

"One. Deflect Shiva with one huge hydrogen bomb blast, carefully placed. Estimate of bomb size: minimum four hundred megatons." There were some murmurs, but Chuck kept on. A second paragraph appeared.

"Two. Blast Shiva into small pieces with the same four hundred-megaton bomb. It must be carefully positioned so it will shatter into fragments small enough to burn up in the atmosphere or to inflict minimal damage."

"Minimal damage," muttered Diego. "Nice phrase."

"Shush," Lisa said.

"Three. Use about thirty-five small—they're twenty-megaton—bombs to disintegrate Shiva into small fragments."

"Which means what—?" someone asked in a loud whisper. "Orbiting them or hand-planting?"

"And four, deflect Shiva with about twenty small bombs, planted strategically upon the surface."

"By hand," groaned the same someone from the anonymity of the group.

Chuck Bradshaw turned back to the assembled group. "Of course there are drawbacks to each plan—"

"Murphy's Law," Mort Smith called out.

Bradshaw ignored him. "In every case it will be necessary for Earth to sustain considerable damage—"

"What happened to minimal damage?" Diego muttered.

"—for a number of asteroids and probably fragments

of Shiva itself *will* get through. There is no way now to determine exactly how many will strike or where."

Mort Smith spoke up. "You mean Earth will be, in effect, shotgunned by this meteor swarm?"

Bradshaw nodded. "I'm afraid so. The important thing is that we divert or destroy Shiva. The other asteroids—as big as they are—well, Earth will have to absorb them. Somehow. Someway."

Dink Lowell raised his hand. His face was flushed, but not from drink this time. "Okay, where do we get a four-hundred-megaton bomb? There ain't no such animal. Not as far as I know."

Chuck nodded. "You have put your finger on it, Dink. No bomb big enough. And twenty twenty-megatonners aren't the same. We are getting an estimate now on how long it will take to build one. The prognosis is not good. But if we *can* build one, we think it would be our best bet."

"We have enough thermonuclear bombs, don't we?" Mort Smith asked.

Carl Jagens stood up before Chuck could answer. "The problem isn't getting enough twenty-megaton missiles. We have more than enough. It's in the triggering. Microseconds are involved here. *Could* we trigger twenty bombs simultaneously? The first bomb could easily destroy the others, if there is much of a time lapse."

"When did Carl become a bomb expert?" Diego asked.

"When it became the important part," Lisa whispered.

"We have no triggering devices *as yet* that could guarantee simultaneous and certain detonation," Carl said. "The timing devices—" He broke off as Chuck began to speak. "Sorry, Chuck."

"Yes, well. None of the triggering mechanisms have been tested for prolonged exposure in space. There will undoubtedly be damage from dust and rocks, probably confusion in communications, equipment failure, and other difficulties."

"Other difficulties," Dink Lowell echoed. "New term for pilot error!" There were a few laughs.

"We will have to work mostly *within* the Shiva swarm itself. While we don't have a good reading on that yet, we do know it is more than just a few big rocks. Dust.

47

Pebbles. Lots of little bitty stuff too fine for avoidance radar."

"Can we fine-tune it?" someone called out.

"Maybe. But then the equipment would take a beating from all the small stuff. We are estimating a fifty percent equipment failure at this point." Several people whistled.

Susan Robinson spoke up. "What about kamikaze pilots?"

Several people laughed but Chuck Bradshaw was not one of them. "We considered that. And rejected it. It is a last-ditch resort."

"But a possibility," Susan said.

"Yes. It is a possibility," Chuck said soberly. "But that's not for publication."

"What you really mean is that we don't have anything hot enough to punch with, don't you, Chuck?" Susan said, her eyes level.

"That's a possibility, too," he replied.

They looked at each other, then began studying their fingers or the floor. Bradshaw cleared his throat quietly, hesitated, then left.

No one looked up.

2 August: Collision minus 9 months, 24 days

Carl Jagens puffed out into the layered summer air of Houston, dancing lightly in his running shoes to loosen his thigh muscles. He wore blue shorts and a gray sweatshirt with *University of Wisconsin* stenciled on it in black. The training track for the astronauts was a pool of light in the darkening landscape of the base. There were others on the track, but only a few, isolated in their running, serious-faced and sweating.

A lurid sunset was ebbing in the west, orange turning to red and the purple creeping in from the east. Carl felt the familiar tension in his shoulders and knew this was the only way to work it out. The tightness told him it was time for some therapeutic running. He usually worked out on the exercise machines, where he could keep his hand-eye coordination in shape. But he preferred ordinary jogging if the twisting in his back was really bad, and today he'd been feeling it since before lunch.

He started off quickly, wanting to work up a sweat. It always seemed to cool him in these humid early evenings. He could feel the sheen of sweat break out on his forehead, and as if in response, his legs pumped harder and the thick air went by with a tangible feel, a watery touch. He picked up the pace and settled into a quick tempo, passing two anonymous men in hooded sweatshirts who were slowing down.

The world had gone metric long ago, but athletic events kept to the canonical standard. Four circuits of the track equaled a mile. He glanced at his wrist timer: six minutes, seven seconds. Not bad for a man just beginning to feel the slight downward tilt in his abilities, after the long plateau of the late twenties. Not bad, but not all that damned good, either. He was no superman and he knew it. But astronauts didn't need to be. Experience was more useful than muscle. Still, the time would come when the hand delayed a bit too long, when the eye didn't track quite so accurately. That was when you stopped being a pilot and became a groundhog, manning a console or a desk, talking through a mike at men who were doing what you once did. That's what was overtaking Dink Lowell, and look at what it was doing to the guy. The first tangible evidence of mortality: grounding.

The first mile behind him, Carl settled into a grinding, methodical pace. *Thunk thunk thunk*—it came up to him through the bones, his feet churning on with a curious solid sound like chunks of wood falling on an oak floor. A rhythm, a reassuring pounding that swept him around the track beneath the stark lights.

He knew why he was here. The images floated up to him now, arranging themselves. This was the way he put his internal house in order. Carl wasn't given to analysis—nobody who got into the astronaut program was—but he knew this was his own private therapy. Here was where he found out how he felt about things. Here was where the ideas and decisions surfaced.

Shiva. His first reaction—he could admit it now—had been utter fear. He knew what the numbers implied. The searing images inside boiled out now, playing gaudy scenes in his mind's eye.

And the implications: the end of Carl Jagens.

Carl clenched his jaw, relaxed, clenched, relaxed. So he was afraid—so what? He'd been afraid before. On the moon, in orbit, during that snafued liftoff at Vandenberg, the time the gel-gas tanker had veered toward him coming out of the Bay tunnel. Hell, there had been lots of times. The important point was that you went beyond the moment of fear. You caught yourself before your guts spilled out all over the universe for everyone to see. That was the big thing.

Thunk thunk thunk. Distant, hazy memories, schoolyard memories. The bullying of Jerry Osbourne, the senseless fighting and scuffling, the unreasoning fright. He remembered Osbourne's look, every commonplace pinch of it, remembered the resentment, and smiled faintly. You'd think you'd forget, wouldn't you? he asked himself. But he also remembered the satisfying final battle. He'd emerged bloody-nosed but victorious, forever freed from barbaric servitude to the schoolyard vandal. It had taken three years, but he had won. Finally. With finality. He had even been gracious, after, but inside, smug and triumphant.

Shiva.

The unexpected was a concealed opportunity, wasn't that what Benjamin Franklin had said? Shiva was an opportunity. But for what?

Thunk thunk thunk thunk. He kept on, wheeling beneath the glaring lights in the close air, thinking. The whole space adventure was waning, winding down. He had seen that over two years ago. Carl remembered that he had realized that fact on another long run like this one, training in California. He'd put the facts together —ebbing appropriations, a falloff in the orbital manufacturing program, a decline in the Gallup International Poll, fewer requests for personal appearances, fewer clippings. The next step out was such a big one: distant Mars, even more distant Jupiter moons, the impossibly far stars. People didn't want to think about it. Not with their pocketbooks, they didn't.

Thunk thunk. Maybe the exploration of space would eventually lead to an expanded human community, with permanent off-planet colonies, but there was a long slow grind before that day. Nobody in the centers of power had the faith to keep NASA expanding outward at its present pace. And if NASA didn't grow, neither would Carl Jagens. Eventually he'd have to leave astronaut operations and become an executive, planning missions rather than going on them. But what kick was there in working out nickel and dime missions, flights less interesting than the ones you'd already been on yourself, even if they *were* longer or farther?

It was then, on that dusty track in California, that he'd decided to work more with the media people. He knew then that he had a talent for that stuff. He even enjoyed it, sometimes. So he had done a bit more of it, beyond what was expected of all astronauts, and found it worked even better. There was something good about standing in front of a three-D camera and knowing you were in control, that what you said mattered. Yes, mattered to a *lot* of people, the real people, not just to a bunch of NASA execs or to a few of your fellow astronauts, who were jealous of you anyway.

So he had worked with the media, thinking that was the best way out of the closing trap of NASA. After all, John Glenn got out more or less that way. Glenn had overcome that laughable accident, falling down in a shower at home and banging up his head. He had overcome it and won a seat in the U. S. Senate. That was something, to become a senator.

Thunk thunk thunk thunk. Yeah, senators were influential. But it wasn't the power in itself that he wanted. He had abilities to give the world. He had to have power to give himself some scope, a larger canvas to paint on. Even the illusion of power was power. But what had Kennedy said? The men who create power make an indispensable contribution to the nation's greatness. And Sumner, saying that if you live in a town that is run by a committee—be on the committee! And Hammarskjold: only he deserves power who every day justifies it.

That larger canvas, that power to be free to do, that was what he had wanted ever since—well, Christ, it must've been since high school, when he had started doing so well in algebra and built that science project and tried out for the football team. All of a sudden people were saying hello to him in the hallways, people were asking him things, the principal had him in for a little talk, slapping him on the back, and Christ, it had been good. Damned good. Now he wanted the ability to *do* things, bigger things, to try his hand at the whole big world.

But now maybe politics and the media weren't the answer. Maybe Shiva was. This whole thing could revive the space program. A success would make saints and heroes of them all. The card he thought he had devalued now turned out to be a trump.

Thunk thunk thunk. Chest heaving, sweat trickling into his eyes, stinging, blurring the piercing lights beating down. A trump. He didn't gamble, but he liked the language. Some people were trumps, some were small cards, some were jokers. Chuck Bradshaw, for instance. A good paper-pusher, but what the hell did he know about the way things really worked? Bradshaw took orders and saw that they were carried out, that was all. A brick in the pyramid. He would never have thought about romancing Senator McGarry a full year before he was due to be on the Appropriations Committee. He would never have flown to Powell Hopkins's home state when that feisty little man had faced sudden, tough opposition from a big newspaper and television mogul. Bradshaw couldn't see past the next mission. If that far.

Maybe he should go after Bradshaw's job, a vastly extended one . . . no, wait, it was better to be nearer the events. Nearer Shiva. George C. Marshall really ran World War Two, but who remembered his wrinkled face? Who nominated him for president? No, people went for the guy who had been a lowly colonel at the start of the war, who had never commanded troops in battle before, but who was the guy right there at the Normandy thing. World War Two made Eisenhower. Shiva would make Carl Jagens.

Thunk thunk thunk. He passed one, then two men, a woman with her hair in a single thick braid, and realized he had passed them before, easily. He was breathing heavily now, sucking in the cooling moist air. The sky yawned black and solid above the lights. He could see the hazy dome of light from Houston and the blinking red lights of the commuter planes coming in. The tightness was gone. He had his balance back, he knew how he felt. He could work again, undisturbed by doubts.

"Sir! Captain Jagens! Sir?"

Carl slowed, blinked, losing his rhythm. A gray-clad runner swerved to pass him. A noncom was waving at him from the locker room passage. Jagens ran out onto the infield grass and stopped, chest heaving. "Yeah?" His voice came out a croak.

"Sir, I, I was wondering. Last chow call is in a few minutes."

"Oh. Yeah." He waved his hand vaguely at the corporal.

"I've been watching you, sir. Uh, you've been out here an hour and a half."

"Uh-huh."

"That's a lot of running, sir," he said with open admiration. "You guys sure do keep in shape. Sir."

"Right."

Carl looked around, blinking, and wiped the sweat from his brow. He resented the corporal's intrusion. He looked up the track, then trotted across and into the locker passage. He slapped the corporal on the shoulder and went quickly into the building. He dimly perceived that his chest was heaving, his throat raw. His breath wheezed in and out. He was exhausted. But somehow there was no feeling of lassitude. Instead, energy seemed to flow through him. He could have run more if he'd wanted, he was sure of that. Like Apaches, who could run fifty miles, outrun a horse. He was going to be in the best physical shape of any astronaut in the team, he would make certain of that. Yeah. He could still go the distance. He would call the shots.

4 August: Collision minus 9 months 22 days

"Thirty minutes, Mister President."

"Thank you, Steve," the chief executive said, giving his press secretary a quick smile. He sat in the cozy, informal office next to the much larger Oval Office, feeling a little foolish as he always did when wearing makeup. But like every other modern politician, he bowed to the needs and pressures of television. It was still the primary source of information for almost three hundred million Americans and the best political tool available.

John Caleb Knowles looked blankly at his speech. It was a photocopy, one of several. The original had been whisked off to the Presidential Papers file, another copy to the teleprompter technician, and still another to the reproduction room to make copies for the press. He felt locked in, annoyed at being basically unable to veer from the prepared text. But it had all been checked and rechecked by the various aides and departments. *Sanitized,* he thought.

He smiled wryly. Very little of the rolling, noble rhetoric of Roosevelt or the biting directness of Truman was left. Nor the lifting speeches of Kennedy. Everything was polished; no rough edges. Ethnic considerations, security, foreign policy, party policy, prevalent social attitudes—these and more were the fine screens that all modern speeches seemed to be filtered through. Noble phrases, stirring words, directness, heart, *worth* were all strained out.

Not that I am an orator, Knowles thought. But I *do* have some good people working for me. And then there are the filter-people. He sighed, a large, aging, middle American vote-getter with a cramped stomach and an empty heart. What had Eisenhower told Kennedy on his inauguration day? "You'll find that no *easy* problems ever come to the President of the United States. If they are easy to solve, somebody else has solved them." And Truman's *The buck stops here.*

Knowles heaved a great sigh. He glanced up as Myron Murray came in, smiled automatically but weakly, and dropped his eyes again.

"Looks like a very big audience, Mister President," Murray said. "Rumors . . ." he shrugged.

"Congress?"

"Almost one hundred percent behind you."

Knowles smiled. "Almost? Senator Leland?"

Murray nodded. "As usual. If you said the sun was coming up tomorrow, he'd accuse you of pandering to the rooster vote."

"Ah, politics." The President raised his head and looked at a bronze bust of Lincoln. "You know, Myron, statesmanship is harder than politics. Politics is the art of getting along with people . . . but statesmanship is the art of getting along with politicians."

Murray laughed politely. He'd heard it before. "Would you like something before you go on, sir?"

"What kind of something?" Knowles was mildly curious. Murray was the traditional bag-of-tricks man, a high-level scrounger and fixer.

Murray tipped his head. "Drink? Something to bring you up."

"I look down?"

"Yes, sir."

Knowles nodded. "That obvious?" Murray said nothing. The President sighed and shook his head. "No, nothing." Murray left unobtrusively.

Knowles stared at the bronze for a while. "Loneliness is solitude you don't want," he said in a whisper. Leaning forward, he touched a key on the terminal near him. "Grace, will you see if Mrs. Carr is available?"

"Yes, sir."

He sat back, sighing. The wealthy and powerful are said to be lonely, he thought. Perhaps because everyone wants to be their friend. One corner of his mouth bent up in a faint smile. Loneliness is the one thing all people share, he thought.

There was a knock at the door and he said, "Come in."

Barbara Carr poked her head in. "Sir?"

"Come in, Barbara, please. Sit with me?"

"Yes, sir. Can I get you anything?"

"No." He smiled, shook his head, and indicated a chair. "Funny how they furnish the White House, isn't it?" he said conversationally. "Traditional as hell. Right out of the Revolutionary period. Neo-Roman, Chippendale, and all that. And inside the old desks, computer terminals."

She sat down gracefully, smoothing her skirt under her. "New wine in old bottles, sir?" He smiled politely, but wearily.

"You look well, Barbara. Things going all right?"

"Yes, sir. Mister Orr is a good boss."

"Publicity and press relations are a tool, like any other, Barbara. They have to be handled by experts. Political power grows out of the tube of a television set."

She smiled at his small joke and looked around. "The Oval Office has become rather like the old parlor, hasn't it, Mister President? For show?"

Knowles shrugged. "People expect it. It looks more official. I could do a better job down in the briefing room or in one of State's studios, but people like it right from the seat of power."

Her face grew tight. "How do you think they are going to like what you have to say tonight?"

"They aren't. Who would? But what can we do?" He looked at the Lincoln bust again. "Americans have always pulled together when they were in danger, and saw it clearly. We don't really let ourselves be pushed around —by dictators or demagogues . . . or meteor mountains."

"If we can't do the job, there's no one else," she said.

Knowles nodded. "We have vitality and integrity and strength. No matter what anyone says." He smiled at her. "Barbara, it is good to see you. That's a lovely dress. Oh, I've said that before."

"Yes, sir, but thank you, anyway . . . again."

"Have you had dinner?"

"No, I was waiting until after. Steve and I thought . . ."

Knowles waved his hand in disagreement. "No, no, not tonight. Tonight you'll dine with me. Fashionably late, of course, after I finish changing the course of the world. Philippe is one of the best chefs in the world and all he ever gets to cook are big state dinners. Tonight we'll have . . . no, you decide. You call up Philippe and make up a menu to please *you*." At her expression he smiled. "Please by my guest, I . . ." He stopped and looked away.

"Thank you, Mister President, I, I'd be honored."

Someone stuck his head in the door behind the President. "Five minutes, Mister President."

"Thank you." He looked at Barbara. "Just the two of us, eh? A little California wine as well?" He rose and she quickly uncrossed her ankles to stand as well. "Do you know that someone once said that Americans insist on living in the present tense?"

"It's the only tense we have," she replied, smiling.

"Good thing, too, or we wouldn't have the system to combat this Shiva thing." He stepped on the door, then looked back with another smile. "On the other hand, think what our culture would be like if there had been no whorehouses in New Orleans."

He left her smiling and puzzled. After a few moments she slipped through the door into the Oval Office. Light and television cables snaked across the floor and one end of the room was brilliantly lit. President Knowles was seated in his large chair, behind the gnarled Lincoln desk. A makeup man was bending over him and the chief executive sat patiently, his eyes closed. Barbara moved behind the cameras and nodded at Steve Banning, Senator Mathison, and Congressman Hopkins, who were looking at her from one of the couches. She felt conspicuous and moved quietly toward the back of the room.

Gilbert McNellis, the Secretary of State, was talking to Michael Potter, the Secretary of Space. She brushed by them and noted they automatically shut down the conversation at her approach, smiling perfunctorily at her. She stood near General James McGahan, who nodded soberly to her.

"Thirty seconds."

Knowles sat up straighter, took up some papers in his hand, and looked straight at the camera. Barbara saw it happen with a certain surprise, although she had seen it many times before: the transformation of John Caleb Knowles from tired, worried, aging politician to the President of the United States, calm, intelligent, powerful, merciful, the man in command.

She looked at the monitor; images of government, traditional government. Long shot, White House. Close shot, White House, Oval Office windows. Close shot, Presidential seal. "Ladies and gentlemen, the President of the United States." That introduction, so simple, so unadorned, had always thrilled her, no matter what person held the office.

Dissolve: John Caleb Knowles at his desk.

"My fellow Americans, I come to you tonight with disturbing and perhaps even frightening news . . ."

Douglas Kress punched the remote control stud in the side of his armchair and the three-dimensional holographic image dwindled away. The dollhouse White House, illuminated all around by floodlights, folded in on itself, turned blue and vanished. The holographic stage automatically folded up as well and the carpet-backed panels slid into place.

Kress stared at the empty space. *A falling away of all things,* he thought. The secular world fading away in the great hour of crisis. The shrinking White House was just one more sign of what this event truly meant to the world. The Lord had a way of making these small signs, subtle but clear. Only the truly devoted could read the significance of them, at first.

Kress got up and stretched. He felt his back and shoulder muscles relax. They had cramped while he was watching the three-D. Now they sang with new energy. *Informing grace*, he thought. The moment has come. The final holy days.

He was a big man, accustomed to dominating whatever group he was with, and he was aware of his physical presence. Somehow, now, this living room he stood in seemed too small and narrow for him. Strange how he had never noticed that before.

Kress looked around the apartment. The words of the President—poor, deluded man, obviously afraid, obviously feeling inadequate—still ran through his mind. A revelation which he could not discount, even considering the source.

He could see his wife and children were watching him, as they always did, waiting for his first visible reaction. Their faces tilted up to him caught the diffused light from the small lamps. Faces all blank, faces waiting for an imprint. He would give it to them.

"Our mission has come at last," he said. "Our true mission." His family let out their breath, their faces still blank. He held out his arms to his wife. "Here, darling." Poor dear creature, so afraid; it was so clear. So many things were clear to him now, and becoming even clearer.

He enfolded her in his arms. He watched a small dark mole on her jaw as it swelled in his vision. Blemishes of the body, outward signs of the disturbance she felt within. She had always been like that, not truly liberated from the concerns of the present, not able to see past the tangle of the immediate world. Mired in the body. He squeezed her to press confidence into her frail frame, into the mortal clay that was his charge.

Strange, the perceptions that came to him. Her neck stretched up to kiss his throat, her body compressed, her breasts flattening against him. So weak and easily shaped, she was. He looked beyond her, at the children. Their faces were now filled with hope and trust. Already he could sense the power flowing out of him and into those around him.

He looked out the window at the plain bleak street,

shadowed by nightfall, banded with pale light from the ranks and tiers of apartments. He could feel the emptiness out there waiting for him. Waiting for the humming fresh force that he could bring.

"There is no doubt in the world now," he said. "We see what this means."

His wife drew away from him to peer up into his eyes. Her lips parted to make a sound, a hesitant sound laced with doubt.

"They will try to stop it," he said. "It is the way they think, those technocrats. But they cannot. This is the divine justice we have so long spoken of."

"Justice?" his wife asked in a hollow voice.

"A cleansing, my dear."

His son, who was seven, sat up. "That big rock is going to hit the earth, Daddy? You think the President won't stop it?" The boy seemed puzzled. Well, that was natural, Kress thought. The holographic newscast had confused the boy about what was important.

"The terrible fires and death we have witnessed these last few days," Kress said, "were a portent, my son." He could feel his voice grow and fill his chest; the gift of projecting himself. He had been grateful to the Lord for this gift in the past. It had helped him through this life. He always rose rapidly in every church he joined, charismatic, magnetic, rising until they rose against him, tools of darkness, to drive him out.

But it was really he who drove them out, driving away their tainted church, their blind prejudice, their unreasoning animal reactions. At last he saw what his gift was really for.

It was for these days ahead. For the Time of Last Things.

"People died, Daddy. Are more people going to die?"

"They must." He released his wife as he spread his hands. "There will be no stopping the hand that is descending upon us now."

"But, Daddy, the President said—"

"Delusion! That man is the captive of the godless powers who secretly run this country. They cannot see the truth behind these events." He fixed his young son and the boy's younger sister in an eagle's glare and they shrank back, staring.

His wife spoke timidly, touching his arm. "But, dear,

the President said they had a way to stop it, maybe not absolutely certain, but almost certain and—"

Kress laughed, a rolling laugh that swelled and filled the room. He stepped away from her, speaking toward the wall where the flat photographs of his family were hung. "They will fail," he announced to his ancestors. Then he turned back. "To oppose what is coming is a sin!" He put out a hand toward her. "My wife, if they truly mean to try to stay God's hand, of *course* we will halt them." He drew himself up. "All the righteous will band together!"

"Daddy," his daughter said in a small, squeaky voice, "does that mean those rocks can fall *here?*"

He looked down upon them and felt the air in the room thicken and grow heavy. The hum of the waiting town outside murmured at the windows. The world was compressing around this room, awaiting his reply. Scratchy wool filled his throat. Were pivotal men always aware of these moments? They must have been.

"Daughter, the stones from heaven will fall everywhere." He gestured out to the world. "They will burn and blacken and cast down all the false powers. Our great cities will lie in ruins. Our vain, elaborate machines will shatter and fail."

"And *us* . . . ?" His wife spoke in a thin voice, clutching at the front of her dress. He noticed that her lower lip trembled and her face was flushed. Often when people listened to him their faces drew the blood from their limbs and their flesh reddened with the power of the truth that came out of him. When that happened he knew he was once again the vessel the Lord intended.

"A return to the simple, raw struggle for survival. For the fortunate, chosen few. Blessed by the Lord." Odd how his voice filled the room, pressing everything flat, even human flesh.

"What, what if a rock hits here, Daddy?" his son asked.

He made a gesture of dismissal. "We will die. But we will perish in God's service, my son."

They fell silent. Kress felt them draw away from him. The fear flickered in their faces. He smiled, forgiving them. He could hear the humming of the city outside, even faint voices urgently calling out. He could feel the people who needed to hear the truth, who would cling desperately to the word if it was only made manifest to them. If they felt it, truly felt it, they would not cooperate with the puny efforts of the scientists. They would accept the natural order of things. They would be ready to receive the new world the Lord was bringing, bringing with His fire from heaven.

But to reach the people, Kress suddenly saw, he would have to speak with renewed power, with an amplified voice, with a presence larger than life. He would have to speak through the atheist siren call of television and use its illusion of reality for his own ends. For the Lord's ends. To truly carry the word would tax him to the limit; he was certain of that. For years he had spoken in the churches and the tent revivals, the storefront missions and the forums in the park, but this was more, vastly much more. It would sap his strength, test his faith. And the place to begin, to practice, to hone the weapon he must wield, was here: in his own home, to his own family.

"Yes!" he said suddenly, the voice rolling out of him. "We must be ready for death. That is what the fire stones say to us." They peered up at him. Open faces. Slates to be written on. He spread his arms wide, palms up. "Come. Let us pray."

After a moment they bowed their seeking faces and Douglas Arthur Kress felt the energy surge and dance and sing in himself again. A shiver of joy ran over his skin. Electricity of the spirit. Spiritual resolve. Yes. Yes.

The exhaltation brought increased sensitivity. Everything was brighter, clearer: the worn spot where the floor panels folded over the holographic well, the stain on the wall near the kitchen, the sloppily repaired chair leg, his wife's ill-fitting dress, the pimple on his son's chin. He looked up, seeing the low-energy light, the shadows, the stains.

He had found himself, as men did in moments of stress. He had found the grandest mission of all—service to the Lord.

"Let us pray."

5 August: Collision minus 9 months, 21 days

Myron Murray came in hurriedly, holding a black video cassette in his hand. "Sir, this just came in," he said, going toward the four-screen complex at one side of the Oval Office. He flipped up the panel that concealed a video cassette player and slapped the unit in. "Simultaneous translation on the official Russian channel, beamed by satellite all over the world."

Knowles put down a report and laced his fingers together. His stomach gave a tight lurch but he kept it down. The screen blipped and he was looking at a swift montage of Russian power: Red Square during a May Day parade with the immense bulk of the KV2 "Lev" or Lion missile, the main Russian space station with North America beneath it in the background, a very low pass by a wing of the newest jet fighter-bombers over Moscow, peasants in the fields, giant harvesters churning wheat, tractors, a smiling baby in a mother's arms, another Red Square shot of massed might, then a huge banner of Marx, Lenin, and Yaroslav Kalinin.

Dissolve. Yaroslav Kalinin himself, in a plain uniform, without insigne, but with the Order of the Red Star on his chest.

"Comrades throughout the world . . ."

Myron Murray spoke over the translator. "This is all propaganda stuff, of course; reminders of Soviet power and Marxist idealism."

"Our brave undercover operatives and their sneaky spies."

"Sir?"

"Never mind."

". . . Soviet science has once again supplied the proper response to a threat from without. Almost overnight comrade scientists, working against great odds and under incredible pressures, have produced the exact device necessary to destroy this menace from space, this meteor the Americans call Shiva—"

"Neat, neat, linking us with—"

"Shush, Myron."

"—a miracle of Soviet science and Soviet will. We freely offer this four-hundred-megaton atomic device, the cause of saving mankind. The Central Committee does—"

"The rest is puffery," Myron said, looking at his boss with his hand on the controls. Knowles waved his hand down and Murray shut off the cassette.

"So, they had one after all," Knowles said softly.

"They said they built it for this, but . . ."

"The CIA *thought* they might have built a doomsday device during that last crisis, five, six years ago, but they could never pinpoint it." Knowles chewed at one corner of his mouth and looked at the fine wrinkles on the back of his left hand. "They never had to threaten us—or China—with it, but they had it, like an ace up the sleeve." He sighed.

"Get onto State and Defense and see about transporting it to the Cape. Get the specs, the whole thing. They are going to need all that to design a craft to carry it."

"Yes, sir." He left swiftly and Knowles picked up his discarded report. But he found he was looking at the words and not seeing.

A four-hundred-megaton bomb.

Twenty times bigger than the standard twenty-megaton missile. It could wipe out the East Coast quite effectively, send radiation throughout the world, destroy the—

He broke off that line of thought with an abrupt shake of his head. He felt his stomach lurch, but he forced himself to be calm. He couldn't lose his head. He was the President. Everyone looked to him for guidance. He chewed at his lip, feeling guilty. He was only a man, one man, not a god, not a superman. They should only expect so much from him.

Yes, only so much.

9 August: Collision minus 9 months, 17 days

Lisa Bander was breathing heavily, her eyes flaring, her fists bunched into tight balls at the ends of her stiffened arms.

"Carl, we must have *some* options!"

He looked at her, an exaggerated expression of pity on his handsome face. "Oh? Why? The Soviet bomb, properly placed, will divert Shiva. We have always accepted the fact that some meteorite damage must be taken. There are simply too many minor asteroids to handle. Shiva is the priority target. Bump that and the main danger is over."

"But what if it doesn't *work?*" Lisa said, controlling

her voice. The argument had gone around and around for hours.

"It *will* work. With me in command it will—"

"Wait a minute," Dink Lowell interrupted. "Who put *you* in charge?"

Carl Jagens fixed the smaller ex-astronaut with a hard look. "Who is better for the job? Who knows the system better?"

Diego Calderon said, "No one is disputing your technical ability, Carl, nor your experience."

"I am senior here," the blonde man said, not without pride.

"By about five days," muttered Dink.

"What?" Carl said, quickly turning back to him, glaring. The various scientists unlucky enough to be sitting between them pretended the exchange was not happening. They consulted notes or looked thoughtfully off into the distance, or exchanged embarrassed looks with their colleagues. These astronauts were the people who would actually be doing the work, and required some leeway, once the options had been worked out.

"I said you are not Superman, Carl, just another working astronaut," Dink said, holding up against Carl's glare.

"Which you are *not*, not any longer," Carl said crisply.

"Hey!" Diego said, standing up. "This is a team, Carl, as you damn well know. There's not all that much we can do without the backup on the ground. Dink was docking Saturns before you first lifted off, don't you forget that."

"Yes, and it is time for the newer and better pilots to take over." Carl gave Diego a lofty look, then glared again at Dink.

"Why the hell isn't Chuck back?" Mort Smith asked the room at large.

"Because he has to hand-hold the President and the media, that's why," Lisa said.

Susan Robinson stretched. "Well, I for one, am damned tired of arguing and arguing over and over the same ground. *We* don't have the power to decide on the specifics, so let's adjourn until Chuck comes back. What about it?"

"No, we're wasting time," Lisa said. "We don't have

any hours to waste. I'm for trying with the Soviet bomb to divert Shiva . . . *but* I want a multiple-option backup —as many twenty-megatonners as we can lift, plus all the U.N. devices now in orbit."

Carl shrugged. "As long as we try my method first."

"*Your* method?" Diego said in surprise.

"I helped develop it," Carl said. There was a tight, defensive edge to his voice.

Susan Robinson made a rude sound and stood up. "I'm getting some sleep, I don't know about you guys."

"I'll join you," Mort Smith said, getting up.

"Ho-ho," Susan said flatly and several of the astronauts laughed at his discomfort.

"I didn't mean . . . oh, hell." He clumped out after her. Several of the scientists followed, whispering together in clusters. Diego, Lisa, Carl, and Dink were left.

They sat still, not looking at each other, not quite certain what to do or say. It made Lisa uncomfortable. NASA infighting had never been something she sought, liked, or felt good at. But Carl was very good at it indeed.

Ask the man on the street to name an astronaut and he would most likely say Carl Jagens, or perhaps pick some astronaut who was no longer in the program, like one of the original Mercury or Apollo men. He *might* name Lisa Bander, because of her prominence as the best—though not the first—of the female astronauts. But Carl's constant stroking of the press had given him a prominence in the public eye that was not shared by his fellow astronauts.

Jagen's prominence had been earned. He had been one of a four-person team searching for ice in caves on the farside of the moon. A moonquake had collapsed the roof, injuring Carl and killing one of the astronauts. The spare oxygen was in the spidery frame ship outside, their tanks were running low, and their communications were out. They had worked like demons, but Carl had been the only one to pace himself. He didn't panic and he lasted a half hour longer; the rest had collapsed, panting, blue, and almost dead. That half hour made the difference. Carl got through the rubble, returned with the spare tanks, and saved the other two survivors.

Paul Morrison had been the first astronaut actually

buried on the moon. There had been considerable television coverage and Lisa was almost certain Carl had stood where he had, mourning, because behind him were the unfurled flags of the United States and the United Nations, ripples frozen in an unseen wind. The other astronauts, most of them now out of the program, were grouped around, but it was Carl who knew how the cameramen framed things.

Lisa had to admit that Carl's anticipation of the direction of the various political, technical, and scientific developments had kept him constantly in the public—and NASA's—eye. He was so well-known that any Shiva team that did not contain him would be suspect and any team that did not name him their leader would be scrutinized by a Congressional committee, in all likelihood.

None of Carl Jagen's maneuvers with the media and the NASA superstructure had endeared him to his fellow workers. They didn't mind his exacting and demanding nature—theirs was an exacting and demanding field—but it was his *way* of demanding and exacting that irked many. Still, he had a few admirers and adherents; it was just that few of them actually worked with him.

Lisa raised her head and looked at Carl. "Well, you certainly polarized the effort. It's either your way or certain failure."

Carl smiled at her. He rose from his seat in the small auditorium and walked toward the stage, turning to look at the others.

"It *is* the way to stop Shiva."

"It is *a* way to stop Shiva," Diego said.

"You gotta be right the *first* time, Carl," Dink said. "I think we should have a backup option."

"As many twenty-megatonners as possible," Lisa said.

Carl smiled. "I agree. My team will go in with the Soviet superbomb and your team," he looked significantly at Lisa, "will do the cleanup. The largest meteors of the swarm and so on."

Lisa sighed. "Aha," she said softly, "one big dramatic blow, one great decisive explosion."

Carl nodded soberly. "Yes."

"If you can sell it to Chuck," Dink said.

Carl waved his hand as if that was a minor point.

"It *is* the way and Bradshaw is intelligent enough to see it. Look at all the systems studies done—"

"They aren't finished yet," Dink said sharply.

Carl shrugged. "I went to Boston yesterday and talked to the people doing the study. I talked to the insiders and got the feel of how the report will read when it comes out."

"Aha," Lisa said again, softly. "The secret of success. Talk to the right people . . . at the right time."

Carl ignored her and looked at his watch. "I'm going now. You get some sleep. You'll see I'm right." He presented them with a wide, confident smile.

"Yes, sir," Lisa said and Carl gave her an annoyed look as he strode from the room.

"Ah, all the world loves a hero," Dink said.

"Carl is probably right, y'know," Diego said.

"I know, I know," Lisa said. "But it is *one* way, not *the* way. That man—!"

"Don't let him get to you," Diego said.

"He's a team player," Dink said. "As long as it is *his* team." He sighed and got up. "Might as well get some sleep. We terminal jocks have to get our beauty rest." He waved and moved off between the rows and out the door. " 'Bye, Beauty . . . bye, Zorro . . .'"

Diego turned around and looked at Lisa, several rows behind. "Well?"

"Well what?"

"Dinner at Culberson's? Rare wines? A candlelight affair? And . . . ?"

Lisa nodded with a weak smile. "Dinner, yes, Colonel Calderon, but right here on the base. I want to get in early. I have a stack of tapes to study. Stuff on the Soviet bomb they are sending us."

"Uh-huh. I can see what kind of relationship this is going to be. One little world-destroying rock and you have a headache." He threw up his hands. "So it's base chow again?"

"For a while," Lisa replied. "Probably for eight months or so."

Neither of them smiled.

Lisa smiled and sat down to face the panel of four reporters from all the networks. She sensed, rather than saw, the cameras zooming in on her, which made her nervous, but she betrayed none of it.

"Major Bander, it is very good of you to appear here with us today," Py Rudd said. "We all know you are very busy."

"I'm happy to, Mister Rudd. The people are vitally concerned with what we are doing here."

"Yes, but we don't want to interfere." Lisa smiled. The networks had been badgering Lyle Orr for weeks to get inside for a really close look. He had finally agreed, but to do it with all the networks at once. They had erected a small set on the floor of the Vertical Assembly Building at the John F. Kennedy Space Center, at Cape Canaveral. Rockets towered behind them, rising into the darkness. Here and there teams could be seen working in pools of bright light.

"Major Bander," Nancy Darrin said in her no-nonsense, don't-ever-lie-to-me voice. "There are still a great number of people who simply don't believe that a rock—even a two-kilometer rock—can possibly do such damage as has been predicted."

"Are you one of those, Miss Darrin?" Lisa asked.

"I'm just reflecting the thoughts of millions," the CBS reporter said, her eyes narrowing dangerously. "Please do not evade the question, Major Bander."

Lisa smiled. "There was no intention of evading the question. It would seem to me the simple physics of it has been explained time and again, but perhaps I could go over it once more and introduce some new elements I am not sure have been discussed."

"Please do," Nancy Darrin said with acid politeness.

"You have only to look at the moon to see that asteroids have struck repeatedly. The craters of Copernicus and Tycho, for example, can be seen with the naked eye from Earth. While many of the craters on the moon and on Mars are volcanic, many are impact craters. There is the Caloris Basin on Mercury, for example, which is more than eight hundred miles across.

The estimate is that a fifty-mile-diameter planetoid struck the planet about four billion years ago. Directly antipodal, that is, directly *through* the planet Mercury, opposite the Caloris Basin, is an area of weird terrain consisting of jumbled blocks, broken craters, and mountains that seem to have been literally shaken apart by the tremendous impact. The basin itself has been completely cratered. It is the planet's single largest feature, indeed, the largest surface feature of *any* planet in this solar system."

"Yes, yes," Nancy Darrin said quickly, "but that was back at virtually the beginning of the solar system. There was a great deal of material floating around then. Most of it has been absorbed by now. There's nothing out there that big."

"It doesn't have to be that big," Lisa responded. "Shiva is quite big enough, thank you."

Py Rudd smiled. "There are fifty-sixty-mile craters all over Mercury, and one a hundred and ten miles wide near the South Pole, but," he smiled in his loose-lipped manner, "that was then; this is now."

"The point is, Mister Rudd," Lisa said, "that impact craters are nothing new on *any* planet. The planetoid that struck Mercury, for example, sent a shock wave through the entire planet, with an estimated force a *trillion* times that of the mile-wide crater in Arizona. It lifted the planet's *far* side about ten meters, then shook it with afterquakes. Our own Mare Imbrium and Mare Orientale, on Luna, are nearly as large as the Caloris Basin. They, too, seemed to have affected surface features at their respective antipodal points. Almost all the craters on the smaller planets and satellites are impact craters." She smiled benignly at Nancy Darrin. "In fact, crater-scarred surfaces are the rule rather than the exception among the planets of the inner solar system. Radar mapping of Venus has shown us similar cratering beneath the cloud cover. But here on Earth the weathering has eroded away much of the evidence." She tilted her head and said, "In fact, Robert Dietz many years ago suggested the term *astrobleme,* or 'star wound,' for such craters."

Christine Mahlon, from PBS, asked a question in her soft voice. "Major Bander, can you give us some *examples* of the effect of such a strike in *other* terms?"

Lisa thought a moment. "Very well. Consider the enigma of the mammoths. These ancestors of the modern elephant have been known from the Miocene onward, and survived until about six thousand B.C. Their frozen carcasses have been found containing undigested stomach contents. Now this is very puzzling. Consider the days when we hunted the great blue whales. When they were killed in Antarctic Ocean waters but not dissected for a few hours, the whale's flesh was quite literally roasted within the insulating shell of blubber by the heat of its own putrefaction. Even for the mammoth, which was much smaller, the effect would be retarded by the operation of the square/cube law. But it still should be comparable."

Lisa saw the frown on the face of Nancy Darrin, who said, "Yes, yes, but what has this to do with Shiva?"

"The well-insulated stomach contents should so ferment as to become unrecognizable," Lisa said. "Yet mammoth carcasses found in Alaska and Siberia—lying in frozen jumbles of muck and tree trunks, in the permafrost—had stomach contents *undigested* and *unfermented.*"

Nancy Darrin looked disgusted. "Major Bander, is this some old Von Daniken nonsense?"

Lisa smiled slightly and spoke to Christine Mahlon. "I read that when they built the Alaska Highway there was one stretch where the bulldozer drivers had to work in gas masks. They uncovered and cut through so many carcasses that the area stank like an uncleared battlefield."

Nancy Darrin sighed noisily and looked up at the lights. Christine Mahlon gave her a look, then asked, "Yes, but how does this—"

"The trees, you see. Trees simply cannot grow in permafrost. The vegetation with which these carcasses are mixed belonged to zones hundreds of kilometers closer to the equator. And how would a beast as large as a mammoth survive on the tundra, as we know it now? There simply would not be enough food." She paused and looked down the line of newspeople. "Well, the fact is . . . I would hardly be surprised to learn that calamitous changes have occurred in the past. Perhaps from meteoric strikes, perhaps from other reasons. But

70

it *does* seem strange indeed that these changes should occur just at the racial demise of the mammoth."

Christine Mahlon tapped her pencil on the desk. "Are you saying, Major, that the climate changed so *fast* that these woolly mammoths were caught in tropical or at least much more temperate zones? And froze to death so *fast* that the fermentation of the contents of their stomachs was *frozen?*"

"I don't *know* that that is the case, Miz Mahlon, but those are the facts. It is *possible* that the Earth was struck so hard that it rolled on its axis and assumed its present-day configuration."

"You mean Florida could become, say, the North Pole, and Nome some kind of hot spot?" Christine Mahlon asked incredulously.

"Perhaps. In a manner of speaking. It is a theory, of course. Such a theory would account for many unusual facts, such as the ones mentioned." Lisa saw Hugh Michaels, the ABC science reporter, lift his hand, and nodded at him.

"Major Bander, how does volcanic action compare with these meteor impacts in force?"

"Not very well, Mister Michaels. Endogenous—or interior-generated—phenomena are just not in a league with asteroid impacts. Even the big Martian volcano is barely within the same category of major astroblemes. The asteroid that created the Vredevoort Ring structure in South Africa, for example, creating a crater over forty miles across, is estimated to be slightly *less* than Shiva, or about a mile in diameter, impacting at about twelve miles a second . . . resulting in an explosion estimated at about fifty *million* megatons." Lisa smiled politely at Nancy Darrin, as if directing her information toward that person who most needed it. "It wiped that portion of Africa *clean.* It threw enough debris into space to cause a planetwide ice age that lasted centuries. Rock layers tens of miles deep were peeled back like a . . . like a thrown-aside blanket. It opened a hole in the Earth's crust halfway down to the mantle. Blast-induced melting and lava, coming up from the interior, quickly filled the cavity. Shock waves and air blasts circled the Earth." She shrugged. "Luckily the only life on Earth consisted of single-cell plants in the

71

oceans. If there was anything higher in the evolutionary scale, it was destroyed."

A long silence followed Lisa's remarks.

The Soviet involvement in the Shiva mission created problems. No matter how vital time might be, diplomacy required a certain amount of unavoidable ritual. The Soviets called for an international meeting to settle issues of astronaut selection and crew ranking. It meant little or nothing of course; the important matters were worked out well in advance. Still, part of both U.S. and Soviet policy was to appear open and aboveboard. The media had developed a virtually infinite appetite for Shiva-related news. The State Department had no real input in the planning, but it did have enough power in the government to enlist a few astronauts in the ceremonies.

It all took time, and time was the one thing they had very little of.

NASA protested, and the astronauts wanted no part of it. But pressure mounted. The secretary of state argued forcefully with Knowles, and Chuck Bradshaw recognized a time-wasting battle when he saw one. He approved leave for five days' attendance at the London conference. The astronauts were to draw cards for the chore. But then Lisa Bander volunteered. Relieved, the others went back to work.

It was, as she expected, a circus. Photo flashes followed her everywhere. Video cameras tracked her every move. Hotel corridors were always lined with spectators —all official in some Byzantine way, and all useless— who pushed forward for a glimpse. Men pressed notes into her hand, or bribed room service waiters. They all wanted exclusive stories, had the answer to releasing her pent-up anxieties, or just wanted to touch the hem of greatness.

Getting from hotel to conference site was a parade. The streets were filled with faces. Dignitaries with unpronounceable names shook her hand until it was sore. Everyone she met seemed to mouth the same empty phrases, their eyes glistening with hope or sad with resignation. In the huge conference auditorium delegates from dozens of unlikely nations vied to make the most striking, Churchillian speeches. There were Biblical references, rolling sentences rich in adjectives, sly reminders of how *their* countries were helping—whether they were or not—but scarcely a mention of hardware or mission options.

Lisa's own remarks were greeted by the multilingual media as "simple, eloquent, direct" and given a two-minute recap spot on the evening news, overlaid on a pressroom scene of her shaking hands with the secretary of state, Princess Victoria and the new premier of France.

After the third day she called Bradshaw and told him about her sore hand. That did it. State relinquished claim to her time, even though the Fourth Estate gave up most reluctantly.

Rather than zip back to Houston, Lisa remained the last day in London. She called up an old friend, Kingsley Martin, and arranged an afternoon auto trip out of town.

Lisa left by a side door of the hotel, a scarf over her head, an unneeded umbrella angled over her face, and bracketed by her ever-present security men. A sputtering alcohol-powered auto with no government markings pulled up as they emerged. A man leaned forward and opened the door, smiling up at her.

She recognized Kingsley Martin as an updated edition, filled out in the waist and shoulders, smile tilted slightly askew in that wry way of his, but with his eyes questioning.

"Hi," she said, getting into the back seat. Without hesitation or much thought, she kissed him. The security men swept even blanker expressions over their noncommittal faces and peered up and down the narrow lane. One of them gestured and another car, a luxurious vintage Bentley, rolled up. Lisa saw one of them squinting up at the windows and parapets of the buildings around, as though afraid some video monitors might show a famous lady astronaut kissing a stranger. They were perhaps more worried about that than if some crank tried to take a swing at her. A crank they would probably be able to stop.

A security man got into the front seat and muttered something to the driver, undoubtedly another security man, and the car surged noisily away.

73

"Hi to you," Kingsley said, putting his arm around her. "Still's got some zip in it, I see."

"What has?"

"This." He kissed her again.

"Some things get better with age, like wine," he said after a moment, letting her go.

"Indeed." Lisa smiled warmly at him, a smile she recognized she had never used on anyone else. Kingsley Martin had been the first big love of her life, and although it hadn't worked out, there would always be a bond between them. He had gone back to England at the end of it, partly because there was a Fleet Street job awaiting and partly because the breakup with Lisa had soured him on things American. That had been almost nine years before. They had not met since.

She studied him as the little car whined its way out through the towns around London. A light winter fog pressed in at the windows and then dissipated as they left Croydon. From time to time the security man muttered into a radio and the driver kept the Bentley in the rear mirror at all times. The luxury car was supposed to be a decoy, if anything happened.

Kingsley launched into a description of his working life, recounting the agonies of writing a regular column for the *Observer*, relating curious and amusing anecdotes about the great and near-great, swearing at his senior editor.

He's putting me at ease, Lisa thought, appreciating the good will behind the effort. Few people in the last few days had that talent; for diplomats, they'd seemed surprisingly insensitive. She laughed easily at some of his stories and raised her eyebrows at others. They held hands.

Soon they were among the rolling hills still tinged with summer's green. Lisa reminded herself that here winter's gray never won a final victory, though it managed to strip the trees to naked branches. Kingsley rattled on, his voice lilting as he impersonated heavy-handed executives, ambitious stars of the new holographic amusement field, slovenly actors, and prominent politicians on both sides of the Atlantic. He led an interesting life, she knew, observing the shifting scene of a great city, from Parliament and the posh hotels to the seamy Soho nighteries.

74

"There!" he said suddenly, pointing. "Down that lane."

The security man braked and the other man muttered into a mike. The car pulled off onto a side road strewn with leaves, which crinkled under their tires.

"Wonderful spot down this way," Kingsley said. "Strordn'ry."

They stopped in a thick patch of woods that seemed to have avoided autumn's dead hand. Fog shrouded the low dips in an otherwise smoothly curving hillside. The security man in the passenger seat said, "Just a moment, if you please." He spoke again into the microphone. Several men got out of the Bentley and spread out into the woods.

"Ah, security, security," Kingsley said, smiling and squeezing her hand. After a few moments the security man pressed a finger to the receiver in his ear, muttered into the microphone, then nodded back at them and jumped out to open the door for Lisa. She climbed out, followed by Kingsley.

Lisa inhaled deeply. "How did you know it would be like this? It's beautiful," she said.

"Bit of local color. Something odd about the wind and humidity here. Or the soil. Or something." He turned toward her, thumbs hooked in his vest pockets, and they started walking. "You know the technical stuff isn't my long suit. Never was."

She nodded, smiling faintly. "I knew you were a wordsmith the first moment we met."

"Right, that's my line. I did a few holographic spots out here, for that 'Viewing Askance' show of mine. That's how I know it."

"Ah."

"Damned good research staff, actually."

"Um."

Kingsley turned abruptly and glared at the security man dutifully tagging along a few steps behind. "I'm certain you fellows do not need to tread directly on our heels."

The security man's face remained bland. With his eyes on Kingsley Martin he muttered into his radio, then stood with a finger pressed into his ear receiver. He nodded.

"Yes," Kingsley said, turning to Lisa. "We'll be along

presently. Do give it a rest." He took Lisa's arm and they started along the leaf-covered lane.

The security chief was joined by another man. They stood uncertainly for a few minutes, looking after their charges, then the chief spoke quietly into the radio. He and his companion put their hands behind their backs and turned slightly away, moving off the road into the grass, on either side. Lisa glanced over her shoulder to see them following at a greater distance, flanking their meandering route with studied casualness. The sight brought forth a pearly laugh.

They went along the lane. Blades of sunlight lanced through the trees. The wind rustled from time to time. A bird flew over, racing hard, banking into the woods.

"We were right about each other, weren't we?" Lisa said quietly.

"How so?"

"We've each turned out the way the other expected."

"You the astronaut wallah and me the opinion monger?" Kingsley furrowed his brow a moment. "Yes. Perhaps it's demeaning to be so predictable, but yes, you're right."

"So it was best we split up."

He stopped suddenly, breath fogging the air. She took a step or two before she turned back to him. "I wish I knew, Lisa."

"Well," she shrugged, "it's worked out."

"You mean we've made other lives."

"Well, yes."

"That doesn't mean we were right. It simply means we survived."

Lisa didn't know what to say. They continued walking, but with a trifle more energy. A self-conscious silence hung between them. For a few moments Lisa watched one of the security men moving through the trees far to their right.

"What's that?" Lisa pointed at a wrought-iron fence seen through the trees to their left. The fencing was so rickety it had bowed to the ground at spots.

"Old cemetery," Kingsley murmured, distracted.

"Let's go see."

They found the creaky gate that gave onto the cemetery grounds. Gnarled undergrowth grew along the footpaths and lapped against the limestone tombs. Here the thinned trees let in more of autumn's pale light and the land seemed more open, yielding itself up to the shrouded sky. Fog nestled around the streaked marble headstones on the shaded side of the hill. The long rows of boxy tombs looked like small houses. Their vault doors had keyholes, doorknobs, lintels, even working knockers. Grayed green bronze rectangles, cobwebbed and cold. To Lisa the bleached white stonework and ornamental gratings caught an air of the comical, a faint echo of horror movies and distorted realism. She turned to Kingsley, toiling up a gravel path, and was surprised to see him scowling.

"Did you do a 'Viewing Askance' from here, ever?" she asked.

"This bone collection?" he said curtly. "No."

Kingsley stopped at the inscription on a brown limestone tomb. "Barnsworth," he read. "Captain of the Guards in Her Majesty's et cetera. Interred in 1897. Look here."

He gestured at the smashed grating. Lisa peered through the narrow slit into the squarish tomb. "See that? The pile of sawdust on the floor? A rat or something gnawed into the coffin."

"Ah. Yes." It didn't awe or frighten or disgust her.

Kingsley tramped on to the next tomb. "This one's nice. 'Together now at last.' I should say so."

Lisa took a deep breath and let it out. "Kingsley, do you know why I called you? After all this time?"

He squinted at the carving, biting his lip. "I can tell you what I thought."

"What?"

"That this was a bloody good chance to get an exclusive interview."

"Oh."

"Well, it is, you know. The thought does leap unbidden to the mind. It would make my career." He straightened up with a sudden laugh. It was a high, strained sound. "I'd be at the top of the good old pile for—how long is it? Seven months? Quite a plum."

"That hadn't even occurred to me."

"Well, it did to me." He turned toward her. "I've gotten that way lately, Monalisa."

"I'd forgotten you had that old name for me."

"I had a *lot* of things for you."

"Once."

"You didn't seem to be interested in them."

Lisa shrugged. When he saw the gesture Kingsley turned jerkily away, his shoes spattering gravel against a headstone.

"Pious bastards, weren't they?" he said loudly, a gloved hand gesturing abruptly down the path of tombs and graves. "Look at that one. 'From strength to strength in the everlasting.' Rubbish. Self-serving dreams."

"Who else should a person's dream serve?" Lisa asked mildly.

He didn't seem to hear her. He walked on to the next vault, brushing aside a trailing roseless creeper. "Ha! 'Honor perisheth never!' Well, Mister bloody old Geoff'ry Birdsley-Smith, Esquire, O.B.E., it bloody well has!" He rattled the iron grating. Rust scraped off onto his palms, staining his gloves a brownish red. He savagely clapped his hands together to brush it away. "Filthy stuff."

"Kingsley, I—"

"They were a rotten lot then, and no one knew it. 'I shall wait no more.' Bilge! My pious Mary Ellen Brooks, your bones now used as a nest for rats, your flesh gone to powder, what do you think of your hopeful little motto now? Eh?"

"I don't believe—"

Kingsley stepped back from peering through the grate. "Oh, but *they* believed! Didn't you—?" He turned, arms outstretched to the side, playing to the audience of gravestones. "You all believed. 'Life eternal, saving grace.' Yea, verily."

He danced away, gravel crunching, peering at the carvings. He stopped, called out, "Look here!" Lisa hesitated, frowned, then followed along the path. It was getting colder, and darker.

"Ruddy huge thing, isn't it?" The mausoleum reared up at the crest of the hillside, streaked in brown. Lime stains smeared its corners. Bird nests were under the stone eaves. Kingsley walked between graves up to the structure, and Lisa followed.

"James Foister. Must have been an immense talent, eh, to sport a thing like this?" He walked around toward the side, then back to the bronze door.

Cracks in the cupola, thick with lime, showed where the pigeons had made their way inside. Kingsley bent over and peered through the small grating. From behind him Lisa could see the dim marble interior splattered with their excrement. Feathers and bits of twigs stuck together littered the floor. There were three religious murals on the walls, once probably garish but now stained and faded. The massive coffin in the center was crusted with bird lime, its brass clouded.

"How do you like it now, Foister?" Kingsley shouted through the grate. "Enjoying your bloody immortality, are you?" He lurched away down the path. At the next vault he stopped, hurled an oath, and went on.

"Kingsley—"

He was oblivious to her now. He shouted into the hollow mausoleums, mocking the dead in a high, strident voice. He kicked away the outer iron bars on one vault and they sagged away with a rusty clang. Kingsley laughed and kicked at the bronze door. He did not stop laughing. He whirled on, smacking his hand against the Victorian stonework, yelling insults at the names he read from the inscriptions.

"Talk talk talk! All these meek little messages you label yourselves with—fools! You were so petrified of death you believed *any* damned thing to escape from it!"

"Kingsley—"

"But you couldn't! You're all safe and packed away now—you were wrong, but *you* don't care!"

"Kingsley—"

"At least you dim little souls didn't know what was coming. You didn't know that it was all blankness after all. And at least you didn't know the time, right to the hour, the minute, you—"

"Kingsley!"

He stopped, his arms spinning down. He was panting, eyes blinking rapidly. The silence and the fog rushed in upon them again.

"Kingsley, I came to that awful conference because . . . because I would have a chance to see you again."

He blinked at her owlishly. "You . . . you did?"

"It wasn't likely I could get leave for any other reason, certainly not a personal one."

"I . . . ." He gestured uselessly, limply, at the surrounding stones. "I see."

"That's why. To see you again."

"One last time."

79

"It might not be the last."

He smiled weakly, his chin trembling. His mouth sagged open a fraction with sudden exhaustion. Sweat glistened on his pale forehead.

"Still . . . it might be."

"Yes," she nodded. "It might."

"Well . . ." He sucked in the damp air and looked around. "Yes. Well." He looked at her, then away, then slowly back. Some steadiness returned to his eyes. "And . . . and we do have the rest of today."

"Yes. We do."

Smooth limbs moved the knotted bedclothes. Lisa shifted, raising her right leg and draping it across Kingsley's back. She crooked her calf forward, pressing against his neck. His tongue fluttered her to new heat. A pressing tension built in her, rushing up from her legs. She sucked in a deep breath. The layered air of the hotel room which had witnessed them these last two hours smelled of musk and bodies.

The room seemed vast to her; the corners were far dark places, the ceiling a pale tan sky, the ornamented coping the frayed edge of a plaster cloud. She felt a luxurious freedom. This was a special kind of sex, different from Diego, different from anyone she remembered. It was not simply that Kingsley was technically perfect. He also had a way of responding to her, of communicating so much through a gesture or movement or slight sound. In the English air, heavy with moisture, their bodies glided together with a smooth sureness. He had been softly caring for her the whole time, tending to her pleasure, almost supplicating. He had seemed drawn back, time and again, to that glistening center of her. He looked up at her shadowed face, peering at her as though to judge the impact of his artful work, or perhaps to study her, and understand things she herself did not know.

She arched her back with catlike slowness, enfolding him in her legs, and a blurred purring sound came up through her throat. Perhaps he saw this as atonement for his behavior in the cemetery. She had been revolted by it; he had seen that on the ride back into London. All her years of training made it hard to accept losing control, to accept going to pieces in the face of stress. Here, in this hotel room, that faded. She had put away the disdain and revulsion and let the long evening sweep her up, wrap her in a shimmering atmosphere that was part memory . . .

God, this was so good . . .

. . . and part something else. Perhaps this would help him out of the terror that dogged him. Perhaps she was really of no use to him, except as a mercy fuck. But for one night, for a time when they could reenact the old rituals between them, it was enough.

7 October: Collision minus 7 months, 19 days

Zakir Shastri sat strapped into the chair in the main telescope sphere. He was almost motionless, just sitting and staring into nothingness, thinking. Next to him a computer blipped and ran figures across the face of a screen. Without looking he thumbed the hard copy printer and the machine began pumping out the cards. He disturbed a pen, which floated slowly upward. He watched it, thinking.

Shiva was such a disturbance. It wasn't his real work. But of course, he was on the spot and should help as much as he could. But they were very likely going to miss the simultaneous observation of Cygnus A, that immense radio object, and the strange galaxy at its center. Cygnus A had been the subject of intense curiosity for more than a generation. It had taken Shastri and others almost a year to put together a consortium of groundside telescopes and radioscopes, plus the Orbital Astronomical Observatory's full armory. They had been planning to "take a picture" of Cygnus A on every level of the spectrum, with a multiplicity of viewpoints and overlapping areas.

His was to be the crucial measurement. He would use the eighty-centimeter telescope to search for a possible bright ring at the center of Cygnus A. If found, and correlated with the quickly varying radio emission, it could be definitive proof that at the galactic hub there was an immense black hole. Proof that black holes lay at the root of all the phenomena astronomers had observed for many decades. A superb capstone to his life's work, yes; but Shastri knew with bitter certainty that his involvement with Shiva would be the tag by which the public would remember him.

But if that bright ring at the center were to be found, it would crown his professional life. To see at last the accreting disk of stars and dust that fed the black hole; to watch them gobbled up and, falling inward for their last fiery instant, belching great plumes of radiation and matter; to see the mechanism that made the quasars blaze, that consumed the cores of the early galaxies.

There was a beauty in it, a vast cold loveliness. But for now it would have to be forgotten. Perhaps forgotten forever, as far as mankind was concerned.

Shastri sighed. Too bad there hadn't been the funding for the composite telescope, that great grouping of thin plastic disks that would have formed a giant lens kilometers across. It wouldn't have been much money. All assembled in space, each great disk floating free with a microcomputer behind it and tiny attitudinal jets to change focus. Even the radio astronomers had not been able to get funding for any of their projects, such as the huge "cup-and-saucer" telescope. The "cup" would be the radio reflector while the "saucer" would be a shield from Earth's radio interference. The Indian scientist sighed again. *Such dreams.* So much information for so little money. Cut a plane or two from the massive defense budget, that was all. Every week or so a pilot made an error, or one of the thousands of parts failed, and a plane crashed. Built out in space, the telescopes would be virtually immortal.

Shastri rubbed at his face, his eyes tired, grateful for the absence of gravity on his aging body. *Such fine dreams . . .*

The printing on the screen stopped. The last slim card slid out into a tray. Shastri caught the floating pen and picked up the cards. He made a notation on one, then reached down and pulled one of the big sensitized plates from the case. Squinting at the edge markings, he made a minor adjustment on the sensitizing circuit. Swinging around, Shastri slipped the plate into position, locked it down, and pulled out the black metal slide.

Beep. Beep. Beep.

With a grimace Shastri turned and thumbed the intercom line. "Yes, what is it?"

Fakhruddin Radhakrishnan stuttered, "S-sir, it's M-Mister B-Bradshaw, the h-head of N-NASA."

"I'm taking some plates. Tell him to call back."

"He's s-says it's ur-urgent, s-sir."

"Oh, very well." Shastri snapped off the line, deactivated his sensitized plate, but left the tracking computer on. He needed to obtain as many plates as possible.

Shastri came into his office quickly, with practiced moves, his motions elongated and certain in the light Observatory gravity. Radhakrishnan got up and offered him a seat before the screen. He looked flushed, excited, and eager to overhear. Shastri pulled himself into the seat before his littered desk and clipped on the light restraining harness as he said, "Yes, Mister Bradshaw?" He swung the television pickup lens around to frame his features in closeup.

Chuck Bradshaw looked up with a quick smile. *"Doctor Shastri, how are you? Are you getting everything you need up there?"*

"Yes, Mister Bradshaw. It is most gratifying . . . " He paused and a smile appeared briefly on his lips. "After all these years of delays and curtailed funding, it is most heady to have such prompt action."

Chuck grinned again. *"I know what you mean, Doctor. Now the new 'scope will be installed, tested, and working in plenty of time?"*

Shastri nodded. "No problem, Mister Bradshaw."

Another voice came over the speaker. *"Doctor Shastri, this is Lyle Orr? I'm PR for NASA? Sir, I wonder if you could give us, in layman's language, an explanation of how this new 'scope will work? We'd like to tape it and release to the media tonight, sir?"*

"Um. Why, yes, Mister, um—"

"Orr," whispered Radhakrishnan.

"—Orr. Um, are you ready?"

"Anytime." On the screen Chuck Bradshaw moved out of the chair with a little gesture of "Don't go away" to the Indian astronomer, and thin, nervous Lyle Orr, the PR man, slipped into the seat with an uneasy smile. He brushed his hand over his transplanted hair, cleared his throat, and assumed a serious expression. *"Doctor Shastri, could you explain this new telescope you are installing at Station Three, the American Orbital Astronomical Observatory?"*

"Um . . . yes. Well. The original discovery of Shiva was made with a liquid-helium-cooled bolometer with a one point six micrometer filter. By comparing the asteroid with a 'standard star'—in this case Alpha Ori—we here and the staff at Thales Center compared the the electromagnetic spectrum." Lyle Orr was looking uncomfortable and his smile slipped, but Shastri went on unperturbed. "Thus we achieved a relation, giving the surface albedo of Shiva, by measuring how much radiation it was reflecting." Shastri smiled thinly. "Actually, it was *reemitting* the flux originally falling on it from the sun."

Lyle Orr started to say something but Shastri went on quickly. "Photometry experiments at other wavelengths gave the spectral reflectivity, which in turn suggests an iron-rich surface, instead of the more common carbonaceous chondrites. Shiva was observed first by apparition, that is, optically and—"

Lyle Orr's eyes opened wide and he interrupted hastily. "*Uh, uh, excuse me, Doctor! You, uh, you mean that Shiva is a big lump of solid iron?*"

Shastri frowned. "Yes, I believe I put that in my original report. We don't *know*, of course, but our tests have proven out on other Apollo objects and . . . " He looked a little confused. "I do believe I put all that in my original report. Almost certainly carbonaceous chondrites. At least a major portion of the surface."

Chuck Bradshaw stuck his head back into the range of the pickup lens. "*Are you certain, Doctor?*"

Shastri's momentary confusion turned into cool professional *hauteur*. "Within the present limits of our science, yes, Mister Bradshaw. Didn't you read the report?"

"*I've a lot to do, Doctor.*" He looked at Orr. "*Boy, does this change things.*" Orr looked sick. Bradshaw gave the astronomer a smile. "*Listen, Doctor, we'll get back to you, all right?*"

"Very well. But I am quite busy installing the new, larger bolometer. We will be able to do a much more precise job once that is operational."

"*Yes, I'm sure. Talk to you later?*" He gestured to Orr, who sat forward, his face compressed with nervous anxiety.

"*Um, wait, Doctor, don't go yet. Listen, uh, all that we taped just now . . . um, listen, I didn't understand a*

84

word. Well, I mean, I understood the words, but I didn't understand what they meant."

"Mister Orr, deliver the tape to someone there, someone in your celestial navigation section. Have him translate. I'm really quite busy."

"*Yes, I understand. Um. Well, yes, all right. Iron, huh?*"

"In all probability, Mister Orr."

"*A two-kilometer iron cannonball.*"

"Imprecise, but metaphorically correct, yes."

"*Jesus.*"

"Good day, Mister Orr." Shastri switched off the set and unclipped the strap. "Back to work," he grumbled. As he went out the door he muttered, "I told them days ago. Why do they think we *make* reports, anyway?"

27 October: Collision minus 6 months, 30 days

Brother Gabriel raised both his hands and the sound leaped up from the crowd, a rippling sonic wave that almost hurt. *It's that easy,* he thought, marveling at the sense of momentum it gave him. He was at the focus of it all, the nexus, the locus, the target of the attention of almost a half million people.

He turned, hands high, the sleeves of his simple robe falling back, the faint lighter disk where his watch had been still on his wrist. He bathed in the sound, turning, turning.

On either side of the rented portable stage there were tall towers, scaffoldings to hold the powerful lights and some of the television crews. He frowned, bringing down his full patriarchal brows, as he looked into the glare.

Dusk was falling. It was dark in the bowl of hills, but the sky was still light and some of those highest on the western edge were backlit by the setting sun. They had come to see him in the flesh, intrigued by the increasing television coverage.

Brother Gabriel, the man who had been Douglas Arthur Kress, was not unaware that the simple setting in the rolling hills was somewhat reminiscent of all the Bible films about Christ, only updated. Behind his beard Brother Gabriel smiled. If Jesus had had ten-thousand-watt quartz lights and wireless body mikes he would have used them. We might have had the Sermon on the Mount recorded: $6.95 record, $7.95 eight-track stereo cassette.

Months ago it had seemed that no one would listen to him. People were buried in their own lives, strapped to inertia, habit, and indifference. The news of Shiva caused a ripple, though there were many local splashes. But it was more than a month later before anyone began to come to him. He had started simply, in parks and on public access television, presenting his cause on an electronic soapbox.

They began coming, in twos and threes, families and lovers, the failed and the successful, expressing their feelings in halting sentences, or repeating his own words back to him. It was then that he truly felt the pulse running through the true heart of these people, the conviction that Shiva was the Lord's ordained way to set things in order once again. A purging, a restart, a new beginning. The Lord God Jehovah was going to try a third draft. He'd done it before, with the Great Flood.

So the ministry of Brother Gabriel had begun. Small meetings, tent revivals, TV talk shows. Then the breakthrough at the Civic Auditorium in Dallas, followed by the Vanguard Stadium in Phoenix. The assassination attempt that had cost sixteen lives at the Riverfront Stadium in Cincinnati had pushed him into even greater prominence. In Oakland, at the County Coliseum, there had been a riot between his followers and the disorganized opponents of what he preached and believed. An unknown number had died, somewhere between a hundred and two hundred, with a thousand injured. But it had all led directly to these hills, covered with the willing and waiting throng, with the network cameras in the light towers and on platforms out in the darkness. They were waiting for him.

He stepped into the center of the light. He seemed to glow as his hands came down. White-robed and bearded, almost the typical Hollywood prophet, yet . . . yet . . .

The vast crowd grew quiet. There was a hissing sound that slithered over the uplifted faces as people hushed others more enthusiastic than attentive. He waited.

Then he pulled a piece of paper from his sleeve. "Brethren . . ." The crowd sighed. There were a few faint, far-off cheers. The loudspeakers carried his words to the farthest hills. "Brethren, I have here a piece of legal paper. It was just presented to me by officers of the law." There were shouts but he waited them out, turning so that everyone in the great natural amphitheater could see as well as hear him.

"This paper is from the governor of this state. He orders us—that is, me—to disperse this holy convocation." There was an angry roar that started low and grew with alarming speed. Brother Gabriel raised his hand and they quieted again. "He says it is of imminent and precipitous danger to the inhabitants of this state!" There was another roar, quicker and louder, but it died away as Gabriel turned, holding up his hand. Every hair of his beard and flowing hair seemed to glow in the brilliant floodlights. "He says we are an unlawful assembly!"

The roar came again, as though programmed, sweeping down from the hills, echoing, thundering. Brother Gabriel leaned back, chuckling deeply, and the microphone in his robe sent the sound rolling out through the dozens of amplifiers into the hills. The bass tones echoed back to him as the crowd grew quiet again. People shouted advice to him and asked him questions but he ignored them.

"Well, I think I know what we think of the governor," he said, pausing for the roar. "He'll have as much luck stopping us as the *fed*eral government will have stopping Shiva!" Again the murmuring roar from the hills came in response.

He raised his hands, throwing away the paper, which fluttered to the stage and lay there. "*We* are the people! *They* are the past! *We* are the new! *They* are the old, the tired, the used-up, the corrupt!" The answering roar washed over him in a tidal wave of sound. He dropped his hands, but gestured with them as he spoke.

"The essential truth today in this country, in the *world*, is that our government is standing in the path of God Himself. There is no other way to think of it. Unbelievable as it is, the politicians in Washington propose to expend our substance needlessly." He paused to let the crowd vent its feelings once again. "They even now marshal our precious natural resources, our finest minds, our best workers—all to stop a natural event that *cannot be stopped!*" Before the crowd could react, his voice thundered again. "*That should not be stopped!* That *will* not be stopped!" The crowd's roar smashed over him. Fists waved. "That is as certain as the laws of this universe, which were ordained by God, the Maker of All Things, the Infinite, Eternal God of Creation!"

He paused, letting the crowd have its time, its interaction, letting the rhythm ebb. He began again, on a lower, more restrained note. "You know, the scientists say there are two laws bringing Shiva to Earth. One is the Law of Universal Gravitation. Well, that's fine," he smiled. "But the other—that's the one that some of you may recognize as F equals M times A—they have another name for it. They call it *Newton's* Law! As though someone named Newton *made* that law!" He chuckled warmly with them. "And isn't that typical, my friends? Perfectly, predictably typical? The law was made, not by Mister Newton, but by *God!*" His voice surged up at the end, sending a gasp sighing over the hills.

"Yet the scientists persist in naming these holy forces for the mere *men* who first stumbled upon them." He turned, his voice natural, reasonable, as he gestured toward a new quadrant of the throng. "You see, when you think of it, that even the way we talk about these things is filled with our own arrogance."

He knew it was time to begin building again. "Because, as we all know, the pain and horror and despair all around us these last few years, even before we heard of Shiva, came from *man.* Not God! Man!" He turned in the bath of sound, feeling the tingle of hot lights on his face.

"Our error has lain in putting man before God. In forgetting about *natural* processes. In putting ourselves before the ecological wholeness around us. So is it any wonder that we are discontented with our crowded cities, stinking in their own waste? That we turn brother against brother? And that crime mounts, in intensity and variety? And divorce splits man from woman, children from parents? God didn't make us for these monstrous cities! For these freeways! For this smog! For polluted air, polluted waters, polluted *food!*"

Brother Gabriel turned in the light. It was darker now and his was the only light. "He made us for the *natural* world. And Shiva is a natural event! Shiva has come to this good green Earth before, and it will come again. So it is written, my friends, written in the laws of the universe, as surely as the sun shall rise tomorrow."

He turned again, quickly. "Do we try to stop the rising sun? Of course not! We don't fight the sun. We *use* the sun. We seed our crops, as man has always done. And the sun comes. And it makes our seeds give forth from the good, green Earth what we need to feed and clothe ourselves. That is *natural*. That is real! That . . . is . . . the . . . way!"

The enormous crowd murmured with a deeper tone. *They're getting it*, he thought. *They're picking up the momentum*.

"What we need—what we *must have*—is a godly approach to Shiva. This is a *natural* event. Let us greet it *naturally*, brothers and sisters." He paused, feeling the silent, waiting crowd, letting it build. "And we ask ourselves: what is natural to man?" He turned, silent, as if awaiting the answer. "We all know the answer. The *good* things. Our families. Mother, father, sister, brother. Our families. And our homes. The home, which is the seat of all the old ways, the things we love, the secure ways man *once* had. We have to learn again to rely on these natural, human things, things cut to human scale, human needs. Not on rocket ships. Not on electronics. Not on complexity and redundancy and vast dehumanizing industry. Not on trying to stop the rising sun."

The bowl of hills filled slowly with a rumble of assent. They were following his sentences with cries of, "Yea, brother!" and "A-*men!*" Brother Gabriel spread out his hands, standing in the center of the focus of lights, and let it come out of him.

"The answer to Shiva is the old way, the ancient, tried ways of man. No useless attempts to stop it. Not futile rocket ships. Not frantic building of hell-bombs! Not nuclear destruction! *No!*" His thundering words merged with the crowd's roar of agreement. Half a million mouths shouted back with one will. Brother Gabriel turned slowly in the light, seeing a television crewman waving an enthusiastic fist, feeling the vibrations of sound and mind. They were truly with him now, truly caught up in the Word.

"Far better to *prepare!* Secure your homes and families. Wall up your houses against the coming storm. Store food and clothing. Fill your larders. Waste not your time and substance! Do not fritter away your essence on futile attempts to stop the laws of nature in operation!"

He overrode the crowd with the power of his amplifiers. "When Shiva comes, our cities may well be laid low. But the *people* will remain, the *believers* will remain. Life will go on. We will be simple farmers again, my people. Simple and good. Uncomplicated and virtuous. We will live amid green fields and warm close family and friends. In villages and towns, where you will know everyone and they will know you. Amid the wheat and barley and corn that we have had as ancient partners on this good Earth. *Natural* things. No rockets! No bombs! No poisons in the milk of mothers!"

He stretched himself up, hands clawing at the dark, empty sky. "And when you see another wasting our substance on rockets and bombs—stop him! Make him see the way! Show him that Shiva is God's way to bring man to his senses! *Stop him!* Let the ancient stone from the beginning of time fulfill its final destiny, God's destiny! *Stop them now!* And you shall be blessed, eternally!"

A shuddering chorus of assent swept down from the hills, a wall of sound that physically battered him. The vast, deep, demanding voice of the people. His people.

He smiled and shook his fists. Brother Gabriel could feel God moving through him, exalting him, using him as a vessel. Now the power was in the multitude before him. They could do it. Guided by him if need be, they could stop the government madness, the ungodly, unholy, futile attempt. They *must* do it.

And he would lead them.

Yes.

That, too, was God's way.

31 October: Collision minus 6 months, 26 days

Diego came into their room and sat down on the military-neat bed and took off his boots. He unlaced them methodically, unsnagging the laces from their keeps and smoothing out the kinks in the leather with his fingers as he went. When he got them off he sighed and rolled onto the bed, flexing his toes.

"Tennis shoes would be more comfortable," Lisa said. She had watched the ritual in silence from her writing desk, where a spec manual lay open. A terminal screen was on, but empty, at her elbow, flickering slightly.

"I like boots," Diego said, his arm across his eyes.

"Okay," she said. She turned back to the manual and resumed marking sections with a yellow flow pen.

He put his hands behind his head and looked around. "Why do they call them quarters, anyway? They're about dime size." Lisa smiled but said nothing. Her terminal screen flickered. "Hope they'll be bigger when we move to the Cape," he said and she nodded.

"Hard day?" Diego asked after a few moments.

"Ummm." She punched something out on the console, squinted at the response, made a note, and cleared the screen.

"I was talking to Orr," Diego murmured.

"Ummm."

"He was looking at the follow-up reports on that London thing."

"What for? It was just cosmetic." She didn't look up from marking.

"He wanted to ask something about it, but he said he didn't want to mix in."

"Mix in."

"About that newspaper guy."

"What—? Oh." She stopped marking.

"Security has a whole report on him."

Lisa put the cap back on her pen, then turned toward him and put one elbow on the back of her chair. "Why?"

"Everybody who sees one of us gets the works, I guess." He made a circular gesture with the hand across his eyes.

"Oh."

"Especially if they get out of sight of the watchdogs for long."

"The cemetery," she said.

"No," Diego said carefully, "that's not what Orr wanted to know. About later."

"Back at the hotel."

"Yeah." He dropped his hand down, stretched out on the bed, and put his hands behind his head, elbows up in the air, and looked at the ceiling.

"We went back to the hotel and spent some time in my room. That's all Lyle is going to get."

"He already knows that much."

"Okay, Diego."

They stayed that way for a while and nobody said anything.

"I just don't like to find out about it that way, that's all," he said.

"Find out what? That I wasn't born the moment you met me?"

"That's one way to put it."

"I don't think you understand."

"Oh, I understand," he said, looking at the ceiling. "I do speak the language, you know. I understand it all very well."

"Oh, Christ."

"So you don't have to explain it to me."

After a few seconds she said, "Maybe I do."

"Yeah?" He suddenly sat upright, swinging around toward her, putting his stockinged feet on the floor, sitting very straight on the edge of the bed. His eyes moved restlessly, but he didn't look directly at her. "Okay. Explain it."

"None of it means I don't love you."

"Is it love we're talking about here?" He stared fiercely at a stack of books against the wall, most of which had slips of marking paper dripping limply from them.

"I am."

He looked down at his boots, frowning faintly.

Lisa said, "I really am."

"Who is he?"

"Someone I knew." She blew out a long breath and studied her pen. "First love, I suppose. I thought it was over but I guess it isn't, and anyway, when the opportunity came up and Barrows mentioned that it was in London, that was the first thing I thought of."

"The first thing."

"Yes." She looked at him, her fist closing tightly around the pen. "I'm not going to tell you he just called up because he'd seen my name in the papers and we got together for a drink."

"Good thing you didn't," Diego said moodily. "Barrows told me the whole itinerary and I know you didn't have a drink."

Lisa made a wry, mirthless smile. "They're very thorough, aren't they?" She chewed at her lower lip a second and stared at a corner of the ceiling. "So they know I spent some hours in my hotel room with a man I once knew." She looked at Diego, a frown line between her brows. "They must suspect I had an affair with him years ago and they are right. That must be buried somewhere in my file, if only in the 'Unsubstantiated Reports' section. NASA checked him out then, too."

"I guess," Diego muttered, his voice tight.

"So why did Orr ask you about him?"

"Well . . ." Diego stopped to remember, his shoulders hunching as he gripped the edges of the bed. "Orr said he wanted to be sure you hadn't done any background briefing for this guy, because we're not supposed to talk to the media anymore and . . ." His voice trailed off. He grinned sheepishly. "Yeah. Pretty phony, huh?"

"Lyle didn't want you to find out from me what I'd told Kingsley," she said.

"Right. But he still . . . well, I didn't like it."

"I know you didn't, Diego," she said softly, looking at him. "But I have a life that's just as big and complicated as anybody else's, and there are threads in it I want to try to tie up."

"Because of Shiva?"

"Partly. And because of you."

"Oh. It's because of me you parlayed this London thing into a quickie with an old friend."

"That isn't quite the way I would put it," she said evenly.

"Well, that's the way I'm putting it."

"I keep telling you, it was something I had to straighten out."

"While Orr was telling me about it I felt like shit."

"I'm sorry."

"He was very business-as-usual about it. Said he wanted to check out what you'd told the guy and Security was on to him so he came to me rather than to you because he knew you would be a little embarrassed about it. He had to account to Security about those hours."

"He said."

"Yeah, he said."

"And you still feel like shit."

Diego sighed and something in him became a little less stiff and he rocked forward a little, gripping the bed. A slow smile spread across his face.

"I still feel like shit, but for different reasons." He shot a quick glance at her, then looked back at the floor, with its government-issue green carpet. "When he told me all I could think was that this Anglo asshole was putting the horns on me."

Lisa smiled. "Horns?"

"Cuckold? That's the word, isn't it? The husband wears the horns and everybody can see. That's what this—" he made a sign with two fingers, "means, where I grew up."

"Lyle didn't. Kingsley did, if that's the way you want to look at it."

Diego made a face. "I never *heard* of this other guy before. What do I care about him? But Orr—that made me mad. He knew and I didn't." The bedcover rustled as he gripped it tighter.

Lisa got up and came over to him and they embraced awkwardly, sitting side by side on the bed. "Dumb macho bastard," she said into his throat.

"Huh? What?" He swayed back a bit and frowned at her.

"You were pissed at Lyle Orr knowing, that's all. There was nothing about what Kingsley meant to me in it."

"Well . . ." Diego frowned at her hair and seemed to be thinking.

"That's right, isn't it?"

"Maybe."

She laughed. "That's what I love about you. You've got all these old things that aren't going to change, no matter what veneer the university and then NASA have coated you over with."

"Love me, love my veneer."

"Unfortunately, you're right." She hit him playfully on the arm as she leaned back. "You were all set to come in here and rage at me, weren't you?"

"Yeah," he admitted. "But it's gone now."

"That's why they did it, too, you know," she murmured as she came back into his arms. Her voice was serious and Diego frowned.

"Told me? Lyle wanted to get to me?" He thought a moment. "Ah. Yeah."

"They envy us."

"They do?" He pulled back his head and grinned at her. "Or maybe just me. They'd all like to lay you."

"Oh, I doubt that."

"Don't. It's true. If you think being an astronaut had its attractions and groupies before, now it's incredible."

"Come on."

"There isn't a man in the Shiva operations who hasn't thought about what it would be like with you."

"They've all got women."

"Doesn't matter. They're all men."

"More macho bullshit."

He smiled at her and this time he seemed much more certain of what he had to say. "That's the way we are. Really."

"Wetback wisdom."

"Lady, there really are some things you don't know."

She bent down and pushed his boots under the bed. "Show me," she said.

Astronaut training stepped up to an even faster pace and became an all-encompassing world for Lisa. Around her the staff was good-humored and efficient; the other astronauts were their usual, steady, competitive selves. They lived apart from the rest of the world, cushioned and protected much of the time. The outer world crept in, however, in odd little ways: a technician with eyes red from crying or drink, a suddenly absent co-worker, too-shrill laughter at weak jokes, a glimpse of silent, watchful civilians standing out by the gates. Just standing, just watching. Some had pitched pup tents, built fires, or made little homes around recreation vehicles. And watched.

It was impossible to keep thinking how important Shiva was; you had to get through the day at a livable pace. Each day was a maze of sensors, wiring diagrams, systems analysis, switches, pipes, tanks, connectors, hardware and more hardware, a lot of it cobbled together only the day before, untested and uncertain. There were intensive lessons in orbital planning, a constant reevaluation of the surface configuration of Shiva as the radar

95

pictures sharpened, even instructions in food planning and air management.

At times Lisa thought of Kingsley Martin and the days in London. They had made love, yes, but the scene in the cemetery loomed over all the other memories.

He called. The Astronaut Office gave forth a summary of calls Diego and Lisa received on their private number; even those were intercepted now. His name appeared with increasing frequency. She did not reply, though it would have been no problem, even under the tight security that existed. Diego never commented, though he read the summary every day or so.

And then, without thinking consciously about the question, she simply let the knotty problem drift away. She stopped reading the printout of personal calls. She concentrated on the rush of training, of schedules and systems, and study. After a while the memory merged with the blurred background of the rest of her past.

2 December: Collision minus 5 months, 24 days

At the sound of the discreet buzzer John Caleb Knowles turned from his contemplation of the rose garden through the thick glass windows behind his desk. "Yes?"

Grace Price, his secretary, was looking flustered on the small screen. "Mister President, uh . . . Carl Jagens is here."

"Who? Oh, yes, of course."

"He would like to see you privately, sir." Anticipating the President's next question, she hurried on. "Congressman Fox and the Undersecretary aren't here yet. You could give him two or three minutes . . ."

Knowles smiled at the pleading in her voice. "All right, ask him to come in, please. But tell me as soon as Fox gets here."

"Yes, sir." There was a smile in her voice.

Almost at once the door opened and Jagens came in. Knowles rose to shake hands, taking in the astronaut's uniform, the stark dark blue and white of a full naval captain. He didn't have many ribbons, but few of the astronauts did, for America had kept out of all but a few short and seemingly necessary brushfire wars for some years.

"Mister President, it is most kind of you to see me on such short notice."

"That's quite all right, Captain Jagens. You are one of our heroes, you know." The President looked around, then gestured toward a door in the gently curving wall. "Let's go into the small office, shall we?" The President led the way and they settled down in the adjacent room, a plainer and much smaller office.

"Sir, I've come directly from Houston. I had hoped to meet with Chuck Bradshaw, but . . ." he shrugged, "we crossed en route."

Knowles looked at his watch, an old but effective method of speeding up preliminary remarks. It didn't seem to affect Jagens, who moved ahead confidently, but without hurry.

"There are two major factions, sir, within the group that has the responsibility of the final action against Shiva. I believe strongly in the use of the Soviet device. It's the only certain way to deflect . . . possibly even destroy . . . this menace. I believe strongly in a solid backup force, a second team, that will concentrate on the mopping up—the secondary targets and so on."

"So what would you have me do? That is a technical matter . . ."

"The other faction would so fragment our efforts with multiple options that there is a likelihood of the operation failing entirely."

President Knowles raised his eyebrows. "Bradshaw is a good man, he'll see that."

"Yes, sir, he is." Carl leaned forward and for the first time Knowles was aware of how small Jagens really was. He gave the impression of being a much bigger man, but although the largest, physically, of any of the space pilots, like most astronauts he was shorter than average, compact. "Bradshaw *is* a good man, sir, but he is hampered by factions within the team itself." He smiled charmingly. "I know everyone in the world—certainly in the United States—brings you their woes, but this is a *crucial* matter. One only *you* can decide."

Knowles was not certain just what was about to be decided here, or even if there was a necessity to decide anything at all. "Well, what you outlined seemed fine to me."

"Thank you, sir!" Jagens said happily.

"Now wait a minute," Knowles said, his voice roughening. A lifetime spent in snowballing others had made him sensitive to the process himself. "I just ventured an opinion. I'm hardly qualified to—"

"Mister President," Carl said earnestly, fixing the politician with his steady eyes. "This is the most important decision *any* man has *ever* made."

Knowles kept his voice calm. "I realize that, Captain Jagens. My decision was to go with whatever Chuck Bradshaw's team came up with."

"It's King Solomon time, Mister President," Carl persisted. "You know what's been going on at NASA and Defense."

"What do you mean?" Knowles looked at the astronaut sharply. No leader liked to admit he didn't know everything; except, of course, when it suited him to.

"There's confusion. There are these factions clawing at each other. I'm afraid there are people horning in who, well, who don't belong."

"Who, for example?"

Jagens shifted his position in the chair, the vertical crease between his brows deepening. Knowles was good at reading a man's unconscious signals and Jagens looked to be genuinely uncomfortable at the prospect of naming names. But was that awkward motion a contrived signal or not? Something about Jagens made him wonder, and the President wrapped another layer of detachment around himself.

"Some senators," Jagens said. He raised his eyes up from the patterned carpet to look at the chief executive for a brief moment. "A few in your Cabinet."

Knowles nodded, his lips pursed. He'd heard a few bits of in-house gossip about this, but it didn't seem serious. But then, a really earnest meddler would cover his tracks. He knew Shiva was on everyone's mind, and it wasn't unreasonable that somebody in the Cabinet would be overstepping his or her bounds. But how could he verify that in the time left?

"I understand." That was the right note: bland, neutral, slightly judicial.

"We're losing time over this, sir. I think Chuck Bradshaw is doing the best he can. He doesn't want to come running to you with every little thing. But these outsiders are hamstringing the operation."

"I could look into it."

Carl frowned, his eyes intent on the President now. "Sir, with all due respect, I don't think that's your job. You haven't got time to run down all these kibbitzers."

"My staff can." What was he getting at, exactly?

"I wonder. This isn't like an ordinary issue, Mister President. People feel their lives are on the line."

"They're right."

"I think the logjam will break up once there's firm leadership."

"Meaning—?"

Jagens shrugged his shoulders. "We're losing time haggling. The decision is the crucial thing—people will fall in line once it is made. We who fly out into space are merely the instruments of that decision."

Knowles blinked. "Excuse me," he said solemnly. He stood up and walked out of the small office, straight-backed and serious. He liked the feeling of closeness in the small office, a feeling that was impossible in the big Oval Office next door. It was easier for him to think in cozy places, he thought. The Oval Office had too many memories; too many decisions had been made there by others. They watched him there, judged him, and made him uncertain. He liked the little office, with no reminders of history.

He went through a short corridor and into the small bathroom. He put his hands on the rim of the basin, looked at himself, then away, to stare at a towel on a rack. He had to sort out the signals he was getting from Jagens and the information he had on the Shiva program from a hundred other sources. Some of what Jagens said was true. Things had clicked into place while the man talked. It was one of those nebulous matters that you grasp intuitively before you have the facts to back it up. Sometimes you could see an issue more clearly if you were far enough away from the day-to-day infighting, from the petty problems that assumed alarming proportions and distorted one's vision. That was what executive power was for: to make decisions from a remove, with the judgment unavailable to those farther down. The big picture, the view from on high, the master plan.

Knowles had often used this little ruse of going off to the bathroom for a chance to think. Nobody ever questioned your leaving, and it was an invaluable break.

When he had been a senator he had used pocket phones in the john to check facts, to gather backing, to influence. This whole matter was one thing he wanted to mull over without Jagens, or anyone, watching. The man had a presence that Knowles recognized: Jagens' warmth came on like a light switch and made the listener want to agree. Very effective.

Decide.

He looked at himself in the mirror. Oh, Senator Stevens, I think *you* won the election by losing! He leaned on the basin and looked at his seamed face closely.

Decisions.

He'd risen to the top because people said he wasn't afraid to make decisions, but he knew that wasn't true. He'd been lucky, that's all. His failures had been in the dull, unimportant matters and his successes in the things people paid attention to or affected their lives. What could affect us more than Shiva? he thought.

Decide. Be a hero. A world-saver.

It *sounded* good. One big hit, with mop-up teams. The mop-up teams *could* be used to add further deflection, if necessary. Couldn't they? He made a note: check with Bradshaw, Kinney, McGahan.

Decide, damn you.

Maybe it was a good idea to put a little body English on the whole process? If the President of the United States came forward with something solid, a clearly worded, strong statement, the people below might line up without making a major scrap about it. That was a smooth way to do it. People were shaken up enough already.

He sighed and looked himself in the eye. Whatever happened to that eager young congressman, out to change the world? Was he still around somewhere?

The President of the United States straightened his suit coat. He wondered for an instant why he always wore the standard businessman's uniform, when he could just as well wear anything he liked. Kennedy made copy by refusing to wear a hat and Carter had gotten publicity out of his cardigans. Was he getting to be like Nixon, wearing a blue business suit to go walking on the beach? Well, it was all a matter of the persona, he supposed. You started out appearing to be something and pretty soon you convinced even yourself.

He would know it had gone far enough when he woke up some morning and his first thought was not about what John Caleb Knowles was going to do, but of what The President was going to do.

He fingered his tie, reached over to flush the toilet without thinking about it, then returned to the small office. Carl Jagens came to his feet stiffly, but swiftly. Knowles waved him down, sitting opposite the astronaut and adjusting his coat.

Jagens smiled wanly. "Everyone comes here with a bitch of a problem, don't they?"

"It does seem that way, I admit. Well, Captain Jagens, I have made my decision. Now it *is* Chuck Bradshaw's department and his responsibility, but I *will* go on record as liking your plan. It seems eminently practical."

"Thank *you*, Mister President! I know you're busy and I *am* sorry to have disturbed you, but I thought you should know the way the thinking is going."

"Yes, well Chuck was here this morning, but according to him we had not narrowed it down so precisely."

Jagens was nodding soberly. "Yes, sir, that was true. When Chuck left . . . well . . . we are on top of this and things are moving very swiftly. I won't keep you, sir, and thank you, thank you very much, Mister President!"

After Jagens had left Knowles thought a moment and wondered if he had handled it correctly. He brushed the thought aside with an impatient gesture. You act, then you move on. That is how it is done, how it has to be done. There isn't time for second-guessing. Senator Fox was announced and Knowles returned to the Oval Office. He knew Fox liked the image of conferring with the President in the historic chamber.

Fox came in, appropriately self-important and Knowles plunged into the problems of feeding and housing the millions that would undoubtedly flee from where they were to where they thought they would be safe.

As if there *were* a safe place.

"You mean Frank Ernhalter and Dorrie Jones *both* split?" Chuck Bradshaw stared hard at Lyle Orr, who nodded miserably.

"Yes, sir. They disappeared sometime last night. We don't have a clue how they got out, unless, somehow, they smuggled aboard that patrol that swept the outside of the fence around midnight. They could have dropped off anyplace in that palmetto mess and been long gone before—"

"They do any damage?"

Orr shrugged. "I don't think so, but they're checking. I think they split on, you know, religious grounds. Uh . . ."

"Yes?"

"There's been some talk about a purge. You know, a screening, to determine who might be secretly an Armageddonite, or even a Shiva Dancer, for that matter."

"What the hell is a Shiva Dancer?" Bradshaw asked.

"The Dancers of Shiva are, well, organized hedonists, I guess you'd call them. Started in India, spread all over. They, um, dance and do, you know, in the streets."

"World's going to hell."

"Yes, sir."

"Some people give up too easy."

"Yes, sir."

"Where are the old—" He broke off and thumbed the intercom as it sounded its second buzz. "Yeah?"

"Boss-man, take a look at channel two."

"Why?"

"Uh . . . just look, huh?"

Grumbling, Bradshaw asked Orr to turn on the television set across the room. The screen expanded and Bradshaw recognized the voice of Arnold Binns, CBS's trouble-shooting reporter. ". . . the effect here has been phenomenal." The screen showed, live, a milling mob in a Paris street, screaming, running, fighting police. Many of the people were naked, or half-naked. As the camera lens zoomed in from a high vantage point Bradshaw could see two men carrying a huge framed painting, a pastoral scene of some kind. As he watched a woman ran up and slashed the painting with a knife. The men stopped, aghast, then kicked her unconscious. No one paid any attention.

"Similar riots have been reported in other French cities. All communication with Lyons and Marseilles has been cut off. There is a rail disaster near Dijon," Binns reported. The camera swung to the right at the sound of an explosion, and Bradshaw could see Binns, with a

102

microphone, leaning over the balcony railing. Smoke was pouring up from a nearby street.

"France is in turmoil and the police are unable to stop it. There are reports of police *joining* the looting in Toulon. This is Arnold Binns, in Paris."

The CBS anchorman switched the network, via satellite, to Japan, where it was night. Fires were burning in the background and a few people were running past Henry Stater as he stood in the glare of the television lights.

"There is some looting and rioting here in Yokohama, but most of the Japanese seem to be accepting the possibility of Shiva as *karma*, as fate. The Buddhist temples and Christian churches are full, the police have the matter well in hand, but liquor stores report unusually high sales. The Prime Minister has promised a return to normal within three days. This is Henry Stater, for CBS, Yokahama, Japan."

"Turn it off," Bradshaw ordered. The screen collapsed to a dot and Lyle Orr straightened with a sigh, his face sour.

"Jesus."

"The condemned people ate a hearty meal."

Orr looked at Bradshaw. "Yet . . . Jesus, Chuck . . . some of the polls say forty percent of the people don't even *believe* there *is* a Shiva."

"Maybe they're looking for an excuse. Some people don't have anything to lose. You've got to educate them."

Orr hesitated. "But . . . but *should* we? If they act like this without really being *certain* of Shiva, what would they do if they were positive?"

"If they *know*, they won't interfere. We're the world's only chance."

Orr nodded his head and took the doorknob in his hand. "Yeah, yeah . . . I guess you're right."

"Get out of here. I've got to prepare for the meeting."

Orr sighed deeply. "Yeah, sure, Chuck, right." He left and Bradshaw stared at the closed door for a long time.

Zakir Shastri peeked somewhat shyly into the reception room and saw Carl Jagens look up from his clipboard. "You're the astronomer, right?" the astronaut asked.

Shastri nodded, stepping into the room. "I . . . I was to wait somewhere, I thought . . ."

"This is it," Carl said, waving a hand expansively. "Sit down. Some doughnuts over there and the coffee is passable." He set down his clipboard and made a face. "That thing's become part of me lately." He tapped the clipboard. "But it's a help in memorizing all these mission subsystems. Gotta memorize them; if things start happening too fast, you can't dig out a manual to consult."

Shastri nodded nervously as he sat down carefully on a folding chair. "I really do not know why Mister Bradshaw asked me to do this," he said.

This guy's frozen up, Carl thought: *He looks scared.* "Here, I'll get you some coffee." *Well, he's the guy who discovered Shiva. He's seen it, direct. Maybe he's got a right to be scared.*

When Shastri took the mug, his hands shook, but he seemed unaware of it. "Thank you, I seldom drink stimulants. But lately . . ." He finished with a sigh and Carl nodded in sympathy as he sat back down.

"Yeah, it's been a little out of the ordinary, hasn't it?"

"Indeed." Shastri took a breath, then suddenly his face crinkled, like the folds in a worn brown paper bag. "There are people everywhere, asking questions," he said in a strangled voice. "Wanting to know things no one knows . . ." He looked at Jagens with sad eyes. "I am *only* an astronomer. I cannot read the future."

"They want someone who's certain," Carl shrugged.

"But science is not certain. Science tells one what is probable . . ."

Carl felt a sudden rush of warmth for this small, lean man. He was in way over his head. A rock had come out of nowhere and pushed him out of his ivory tower and into the tangle of life.

"Look, you're nervous about this press conference, aren't you, Professor Shastri?"

Shastri looked shyly at him. "Yes, I am afraid I am, Captain Jagens."

"Call me Carl. May I call you Zakir? Thank you. But let me tell you something. I was that way, once."

"You *were?*" Shastri was plainly disbelieving.

"Sure," Carl shrugged. "Everybody is. But I learned

that you don't have to be. Just remember that nobody knows as much about your subject as you do. They may fail to understand, so you have to explain it again and again. But they can't prove you wrong. Be tough about that. Insist on telling them the truth. Don't let them stampede you."

Shastri scowled in puzzlement. "It is true, I know more. But those are important people out there. Television people. NASA and government officials."

"Them?" Carl made a casual laugh. "They're dummies."

"But they have—"

"They know *nothing*, compared to you. Half those teevee commentators probably think the sun goes around the earth."

"Well, I doubt . . ."

"No, really," Carl interrupted. "I *know* two of them who don't understand why the moon changes from full to a crescent."

"Truly?"

"Yeah. No kidding. How many do you think understand a gravity well, much less Roche's Law? Probably the science reporter from each network and that's *it*."

Shastri smiled slightly. "No matter how sophisticated we become, education does not seem to reach many."

"You bet." Carl saw confidence rekindling in Shastri, a confidence Carl knew had to be there; you don't get to be a top astronomer—a top anything—without an inner core of certainty.

"Say, look," he said, "tell you what. If any of those sensation-mongers gets on you, I'll give our press man the sign. He'll shut the guy up for you. Okay?"

"One can do that?"

"You betcha," Carl grinned wolfishly. "I'll watch for you. Sometimes, when you're in the middle of thinking how you are going to answer a question, you don't realize that you may not have to answer it at all. I'll keep track of that."

"I . . . I appreciate your kindness, Captain, uh, Carl." Shastri sat more erect and breathed in sharply. "That is of great help. I shall simply stick to the scientific issues."

Carl grinned again and waved a hand. "There will always be some dipstick that asks the kind of question that requires a four-hour answer. Just refer him or her to a basic text and move on. There'll be someone who will want to tie it to astrology or some Biblical prophecy. Just pass 'em on. Say that is not your field of expertise. Pick the next questioner quickly before they start arguing with you."

Shastri smiled fully, but the smile faded as some thought overcame him. "You know, there have been threats against my life."

"I heard."

"And against your life, too, I should imagine."

Carl grunted assent. "There's always some dingaling who thinks it is against God's will to fly in space, or to prove that the earth is not flat, like they thought in olden days."

"I think those threats . . . well, that unsettled me for a while."

"No wonder."

"But . . ." Shastri stopped and peered closely at Carl. "I see now what my task is. To ignore the threats. To wave away the attentions of these television people. To do the science and forget all else."

Carl spread his hands, palms up. "You got it."

Shastri suddenly beamed, sitting up erect and clasping his bony knees. "I thank you, Captain Jagens. You have pointed out to me my proper path."

Carl felt a simple pleasure in the man's thanks. There were precious few moments like this, these days. In the hustle he had forgotten the simple, human dimensions of the world. He resolved to notice a little more, if there was ever time again to do it.

"You're welcome, Zakir."

"The President himself has given his approval to the Alpha-Omega plan," Carl Jagens said into the forest of microphones. The newspersons were gathered around in a tightly packed semicircle, and the video cameras were behind and above them. In a few words he outlined the plan.

"The Alpha team, which I hope and pray is commanded by myself, I must admit," he shot the cameras a wide grin and several people laughed in appreciation, "the Alpha team will utilize the Soviet bomb, the four-hundred-megaton device, to deflect the Shiva menace. The Omega team will concentrate on the secondary targets, the minor but still very deadly asteroids of the type that have already caused worldwide damage and death."

"Who will command Omega?" called out the NBC reporter.

Another wide, confident Jagens smile. "That has not yet been determined. I must remind you that no plan has been *definitely* set, and no team commanders chosen. I hope to be included, of course, but that decision is Chuck Bradshaw's."

"What does the President know about space stuff?" the ABC reporter asked.

"The President is fully briefed, with daily updating," Carl said. "I myself was just with him and he is amazingly aware of every aspect of this project. And, I assure you, this is a cooperative effort unparalleled in human history!"

"Will there be women among the Alpha-Omega teams?" the PBS reporter asked.

Carl Jagens turned toward her, saw Grace Price higher up on the steps, and gave her a dazzling smile. "Yes, I'm certain there will be," Carl said. "Although we have no idea who will be chosen at this point in time. The basis for selection will, of course, be the effectiveness of each individual and not his race or sex."

"Nicely done, Carl," someone said.

"Ladies and gentlemen," Carl said, then smiled into the cameras directly, "and you watching at home. Feel confident. Everything that can be done *is* being done. I, personally, vouch for that. President Knowles is behind us one hundred percent and we have the best possible team available."

"What about the Russian cosmonauts?" the CBS reporter asked.

Carl looked at him sharply. "What do you mean?"

"It came over the wire an hour ago. Conditions. With the bomb comes a Russian team. They go along or no bomb."

A local reporter called out, "How will that affect your Alpha and Omega plan, Captain Jagens?"

"There are many well-qualified Russian cosmonauts. I've met a number of them, here, on the moon, and at Station One. I'm sure that they will send their A team. Thank you, everyone, thank you. I must get back to Houston. We have a great deal to do." He pushed through the crowd, smiling, exchanging a few words. When he got to the black government car he looked back at Grace Price and sent her a smile. He well knew that even the most blasé had someone—some type—that got to them, even presidential secretaries.

Carl was conscious of his maleness as a tool, just as fame itself was ultimately another tool. It helped you get things done. Especially if you were not squeamish about using it. Sometimes the people you had to influence or get along with were women, and then you used a different approach, if you had to.

But Carl had read the history of the program when he was first getting into the Astronaut Office, and had talked with the old-timers, and he had learned from it. The Don Juans didn't rank quite as high in the Mission Selection Ratings as did the men and women with more conventional records. It took time, too, and that cost you. When the funding got tight, or dried up in periodic cutbacks, it was the little things that cost you dearly. Time was one of those. Women were an unneeded luxury. Even if there were plenty of women hanging around hotel lobbies and turning up at cocktail parties beside the pool and smiling brightly at official functions—so what? One of the reasons they did it was to brag about it. Carl knew such gossip could hurt a career; it had done so before.

Not that any of the astronauts, male or female, were saints, for they were of and in their times. But there was no point in being vulnerable. So Carl kept his sex life well away from the cameras, away from the good-buddy locker room talk that always ended up giving away more than you realized.

When Carl got whatever he wanted—which was sometimes just an appointment squeezed into a busy calendar, or maybe a copy of a confidential report—he saw no point in keeping up a fiction that had served its purpose, unless there was the possibility of further use. He simply moved on. Maybe a drink or two together, a bit of social stuff, something to grease the parting. It wasn't as though he cast women aside like sucked oranges; he was aware of the dangers of a negative image. But that was all. Just as he had never had any homosexual encounters—and his opportunities had been frequent—because the public or even private knowledge of such things, even in that "enlightened" day, might do him harm, Carl was careful of what he did. He always gave value, though not always full value.

Grace Price had got something out of it, too: personal attention from the hero of the moment. Or maybe it should be hero-to-be, he thought wryly. Life was made up of such fair trades.

Carl leaned forward to look out the limousine window. He couldn't see Grace, but he waved to her anyway. *Just taking care of business,* he thought, and sat back with relief.

In the Oval Office Myron Murray shut off the cassette, glancing at Steve Banning, who raised his eyebrows and made a face.

"That son of a bitch," John Caleb Knowles said without heat. "He sandbagged me. Now I must go along with him."

"You can't repudiate a hero," Steve Banning said. "Not without a lot of explanations."

"Besides, Mister President, he might be right," Myron said softly.

Knowles nodded. "Yes, he might. I hope to God he is. Or *someone* is."

In Houston Lisa Bander sat up in bed, clasping her knees and looking blankly at the screen, her tape reader ignored.

"That sneaky bastard," she said aloud. "Now it's *his* plan."

She shook her head wearily. This kind of infighting was not for her.

She shoved the tapes aside and slid down in bed, turning off the light.

But who *was* going to head up the teams? Or even be on them?

"Oops! Sorry!"

Diego grinned apologetically at Amani Kamarage and started backing out. He couldn't see who the big black Tanzanian was embracing and he didn't think he wanted to.

"Oh, hey, wait, Colonel!" Diego saw small Walt Solomon peer around Kamarage's arm. The little computer expert ducked under the muscular limb and came toward the astronaut without a trace of embarrassment. "What can we do for you, Colonel?" He was all business.

Inwardly Diego shrugged. Homosexual behavior was not the secret shame that it had been in his youth, but still, he hadn't seen any overt acts on company time, at least not in NASA. But that was their business. Solomon and Kamarage were top men. He held out a pair of tapes. "Could you flash this up to Boston, Walt?"

"You bet. Be there within the hour." He took the tapes, quickly scanned the labels, then spoke with a studied casualness. "Say, Colonel, there's a party in Barracks C-3 tonight. Care to come? Just some of the fellas."

"Thanks, but no thanks, Walt." He took the slight sting out of it with a smile. "I gotta cram, y'know. They have more things for me to learn than there are dots on a reading chip."

"Sure, Colonel. Just asking. We know you're busy. Well, I'll code these right now." He waved the tapes and turned away. Kamarage was bent over a scanning scope, checking a blowup on a ferrous tape. Solomon slapped him on the butt as he passed.

Lisa put down the tape reader and looked up as Diego came into their quarters. He was carrying a hastily assembled dossier, which he dropped on her desk with a grunt. Then he threw himself into the small couch opposite her and rubbed his face hard, sighing deeply.

"Well, there's the latest on Shiva."

Lisa picked up the folder and opened it. "Um," she said. "A relative spectral reflectance index of one point four. So our Shiva is not a simple rock."

Diego nodded, his eyes closed and an arm across his face. "Lots of iron on the surface. Nothing special there, that's the most plentiful metal in asteroids so far."

"Some silicates," Lisa murmured, "but the majority of the swarm could not be simple stone. Hmm. The reflectance index indicates it is compatible with the 'stony iron' meteorite class."

"Look a bit further," Diego suggested. "Glenn Veeder at JPL has determined that Shiva is predominately iron."

"Yes, I see." She read silently for a moment. "He says, 'This implies that it was the core of a larger asteroid which had—presumably during the early formative stage of the solar system—broken into fragments for some reason.' Oh, then the satellites in the swarm are part of the original proto-Shiva?"

Diego grunted. "They're digging up what they can on the impact sites, but that's not going to help us much. Apparently, the softer parts of Shiva have been slowly eroded away, leaving this hard iron chunk."

"Was Shiva a planet, do you think?" She smiled. "Something from the Asteroid belt, part of a planet that maybe used to be there, between Earth and Mars?"

Diego shrugged. "Veeder doesn't think so. Probably never was a planet with a molten core in the sense we know a planet. You know iron appears in asteroids for a number of reasons."

"Uh-huh," Lisa said. "Radioactive elements eventually decay into iron, since iron is stable."

"Or some warming process that seems to have occurred early in the solar system's history—the 'T Tauri stage,' which heated up bodies, boiling away light elements and melting some metals, so they ran together, coating the surface of asteroids."

"*Or* radioactive decay of some isotopes, which may have heated the asteroids enough to do this."

Diego dropped his hand from his face and looked at her wearily. "Lots of possibilities. It is definitely confirmed that Shiva is slowly tilting down into the plane of Earth's orbit. Perhaps it is something to do with perturbations from Jupiter and Venus, but they aren't certain. It's even been suggested this is a cyclic thing, that every few million years the plane of their orbit passes through the solar plane. I dunno. It's all there in Veeder's finest jargon."

Lisa looked further into the dossier as Diego stared at the smooth plastic ceiling. Then she closed the file and slowly squared it with the corner of her desk.

"So," she whispered. "An iron ball is descending. In eleven months from the Tunisian strike we can expect it again. Closer."

"At about ten kilometers a second," Diego said in a flat voice.

"One good thing," she said after a few moments.

"Oh?" Diego lifted his covering arm and looked at her. "You found some good news?"

She nodded with a slight smile. "It's only rotating once every two hours."

"I missed that. How did they figure that out?"

"They followed the light curve, the oscillations in the reflected light. But rotating that slowly means we won't be thrown off by centrifugal force if we have to land to plant the warheads."

"We?"

"Well, whoever is selected. Any news on that yet?"

"No, but Carl is acting as though *he's* going to be the one to do the picking. You know Carl."

"Well, bringer of glad tidings, have you had dinner?"

"No, nor lunch, except for one of those machine-made sandwiches. You'd think with space stations and solar energy disks ten kilometers in diameter we'd be able to concoct a coin-operated sandwich machine that didn't give us soggy sandwiches."

"You expect miracles, my darling. Next you'll want a responsive bureaucracy, calorie-free snacks, and a cure for the common bore."

"You know what I hate most about being an astronaut?" Diego said as he swung his feet to the floor and sat up.

"No, my grumpy compatriot, what?"

"The food in space. When I used to watch the stuff going up from Vandenberg out in California I knew about squeeze tubes and eating in zero gravity. But I thought by the time I grew up and became a daring, dashing space pilot they'd have solved that." He shrugged and shoved on his knees to stand up. "What a disappointment. It's just freeze-dried chicken à la king. Great. Really great. And with this we are ready to meet the aliens from outer space."

He took Lisa's hand and she rose. "Xenophobe," she said happily. "You don't like anything with less than two legs and more than four."

"Damn right, especially if it's intelligent."

"Nothing intelligent on Shiva," she said as they went out. "Too dense to be some kind of ancient alien starship, some cosmic derelict."

"Uh-huh," he grunted. "Except that we don't know how dense aliens might consider a properly made starship."

"Oh, thanks," she said. "One more thing to worry about."

The selection of the Alpha and Omega teams assumed global significance. Everyone had an idea as to who should be included, or specifically excluded. Newsfax editors, television commentators, politicians, movie stars, authors, even the inmates of San Quentin's Death Row had their lists. Some of the lists even included astronauts. Church groups called for the believers, politicians plugged for their state's spacemen, the Armed Forces and the various ethnic groups all noisily contributed strong "suggestions."

The NASA astronauts themselves were polled. But that was nothing new. Team evaluations had been made since the very beginning of the space race, from Mercury and Gemini and Apollo on. But the astronauts, and even more the National Aeronautical and Space Administration hierarchy itself, were all under tremendous pressure. Diego and Lisa were made very much aware of how the system worked.

Name-the-crews games were played constantly, in the public media, in homes, in the privacy of NASA locker rooms. Politics and favoritism were very important. Diego pointed out to Lisa that it was not all that different from any job where personalities played a big part, where it helped to be in the right place at the right time —with the right image and experience—and where many nontechnical factors, such as service relationships, first impressions, sex, pressure from friends within and without NASA or the government, helped determine the final selections.

Trial balloons were leaked with different sets of astronauts. Carl Jagens' sophistication, his powerful friends, and public image made him a favorite on almost all lists. The NASA bosses knew him, governors and senators knew him, millionaire oilmen and fading royalty knew him. They all wanted to be able to say, "My friend Carl Jagens saved the world," or "He was here just two nights before he went out to stop Shiva." Other astronauts—and nonastronauts—came and went on the various trial teams.

There was a sudden, flashy movement that started on the West Coast to put a certain he-man movie star on the Alpha team on the basis that he had stopped worse disasters in his thirty-film career. All too many were serious about it. Beauregard Boyce Lee, the fire-spitting preacher, was another favorite son candidate, as were several senators, two newsmen, a female anchorperson, and a consumer advocate. The fact that these people were even mentioned was a great vote for the people's trust, but did not say much for their sense.

To the world the American astronauts and the Russian cosmonauts had a certain image. The Russians were short, stocky, phlegmatic, quiet, "peasanty," and tough. They had been that way since the 1950s. "They all look like Gagarin—even the women," Py Rudd had once said, not too diplomatically.

But the American astronaut image had changed. In the 1950s and sixties they had all appeared the same: compact, short-haired, jut-jawed, clean-cut, loyal, faithful, patriotic, and team players. While that had not actually been the case, it was the impression, the *image*. With the slump in interest and action in the seventies no one paid much attention, but when the 1980s brought the shuttle program alive, and when the United States pushed out, however tentatively, to other planets, the public became aware that the old stereotypes had changed.

The Martian astronauts and the shuttle pilots, even the moon-based teams, were far more ethnically diverse, and they had been, of course, sexually diverse since the late 1970s. Blacks, Chicanos, even the one gay astronaut had changed forever the WASP image. Lisa Bander's beauty was well within the established NASA tradition, for several of the earliest female astronauts had been genuine beauties.

But it was not her beauty that was going to get Lisa on any of the teams, it was her record. The crew evaluations, which were standard ongoing procedure, had always rated her high. The astronauts were as honest as possible when giving these evaluations, and tried to disregard personal likes and dislikes as much as possible, for a stupid rating sheet might fault them for poor judgment.

Betting pools were begun within the NASA complex—as well as nationwide—and many jokes were made as various astronauts had their odds raised or lowered. But everyone was very tense, for not only did their own careers hang on team selection, but quite possibly the lives of everyone on Earth.

One day Lisa found a Xeroxed "Rules of Shiva Team Selection" on her desk. She laughed—however wincingly

—and found that hundreds of the sheets had been distributed overnight. The "rules" read like this:

1: If you are Carl Jagens, you don't have to be terribly competent as your buddies will get you selected.

2: Ethnic types should resign from consideration; no one would ever believe a Polish hero. (A Polish pope was difficult enough to accept.)

3: Political influence is considered counterproductive as Big Carl owns them all.

4: If you can't say anything good about someone, don't hesitate.

5: Do unto others as they would do unto you, but do it first.

Diego stopped reading. "Not funny," he muttered. He balled up the sheet and arced it neatly into a wastepaper basket. He looked moodily over at Lisa. "They'll never select *both* of us. I imagine they'll pick you, though."

"The token female?"

"Maybe. But not both of us. We aren't that lucky."

"Oh, stop grumbling. Let's go to a party."

But there were no parties on the base that night, and there was no way to get out the front gate. Reluctantly they dug out books and tapes and settled into a few hours of study. When they went to bed they were too drugged with weariness to make love. They held each other and were soon asleep.

In the morning they couldn't remember their dreams, but they hadn't been nice.

23 December: Collision minus 5 months, 13 days

Lisa Bander sat by herself in the lounge, a cup of coffee growing cold before her. She stared out of the window at the rectangular white buildings around her. Between them she could see the flat Texas plain to the north, covered with encroaching houses and the busyness spawned by the Johnson Space Center. Strips of greenery marked the residential streets, and beyond them, the tall spires of Houston, the city built on oil.

A long way from the mountains of Colorado, she thought. This is like some manufactured landscape, board flat, buildings from a kit. But it was the brain of NASA. The Cape Canaveral facility was just the obvious, dramatic focal point, but the smartwork was done here, and at NASA facilities all over the country, fed by still more facilities around the world, in space, and on the moon. If Shiva was to be stopped, the script would be written here, she thought, even though it may be enacted millions of kilometers out in space.

And no doubt televised, with armchair quarterbacks and network critics oracularly second-guessing. With breaks for commercial messages. With chances for global exposure for the lucky politicians.

Lisa exhaled forcefully and tasted her coffee. Cold. She didn't get up and go over to the coffee machine, she just sat. A tremor went through her.

Isolated, she thought. We're isolated from everyone. We have to be, I know, but out there, in the streets, people are rioting. Afraid and ignorant, they are panicking. They kill, loot, rape, go catatonic, wander aimlessly, commit suicide . . . and pray.

She had almost stopped looking at television. First, because she didn't have much time, and second because all there was, besides the canned sitcoms and old movies, was bad news. Fires, explosions, murder. The crazies roamed the streets, shouting about God and Satan and Armageddon. The most frequent movie shown was the old George Pal film *When Worlds Collide* because it had a happy ending. There were plenty of others, but sometimes a station was firebombed because some person had been frightened.

Chaos.

Even in the Army. Mutinies on ships, desertions, sabotage. The Royal Navy lost the *Repulse,* to a crew aping the *Bounty* crew and taking off for Tahiti. The Russians lost two, sunk by their crews as the men disappeared to rut away their last weeks. The French had a ship scuttled in Le Havre, the Bolivians another. *Coup d'état* was an accelerated game in South America. Mort Smith's mother had been found murdered in her Fort Lauderdale apartment. Martial law was still not nationwide but it was not far away. President Knowles was keeping it cool in Washington, although there had been riots with hundreds killed. At least they hadn't dynamited the Capitol or the Washington Monument, as had been attempted.

A world gone crazy. Literally crazy. Or on the fragile edge, like Kingsley. She couldn't blame them. Sometimes

116

she, too felt like running out, tearing off her clothes, and joining the mindlessness of the orgies. Or praying. Or crawling into a hole, or a bottle, and just disappearing. Or . . . going on doing what she did best and knew was important. And the only chance.

She looked up as Dink Lowell came in. "Hi, Beauty. Where's Zorro?"

"He'll be along soon. How are you doing with that desk?"

They walked back to the window seat and sat down. Dink shrugged and flip-flopped his hand. "Different. My head says it's important and all that, but my heart . . ." He sighed and gave her a lopsided smile. "You make different kinds of decisions, that's all. The scenery is lousy. It averages out. Instead of days of boredom and a few moments of stark terror it's days of boredom and a few moments of intense apathy."

"What kind of different decisions?"

"They're less precise. You deal more with people than machines and the laws of nature. People are never precise, nor do they react as predicted."

"Poor Dink."

"It will happen to you, too, Beauty, unless . . ."

She raised her eyebrows. "Unless?"

"Unless we flub the Shiva deal. Then all bets are off." He shifted in his seat and rearranged his expression to a more pleasant one. "Listen, have you heard about the movements? Yeah, for and against."

"For and against what?"

"Shiva."

"How could you be *for* Shiva?"

He grinned. "Easy. If you hanker for power and fame, you start a religion. For or against. Though I must say the pro is far more organized right now." At her expression he went on. "There's some dude that calls himself Brother Gabriel. Believes that ol' debbil Armageddon is here." He smiled at her expression. "Well, he might be right. There's a lot of Bible prophecy interpretation going on these days. Bending the rules a bit to make it fit, but they're doing it. This Brother Gabriel, he's something. A real fire and brimstone character. Thought he would have gone out of style ages ago, but maybe there isn't anything new under the sun."

117

"Shiva isn't. It's primordial matter. Been around longer than Earth."

Dink waved her words aside as he took a long swallow of coffee. "Uh-huh, uh-huh, but this Gabriel dude has been gathering followers like he invented sex. Nothing we can do—or *should* do—will or can possibly stop Shiva, stop the destruction of Earth. The end is near and all that." Lisa made a face and took a sip. "In fact, they are saying that it is against God's will even to try."

"Oh, well, there's always the Anti-Technology League."

"No, no, he's *for*. Shiva will purge the Earth and all that. He's getting *a lot* of notice. He's starting some kind of march, too, from Chicago down to the Cape."

"To stop—?"

"Uh-huh. 'Course if they have to, they'll call out the army, but I don't think it will come to that. Brother Gabriel is not using any sort of invention to get there. A real march." Dink grinned and chuckled. "Except for one invention, which he uses with excellent results: television."

Lisa nodded, her face sobering. Dink peered at her. "Want to hear about the others?"

"What others? Not more bearded prophets?"

"No, the hedonists. They buy the end of the world, all right, but they are going out—not in a blaze of religious fervor—but in a sweat of orgasm."

"You're kidding."

"Nope. People quitting jobs all over the place. Just dropping the tools or walking away from the desk or whatever. Out in Los Angeles there was a big hedonist rally that turned into an orgy . . . and some of the cops joined in! Ten, twenty thousand in Griffith Park, rutting away like some saturnalia."

"My god," Lisa said. "*Why?*"

Dink shrugged. "They figure we can never stop Shiva, so . . ." He made a face. "I understand the feeling. The news said the murder rate is way up and suicide has tripled."

"Some people fight. Some give up."

"And some adjust," Dink added. "Hey, there's Zorro." He half-stood to wave and Diego saw them. He held up a hand and went to the coffee machine.

"Well," he said, sitting down next to Lisa. He leaned over and gave her a quick kiss. "Well," he said again.

"Yes?" Lisa asked, impatient.

"They've made the selections for the Alpha and Omega teams. But they are leaving the selection of commanders up to each team."

"*And—?*" Lisa frowned at him.

"We're both on," he said, but there was no joy in his voice.

Air went out of Lisa in a sigh. "I don't know whether to be happy or not. What team are we on?"

Diego looked uncomfortable and glanced at Dink. "Uh, I'm on Alpha. And you're . . . you're on Omega."

Dink said an obscenity, but Lisa smiled faintly. "Hey, at least we're going. I thought maybe Carl was going to get the President to give out the assignments and we'd be down here with . . . oh, I'm sorry, Dink."

"Hey, forget it. I've made my adjustment. Better you two should go. But hey, Zorro, can't one of you switch?"

"I'd love it. Get away from Carl—and he *is* on the Alpha team, of course—but Chuck already said no. I asked."

"Well, ask again," Dink said. "I'll go see him and—"

"No, forget it." He gave Lisa an unhappy look. "Billinger gives Alpha about a one-in-ten survival chance, but Omega has about one-in-four. You're better off there and—"

"Don't they know we—?" Lisa was beginning to become angry.

"Yes, they do," Diego said, putting his hand over hers. "Which is, I think, why we're on different teams. You know they've never been happy with our—what's the chic word?—relationship."

Dink snorted. "The good ol' lily-white NASA image. Everyone married and safe. No bachelors if they can help it. And two *lovers*—my God!" He threw up his hands and glowered.

"It isn't only that," Lisa said, and Diego patted her hand again.

"Yeah, yeah," Dink grumbled. "Good ol' chauvinistic NASA. They predicted problems with female astronauts and with *unmarried* female astronauts, gawd!" He made a face. "Remember the noise that came from the boondocks when they brought in the first female? You'd think the modules were outfitted as whorehouse bedrooms—! Every female astronaut was a Jezebel, a temptress, and harlot." Dink spat. "It's not the 'female question,' as they call it, but the 'idiot question.'"

"Aw, Dink, you know it's not just NASA," Diego said. "They get a lot of pressure from church groups and self-appointed bluenoses. Even the wives of some of the astronauts. Ever since that Russian cosmonaut gave birth they've used it as a red flag, if you'll pardon the pun."

"Yeah, yeah," Dink muttered. "Hanky-panky in outer space. We lost Gail Summers and Kathleen Stuart because of that nonsense. But I still think you oughta get transferred to Omega. Be with Beauty here, protect her."

Lisa gave Dink a withering look. "Oh? Protect me? Am I an astronaut or not? If I am, I don't need 'protection,' and if I'm not, the question doesn't arise."

"Aw, you know what I mean—"

"No, I don't, Dink. Am I some kind of second-class astronaut that only gets to operate the backup systems?"

"Okay, okay, I apologize. *Jeez.* You take care of Zorro, then. God knows he could probably use it. He was never too good at celestial ballistics or UFO identification."

"That's a contradiction in terms," Diego laughed. He paused, smiling faintly. "Chuck gave me the impression I'd be scrubbed if I gave them too much flak about this."

"Well, it won't hurt," Lisa suggested. She stood up and her chair scraped back with a squeak. "Come on, let's ask."

Chuck Bradshaw glowered at them. "Get out of here, I'm busy. You know the deal. NASA has never liked having personnel deployment questioned. Either you take the assignment or you step down. You know there are plenty of people waiting for the spot."

Diego's shoulders slumped. "Okay," he muttered. "I do want to go."

"Then shut up and get back to work." His glare included Lisa. "I apologize for my short temper, but not for anything else, understand?"

"We know you're busy," Lisa began.

"You don't know the half of it. Every fruitcake and nut case in the world is trying to tell me how to do it." He slapped a pile of papers on his desk. "Senators,

kings, ambitious politicians, country people, hustlers—!"
He made a growling noise. "Some bible thumper named
Beauregard Boyce Lee wants to take the word of God
to the heathen rock. Reputable scientists are sending me
crackpot ideas. Stop the Earth and let it go by. A wall
in space between here and the moon." He rubbed a
hand across his face and sighed. "Oh, a lot of them
mean well, but, Jesus—! And *some* of them are too
damn big to offend. Would you believe the senior senator from Arkansas wants to shove the moon in between
us and it?" He waved his hand at them in dismissal.
"Get the hell outta here. Get back to work before I replace you with Reverend Lee."

They nodded gloomily and left. Out in the brightly
lit corridor she sighed. "It's blackmail. There's a damned
feudal system around here—!"

Diego smiled wearily. "Uh-huh, but it's the only game
in town, babe. Besides, I told you it wouldn't work."

Dink Lowell joined them as they emerged from
Bradshaw's offices. He didn't have to ask how they
made out. "Hello, hello," he said. "The teams are supposed to meet and elect their leaders next week." He
smiled at Lisa. "I'm on the Omega ground control team,
so I get to vote, too, if there's a tie."

"How can there be a tie with five on the team?" she
asked.

"Someone might stuff the ballot box."

3 January: Collision minus 4 months, 23 days

The carved and polished door opened into the street,
emitting a cloud of scented air. Lisa and Diego came
out, laughing. The delicious odors of the restaurant
spread out over the sidewalk around them. Diego
glanced at the evening sky. Past the great spire of the
Exxon Energy Building the moon was almost full. Little
yellowish rectangles showed in the massive dark towers
around them. There was almost no traffic, although a
number of people hurried along the street toward the
subway entrances.

Lisa heard the engine start up and looked down the
street at the U. S. Army sedan, sedate in its olive drab-

ness. It came smoothly up to them, but she shook her head. "Let's walk awhile?"

"Okay." Diego nodded and bent over. The bullet-proof glass whispered down and Diego spoke to the uniformed driver. "We'll just walk along here to Travis and turn left. Give us about fifteen minutes and come along, okay? We'll stay on this side of the street."

"Sir, there's been reports of riots on Alamo Boulevard. It's either the Gabriels or some like 'em. Smashing windows and such. Best you get in, sir."

Diego grinned. "Thanks, Sergeant, but the lady wants to stretch her legs."

"We'll be strapped into a module long enough," she muttered.

"You wait here, or go along a bit and find yourself a bar. Give us fifteen, though, all right?"

"Yes, sir. But you be careful, y'hear? Sir."

They strolled along for a block or so. The windows were all taped, or had been replaced with expensive "unbreakable" glass. In some cases metal plates, painted and decorated, had simply been substituted. The pedestrians glared at each other suspiciously. Lisa and Diego had worn nondescript civilian clothing and she had braided her hair to change her appearance. The cold wind cut at them.

"I feel like I'm playing hooky," she said.

"Uh-huh. And with Chez Abney's superb cooking sloshing around inside—yum!" He smiled at a passing woman, who frowned back and hurried on.

"Look how many people are carrying clubs," Lisa said.

"It's amazing how many people are taking baseball bats home to the kids," he said, and shrugged.

"It's Gabriel's fault," Lisa muttered as they moved back against a storefront to escape a gang of six or seven twelve-year-olds running along. One was carrying a television set with a dangling, ruined cord. Another was waving a woman's dress. It had a few spots of blood on it. They jeered at everyone, but steered clear of Diego, who was looking hard at them.

"No, it's Shiva's fault," he said, looking over his shoulder at the retreating gang. "If something inanimate can be held at fault. It's an undeserved death and they resent it."

122

"Then why do some people hang in there and others go to pieces? Why do some turn religious and others pagan?"

He smiled. "There are some very religious pagans, you know, you Judeo-Christian chauvinist. Listen, why do some people put on their pants with the left foot first? Hell, Lisa, people respond according to their stress patterns. If they were built strongly, they hold up; if they have flaws, they crack." He shrugged.

"California pragmatist."

"Uh-huh. In some people character is skin deep."

"But, my God, Diego, this is . . . ." She took a deep breath and stopped to stare sightlessly into a window full of bizarre East Indian Halloween masks. The Shiva name was influencing a lot of areas, including fashions. "This is total world destruction we're talking about. Why shouldn't people be scared?"

"Why not, indeed? I am. You are. Even Carl. Well, maybe not Carl. You have to have imagination to get scared. But people react differently—they get drunk or get laid, they crawl into bed or curse the gods, they . . ." He waved his hand around. "They cry or go catatonic; beg or pray or start a fight. With no rational outlet they go bonkers."

She took his arm and they started walking again. At the corner of Travis they turned. At once they saw an orange light flickering off the metal sheen of a skyscraper. There wasn't a single light shining on that side of the littered street.

"Power's off," Lisa said softly, stopping.

"And a fire."

They heard a shout, then a low roar, and almost without warning a small mob streamed out into the street. Far down the avenue a single car screeched to a stop, then rapidly turned and sped away. Diego pulled Lisa back toward the corner. The mob was milling, running this way and that, until a single woman ran out from the side street. There was an explosion behind her and she cried out, "Destroy! Destroy the unbelievers!"

Diego pulled Lisa back around the corner. He glanced down the way they had come. No Army car. "Uh-oh."

"That's great stuff she's screaming," Lisa said, her eyes alert and searching. "Wonder who writes her screams?"

"No one loves a smartass," Diego muttered, looking

123

around. "Now that we need him, where's the driver?" Without waiting for Lisa to answer he answered his own question. "Where I told him he could go, damnit."

"Let's get out of here, that bunch is getting closer. If they recognize us . . ." Lisa shivered as they hurried back down the street. But the mob behind them was running and another group boiled out of a side street ahead. They came to a halt, now caught between two groups.

Both astronauts were remembering what had happened to Major Miller, who had come into downtown Houston in full Air Force uniform only two days before. Bradshaw had given in to pressure by the base-bound personnel who were going stir-crazy, and let Miller have leave. A mob of Gabriels had recognized him, run him to ground, killed his two Marine guards and hung him from a lampost. Then they set him on fire.

Military and city police had swept the Gabriels out of town, but Bradshaw was still very nervous about letting anyone go. Strict enforcement was sending people up the wall and was a measure no one wanted to take. But the roving bands of Gabriels seemed to form out of nowhere, inside police roadblocks, run rampant, then dissolve before or soon after the police arrived.

"Well, well . . ." Diego said tensely. The two mobs were coming together. Glass was being broken. There was another explosion around the corner and more yells. Someone fired a gun and a window ten stories up shattered, showering glass down. Lisa and Diego crowded into a storefront as the deadly shower crashed into the sidewalk and street. "Well," Diego said, "if you can't beat them, join them." He stepped out onto the sidewalk, the glass crunching beneath his feet. Lifting his fist into the air he shouted one of Brother Gabriel's favorite slogans. "They have no right! They must not interfere!"

There was a ragged chorus of shouts. Lisa stepped out and added her angry scream to the growing tumult. "Down with the scientists." To Diego she said, "I feel like a traitor."

"Don't. You'll survive. You're too valuable to lose."

"There are plenty of other astronauts in the backup teams."

"To hell with NASA. Too valuable to *me*. I haven't used you up yet!"

"Why, that's the nicest thing you ever—*uk!*" She ducked as another shot spattered along the concrete overhead. More shots were being fired. Neither group seemed to care that they were showering their own kind with glass and ricocheted slugs. Diego let out another yell, this one a wordless cry, and they were swept up in the joining of the two mobs.

"Eternal bliss, brother," a wide-eyed man said to Diego. In his hand was a length of pipe. Without warning he struck out, smashing through the bars of the shop window behind them, ripping through the cross-hatching of glass tape and shattering the window. He uttered an orgasmic cry and struck again. Diego pulled Lisa away, but someone struck out at him with a two-by-four, hitting him in the shoulder and driving him to his knees.

Lisa was torn away through the shouting mob, but elbowed her way back and lifted Diego to his feet. "Come on!" she cried and started stiff-arming people. Diego shook his head, then pushed ahead to make a passage for them both.

The mob was carrying them along and Diego was trying to get them out of it, into a side street and away, but the mob was too dense and too erratic. They ran across the street, then along toward the center of town. Sirens were in the distance. A wide-eyed woman brandishing a bloody butcher knife appeared suddenly before Diego.

"Bless you, brother!" She started to bring the knife down but Diego punched her hard in the stomach. She fell to the side, vomiting, and he half-tripped over her legs as the crowd shoved them along, heedless of the fallen woman.

An Army tank appeared several blocks down, wheeling into the street. Some troops were behind it. It rumbled up the street and the crowd, screaming incoherently, rushed toward it. Another tank came into the avenue, followed by some personnel carriers, which stopped to disgorge troops in riot helmets.

Diego and Lisa were swept along, bruised and out of breath. A surge parted them and Lisa was carried away, toward the middle of the street. Rocks and pipes were flying in the air, clanging off the tank. The first of the gas grenades exploded and the front rank tumbled beneath the knockout gas. Diego could not see Lisa and fought his way into the street.

"You Messican!" a big man cried out and swung a knotted fist at Diego, catching him in the side of the neck. Diego staggered, almost fell, then ducked under the next blow and karate-chopped the man in the neck. Two more grenades exploded and more of the front ranks collapsed. The tank had rumbled up to the first line of prostrate rioters and stopped. Then Diego saw Lisa. She lay partially under two sprawled men. She wasn't moving. Diego ran toward her, stumbling over arms and legs.

Another gas grenade popped and Diego fell.

The blackness was almost instantaneous.

Lisa sat on the edge of a bunk in the Johnson Space Center Emergency Clinic, holding her head. Lyle Orr, the staid publicity director for NASA, offered her a cup of coffee.

"Where . . . where's Diego?" she asked, taking the mug.

"Coming out of it. He has some bruises, but nothing serious. Jack is with him."

Lisa nodded, sipping at the coffee. She swayed slightly with her eyes closed. "Those are some gas grenades . . ."

"Got to use them. Those mobs are getting worse every day. Especially here, at the Cape, and out near Edwards and Vandenberg. Washington, too." He shrugged. "Chuck had to seal all the bases. No easy passes anymore."

"For the duration?" she asked, squinting at him.

He nodded and shrugged his shoulders. "Had to. You okay now?" She nodded slowly, holding one hand to her temple.

"Let me see Diego."

"Sure. This way."

They went into the next emergency room, where a weary but smiling Diego greeted her. "Hi. You all right?"

"Weak but willing. Any broken bones?"

"Naw. Just some cuts and bangs." He jerked a thumb at Jack Barrows, his PR assistant. "He tells me all the NASA facilities are buttoned up. Sorry, babe, I was go-

126

ing to take you out for some good chow again, tomorrow."

She embraced him. "It's the government gourmet cafeteria from now on, lover."

"We're keeping this quiet," Jack said, looking at his boss.

"That's right," Orr said. "So you keep silent about it. We don't want people to think we are so vulnerable. It was lucky one of the officers recognized you both as they were hauling everyone off to the slammer."

Lisa grimaced, thinking how dangerous it might have been, trying to identify themselves in a cell full of Gabriels. "I feel so stupid," she said.

Orr shrugged. "The Gabriels are the stupid ones. How they can imagine Shiva is going to purge the Earth, I don't know. It's not like some, who are going into the Rockies and the Andes and the Himalayas to be the seed colonies of a new society. They've got their heads stuck in philosophic holes." He grunted and started to leave. "Just take it easy after this, huh?"

Diego grinned. "On the ground, sure."

11 January: Collision minus 4 months, 15 days

Once again Carl Jagens dominated the room, both by his manner and by verbally directing each astronaut and backup team member to one side of the conference room or the other. Most of them obeyed quietly, or with a little sigh of acceptance. Since Carl seemed willing to accept the responsibility of leadership and the troubles that went with it, they went along without much grumbling.

Diego Calderon gave Lisa a look as he moved to the left side of the room to join those who had been selected for the Alpha team. Only three people sat apart and Lisa recognized two of them right away: Zaborovskii and Nissen, two of Russia's top cosmonauts. She had met Zaborovskii in person, a compact bearlike man cursed with perennial five o'clock shadow. But Olga Nissen she knew only by reputation. The Russian woman gave Lisa a penetrating but unreadable look. Then her eyes moved on to the next astronaut entering.

Carl Jagens consulted a clipboard, then set it down

firmly. "All right, everyone, settle down. First, I had best introduce our Soviet counterparts, who will be assisting us on this mission."

Zaborovskii frowned at that and gave Jagens a dark look, but the tall, blond astronaut gave no sign of noticing the disapproval. "First, let me introduce Olga Nissen." There was a regal nod from the darkly blond Nissen and a smattering of applause that quickly died away. "Aleksandr Zaborovskii you all know, I think." Several of the astronauts gave little casual signs with their hands and the Russian nodded politely.

"And last but not least, Dmitrii Evgenovich Menshov."

That's Menshov," Lisa said in a whisper and several of those around her nodded, studying the famous but curiously unpublicized cosmonaut. He was small, even for a spaceman, with the most ordinary of faces, plain and pale. A peasant's face, Lisa thought, not like Zaborovskii's Russian bear mug or Nissen's faintly patrician facade. Yet this was Russia's great space hero, the rescuer of *Prastranstvo Gotup,* the sole survivor of the *Gromyko* crash on Luna, the one cosmonaut with the most "firsts" in the last decade. He seemed unimpressed by the scrutiny of the Americans and looked back at them blandly.

"And you all know Commander Roberts of the Royal Air Force, and Colonel Mezieres of the French Air Force." The tall Briton nodded. The slender Frenchman gave a slight, debonair bow.

"We are an international team," Jagens reminded them needlessly, "and reflect the concern of the world. Now for the benefit of our Soviet collegues I would like to introduce the American teams." Jagens went quickly up one side and down the other, giving name and rank and service affiliation if any. The Russians followed the introductions intently and Lisa felt as though she were being somehow photographed for some secret file.

"Now, to business," Carl said. "We are here to elect leaders and assistant leaders for each team. Colonel Zaborovskii, you are assigned to the Omega team." He gestured toward Lisa's group. "Major Nissen . . . Colonel Menshov . . . my team."

Diego snorted at the proprietary air, earning him a quick glare from Jagens, but the Russians rose and dutifully joined their assigned teams. There were five astronauts or cosmonauts in each team, with twice that many backup pilots or ground control members. Lisa looked at the immediate members of her team. Zaborovskii, herself, Julius Short—one of the few black astronauts—Blaine Brennan, and Nino Solari. She smiled at the deliberate ethnic and racial mix, then looked over at the Alpha team.

Jagens, Diego, the two Russians, and Ikko Issindo. The backup teams reflected the same political mix, although she admitted there was no one there who was not first-rate. She felt a little surge of ego but it was quickly suppressed.

Blaine Brennan said, "Well, I nominate Lisa Bander." For some reason they all looked at Zaborovskii, who remained expressionless. He simply returned the look, then moved his stare to Lisa.

"I second," muttered Nino Solari.

"Why me?" Lisa said, genuinely alarmed.

"Why not?" grinned Brennan.

"That's not very good logic, Blaine," Lisa replied, but the Irishman just grinned and turned toward the backup group.

"Am I right or not?" Several of them grinned and nodded.

"Any other nominations?" Lisa asked quickly, but no one spoke up. She looked at Zaborovskii. "Colonel?"

He shrugged. Brennan raised his hand. "Who's for Lisa?"

All four of Omega team put up their hands and Lisa gulped. "But, but—"

"Be quiet," Brennan said. "Now for assistant leader—?"

"Colonel Zaborovskii," Lisa said quickly.

"Brennan," said Solari. They looked around. There were no other nominations.

Lisa blinked, then asked, "All right, those for Colonel Zaborovskii—?"

She put up her hand, as did Julius Short. The Russian did not vote.

"Those for Brennan?" Solari put up his hand, then very obviously reached over and pulled up Brennan's hand.

"Hey!" the Irishman said.

"All right, let's put it to a full vote," Lisa said, looking at the backup team. The Russian won, by a slight edge.

He nodded slowly as Lisa announced the results. Then they turned toward the Alpha group.

Issindo had nominated Jagens, Nissen had nominated Menshov. Diego declined to vote and it was thrown open to the whole Alpha team. Carl Jagens won by a strong majority, and in a move that came as a surprise, Diego Calderon was elected second in command. The Russians kept expressionless faces throughout the proceedings.

Carl Jagens stood, confidence and authority shining from him. "All right, all right. I'll announce the results to the press in a few minutes. Omega—what about you? Who was elected over there?"

Blaine Brennan took obvious pleasure in announcing their team leaders. Jagens's face clouded for a moment. Then he gave Lisa a broad smile. "Welcome aboard, Miss Bander."

"Major Bander," Brennan said softly.

"Yes, of course. All right, let's get to work. Calderon, you take Alpha to the Cape this afternoon. I'll follow tonight or tomorrow morning. Lisa?" He called over to her lightly. "We'd better get everyone down to the Cape and start putting together our act." Carl used the none-too-subtle air of a command, and Lisa bristled. Then she just nodded. It was the proper thing to do at this point. There was nothing at Johnson Space Center for them now.

"All right," Jagens said with great satisfaction. "We can really *start* now!"

Diego came over to Lisa and took her arm. "Congratulations, honey."

"Uh-huh," she muttered softly. "Are you certain this isn't the kiss of death? I'm not certain it should be me that has all the responsibility . . ."

"Oh, stop doubting yourself. Do you think ol' Play-it-safe Brennan would go for it if he didn't think it was the best thing?"

"Why didn't NASA just *assign* the team leaders?"

"You know why. Image. Press relations. World opinion. America the free and all that."

"You mean they are *seriously* thinking of something like that *now?*" He was guiding her toward the door.

"Sure. Besides, is there a better way? We all know

each other—the Reds excepted—better than the gods of NASA, don't we?"

"Oh? Is that why Carl got elected?"

Diego shrugged. "He *is* good, I'll give him that, even if . . . well, he does get things done. One way or another."

"He gets things done *his* way." They were interrupted by people congratulating them, then Lyle Orr took her arm.

"Excuse me, Diego. Congratulations, Lisa. Oh, you, too, Diego; I'm sorry."

"What is it, Lyle?" Lisa asked, looking at the thin PR man with the obvious toupee.

"News conference, my dear." He grinned quickly. "You don't want Carl to get *all* the publicity, do you?"

"I don't care, Lyle. I'll do my job."

"This *is* part of your job, Major Bander. You were a perfect choice. We'll get a lot of mileage out of your selection as—"

"Oh, for Christ's sake, Lyle!" Diego growled.

"Well, it's true, Colonel Calderon, and you know it. And by the way, Lisa, you'll be going to a light colonel this week. Maybe a full chicken, who knows?"

"*You* go to the news conference, Lyle," Lisa said, pulling away.

A surprisingly tough note came into the publicity man's voice. "No, Lisa, *you* will. That's an order from Bradshaw. We want to scotch the rumors about NASA's treatment of women and this is perfect. Besides, the public should know." He gestured down the corridor toward the press auditorium.

Lisa took a long time to answer. Her eyes searched Lyle Orr's face. "I'm still a symbol, huh? Is that it?" Orr shrugged. "I'm never, ever going to be just Lisa Bander, astronaut. I'm always going to be Lisa Bander, the *woman* astronaut."

Orr made an apologetic face. "Don't blame me, Lisa, I just work here. I do what I can to give us a good face, to direct the attention, to plug the leaks. It's my job. You have a job and I have a job." He reached up and smoothed his hair. "Part of my job is seeing we get full mileage out of everything. We'll give the Russians as much coverage as we can and slant it so that they are *assisting* us."

"How much did you influence the team selection?" Diego asked, his face hard.

Orr shrugged again and took Lisa's elbow. "We picked the top ten percent, then went over them for . . ."

"For the minority shuffle?" Diego asked bitterly.

Orr was not apologetic. "Yes, of course. You'll find a nice religious mix . . . though I'm not too happy with Issindo being a Baptist; we already have one of those in Alpha backup."

"You left out gays, midgets, and senior citizens," Diego said.

"That's not funny, Colonel Calderon. We do our best. If you sat in my chair for a few days you'd understand that there are obligations, pressures, compromises. Congress holds the purse strings, Diego. I'm really sorry we lost Bernstein last summer. Schumacher didn't quite make the top ten percent. That would have been an excellent choice." He frowned to himself, his lips pursed. Diego made a gritty, gurgling sound and Orr nodded. "Yes, the usual contempt for the earthbound. But you forget who goes through hell to get the funding, to keep Congress and the presidents happy—"

Lisa pushed her way between the two men. "All right, you guys . . ." To Diego she said, "Come on, let's go to this damned news thing." To Orr she gave a smile "Maybe you'd better get a little good publicity out for the PR department, Lyle?" She hurried off, half-pulling Diego behind her.

Carl Jagens gave them a quick glance as they appeared. His dark look said he didn't care much about sharing the spotlight, but he recovered quickly.

The room was brightly lit. On the small stage was a speaker's stand and behind that a row of chairs before a blue curtain that covered a large briefing screen. Carl stood at the podium, both hands clasping the sides as if he was not going to be dislodged.

"Ladies and gentlemen, let me present my own Alpha team second-in-command, Colonel Diego Calderon." Cameras swung toward them and the men and women of the press pushed forward. But Diego fended them off, made a passage for Lisa and himself, and they stepped up onto the stage.

"And . . . as commander of Omega team, the mop-up

132

group, Major and soon to be Lieutenant Colonel Lisa Bander." There was some applause but mostly questions, which flooded over Lisa. She had been the focus of media attention before, but never so massively. There was a touch of aggression in it, and she felt an odd shiver of fear.

Carl Jagens's voice cut through the tumult. "Excuse me, excuse me, folks, but there is still one more. Just coming in, the assistant Omega commander, Colonel Aleksandr Zaborovskii, of the Soviet cosmonauts! Come on up here, Alek."

Lisa glanced at Diego, rolling her eyes slightly at Carl's glad-hand American heartiness. But she sighed with relief, too, as the focus shifted from her to the Russian.

They spent more than an hour answering questions, with Carl acting as moderator, and answering most of the queries himself.

Eventually Lisa and Diego were able to get away. Past the security men, she slumped against a corridor wall. "Oh, God," she sighed and grinned weakly at Diego.

"How'd you like that one about us getting married?" he asked.

She shrugged. "And I just loved the way Carl butted in and undercut Zaborovskii. I don't think our Russian bear cared much for that."

It was Diego's turn to shrug. "Maybe he's just not used to the give and take of a free press. Maybe over there they know all the questions in advance. Come on, we've got to pack and get ourselves to the Cape."

"Why not Vandenberg, I wonder?" Lisa asked as they hurried along.

"Cape Canaveral is more dramatic." When Lisa looked sharply at him, Diego grinned. "I'll bet you that's the reason. The Kennedy Space Center facility has always been the home of our space effort and Vandenberg a kind of test facility and unglamorous second-string affair."

"But sixty percent of the shuttle traffic goes in and out of there and Edwards—"

He grinned at her. "But *visually* the Cape is better. A reminder of American might, of historical precedence. Prettier, too."

"Oh, my God," Lisa said bitterly. "Cosmetic imagery.

It's a wonder they don't sell ads on the side of the ship and get all that teevee time—!"

"Shush, don't suggest it. You know how they keep coming up with an idea to have a solar-powered synchronous satellite around the moon, projecting ads on it. Or selling hype space on stamps to relieve the postal department's woes. Or having patches on the spacesuits like race car drivers."

"What race car drivers?" She frowned as they went through a door into the heat of a Houston autumn. "That's one sport that got knocked out by the energy shortage. Or do you mean the blimp racers or those vane sailors?"

"Well, you know what I mean. Crank a little good old American sell into the program. Remember how they had to pass a law to prevent active astronauts from endorsing products? Hey, there's Dink."

The short, grinning ex-astronaut came up the path to them. "Well, video stars, howdy. Zorro, you were great on that loaded question about the truckers."

"Yeah, yeah," Diego muttered. "But I couldn't help it. Those guys getting in a huff and going on strike because they've cut long-distance trucking to help the energy situation. Why don't they just give up? Everything has been going by rail for several years, but they blame this last squeeze on us . . . as if Shiva was our fault."

"Aw, that's the President's problem. Well, Beauty, Carl did it to you, again."

"Uh-huh. You know Carl. He's going to corral Knowles into whatever scheme he has going."

"What can he have going?" Diego asked. "It's pretty straightforward from now on. We put together a strike force . . . two of them . . . adapt a lifter for the Russian bomb . . . triple-check everything and lift off for rendezvous at the optimum time. What's to get mysterious about?"

Dink grinned lopsidedly. "Probably out ordering his bronze plaque himself, to be certain the wording is right. Not *too* complimentary, you know."

Diego and Lisa sighed together. "I wish he'd put all that energy into the problem," she muttered.

"What? And leave show biz?" laughed Dink.

"The President will see you now, Captain," Grace Price said with a smile, replacing the intercom handset.

Carl Jagens slid off the corner of her desk and smiled happily. "Thank you, Grace." He pulled something from the pocket of his naval uniform and gave it to her as she rose to escort him to the door. She hesitated, looked at the object. A fine chain fell limply and she caught it.

"Oh, it's lovely!"

"A moon rock," Carl said softly. "Picked it up myself near Eudoxus. I thought it was quite attractive. It's legal. They let us keep a few, but they get first pick, of course. I had it polished and . . . waited for someone to give it to."

The stone was mostly orange, with tiny red and yellow spots, a cluster of fused droplets which had been ejected from a crater and stuck together. The drops had formed into perfect spheres in the very slight lunar gravity, cooling quickly in the chill of space. Grace Price's eyes brightened. Moon rocks were still rare enough to be valuable, but as a gift from Carl Jagens, it was priceless to her. She blinked up at him, her usual urbane stainless steel surface ruptured. "Th-thank y-you, uh, Captain Jagens, I—"

"Carl, please," he said, taking her elbow and guiding her toward the door.

Grace blinked, clutched the stone on the chain in her fist and opened the door. "Mister President, Captain Jagens."

"Captain, Captain," the President said, rising and coming around the desk to meet him. "How are you? Care for a drink? Some good California wine? Juice? A beer? You know Myron Murray, General McGahan, Steve Banning."

"Sir," Jagens said to the general formally. "Mister Murray, Mister Banning."

"Hello again, Captain Jagens," Banning said, his usual cheerful expression absent.

"What can we do for you, Captain . . . or may I call you Carl?" the President said, slapping a hand on Carl's shoulder. "Come, sit down here. You know, Carl, you put me on a spot with that news conference after you left here the last time."

Carl Jagens looked surprised. "Sir? But you agreed that my plan was the best. We discussed—"

"Oh, bull waste, Carl, you sandbagged me," President Knowles said with a grin. "I was snowed and you know it. But no hard feelings. We're committed. But . . ." his eyes slitted over his continuing grin, "don't do it again, boy."

"No, sir."

"Well, then, what *can* we do for you that isn't being done?"

"Well, sir, uh, you asked *me* here."

"Eh? Oh, yes, I guess I did. Myron?"

Murray stepped closer, opening a thin leather binder with a few sheets of paper in it. "Mister President, you wanted to talk to Captain Jagens about the tour."

"Um, yes, of course." He looked at the astronaut with a smile, then changed his expression, as if caught doing wrong. "Yes, well, you know the stock market has gone all to hell. The rallies haven't held, the bargain hunters started selling, and so on. It has been devastating. That's why I had to close the banks, you know."

"Yes, sir," Jagens said respectfully, frowning slightly. The announcement had been a bombshell. All credit cards had been automatically voided.

"The Arabs have done the worst damage," Knowles said. "Pulling their petrodollars out without the slightest idea where to put them. The Swiss have stopped trading in currency, the London gold market has gone out of sight—!" The President slapped the arm of his chair angrily. "Country's going to hell, going to hell! You can't eat dollars, you can't keep warm with gold."

"Yes, sir." Jagens gave Murray a quick look, but the presidential aide was looking at Knowles. "What can I do to help?"

"You can go on a tour, Captain. Hype confidence. Tell them—Americans, everyone—tell them we'll do it, stop Shiva."

"We will, sir."

Knowles squinted at Jagens, suddenly quiet. "We will, huh?"

"Yes, sir, I believe so."·

Knowles looked at Steve Banning and the general. "He says they'll stop it."

"If Captain Jagens says so, sir," Banning replied, "then I am prepared to believe it."

Knowles looked at him for a moment. "Steve, you have been pitching bullshit so long you don't even recognize it when you step in it."

Jagens was hurt and tried not to show it. Knowles swung his gaze back to the astronaut. "But, of course, there are always miracles. Maybe the strike won't be as bad as they say. Maybe the whole thing is another bureaucratic screw-up."

"Sir—" protested Jagens.

"But we must go through the motions, I know that, you know that," Knowles said.

"Sir, the danger is real, very real," Jagens said.

"Oh, it's *real*, but maybe not as bad as everyone thinks. You should look on the bright side. That's what we want you to do, Captain. Go around telling them. Full media coverage. *Special* media coverage, I'll see to that."

The idea was intriguing. *The* spokesman for space. They hadn't asked Chuck Bradshaw, Carl noted.

"You and the leading astronauts," Knowles said with a wave. "That woman, whatshername, the pretty one, Bander. That black Marine, too."

"Major Short," Murray said.

"Yes, and Calderon, of course. Good mixture. What do you say, Captain?"

Carl took a deep breath. The idea of his being the sole focus had intrigued him, but the others diluted it. And they didn't really have the time, as important as such a mission might be. The economic balance of the country had to be restored. Already some cities were issuing scrip to their firemen, police, and other vital workers. Redeemable when the banks opened again. If they did. If Shiva didn't hit. Most of the time it worked, as people saw the need, and kept the power plants functioning, the trucks moving, and so on.

"No, sir, I'm afraid we couldn't do that," Carl said. "It's not that I don't agree with the need, it's just that, well, we have more important things to do."

"More important than the economic structure of your country?" General McGahan said sharply.

"Yes," Carl said, looking at him confidently. "The *survival* of the country . . . and the world."

"We could order you," McGahan said. Carl just looked at him.

"Now, now," Knowles said placatingly. "I think we can get someone else. One of the third-string astros, the Secretary of Energy, the Secretary of the Treasury."

"You could go on the road, sir," Murray said, but Knowles shook his head.

"No, I'll go on the tube, that's all." He slapped the arm of his chair again. "This is my post. Right here." He smiled at Jagens. "Well, blame it on those Arabs. With one side of their mouth they say it's the Will of Allah. If Shiva hits, Shiva was intended to hit. If it doesn't, it doesn't. If they are to die, they will; if they are not, oh, crap, they drive me crazy. Do-nothings! With the other side of their mouth they are saying 'Give us our money back.' Bastards. Thirty years they've been buying up America, them and the Japanese. Investing, investing, investing. You can't pull a few billion out of a country, not even the United States of America, and not have it hurt!"

"Sir, I just think we are more valuable—"

"Of course you are, my boy, of course you are. No question of that! Silly of us to drag you up here. You get right back down there and do your damnedest. Yessir, your damnedest!" He reached over and slapped Jagens on the arm, then stood up.

"I'd like to help, sir, but I feel—"

"Yes, yes, of course. We understand. You're the one who knows best about these things. You just stop that rock now."

"We will, sir."

"Uh? Oh, yes, I'm sure you will, yes. Good luck."

Myron Murray came out into the corridor with Carl. Jagens looked back as the tall door was closing and saw the President sitting down behind the big carved desk. He looked smaller than Carl remembered him.

Grace Price smiled at him, sticking out her chest in a peculiar manner, until Carl remembered the moon rock pendant. She wore it around her neck. He smiled back and Murray guided him along.

"If there is anything you need, Captain, anything. Just call."

"Thank you, Mister Murray. Ah . . . the President, he's—?"

"He's fine, Captain. Concerned, like all of us, that's all."

"Oh, yes, of course, naturally."

Who wouldn't be concerned? Especially the President.

"Colonel Calderon, glad to have you on my team!" Carl Jagens was smiling as he extended his hand. Diego took it, hesitating only a second, for the news cameras were on him. He muttered something incoherent and the tall, blond astronaut put his arm around Diego. "One of the best men in the whole program!" he announced heartily.

"And here . . . the leader of the backup team, Lisa Bander!" Carl's magnanimous wave brought the lights and cameras to bear on Lisa. She noticed at once that Carl's wide smile still left his eyes cold. She smiled and made a gesture, a kind of casual salute.

"We've come here to Cape Canaveral," Carl said in a practiced tone of command, "to get ready for the assault on Shiva. The nominal mission plan has been set, and approved by President Knowles, and we will implement that plan . . . or die in the attempt."

Jagens did not say the last words melodramatically, but offhand, as if that were the expected result of failure, and because of his casual delivery, the words had a sincerity. Am I cynical, Lisa wondered, or do I think Carl practiced saying that? Maybe he rehearsed in his room, before a mirror?

His quote was the one on the evening news, with the shots of the rest of the Alpha-Omega team run silent beneath the network anchorperson's voice. It was a tape-clip that would often be played over the next few months, Lisa suspected.

1 February: Collision minus 3 months, 25 days

"No, Brennan is still out and that's final," Bradshaw said. Carl Jagens and Lisa Bander exchanged looks. She tilted her head toward Carl; Brennan's replacement, Schumacher, was now on Omega team.

"All right," Carl said without emotion. "Brennan's the better man, but if that is the way the powers want it, all right."

Bradshaw looked at him suspiciously. "Carl, you're being too easy to get along with."

Jagens smiled pleasantly and raised his eyebrows to Lisa, who was looking as surprised as she felt. "All right, Carl, it's your team."

"Save your energies for the fights you can win," he said to her. "Brennan became an embarrassment. After he was grounded, he shot his mouth off again." The blond astronaut shrugged. Turning back to Bradshaw he said, "What's the latest tally on the missiles?"

Bradshaw smiled suddenly and reached across his desk to pick up a message form. "Good, good. Far better than we thought."

"Enough to do the job?" Lisa asked.

Chuck shrugged and rattled the paper. "The French, the Israelis, the Arab Union, and Red China have all contributed missiles."

"Red China?" Jagens frowned, his lips compressed. "What do they want out of it? How many did they send?"

"Six. Cong Ji Fours." He spread his hands. "No strings. They want to be represented, that's all."

"That's *never* all with the Reds," Carl responded. "So what's the total?"

"Alpha will have twenty-two twenty-megatonners and Omega will control nineteen. Plus the biggie, of course." He put the message form down and spread his fingers across it. "A lot of power, people. The greatest atomic fleet in history."

"Yes, of course," Carl said impatiently. "But how are they to be controlled? Who's working on the interfaces? Those Red Chinese missiles must be bitches to phase in. When are they arriving? When do we have operational control?"

Bradshaw put up a hand and lowered his head. "Hold it, hold it." He looked at Lisa and smiled, then sobered up to respond to Carl's questions. "We are sending teams to Peking, the French test facility in the Sahara, and to Cairo. They will interface and the launches will be from there but under our command. The Israelis are no problem, we already have operational interface from their satellite launches three years ago. All the American missiles will lift from Vandenberg."

"And the Russians are coming here?" Lisa asked.

Chuck nodded, his fingers smoothing out the papers before him. "Yes. I don't think they are ready for any experts from the West nosing around their bases."

"And we have nothing to hide?" Carl sneered. "They can just nose around all they want over here?"

Chuck sighed. "They have nine missiles en route right this minute. Their latest and best. *We* can nose around all over them, too. I think they realize the importance of this." He fixed Carl with a hard look. "And you'll grin and bear it. They bumped Menshov up to general, but you'll still be in command."

Carl looked thoughtful for a moment, then spoke in measured tones. "Shouldn't I be on a par? To rear admiral at least?"

Chuck grinned and shook his head. "You just made captain, Carl. You know Naval policy."

"This whole Shiva thing is out of policy. I think—"

"No, Carl. Lisa goes to full colonel. She'll wear silver eagles just like you. You can take that and you can take Menshov's star. The brass doesn't mean a damn. There will be plenty of promotions when you get back, if that's what is bothering you."

Lisa hid a smile as Carl raised his chin. "No, of course not. It just seemed to me that effective leadership would require the proper rank to facilitate matters."

"Yes, of course," Chuck said soothingly. "Well, there will be enough rank, fame, and glory for everyone after this matter is cleaned up. The world, and posterity, will know who did it."

"Well, then," Carl said, abruptly standing. "If that's all, let's get back to work. I've got to take the team through the landing simulations, in case we have to plant the big one right on the surface." He walked to the door, paused to look back. "We don't want to let them score any propaganda points, Chuck."

"No, of course not, Carl."

"I'll be going, too, Chuck, unless you want me for something," Lisa said.

"Stay a moment, will you?" He looked at Carl. "Don't worry, Carl, barring an act of God, you are and will be Alpha leader."

"Alpha *and* Omega," Carl reminded him and Chuck nodded. Jagens left, stiff-backed and resolutely grim. Chuck looked at Lisa and smiled faintly.

"He'll do the job, and well," Lisa said. "He's very good . . . and determined as hell."

"I don't need any reassurances, Colonel Bander," Chuck said with a rueful face. "Not about him."

"Who then?" She tipped her head at the NASA leader.

Chuck shrugged and leaned back, his black leather chair creaking. He laced his fingers behind his head and looked at the walls covered with photos. An old black-and-white of a V-2 rising from White Sands. A large color-print of the upper section .of Orion, *Apollo XVI's* .module, lifting from the Descartes region, looking like a comic strip explosion with scores of varicolored shards flying off in all directions. The picture was lined, as it had come from the remote-controlled television camera. Next to it was a younger Bradshaw, grinning through a helmet, the partially completed Luna One base in the background. Then the lumpy white figure with the American flag standing on the rocky plain of Arcadia, the immense red mountain of Nix Olympica in the southwestern sky. Bradshaw with presidents and movie stars. Bradshaw being sworn in. Bradshaw's family. The walls said Charles Bradshaw had paid his dues. He knew what it was like. He was fit for command.

"Do you think we can do it?" he asked Lisa softly.

"Thought you didn't need reassurances?"

"I'm conducting a poll. Is there anything we've forgotten or overlooked, any procedure that needs beefing up or . . . or anything?"

"If you haven't thought of them, I couldn't, Chuck."

He was quiet a moment and Lisa waited patiently. She recognized it as a rare moment. His defenses were down, if only slightly. Doubts were crowding in. Not that they shouldn't. They were about to conduct the largest scale space operation in history and without one rehearsal. She felt a little like the cartoon: "Five minutes, Christians."

Chuck sighed and clicked his tongue. He was looking at the flat photo of his wife and two kids. They were proud of him, and supportive. He remembered how Gene had got into a fistfight with two larger kids at the school in Brownsville, the ones who had said the whole Mars mission was a fake, that it was all shot in Sedona, Arizona, where the ground was red, too. He remembered his wife, Louise, with that tiny frown line between her brows as she told him everything was fine, that she hadn't wanted to tell him she was pregnant while he was preparing for the Mars flight, and how his gloved hands had gripped the edge of the control panel, twenty million miles away. He hadn't seen much of them lately, he thought. Not even on the videophone. He made a note to call Gene and Frank specially, a call all their own.

He became aware of Lisa's quiet waiting and he flashed her an embarrassed smile. "Sorry. A million miles away." He aimed a thumb at the family portrait. "Thinking about the kids. Haven't seen much of them or their mother." He gestured around him. "This has been home for weeks."

"They understand."

"Uh-huh. Louise wrote me. She saw me on TV, said I should eat better. She had to see me on the tube." He shook his head wearily. "Well, we are going to do it, Lisa, we are going to do it."

"We have to."

"And we will. And after . . . afterward I'm going to take Louise on a world tour. See *everything*. The moon, too, if she wants. The works. Eat, sleep, make love, rest. Then I'll take the kids camping. Sierras probably. Just me and them. A couple of weeks roughing it. No beep-beep, no push buttons, not one damn computer, no vid-calls, no presidents, no—"

"No astronauts, no cosmonauts, no second-guessers, no Monday morning quarterbacks . . ." She smiled at him fondly. "Sounds good to me. I . . . I had something like that in mind." Chuck raised his eyebrows at her and she nodded. "The get-away-from-it-all syndrome, boss. We have this little, well, cabin, up in the Rockies. I thought we'd take a case of Möet and Chandon, some real beefsteaks, some of those Granny Smith apples from Australia, the kind that pop juice when you bite into them . . ." She paused for breath. "And just not see anyone for a while."

"You and Diego?"

"Who else?"

"When it's over . . ."

"When it's over."

They were quiet a moment. Then Lisa said, "My father used to say people said, back in the early forties,

143

'after the war.' Then in the eighties it was 'when things settle down.'" She smiled. "When it's over we'll all go back to doing what we were doing."

Chuck shook his head. "No, we won't. We've marked things from Christ for just about exactly two thousand years. We may mark things Before and After Shiva. Not the calendar, maybe, but . . ." He shrugged.

Lisa said, somberly, "My father also said people marked things before and after Kennedy's assassination. Things were different after."

"Things are always different." Chuck put his hands down on the desk top with a slap and sighed. "All right, Colonel Bander, I thank you for your views, now get your bum out of here and back to work. I have a world to save."

"Yes, *sir!*" she said, hopping up and giving him a two-fingered salute. Before she was out of the door he was barking into the vidscreen.

"Goddamn it, Lawrence, I don't *care* what the latest readings on the flare activity of the sun are, I want a fine-screen readout on the predicted Thirring effect as Shiva comes back in! It can affect the—"

Lisa closed the door quietly. Chuck Bradshaw was back in the saddle.

3 February: Collision minus 3 months, 23 days

When the elevator door sighed open, one of the security men was directly in front of Carl Jagens, hand poised before the opening in his suit, his body blocking the view of the corridor beyond. The security man that had ridden up on the elevator with Carl stepped out, holding the door open, and looked alertly in all directions. He gestured to Carl, who stepped out of the elevator.

As far as Carl could see there were no other security men in sight, though there were the usual tiny glittering video eyes. "It's okay, sir," the security man said to Carl. He nodded at the man who had greeted them, who stepped aside, his face impassive. Carl was led down the corridor of the hotel. He noted the inconspicuous nodes of a sensor net, and more video buttons. It was all thorough and professional. Probably behind more than one door were waiting security teams, armed and ready. The whole seventh floor of Houston's new Milam Hotel was filled with a squad of anonymous, hard-faced government men, bomb snoopers, electronics gear; there were police surveillance teams on nearby rooftops. All on orders from the White House.

The security man stopped at 712 and got out his keys. "You're in charge of this detail?" Carl asked.

"For the next five hours, sir. Then Gutierrez comes on."

"I want to talk to you, ah—?"

"Russell, sir." He held up a hand as the key turned in the lock. "Just a second, please." Russell drew a Colt Python .38 and opened the door, putting a hand out to stop Jagens.

Carl felt mildly irritated at all of the security routine. The whole business made him jumpy and short-tempered. Still, it was worth the trouble, if only to break the routine of living on the base.

The justification for this foray into downtown Houston was the civilian scientist conference he had just attended. Two floors above was the hotel's show-off suite, the Sam Houston, where Carl had just had an opulent dinner. The two powerful senators who arranged it had pressured NASA for the contact, and Bradshaw thought it was a good idea to go along with them and had flown Jagens in from the Cape. All cosmetic, of course. The senators were angling for some further role in the Shiva mission for their committee, which was only peripheral to the main space effort now.

Carl had long held an obligation to one of them and had now paid it off by listening to their ideas. Lousy ideas, of course. There wasn't anything Congress could do this late, except keep out of the way. But the dinner had been pleasant. Lean veal, a delicate cream sauce, spinach salad. A smooth Pinot Chardonnay with a light finish. A hell of a lot better than NASA's wholesome, unexciting chow. And the suite was another world, compared to the remorselessly rectangular Johnson Space Center buildings, with their flat, even lighting, hard surfaces, and governmental decor. Carl liked a change of scenery, and it was damned hard to get away from NASA. Getting permission to stay overnight in Houston, only a few minutes' drive from the base, had taken considerable string-pulling.

The guard came back and opened the door wider for the naval officer. "All checked out, Captain Jagens."

Carl walked in and turned around. "Fine. I want you to tell the rest of the team I'm having a visitor in a short while."

Russell looked at him alertly. "Ah, sir, that isn't on the schedule."

"I know. A last-minute change."

The security man looked a little uncomfortable. "I'll have to have the specs on this person, sir, and call them in. I can't take the responsibility for passing on anyone, unless—"

"Here." Carl took a folded sheet of paper from his jacket pocket and handed it over. The man read it through quickly, then again more slowly.

"Do we have a clearance on . . . on this person, sir?"

"You don't need one, Mister Russell. We're not conducting classified conversations. This is just a social call."

"Well . . ."

Carl looked steadily at him.

With an uncomfortable expression on his face Russell inhaled noisily and let it out. "Well, I suppose it's all right. I'll phone it in as a routine change."

"Good." He smiled at Russell, who smiled back automatically. "Thank you," Carl said, putting a hand on Russell's shoulder and subtly turning him toward the door. "I appreciate that."

When the guard was gone Carl went into the bedroom and pulled out a thick, sealed envelope and tossed it on the bed. Then he took off his jacket, kicked off his shoes and lay down on the bed. He ran his thumbnail under the seal and broke it, then extracted the contents. There was always stuff to look over and sign off on.

This time there were intelligence backgrounding reports, most of them depressing. Absenteeism was getting pretty serious everywhere, but in those areas supporting the Shiva project it was extremely important. The Shiva subcontractors couldn't count on a steady work force, especially among the highly skilled workers. Carl shook his head as he read over the reports. They were couched in the usual government jargon, but the picture came through clearly anyway. People just didn't have faith in their own future anymore. For decades now everybody had talked about a decline of respect for reason—hell, it had become a cliché—but, Christ, *this* . . .

Before now, if he had thought about the question at all, Carl would have assumed that a crisis would stiffen the resolve of the majority of people. But instead, the continuing small meteor strikes were dissolving whatever courage people had. *A century back, we were made of harder stuff,* he thought. But then, a century ago, they'd have been totally helpless against Shiva. Maybe it balanced out.

A knock at the door.

When he opened it the big security man from the elevator was standing awkwardly beside a black-haired woman, who was smiling in an oddly expectant manner. "Miz Conner, sir." Carl nodded and stepped aside to let her in, then shut the door in the guard's face.

She turned and stepped quickly to him, putting her arms around his neck. "Quite a gauntlet," she said. A deep, warm voice. Her body, lush and cushioned, pressed against him. She kissed him hungrily.

"Yes," he agreed when his mouth was free. "They're underfoot all the time."

She drew back from him and her hair cascaded down from her shoulders. It was longer than last time. He liked that and touched the dark curls. He had tried to get her to let it grow long, down to her waist if possible, but she had always refused before. Not fashionable, difficult to maintain. He put both hands into the long black strands and stroked them. She swayed back against him, putting her arms around him tightly.

"I wonder how closemouthed they are," she said.

"Who?"

"Your security clowns. I wonder if word could get back to Henry."

He shrugged. "They're pros. They don't babble. It's the kind they hire." He put his hands on either side of her face and lifted it up. "You haven't told him yet."

"I . . . I decided not to."

"Still making up stories?"

She cocked an eyebrow at him and grinned. "It doesn't take a lot of imagination. One alibi every six weeks isn't hard."

"I suppose not. It's just that—"

"You think he'll see a pattern." She shrugged and

147

hugged him again. "Maybe so, eventually. That would force it out into the open. After—how long has it been? Over five years? After all this time, meeting like this for a night or a weekend, maybe it *should* be out in the open."

Carl felt a cold chill, an involuntary response to a threatened disruption of his routine or his plans. He kissed her exposed throat as he thought. But the warmth of her ripe body kept disturbing him.

They stood together for a long moment, silently telegraphing to each other with body language, then she spoke. "You're not saying anything. What's the legal phrase? 'Silence implies consent.' So you think I ought to tell him?"

He drew back. "No."

"I seem to remember having this conversation before," she said with a wry smile and an expressive gesture. "Every year or so."

"You know the way it is with me, Ann."

"Oh, I do, I do. I've understood you on that level ever since I saw you that first time in Atlanta."

"College romance consummated at last?" He grinned, patting her and moving away toward the small bar. "Yeah, there is that. We've both got active memories. Scotch?"

"Active fantasies," she said, walking into the bedroom. When Carl walked in, holding two drinks, he saw that she had pulled back the covers from the bed, exposing a bold, bright design. "Umm, pretty."

She took the glass he offered and set it on the bedside table untested, then took off her jacket and tossed it on the chair over her purse. She looked at Carl with a serious expression.

"You know, I'm not pressing you. Really. Not with what you have to do. If, if my coming to you is a, a help, Carl, you know I'll do it." She laughed and turned away to pick up her drink. "You could get a hundred thousand or so to do the same, I'm sure."

Ann sipped her drink and walked in little aimless circles as Carl leaned against the doorjamb. "All our play . . . all our fun, Carl, I . . . I want it just as much as you do."

Maybe more, he thought. He smiled wanly, finished his drink, and set it down on the dresser. He picked up one pillow and put it against the other and lay down on the bed propped up. "You know how much I lean on you," he said.

Her face brightened. "Just remember that *tonight* you're not NASA's, you're mine." She looked at him from beneath lowered eyelashes, waiting. He nodded, still smiling faintly.

Her skin was deliciously pale against her jet black hair and when she smiled in a particular mischievous way a slight dimple appeared. "I have a little something for you," she said, putting down her drink.

Carl felt himself relax. Still dressed, he stretched out, eyes half-closed. With the saying of the words, the beginning words he liked, she had begun the old quickening. They were ready to start. God, he needed it.

She smiled at him and reached down to slowly hike up her skirt. She was wearing high-heeled black shoes and as the skirt lifted the black net stockings came into view. Carl hadn't seen this particular pair before. As she turned this way and that, he saw there were eagles on the tendon, just above the heel, black eagles with widespread wings.

His throat tightened as he watched her staring at him, smiling that certain hoping-to-please smile. The skirt inched up, tantalizingly slow. The hose were fastened with black lace garters, embroidered with small red roses. She wore nothing else underneath.

Carl studied the beautiful coming together of pale flesh and black lace, the lush, untrimmed triangle already beaded with tiny diamonds of moisture. He looked into her eyes; they were bright, eager, expectant.

"Go on," he said, his voice choked.

The skirt was tight enough so that when she let go of it it barely moved down. She unbuttoned her blouse, turning this way and that, smiling, teasing. Beneath the blouse was a black lace bra, lacy and open in front so her pink nipples could show through. The nipples were puckered and hard.

Ann unzippered the skirt and in a few quick, practiced movements was out of it. She unhooked the bra and made a show of getting rid of it. If left no marks, which pleased him; it meant she had worn no bra, or had worn it unfastened, until she arrived at the hotel. Probably hooked everything up in the ladies room.

Wearing the high heels, the hose, and garter belt, she came onto the bed and began undressing him. He did little to help her. When he was naked she knelt between his outstretched legs and took him into her hands. She looked up at him, eager yet innocent. "Will you let me?" she said. He said nothing. Silence implied consent. She bent her head over him. He put his hands in the thick mass of dark hair and held her tightly as she moved up and down. She always liked the first one that way.

A security man brought them a room service breakfast. It was not as good as he had remembered it. Good help was difficult to get. The coffee was fine, however. He watched Ann eat heartily, eggs, ham, toast, juice, a ruby red grapefruit, more coffee.

Carl said goodbye to her with Russell standing nearby, looking pointedly at his watch. She left, giving him a lingering, tremulous smile. Carl gathered up his papers, put on his jacket, and followed her.

Russell said nothing in the elevator, and the other security man was equally silent. Not until Carl noticed the elevator sensor node did he think just how extensive the sensor net might have been. They could have put acoustic detectors into the room, possibly even a video button, disguised as a bit of ornamentation or a dresser knob. As he thought about it, he realized there was no maybe about it; such things would be routine.

Somebody had been listening, perhaps even watching, all night long.

When the realization burst on him Carl felt a pressure building in his face and knew he was turning an unaccustomed red. Red with anger, not embarrassment. But after a moment, calmness returned and he was able to relax. The elevator stopped and he got out, preceded and followed by the security men.

The bastards wouldn't dare use it against him. That was the thing about attaining a certain level of fame, even in normal times. The system had to protect you to protect itself. Hell, Kennedy had lounged around the White House pool with a secretary, both buck naked in broad daylight, with Jackie off somewhere for the weekend. The secret Service covered for him. Nobody found out until long after he was dead. They'll cover for me, Carl thought. He knew the system and had followed that logic for years and knew it worked. No reason to get upset just because some blank-faced nobodies got an earful, or an eyeful.

Still, he decided not to tell Ann about it.

As Carl got into the limousine, he thought, what difference does it make? Whether she knows or her husband knows or the world knows? Half the world is rutting in the street or wanting to. In a few months it either won't matter or there will be a whole new world. The civilizations of Earth were going to be different after Shiva, nothing could change that.

He settled back into air-conditioned comfort. Ann was good, he thought. And so well-trained.

4 February: Collision minus 3 months, 22 days

The small amphitheater was almost filled. The full Alpha and Omega teams were there, as well as people from the media, some NASA officials, the Russian ambassador, observers from all over the world, including Red China, a wide variety of scientists, and Carl Jagens.

The tall, blond astronaut made himself highly visible, as was his way, by going from celebrity and high official to yet another cosmonaut, presidential adviser, or media biggie.

Chuck Bradshaw detached himself from the crowd milling around in the aisles, pushing through to mount the stage. "All right, all right, let's get this thing started. Take a seat, please, everybody. Thank you."

He waited patiently, not even betraying his annoyance at Carl Jagens and the protracted delay. Carl was among the last to sit down, smiling and confident as ever.

"Thank you," Chuck said into the microphones. He paused, looked down at the lectern a moment, then raised his head. "This is an updating on Operation Shiva. Doctor Kinney will outline the mission options as we see them now." Chuck retired to a row of folding chairs along the back of the stage as the thickest scientist lumbered up to the mikes. He looked out over the crowd, the lights shining off his scalp beneath his thinning hair.

"Our best chance, of course, has already passed. The

151

lights, please." The amphitheater dimmed and a slide was projected on the screen, showing the last two orbits of Shiva in white on the black of space, and beginning where Shiva was at the moment, the orbit in red for the next eight months. The green-line orbit of Earth intersected. Kinney cleared his throat and said, "The best choice for stopping Shiva would have been to catch it at its aphelion, that is, its farthest distance from the sun. But that occurred just after Shiva's last passage, and Shiva will strike Earth before reaching aphelion again. Because only . . ." He stopped as the murmurs rippled across the audience. The calm voice, so matter-of-factly stating a terrible fate, bothered even Lisa. But then, she thought, it would have done no good to scream it.

Kinney gave his audience a dark look, then proceeded. "Because less than four months remain, Shiva must be met with only slightly modified available hardware—modular boosters, the regular command modules, and so on. There is simply no time to build anything fancy and test it." He looked at the audience as if challenging anyone to contradict him. Lisa remembered a savaging he had taken in a number of articles and television shows, where certain commentators seemed somehow to expect Kinney and NASA to come up with some kind of supership or zap-ray that would take care of things quickly and neatly.

"The four-hundred-megaton weapon provided by our Soviet associates will probably not shatter Shiva, and even if there were a flaw in the asteroid and it blew to pieces, no one could guarantee that the fragments would be small enough to burn up in our atmosphere." Again he looked challengingly at the group before him.

"Yes, well." He looked up at the projection booth, his face underlit from the lectern light. "Next slide, please." A picture appeared that showed Shiva's approach and a number of lines indicating approach routes for the bomb. "A deflection attempt in the last ten to fifteen days seems best. The earlier you hit it, the farther it deflects."

Someone near Lisa muttered, "Linear dependence on time." She looked at the person, and saw a young woman, dark-haired and pretty. There was a small bandage on her cheek.

"There is an optimum combination of intercept distance and weight of the warhead," Kinney said. "The

152

four-hundred-megaton minimum corresponds to deflection at about seven days out. The primary limitation is the performance limit of Earth-based tracking and communications, which occurs at about, um, at beyond fourteen days." He motioned to the projectionist and the slide changed again, showing only one approach path.

"The true aiming point for the warhead is not Shiva alone, but the edge of Shiva." He shrugged his bulky shoulders. "Luckily, a ten percent error in aiming leads to only ten percent reduction in the transverse component of momentum delivered. Also luckily," he added, "the optical sensor on board the warhead booster is the most important, since radar can be confused by debris in the swarm."

He cleared his throat and for a moment Lisa thought he looked very tired. "Shiva will appear as a crescent at the approach . . . oh, next slide . . . an artist's rendering, of course." Against the starfield was a black area with a brighter, irregular edge. "The warhead will approach from the 'night' side, thus only the edge will be illuminated, and that edge is the true target." He paused for a moment, then said, "That is all I have at the moment."

Chuck Bradshaw jumped up from his chair and motioned Kinney to sit down. "Doctor Kinney, thank you. Let me have the intercept slide, please?" On the screen came another graphic presentation of the Shiva-Earth interception, with the trajectories of the Alpha-Omega ships indicated by dotted lines. "As you can see, the sooner the ships leave, the longer they have for warhead-target interaction. We have determined that Alpha Group will launch four weeks before intercept. Firm acquisition will be made first by optical tracking. The arming of the fusing radar will be done only in the last six hours."

"Um, Chuck . . ."

"Yes?" Bradshaw peered into the dim auditorium. "Oh, yes, Jim?"

Dr. Jim Donnelly stood up, scratched his upper arm, and squinted up at Chuck. "Do ye mind telling me again, lad? Just how well this blamed big bomb is going to move this flying mountain of yours?" The chubby, redheaded man sat down, crossed his arms, and waited.

"Lights, please," Chuck said and waited until the auditorium was lit again. "All right, Jim, once again. Targeting Shiva with warheads is complicated by the fact that, near the time of collision . . . that is, collision with Earth . . . it comes toward us out of the sun, and is thus difficult to see. The near-Earth telescopes will be able to see it only near sunset or sunup. It will become visible to the naked eye from Earth only in the last ten hours before collision. It will be low in the sky, hovering over the just-set sun, a dim red eye. In the last twenty days, Shiva will rise only ten degrees above the horizon at sunset. Ten degrees at most. However, in the last ten days, just before sunrise it will hang ten to fifteen degrees above the horizon."

"That's not what he asked," the dark-haired woman near Lisa muttered to her companion.

"Most telescopes, Earth-based telescopes," Chuck said, "will not operate that close to the horizon. They simply won't lower to that angle. Which is why we must depend so heavily upon the Skylab scopes." He shrugged. "Despite these difficulties, Shiva must be tracked as well as possible in the last month, to sharpen the precision of intercept times, distance measurements, and so on. On the final approach, of course, the Alpha team will use ranging radar for the intercept. But until then their best guide will be the orbit of Shiva as computed from the orbital observatory, refined at the Thales facility in Boston, and transmitted to the Alpha Group."

The dark-haired woman leaned toward her shaggy-headed companion and whispered, "And don't you miss a decimal point!"

"Aye," Jim Donnelly said, "I can see the exact placement is important, but just how, *exactly*, is it going to work?"

"Doctor Fedynsky, would you mind explaining that?" Chuck asked.

"Ah, the Russian superbrain," the dark-haired woman whispered. Lisa sat up straighter. She hadn't seen the famous atomic physicist before, but had heard stories about his personal guards, his voracious appetite for vodka, women, American superhero comics, and his unanimously acclaimed genius. Anyone that colorful she just had to see firsthand.

A stocky, middle-aged man with a thick beard and a mane of black hair shot with gray got up from the front row. Lisa had not seen him, hidden as he had been be-

154

tween two halfback-sized companions. He trotted with alacrity up the steps and over to the lectern, his face brightened by a wide smile.

"Ah. Ah," he said with satisfaction. "My friends. You will forgive? My English is not so good. I have tangled tongue. But I have the knowledge, yes?" He grinned quite happily and without any self-conscious humility. "Now. The bomb. This device, it is mine. I have . . . I am father? Yes, father. Now. About eighty percent of the total energy in nuclear explosion appears first as radiation. After explosion, weapon material has temperature of several tens of million degrees. Pressures are many millions of atmospheres, yes? Within a hundredth of a microsecond . . ." He paused, closed one eye, and thought a moment. "Yes. Correct. Within a hundredth of microsecond the weapon becomes nothing but completely or partially . . . um, how do you say, yes, partially undressed atoms . . . plus electrons. And most radiation comes out as, um, soft X ray."

He looked around with a smile and it occurred to Lisa that he was basking in his sudden and worldwide celebrity. Heretofore his face and name had been known only within rather limited and specialized circles. He was not the only scientist who was having trouble—or pleasure —in finding himself the subject of worldwide attention.

"Yes. Um. The energy is conveyed to the surrounding medium . . . in this instance, the asteroid . . . by radiation, the asteroid material itself emits radiation. A shock wave forms." He exploded his hands wide and up, then grasped the lectern again. "The weapons material accelerates outward, forming . . . well, thin shell of high density called the 'hydrodynamic front.'" He hesitated, closed one eye, and thought for a few seconds. "Yes. Correct words. This front acts as a piston. Piston? Yes, piston. As in automobile. A compressional wave becomes a steep-fronted shock wave."

He looked pleased and glanced from side to side. Chuck Bradshaw stepped closer, put his hand over the microphone, and whispered something to the Russian. Fedynsky nodded and Chuck returned to his seat next to Kinney.

"For near-surface bursts," Fedynsky said, "crater depth is about half crater radius. This crater forms from shock wave which . . . um . . . an American word I like

. . . which *rips* the near zone of the asteroid apart. For kill . . ." He flashed his audience a grin, ". . . we should require crater equal to Shiva's diameter. But if Shiva is roughly one kilometer in radius, this umm . . . if Shiva is solid rock, as it should be . . . a bomb of ten thousand megatons!" He raised his eyebrows in astonishment at his own words. "So . . . that is impossible." He shot a look in the direction of his burly body guards. "Even for Soviet science." Then he smiled almost shyly at his audience. "At this time, of course. Later, who knows?"

There was some polite laughter, and Fedynsky continued. "It is deflection then, not 'killing,' that is the best hope with one weapon. The important help is that the heated material near the burst will eject from hot crater, becoming, um, rocket exhaust in a sense." Again, he consulted silently with himself for a moment, nodded in agreement, then went on. "This will push asteroid. So, once you heat it, Shiva will push itself."

He leaned forward, the lectern light shining on his beard. "It is much important—you cosmonauts and astronauts heed me—it is very important to get very near burst. Within fifty meters, if that is possible. This should yield velocity change of about forty meters per second. In this sense the nuclear weapon is inefficient." He shrugged with pained regret. "Compared with simply converting the burst energy into a change in Shiva's kinetic energy, the bomb is about three percent efficient." He looked almost comically sad.

Then he brightened up. "If the bomb hits Shiva before detonation, it will go to pieces in, um, point zero one milliseconds. So, triggering time for the uranium assembly is one point zero milliseconds." He looked around, then back toward the video cameras and smiled. "The uranium assembly is the trigger. It touches off the hydrogen—the thermonuclear shell." He raised his eyebrows toward them as if to see if they had any questions, then he continued speaking.

"So, to acknowledge problems, the nuclear device must be detonated higher than twenty meters to be safe. At the speeds we are talking here . . ." He shrugged elaborately. "You can see the ranging, the targeting must be most precise. Now. Ah. Are there any questions?"

Yes, thought Lisa, *can* we be *that* precise?

"Thank you, Doctor Fedynsky," Chuck Bradshaw said. There was no applause. Early on in the meetings it had been decided, without really much discussion, that the traditional polite applause seemed incorrect in these unusual circumstances. And it took up time. But sometimes people forgot old habits with difficulty.

"Now," Bradshaw said, "if Colonel Menshov would step up here for a moment?" While the small, plain cosmonaut was getting up and moving to the stage, Chuck said, "Colonel Menshov is in charge of the atomic device that we will use as the primary weapon against Shiva. He will briefly describe that weapon."

"Sure he will," the dark-haired woman said in a stage whisper. Lisa smiled. The Russian fanaticism for secrecy extended even to this situation. The bomb was not to be delivered until shortly before loading—although a mockup had been provided for training and adaption purposes —and it would be accompanied by a small army of Soviet soldiers.

Menshov faced the audience blandly, calmly, and with a quiet confidence that Lisa found reassuring. "Parts of the warhead system," he said without preamble. "Fusing. Safe-arm. Destruct subsystems. Plus packaging." He paused a moment. "The safe-arm system. The heart is a rotatable disk or gate which puts a barrier in a cylinder, stopping a burst of fulminate of mercury. The fulminate of mercury shall be ignited by an exploding bridge wire. Redundancy in all these systems is imperative."

Menshov paused again. Lisa was struck with his almost unaccented English, but his words sounded stiff, as if he were speaking by rote. Perhaps he had memorized the speech and trained any accent out of it.

"The packaging includes shock and thermal insulation. The device has end plates bolted into the booster head, fixing it to stainless steel longitudinal mountain flanges in the payload stage final structure." He paused again and Lisa tried to make a schematic in her mind. "Final jacketing and housing are buffered and electromagnetically impenetrable except through the external antenna system."

Antimissile defense, Lisa thought. "The antennae deploy at the rear of the booster to avoid being sheared away." Menshov stopped abruptly, and stood waiting. Chuck came forward.

"Questions?" he asked.

Hughes Michaels stood up, identified himself and his network, then asked, "Colonel Menshov, there is a rumor that your country had this so-called doomsday device *prior* to the discovery of Shiva. Can you confirm or deny this rumor, sir?"

The Russian turned his plain, pleasant face to the ABC science reporter. "The world should be grateful that the Union of Soviet Socialist Republics had the capability of building such a device so quickly."

"I see," Michaels said dryly and sat down. Almost at once a thin oriental with lank, dark hair stood up, waving his hand.

"Teng Shao-chi, the People's Press," he said breathlessly. "Colonel Menshov, what had been your plans for this weapon before the menace from the invading Shiva?"

Chuck Bradshaw stepped forward, put a hand on Menshov's arm, and moved him aside politely. "Please, please. These are questions which are not germane to the problem here. We should be thankful that Russian science was able to provide us with such a weapon. Please keep politics out of this. You can go back to your petty bickering later, after we have taken care of Shiva."

"Petty bickering?" exploded the Chinese newsman in a shrill voice. "The imperialist press has too long covered up the menace of the Soviet bear! Marxist philosophy states—"

"Get him out of here!" Bradshaw snapped. Two broad-shouldered Marines appeared and politely but firmly lifted the reporter up and took him off. Bradshaw looked sad and worried. "Ladies and gentlemen . . . those of you watching in your homes, I . . . I hope you understand we just don't have time for that sort of thing." There was a quick response: heavy applause. Chuck looked relieved, but still concerned. "I don't want to tread on people, but . . . we just don't have much time. Everyone in this project is working very hard. That sort of . . . that kind of stunt we just cannot tolerate. I'm sorry." There was more applause and Chuck recognized more conventional questions.

Lisa caught Diego's eye. People were slipping away

and he nodded. Lisa leaned over and touched Dink Lowell on the shoulder. "Staff meeting at seven tonight, remember." He nodded and she rose to edge along the seats and into the aisle. The dark-haired woman who had been talking was also leaving, along with her companion, a shaggy-haired professor type in his early thirties. They smiled at each other and all four met at the exit.

"Whew!" Lisa said, breathing the late-afternoon air with relief.

"You're Lisa Bander," the dark-haired woman said. "Hi. I'm Caroline Weinberg. This is Wade Dennis. We're at Thales Center."

"Oh?" Diego said warmly. "Then we'll be in close touch with you all the way out."

"And back, too, I hope, Colonel Calderon," Wade Dennis said with a smile.

"Omega has a seven o'clock meeting," Lisa said, looking at her watch.

"Oh, I'm sorry. We won't hold you up," Caroline said quickly.

"No, no, I didn't mean that," Lisa said. "I meant we have almost three hours. Why don't we go eat and relax awhile?" She looked at Diego, who nodded.

"I wish we could go into town," Wade Dennis said wistfully. "I understand there are some great restaurants in town . . . and I'm damned tired of Cape Canaveral grub!"

They all laughed and Diego shook his head. "We're still sealed up here, except for authorized, high priority missions. Brother Gabriel has his pickets at all the gates. A regular tent city. Ellie Roberts came in by car last week, and got roughed up pretty badly. I heard it's gotten worse. They have the army practically shoulder to shoulder around the perimeter."

"We flew in," Caroline said, with a shiver. "It's the same up in Boston. They wrecked the Lunar Research Lab there and would have trashed the physics lab if Coleman hadn't held them off with a laser."

"I heard that," Diego said with a smile. "Heard he whipped up a raygun out of paperclips or something while they were breaking down the doors."

"Ingenuity under pressure," Caroline said. "I heard he was trying to get a patent on it."

"Gabriel's goons or some other group?" Lisa asked.

"I don't know. Probably. Gabriel certainly isn't the only one with antiscience ideas," Wade said. "The Sons of Shiva are just as bad, but their destruction is more random, not focused. They just trash whatever might look pretty falling down. You heard about the old Empire State Building, didn't you? They blew it up last week. They blew out a chunk and it fell over and took a lot with it." He looked sad. "New York is a jungle right now, I hear."

"It always was," Diego said.

"California chauvinist," Lisa said.

"Realist and romantic," he grinned.

"Contradiction in terms, like military intelligence," she retorted.

"Food," Caroline said.

"Food that isn't institutional," Wade said quickly.

Lisa looked at Diego. "Sure," he said.

"Come to our place," Lisa said. "We've got some rations, a stove and everything. Won't be gourmet, but it's better than Cape-style cafeteria pregarbage taste treats."

"Sure!" Caroline said. "Well, I mean, this won't deprive you or anything?"

"Oh, we're Top Priority," Lisa smiled, taking her arm. "You heard them. Whatever we want, we get. Except the freedom to go out of the perimeter. Except good food. Except. Except." She patted Caroline's arm, then released it to take Diego's hand. "They fly in stuff from the air bases around here. Catered by the U.S. Marines courtesy of the U.S. Air Force."

"Well, come on then," Diego said. "We'll catch a tram and gorge ourselves on gourmet eats, government-issue style."

"That great American dish," Lisa muttered, "a couple of cans of something."

"They call us the Omega team because we're the last chance," Lisa said, smiling. Across the table Wade Dennis put down his wineglass and sighed.

"That's it? No waves of ships, no fleets of daring engineers to save the world? Just two little groups?"

Lisa nodded. "Omega will have a minimum of twelve twenty-megaton warhead missiles. Maybe more, but that many are pretty certain. Alpha will have the big Russian bomb and a minimum of six twenty-megatonners. That's what the minimax analysis says is right." She shrugged and took a sip of wine. "But let's talk about something *else*, huh? I'm up to *here* with Shiva right now!"

"Hear, hear," Diego said. "You two are going to be our main computer, huh?"

"Backup and control for your onboard, Colonel," Wade said.

"Diego," he replied. "Diego and Lisa."

"Yes, we're the button-jockeys," Caroline smiled.

"This whole operation is so delicate," Wade said. "No chance for mistakes, no chance to practice. We've been constructing all *kinds* of computer models—you wouldn't *believe* some of the ideas that have been suggested!" He took a sip of wine, his face troubled and serious. "The responsibility you people have, my God."

Lisa smiled at him. "That everyone has, Wade. Backup, ground control, preflight, everything. We all know there's only one chance and no one wants to muff it."

"Except Brother Gabriel," Diego said bitterly. "I just don't understand him, or any of those like him. So he doesn't believe we can do anything, fine. But let us alone to do it. Why throw a monkey wrench in the works?"

Caroline lifted her eyebrows. "My mother . . . she, uh, joined up. Tried to get me to sabotage the computer."

"You didn't tell me that," Wade said.

She shrugged. "I didn't buy it, so why bother?"

"But I always thought your mother was more sensible than that. It kind of shakes you to find out . . ." He looked surprised and his voice trailed off.

"NASA has had some defections, too," Lisa said. "Lower percentage than most, I guess, because most people here are believers in technology and what it can do."

Caroline gave a short laugh. "Technology has two faces."

"True," Lisa replied, "but right now . . . well, what other possible thing could we do?"

"All those people praying," Diego said. "If we go out there and divert that damn thing, they'll claim forever it was their work."

"*If*, Colonel?" Caroline asked, a quiver in her voice.

He shrugged and spread his hands. "If, yeah. No guarantees. But if we don't *try* . . ." He shrugged again and

161

reached for his wineglass, lifting it. "To technology . . ."

"To luck," Wade said.

"To the new world this will be, after," Caroline murmured.

Lisa looked at her and smiled. "Yes, it will, won't it? Hit or no hit, it will not be the same world." She lifted her glass. "To that new world."

Diego's glass sailed through the air and smashed against the air conditioner. "No fireplace," he shrugged. Three other glasses joined his in a shower of glittering shards.

"Very romantic," Lisa laughed, "but who cleans it up?"

"Whoever lives in that new world," he replied.

6 March: Collision minus 2 months, 20 days

"Congratulations, General," Diego said. The Russian's button eyes swiveled toward Calderon and he nodded slightly. "I understand you were in grade quite awhile."

The cosmonaut nodded again. "We do not receive the rapid advancement you achieve here in the West."

Diego smiled. They were walking toward the Flight Simulator along the light cream-colored walls. "I think Captain Jagens believes it to be a propaganda ploy."

Menshov shrugged without comment, as if to say he was not responsible for the idiot beliefs of others. Diego walked beside the cosmonaut for a few more meters, then asked him when *Bolshoi*, the four-hundred-megaton Soviet bomb, was due to arrive.

The new general shrugged again. "Soon. We have the mock-up to work with. It is an exact duplicate . . . only safer." He gave Diego a faint smile. Then in a rare attempt at initiating a conversation, Menshov asked Diego a question. "Is Major Nissen working out well?"

"You bet. I mean, yes, she is. Remarkable woman." He looked at Menshov out of the corner of his eye, but the phlegmatic Russian was as expressionless as usual. "Are they going to give her a boost in rank as well?"

"It is not needed." Menshov pointed ahead. "We must hurry. They are ready to simulate the approach from a parallel track."

Diego grunted assent. Menshov was as uncommunicative as ever . . . or almost so. It was as though he was under orders to utter only so many words a day. But maybe, Diego thought, it's me that talks too much.

In northern Africa crowds began to assemble. Local authorities could not understand the sudden influx of intent, humorless tourists who sat in cafes and talked earnestly to each other, or stared moodily into space, ignoring the restaurants and nightclubs and prostitutes.

Within weeks the trucks hauling stone and cement appeared, rumbling through the towns and villages. The story came out with a rush. Thousands were streaming into Egypt and Libya intent on one mission: to build a last, immense pyramid. When asked about their motives the blank-faced workers mumbled and turned away. They were not planning to build a redoubt and hold out in the pyramid, insulated against Shiva's holocaust; there was no room inside for them all. The pyramid was to be like all the others: a giant tomb.

The day before Shiva struck, the workers—who came from many countries and many classes, from illiterate dock workers to fat Lebanese bankers—would draw lots. The winner and his family or chosen ones would lie in the hidden chamber, amid gold and jewels, and vacuum pumps would suck the air from the sealed chambers. There they would rest forever, immune to the world's slow rot, buried in laser-cut stone, preserved, free of Shiva's hand.

27 April: Collision minus 29 days

"My son, the view is lovely from this hill."

"*Si*, it is." Diego scuffed his toe at the sandy path. They were standing on the family burial plot. Bakersfield lay behind them. All around them like a stubby forest were the bleached white markers of departed manual laborers, farm workers, clerks, children. The florid script on each gravestone spelled out no Anglo names. Some stones gave simple names and dates; others quoted short lines of scripture or a blessing. On one, a revolutionary slogan from some forgotten cause was carved. There were lots of crosses, some of wood, with painted designs and the names laboriously spelled out in rusting nails. There were few angels or saints, for such sculpture was expensive.

Directly in front of Diego his grandfather's slab of rough-edged granite seemed heavy and permanent. The flat surface was almost mirror-smooth, glossy and unreal. His grandfather had been wrinkled and leathery, smelling of dirt and tobacco. *Francisco Diego Calderon.*

His grandmother's name, dutifully carved below, seemed almost an afterthought, a footnote. To both sides were ranked great-uncles and aunts Diego remembered only from long Sunday afternoon reunions after Mass, vague presences who sipped beer while he played outside with his cousins. Each had had a solemn, sweet-smelling funeral that Diego recalled only because he had twitched and whispered at them and had finally had to be sent out of the room.

His father's funeral he could still see in precise detail: suffocating wreaths of flowers, aunts in black lace looking like extras from a film, a musty layered air in the room, the polished coffin, the gleaming satin, the candles and rustling fabric as women knelt. The priest, solemn and brown, sprinkling holy water lavishly. The strange feeling around his eyes.

Diego walked on a few steps. The stone for his father was not even dusty. There was a neat space for his mother's name. "Here I will be," she said from behind him. "Much room is left."

"Yes." *If we fail many will never be buried in any ground, holy or not.*

The view from up here really wasn't lovely at all, Diego thought. A ribbed gully in the distance carved a snaky path through a scratchy landscape. Low scrub hugged the dry, rocky soil.

"Much," she said, nodding from emphasis. She knelt awkwardly on one knee and dusted across the stone, then placed the small bouquet on it. Her head bent in prayer.

Does she expect me to pace off my two meters and peg the corners, claiming space before the rush?

"I will be here soon."

"No, mother."

"I am an old woman."

"No, you're not. Not at all. Why—"

"No." She shook her head energetically; she would

164

not be deprived of this fraction of her identity. "And the thing from the sky. It will be here soon."

Diego started to speak in Spanish, but stopped at the first word. His parents had enforced a firm rule: nothing but English was suitable for talk among the family. In the streets Spanish was necessary, but not at home. This world belonged to the Anglos, and their language was the key into it.

"It won't come, mother."

"Perhaps."

"That's why I am able to get so little leave. We work night and day. I got permission for this visit only because you said it was so important." *And that I could check with Sanders at Vandenberg on the way back.*

"It is." She poked a thin finger at the hillside, then started to rise. He helped her. "You must choose now."

"I don't need a plot, mother." *Madre de Dios.*

"You do not know. You could go out there—"

"Mother, it's all going to work out, you'll see. We have the entire resources of the *world*—"

"This thing is dangerous. Do not think you can fool your mother. If you die, I want to know where you will rest on this earth."

"If I die, mother, far out in space . . . " His voice trickled away like sand. Did she understand that if he bought it, Shiva would probably strike Earth within days afterward? And even if they succeeded he could die. A spaceman's burial. It had happened before. A long orbit into the sun. Fitting. Tidy.

"I may be gone as well, my son."

"Well . . . " He tried to smile reassuringly.

"Who would tell them where? Each family here on the hill keeps its own records. Who would they ask?"

He sighed. "The view is lovely."

"*Si.* We will all rest here, together." She seemed very satisfied.

She honestly thinks somebody would bother to bring my body back to Earth, he thought.

"Yes," he said, "a lovely view."

"You should have been here for your uncle Esteban's funeral."

"I was on the Moon, mother, you knew that."

"They should have brought you back. People asked."

"Ah . . . yes, mother."

"Sir, we can't hold them much longer." The young captain was pale, his uniform dusty and sweat-stained. He gripped the radio with white fingers. He had to press a palm to his other ear to hear what headquarters said.

"We're sending reinforcements from gate seven, Saperstein. If it looks as though you are going to be overrun, fall back to your prepared positions and don't hesitate to fire."

The young captain gulped. "Fire, sir? But they're . . ."

"You have your orders, Captain. Colonel Morgan is coming. If you can't give the order, he will. Those goddamn Gabriels must be stopped. At any cost, you understand?"

"Yes, sir, but—"

The line was dead. Captain Saperstein clicked off and stared wearily out of the sandbagged slit in the guardhouse. A Patton II tank stood smack in the middle of the road. No vehicles could get through, the fence was electric, but still Saperstein shivered.

The noise from the crowd ebbed and surged. Chants came and went, punctuated by shrieks. Every few moments someone was knocked against the electric fence and sparks flew. Sometimes the bodies staggered back caught by the crowd. Other times they hung there and fried. Patrols in riot helmets stalked the inside of the double fence and used long insulated poles to pry the bodies loose.

Some of those who electrocuted themselves were suicides, who hoped to build a ramp of bodies over which the Gabriels could scamper, but it hadn't happened yet. The Army patrols used gas and the fence line was littered with dead and unconscious bodies.

Captain Saperstein came out of the guardhouse cautiously. A homemade Molotov cocktail arced over the fence and splattered against the tank treads, spilling jellied gasoline. A corporal, wearing a gas mask beneath his riot helmet, came around from behind the tank and sprayed the fire with foam. Drying gobbets of foam dirtied the whole front and top of the dusty tank.

Saperstein looked at the next line of defense, a sandbagged and bulldozed revetment a hundred meters back. He could see the medics standing by the ambulances and the massive Bradley-C tanks that had been brought down from North Carolina and Georgia. Far beyond them were the red gantry towers.

"Sir?"

"Yes, Cooper?"

The middle-aged sergeant pointed down the fence line. "Checkpoint Gamma, sir. I think they are going to rush it."

Saperstein frowned, trying to make out the situation. "What does Lieutenant Stevens say?"

Sergeant Cooper shrugged. He was a tall, red-faced Southerner who had often refused appointments to OCS and his dedication to the appreciation of beer was well-known. He was not wearing any of his many ribbons on his green tunic. "He says it could be a diversion, but that he thinks he's spied some ladders in the ditch opposite. They must have brought them up last night."

Saperstein sighed. "Jesus, what an assignment. Okay, move the squad with the gas down there, but leave the fence patrols here. Alert Captain Miller, will you?"

"Yes, sir."

The mob beyond the fence became suddenly noisy, a wave of sound that swept forward from the rear ranks. Saperstein stepped up onto the bumper of a jeep to get a better look. He grinned at the pale-faced young private behind the .50-caliber machine gun. "Stay tight, son."

"Uh, yes, sir."

How many were there, Saperstein wondered. A hundred thousand, more? The Gabriels spread out in clumps and groups all along the miles of fence, causing the Army to spread itself thinly. But there were at least twenty thousand directly opposite the main gate.

Twenty thousand Americans. Twenty thousand scared people. Saperstein chewed at his lip. How easy it would be to become one of them, to surrender all volition, to trust, to *believe* that it was all for the best. But he couldn't; he knew he couldn't. He was a survivor. Survivors don't give up. They may get killed, but they don't give up. Scared, yes; give up, no. As long as there was a chance that NASA could do something—anything—

he'd have to hang in there and see that they had their chance.

His thoughts went to Jackie and the kids, down in St. Petersburg. Were they well? Were they even alive? He pushed the thoughts away. The sudden noise from the mob had peaked and a silence came. Far off, Saperstein could hear a murmuring, then a cheer.

"Brother Gabriel! Brother Gabriel! He's coming! Brother Gabriel is coming!"

Saperstein stepped down from the jeep's bumper and his hand checked for the .45 in his holster.

30 April: Collision minus 26 days

It was not a very big meteor, really. About fifty-thousand tons of nickel-iron. It struck just south of the Gulf of Chihli, west of Tsingtao, in the Shantung Province. The explosion broke every window in Tientsin two hundred miles away. Hwong—the Yellow River—poured into the crater from the south and a great tidal wave came in from the gulf to the north. The shipping on the Yellow Sea to the southeast was destroyed. It was reported in objective tones and media phrasing from Station Six.

Shiva had sent in its calling card.

A shower of smaller meteors fell across Mongolia, the Gobi Desert and the lower regions of Siberia. The destruction was minor on a physical scale, but the triggering of emotions across the world was major.

The mobs gathered. Looting and raping and wanton destruction took a drastic upsurge. In Sydney, Australia, the post-Victorian attitudes were destroyed by a mass orgy, which ended in a mass prayer. In Nicaragua a peasant girl reported seeing the Virgin standing atop a great flaming ball, and thousands trampled the village to gravel trying to pray there. In the Ukraine four thousand people were shot because they left their farms and packed the few churches. In Turkey a suicide cult was founded, gathered thousands of members, and extinguished itself in days. In Aberdeen, Scotland, a minister's tirade caught on and they marched southward in thousands; their goal—to retake the Stone of Scone, upon which the Scottish kings sat, and which was now beneath the coronation chair in Westminster Abbey. In four days they caused the death of twelve thousand people.

But the riots were not all antitechnology, either. Many Americans fought back, stopping various cults and individuals from destroying electrical substations, power plants, dams, communication lines. Volunteers joined police forces, National Guard units, and military forces to help. Vigilantes hung saboteurs. Thousands of individual acts of heroism took place, noted and unnoted.

Some of these volunteers used the guise of active patriotism to gain vengence, but most did not. Blacks fought shoulder to shoulder with whites—against both blacks and whites.

Outside America protechnology sympathy was strong, but spotty. Individuals reacted to stress in individual ways, as did the nations. A nation is the sum of its parts, and any nation's parts are human beings, with all their strengths and frailties.

The Pope broadcast prayer and advice. On Majorca a famous actress staged what she hoped would be the greatest and most flamboyant orgy of sex and drugs ever held by man or beast. Most of the invited guests were unable to attend. In Pakistan over one million people died in sudden plague; the suspected source was poison deliberately put into the water supply. The emperor of Japan was said to be contemplating the flowers. On Station Five, a sabotage attempt was partially successful and the bulging, spherical station began a long descent to Earth; the personnel were taken off in time.

In Israel the premier was assassinated by Arab terrorists. A brief but deadly war erupted between Israel and the Palestine Protectorate, quickly involving the Republic of Persia. It sputtered and died with neither side a winner. A tribal war to settle old debts all but obliterated several Central African tribes. A PBS newsman committed suicide live on television. There were duels just outside the English Parliament. The Daughters of the American Revolution occupied the Statue of Liberty and barricaded themselves.

The banks were closed in almost every country, and all stock exchanges had suspended trading. Money was suspect and people everywhere were living off barter, the promised redemption of local scrip or theft.

169

Brigadier General Sandra Cohen was badly wounded in a riot as she reported into the White House. A sect called the Armageddonites staged a rally that brought three hundred thousand people to New York's Central Park and almost destroyed it. They believed the world was coming to an end. Two hundred women were raped that day in the park.

In Nagoya, Japan, a Confucianist temple was the scene of a ritual suicide involving a number of top government officials who had failed to stop Shiva. In Denver, Colorado, a young man with the unlikely name of Hubie Joe Kinderman threatened to explode a homemade atomic bomb unless certain demands were met. A police sniper shot him.

A meteor estimated at approximately twelve tons struck the northwestern shore of Hudson's Bay, in the district of Keewatin, creating a two-kilometer-wide crater in the barren land. It was not the first time Hudson's Bay had been a meteor-impact site.

Shiva had returned in force.

"Look! Isn't that beautiful?" The young girl pointed into the early evening sky, leaning out, holding onto the porch post. The sky was streaked with five lines, short-lived and not much more than blinks. "Did you make a wish?" she asked her uncle.

Clyde Cass nodded, forcing a smile to his lips as he looked at the denim-clad nine-year-old. "Shooting stars, Clementine." He looked over at Clementine's father, who was staring moodily up at the sky. They exchanged looks.

"Starting," Howell Bates said and his brother-in-law nodded.

Mrs. Bates came out onto the porch with a tray of coffee cups. "Little chilly out here for you, isn't it, Clemmie? Maybe you'd better go in and get a sweater, dear."

"Aw, Mom. I don't want to miss any of the shooting stars."

Mrs. Bates looked at her husband. "Don't worry, dear, you won't. Get a sweater now. There'll be lots of shooting stars. Probably all evening."

"Oh . . . all right." The child went into the house.

"Don't slam the . . ." the screen door banged shut with a clatter, ". . . door." Howell Bates made a face,

170

then took a cup of coffee. "You know, Clyde, I think I'd like a shot of that sippin' liquor of yours in this t'night, whaddya say?"

Clyde reached down to the worn wood floor of the porch and brought up a clear glass pint bottle, filled with a brown liquid. He poured a generous dollop into his brother-in-law's coffee, then into his own. He ignored the prim, disapproving look from his sister and took a big swallow. "Ahh . . ." He looked down the street. "Lot of folks out tonight."

Mrs. Bates sipped at her coffee and agreed. "Getting late for Independence folks to be out setting on their porches, I'd think." She sighed. "Wonder what ol' Harry would have said about all this?"

"Dunno," Howell Bates said, "but he'd give them hell about it, anyway."

"Howell," admonished his wife, tipping her head toward the house. "Not in front of the child."

After a moment Clyde Cass spoke up. "Imagine she'll hear and see a lot more'n that pretty soon."

Mrs. Bates nodded grimly "I have to watch everything she looks at now. The *things* they are showing on the news nowadays!"

The door banged open and Clementine ran out onto the steps, and down into the yard, her head up. "Careful, dear," her mother said.

"Oh! Look! That's a long one!"

"The advance particles from the Shiva cloud are now approaching Earth," the newsman said, holding his microphone before his face and looking seriously into the camera. "But all the authorities say there is no cause yet for alarm. All but a tiny fraction of the dust and particles are burning up in the outer layers of the atmosphere. These 'shooting stars' are colorful, but harmless." He turned slightly to indicate the flatly lit computer room behind him. "Here at Thales Center in Boston, NASA is 'logging' every asteroid in the swarm as soon as they are detected." He moved to his left and the camera panned. "We have with us today Doctor Wade Dennis, of the Thales Center's NASA staff. Doctor Dennis, where do we stand at this moment?"

"Well, the main body of the swarm is weeks out, actually. What we are getting here is the forward fringe of the swarm. There *are* a few meteors actually getting down to the surface, but so far they are all extremely minor and have caused little or no damage." He held up some readout sheets. "One struck in the Cherokee Indian Reservation in North Carolina, but it weighed less than fifty kilos. The Russians have reported several to us, ranging from sixty to two hundred kilograms. There have been reported strikes—and these are extremely minor, let me assure you—in Argentina, Mali, Australia, Greenland, Poland, and Italy."

"Doctor, when can we expect the main body?"

"We can't say exactly as yet, Mister Decker. Somewhere around twenty-two days. We'll narrow that estimate down as time goes on, of course. Right down to the second."

"Will these minor meteorite strikes continue until the main body of the swarm intersects us?"

Wade looked uncomfortable. "Well, yes. But we will continue to encounter larger and larger meteorites."

Decker hesitated, then spoke. "You mean, sir, we will be hit with bigger meteors on an ascending scale?"

"I'm afraid so. What we are getting now is . . . is the lightest meteorological shower we can expect until well after Shiva has, uh, passed or been diverted, or, uh . . . whatever happens." Decker said nothing, but the television audience could not see his face. "There's a frontal cone and a trailing cone of, uh, of dust, minor asteroids, and so on."

"Uh, I see," Decker said. "Well, thank you, Doctor Dennis." He turned toward the camera. The word *live* was superimposed across his chest. "There you have the opinion of Doctor Wade Dennis, the man who is tagging and keeping track of the various objects in the Shiva swarm. This is Bob Decker, CBS, at the Thales Center, Boston."

2 May: Collision minus 24 days

Toghrul Arslan tended his sheep along the banks of El Furat, in central Turkey. He was a stolid, unimaginative man, content to be a shepherd and made even more placid by the opium grown by his wives. He did not know or care that the sluggish river he walked along

172

was once known as the Euphrates, whose banks had seen the earliest of man's civilizations. What was past was past; what the future held was written on his forehead. He did not know of Shiva, but he had heard rumors of boxes that caught pictures carried through the air.

Magic, he thought. No good ever comes of magic. As a boy he had sat at the fires and listened to the storytellers. They often spoke of wonders so great they had to be magic, and of magic so powerful it had to be evil.

The heat of the day was rising. The sheep moved slowly, heads down. The winds were warm, coming up from the Syrian Desert and braking against the Eastern Taurus Mountains behind him. His eyes grew heavy as he sat in the shade of the rock. Tonight there would be new rubbery balls of the raw opium ready for trade, and for use. His third wife was relatively new, still supple and moist. His two sons were growing strong. He was rich and content.

The meteor split the sky in a ferocious sound. The bleating of the sheep and his own scream were blotted out in the great roar. There was a flash of blue-white light to the east, then nothing.

Toghrul Arslan stared, blinking. What manner of thing was this? His ears rang, his tender's swift gaze saw sheep lying down and others staggering around. He got to his feet, only to hear the low roar. The ground shook, then was ripped from under him. Rocks clattered down the hillside. He saw blood on the grass, then the world tilted up and he fell, rolled, and clung desperately to the tufts of gray-green grass. The earthquake went on and on and on. A section of ground split, then tilted slightly. The roar was deafening but the terror was even more frightening.

Never again would Toghrul Arslan think of the earth as solid and eternal. The earthquakes of his youth had been as nothing compared to this. He thought about his third wife, in the hut of unmortared rocks down in the valley, and he cried for his loss.

Lily St. Germain stretched out a ringed hand and waggled an empty champagne glass. José Villareal reached for the champagne bottle at once, flashing her a perfect white smile. The wind from Minorca ruffled the silk of their little rooftop gazebo. The handsome young painter poured her some of the bubbly liquid, set the bottle back into the silver bucket with a crunch of ice, then took up her other hand. He kissed the fine web of wrinkles with great care and passion, then lifted his large, liquid eyes to hers.

But her gaze was blurred and inwardly José cursed. Not yet noon and she was already *borracho*. Not the day to ask about the purchase of that superb new alcohol Lancia. The luxury tax alone on that monster was more than he made in a year painting moody canvases. None of his feelings surfaced on his handsome face. He maintained a steadily impassioned expression. It was his best look.

Lily sipped some more wine, reached for a plum with a hand she extracted slowly from José's grip. Then her eyes widened. José swung his head around at her expression. Over the nearby Majorca rooftops he saw a streak of incandescent light, then a great blossoming of still more light. A vast ball, blue-white, gray-white, then orange, grew on the horizon to the north.

"Jesus Maria! What was that!"

Lily St. Germain blinked, her fogged mind struggling to grasp the significance. But it couldn't be true! No meteor would hit *here*, certainly not at Majorca!

She stared at the cloud of steam that rose into the air, then felt José's fingers biting into her arm. "Look! Mother of God, look!" There was a line on the horizon, below the still-ascending cloud.

Tidal wave!

Lily sat up, knocking over the champagne bucket. The bottle broke against the warm tiles and foam spilled around their feet, soaking into the edge of the Persian carpet.

"No!" Lily screeched. She grabbed at José, pulling him off balance. They fell back onto the lounge, toppling it over. José kicked free and ran for the stairs.

Escape!

Run!

He raced down the steps, knocking aside the count, who protested feebly. He straight-armed Angela Fontaine right in her famous bosom and ran for the ornamental grate. He yanked open the black iron grill and stumbled out into the gravel path. He could hear the roar coming now. He sprinted for the shoreline. A boat, a raft, anything! Float, swim, *live!*

José raced past people staring around at the noise, open-mouthed and pointing. He careened off a tourist couple and turned east, toward the docks. There were more screams and others were running. He tripped and fell, grunting as his elbow smashed into the cobblestones, then rolled to his feet. He cradled his arm, afraid to look down, and ran.

Lily St. Germain stood at the parapet, her Falcone original ripped, a bottle of Dom Perignon in her hand. "Come on, you lousy son of a bitch!" she shouted. She lifted the bottle and flung it toward the sea, throwing her self off balance. She fell back, but toppled into a nest of pillows.

The roar was deafening now. She was below the level of the parapet and could not see the great towering wave. She laughed, tears running down her face. "Serve you right, you bastard!" she shouted at the sky. "This'll get Barcelona, too, you nasty, philandering son of a *bitch!*" She dragged herself up to her knees and looked northwest. She wanted to see her ex-husband get it in Barcelona, but the Spanish city was over a hundred miles away, beneath the horizon.

But she could see the wave coming in. She laughed, a bitter, tight-mouthed laugh. She'd meet Death as she had met so many things: drunk.

The wall of water swept over the island, submerging it in foam and crushing everything man-made upon it. When the water ran off at last the fifty-mile-long island was scrubbed clean. There was only rock left and stubs of something that might have been concrete.

A champagne bottle floated in a pool, high on a mountainside. The label was soaked off, the glass scoured opaque. Then the cork popped, spilling foamy golden liquid into the pool, where it mixed and disappeared. The bottle tipped, filled, and sank.

The public reaction was surprise, followed by a rising sense of outrage. The scientists had promised things wouldn't get bad for weeks yet. The world had come to terms with that fact and now these new injuries cut through the thin comforting blanket most people had wrapped around themselves all their lives. "They'll do something," people said confidently. "The government will stop it." Now they felt somehow betrayed. There were angry questions in every parliament, a new surliness in the tone of news commentators, resignations by the score, and red-faced arguments on street corners.

The technical explanation was simple, but for the media, too slow. Answers were needed—fast, reassuring answers. Official spokespersons and unofficial spokespersons commented at length.

In its long history Shiva had probably fragmented along its orbit, leaving clusters of rock that slowly drew away from the center of the mass, tugged by the faint sirens of sun and planets. Some of these celestial shards were in the same orbit as Shiva, but slightly ahead, and all but undetectable with present technology.

The slow tilt of Shiva's orbit down into the ecliptic plane had brought these bits of debris into range of Earth. In the black velvet sea of space the telescopic search for Shiva had missed them entirely. These rocks were, after all, relatively small on the astronomical scale.

A Griffith Observatory speaker made this bland observation in front of a CBS camera and provoked blind rage in many quarters. A teenage gang burned the observatory in full view of the same cameras, only hours later.

But these rocks were *hors d'oeuvres,* spawn of Shiva. The great destroyer itself was weeks away.

Abecher, in eastern Chad, population 21,506, disappeared in a flaming pit.

Stovall, Mississippi.

A tiny town, Piapoco, in the vast uplands of Colombia, received an almost direct hit. No one was even to know of it for weeks.

Nancy Darrin, en route from Houston to Florida, was taken by a gang of rioting Predestiners, raped, and left to bleed to death in a swamp near Good Hope, Louisiana.

"Sir, Colonel Morgan is on line three."

Bradshaw snatched up the handset and punched the button. The screen blipped and the gray-haired officer was on the screen. "Colonel."

"Mister Bradshaw, we've got the final figures on the McDonnell and Stanley defection." Chuck gestured for him to continue. "I regret to inform you, sir, that they

176

took nine reels of computer tape with them, four manuals, three integrated blocks—"

"Oh, *Christ!*"

"We are conducting a search, of course, and may recover the missing items—"

"If they're not destroyed, and they probably are!"

"We're a little short-handed right now, though. I was expecting an augmented regiment in from Fort Bragg, but there's been some sort of foul-up there and all I got was an understrength company."

"If they took tapes, they were in a position to know which tapes to take, Colonel. I'll get on this right now, myself."

"Very well, Mister Bradshaw. If you need me, I'll be in a chopper. Red Leader Four."

"Thank you, Colonel."

Bradshaw replaced the handset and the screen went dark. He sighed, then pulled back his shoulders and glared at Lyle Orr. "Well, what are you waiting for? Get your bum over to your office and start the counterrumors. There will be no purge. Get that?"

"Yes, sir." He hesitated. "Will I be lying, Chuck?"

Bradshaw looked down at his desk top. He turned his hand over and looked at the palm as if the answer were written there. "I don't know, Lyle. I hope not."

3 May: Collision minus 23 days

Caroline Weinberg smiled at the blue-clad regular guard in the lobby and looked with quiet apprehension at the quartet of lounging National Guard soldiers. They stared back boldly, looking right through her clothes, as soldiers and men always do.

"Miss Weinberg?"

"Yes, Archie?"

The middle-aged man stepped closer and dropped his voice to a confident whisper. "Listen, maybe you better have one of these lunkheads escort you home. Or you wait for Doctor Dennis, maybe?"

She smiled at him. "Thank you, Archie, no. Doctor Dennis still has some runs to make and . . ." She looked over at the youths, who were slapping each other on the shoulder and laughing. Their rifles were leaning against the thick glass nearby. "You did say they were lunk-heads . . ."

"Yeah, but . . ." He looked narrowly at them. "Not regular army, y'know. Nothing like when I was in. I was a grunt in Nam, y'know. Caught one in m'leg there, getting out of a Huey." He grinned ruefully at the memory. "A long time ago, huh? Talked to one of these lunkheads yesterday. He thought Nam was World War Two. They don't know nothing these days, Miz Weinberg, do they?"

She shrugged and pushed at the thick glass door. "Thank you, Archie. You know, for thinking about me."

"S'okay, Miz Weinberg, just my job. You *sure* you don't want one a these lunks t'go with you?"

She shook her head. "It isn't far."

"Mess of Shiva Dancers went by here 'bout an hour ago."

"They're all right."

The old guard shook his head. "I dunno. I hear things. They raped some. Trying to get converts to their funny religion, y'know. Think sex is the whole thing, sex 'n' pleasure 'n' God knows what. I'm Roman Catholic, myself, y'know. We don't hold with this Shiva nonsense. Bishop McCartney, he says the Pope's praying for what you are doing."

"Yes, I know." She had the door partly open and could feel the chill wind. "Well. I'll see you tomorrow, Archie, all right?"

"Okay, Miz Weinberg." He waved at her and watched her walk out of sight. In the plate glass windows, turned into mirrors by the early evening darkness, he saw the National Guard soldiers passing around a cigarette. Where was their officer, he wondered angrily. They'd not be worth a damn in five minutes.

"Hey, stop that, you lunkheads!" he snapped at them.

"Blow it out your ear," one of them said nastily.

"Hell, wish I could be out with those Dancers," another said.

"Yeah," grinned another. "Man, that was some fun, huh? Remember that little blonde—no, she was a red-head, remember her? Said everyone was going to die and there were two things she hadn't tried yet." He let out a whoop that echoed in the lobby's chillness.

"Well, why don't we, huh?" one said, reaching for the cigarette.

"Why what?"

"Why don't we . . ." He sucked in smoke and held it, making a funny face. He exhaled and passed it on. "Why don't we just trot right down toward the Commons, huh?"

"They camped there tonight, are they?"

"Naw, too cold, man. They're in those hotels round there, the ones they abandoned, you know."

"Yeah, yeah, yeah," one of them said. He looked around, trying to see beyond the reflections in the glass. "But what about the lieutenant?"

"Fuck the lieutenant."

"But what if they—"

"What? What if they do what? They can't do diddly-shit, man. Where you been? Ain't you been watching the *tube*, man? We're gonna get that goddamn Shiva right up the kazoo, man. The End. *Kaput*. No second season, no reruns, no *nuthing*."

One of them stood up, grinning. "Well, hell, then let's go down and see just how desperate those Dancers are, huh?"

The others scrambled to their feet, and one whooped loudly. "Goddamn!"

"Hey, you lunks can't just *leave!*" Archie complained, standing up from his seat by the little sign-in desk.

"Why not? You gonna stop us?"

Archie put his hand on his .38 Python, then stopped. It was no use. "Leave the rifles, then."

"Leave the rifles, hell," one said grabbing his. "I know a liquor store about four blocks from here. It's still got booze because the National Guard—" He said it loudly and laughed. "Because the great and noble National Guard of the Commonwealth of Massachusetts has been camped practically on its doorstep."

"So how is that going to help us?" another asked, slinging his rifle.

"We're in uniform, right? They won't suspect a thing. We'll collect as much as we can carry and show up at the Commons loaded!"

"Hey!" one cheered. They pushed Archie aside contemptuously and strode out into the evening wind, green-clad youths laughing and punching each other.

Archie looked after them and a great weariness came over him. They were afraid, too. He went to the phone and made a call. It took him fifteen minutes to get through to the National Guard command post. "Don't send me kids, this time," he growled. "This is an important NASA facility, y'know."

"All we got are kids, practically," the officer answered. "We're spread pretty thin, but we'll get you someone. Can you feed 'em?"

"I guess so. But what's the matter with your kitchen?"

"Lost it getting here. Took a wrong turn somewhere from Worcester. Or they took off."

"We got some stuff in the cafeteria yet. I think."

"Hang on. We'll get someone there."

Archie moved to the back of the lobby and put his revolver in his lap. Then he remembered and got up to lock the door. He looked at the bank of screens around his desk. Everything was quiet. He saw a man in a white coat cross a corridor. Outside a trio of drunks went by. One was wearing an evening gown; he also had a moustache.

A meteor the size of a small building burned through the atmosphere and created a second Panama Canal by slicing through Colón. Water poured through, quenching the fire, as earthquakes shook down the jungles. Ethiopia and Saudi Arabia took massive meteor strikes in their barren deserts. Honolulu was destroyed in an afternoon by a tidal wave.

Station One was almost hit by an incoming lump and reported it striking in the Norwegian Sea. Further reports told of hits in the Gulf of Mexico, the Amazon jungle, and Louisiana, all relatively minor. Earthquakes flared up in Chile, Japan, California, Indonesia.

The Prime Minister of Italy committed suicide. Several *coup d'états* were reported in African nations but no one seemed to know what had happened. The Secret Service thwarted an attempt on the life of President Knowles by a member of the Legion of Destiny. The Pope issued another call to prayer.

In Los Angeles, a man calling himself the Voice of God proclaimed "Eden on Earth." He announced that all marriages were dissolved, all legal contracts terminated, all debts forgiven. For five days there were riots and parties. On the sixth day the Voice of God was stilled in the bedroom of an appropriated Bel Air mansion. He was knifed to death by the husband of one of the women he was lying with.

In Vesper, Kansas, Russell Ellis started planting his winter crop of Exxon oil plant. He had been farming for forty-two years and saw no reason to change his plans, even if the new-fangled oil producing plant was a laboratory hybrid. It was planting time.

6 May: Collision minus 20 days

Caroline shivered in the chill spring air that rushed down the darkened street. Broken glass crunched under her feet. The burned-out wreck of a late model Honda was blocking the sidewalk. She skirted it gingerly, smelling the acrid stink. Someone had been inside when it burned and they hadn't cleaned it out very well.

She was afraid. There was no compound around the Thales Center, no easily defended perimeter, just streets, lonely and littered. Someone had made the decision to just post guards in a few apartment houses, and moved some of the Center's people.

Everything was falling apart.

Where was the world headed? Anarchy or oblivion? Somehow Caroline thought those were the only two alternatives. If they didn't stop Shiva: oblivion. If they stopped Shiva, there could still be eternal anarchy. Endless rows of burnt-out houses, riots, hedonistic Dancers, preachy Gabriels, and the Ostriches, the ones who forever denied everything, deplored everything, thought it was all a con-game, a ripoff by Big Corporations or Big Labor or *something*.

She paused at a corner and looked down the street. Something was burning to the south. Fireworks to the east. Helicopters turning in beams of bright light to the west. She saw mist floating down. Scratch one riot. She gave a jump as someone stepped out of the shadows a half-block away. The other person stopped, looked belligerently at her, then stalked off, carrying a baseball bat.

Caroline took out her keys and with the other hand she tugged from her purse a brand new metal claw hammer. She held it tightly in her hand as she moved into the shadows. *All* the streetlights here were gone, shot

181

out and never replaced. But it was the shortest way to her apartment house.

She stopped in the darkness and listened, her senses wary. We are all savages, she thought. How easily I adapted to this nightly routine! A few months ago I'd have been screaming for the cops. But there were no cops, at least not for this. Every man for himself. She'd learned to filter out the noises, the distant, the close, the ones that didn't fit. Two men had jumped at her last week; she'd hit one in the face with the hammer and the other had fled. The bleeding one had cried out hoarsely and clung to her coat until she broke his fingers with her hammer's claw back. She'd run, gasping for breath, glad to be alive, triumphant in her escape. She had not felt the least sorrow for the man she'd mangled. He knew what he had been doing; he'd have to take his chances.

She moved to the corner, crouched low and looked around. Her apartment was only five doors down. A six-story apartment house with air-conditioning, central heating, cable TV, Z-channel movies, four elevators, reasonable rent, neighbors that minded their business, and a landlord who lived on the ground floor. She grinned. Landlords should be required by law to live on the property they own. When the water heater went flooey or something leaked they, too, suffered. But now the first two floors were boarded up with heavy sheets of marine plywood, then epoxied to the hardness of metal. The lobby was a sandbagged fortress with a constant guard of tenants. She stepped out and walked quickly toward the glass door.

She gave the signal rap and one of the tenants peered suspiciously around the sandbagged wall. Seeing it was Caroline, he said something to the others and came to unlock the door.

"Miz Weinberg, you're out awful late."

"I know, Mister Sterling, but we had to do some runs. Those astronauts don't keep nine to five hours, you know."

"Uh-huh," Sterling said without grace, relocking the door and peering suspiciously into the street. He pushed at her, trying to get her to go ahead of him down the narrow lane of sandbags. Caroline looked into the lobby, behind the wall of fortifications.

"Hello, everyone!"

"Um," said Mrs. Murphy.

"Late," said Mr. Poole, disapprovingly.

"Sorry," Caroline said. They were playing cards. Only old Mrs. Keel smiled at her.

"Never mind these numbskulls, dear. They have no *idea* what you do or how important it is."

"Now, Missus Keel," Mr. Poole said, frowning.

"It's true. You're just annoyed at being bothered. Caroline and Doctor Dennis are doing *important* work now."

"Humph," snorted Mr. Sterling, taking his place and picking up his cards. "She's still very late. You know they want us in by dark."

"Oh, you . . . you *nurd!*" Mrs. Keel growled, her wrinkled face turning hard with exasperation. "You can't even *bid* sanely, how do you think you can understand what they do over there at Thales?"

Sterling didn't answer and Caroline smiled over his head and Mrs. Keel made a kissing motion at her. Caroline walked passed the dark elevators and trudged wearily up three flights to her apartment. She turned on the lights, took off her coat, and switched on the television.

". . . an island of sanity in a world of madness," the television reporter said. The picture showed the main dome on the moon, where people seemed to be behaving as usual. "The long history of cooperation and interreliance here has paid off for these inhabitants of man's most durable outpost. Earl Packard, on the moon."

The picture returned to anchorman Victor Mayes. "Elsewhere there is rioting. Two hundred thousand are believed dead in the uprising in Pakistan. An undetermined number have perished in the Tokyo riot yesterday, which destroyed the central portion of the new amusement complex and caused the death of Crown Prince Yoshihiro. In New York today an outbreak of the viral plague took more lives. In Washington, President Knowles is reported in ill health, though the White House denies the President is in a state of extreme depression. A report now from Jane Tomatsu at the White House—"

Caroline shut the set off, bringing a sudden quiet to the cold and dark apartment. The lights they had were weak, mere pools of illumination in a cavelike atmosphere. She opened the refrigerator and took out a sausage, some hard-boiled eggs, and a slab of Proteen. With a knife she sliced herself some sausage, cut the Proteen into bite sizes, then peeled the eggs. A bottle of diet root beer completed her evening meal. Tomorrow she'd have to go to the Guard-protected market, or apply for a priority ration.

She sat down on the couch and turned off the light so she'd have enough energy to run her tape deck. The soothing strains of Respighi's *Fountains of Rome* filled the room, colorful and evocative. She put aside the plate, still with a few cubes of the ginger-flavored Proteen left, and lay back.

Could they do it? If not, what then? Would Shiva miss the Earth? Would things *ever* be the same again? Paris was partially in ruins. Tel Aviv had suffered devastating terrorist blasts. Fire raged unchecked in hundreds of cities, eating away at businesses no one cared to protect. Why are we so fragile, she thought. Is it because there is so little we can do ourselves? Is that the secret behind Brother Gabriel's movement and all the others of the same persuasion? If you can't lick them, join them? Make your helplessness into something positive by accepting, even welcoming it?

Great bubbling pits pocked the surface of Earth and more would come. Against the celestial shotgun what *could* anyone do? Even the power of the atom might not be enough to do the job. Caroline shivered, got up abruptly and found a sweater. It was cold. It was going to get colder.

She wanted Wade to come home. They had moved in together as a safety measure, to conserve energy, they said. But it was more than that. It was desperation. Cool, detached, wryly humorous during the day, during working hours, they were both professionals. But at night, in the darkness of their bedroom, they clung together, made love with a fervor and desperation that seemed to shout back defiantly at the chill stars. *We live!* Sometimes they wept, both of them, but never spoke of it. People cried a lot these days, Caroline thought, breaking into sudden tears in public, great shuddering gushes of release that everyone ignored. But sometimes a spasm of tears triggered a restaurant full of people, or a bus-

184

load, and they all experienced a strange catharsis. For a few moments they felt better. They shared. They acknowledged their mortality, and the fragile mortality of the human race itself.

Caroline smiled weakly into the darkness, looking at the glimmer of fires to the east. If nothing else, Shiva would surely pry man loose from Earth. It would force man to go out into the stars, one way or another. For survival. Even if Shiva was prevented from striking the home world, mankind would never forget. It would spread out so that it could *never* be obliterated.

If Shiva was stopped.

Caroline hugged herself. Wade was late. She wanted him home. She liked him. Love was not something she was all that certain of, not yet.

I like to feel that my man can survive by himself, she thought, that he won't collapse in the face of trouble, or shrivel in the face of everyday problems. But I want him still vulnerable enough to discuss things with me, things that might be close and painful to him. He doesn't have to be a monolith, a fortress. I want a mixture: strength and vulnerability. I like to think I'd be protected if things went wrong . . . and things certainly *are* wrong. I think all women need that. I think they all want a man to look after them on a very basic level. But so do men; they want someone to look out *for*, and to *be* looked out for. I like Wade, she thought; he doesn't find much that threatens his masculinity, he isn't afraid of things that might make him look weak.

But where is he? I need him. Now.

Her fingers touched herself, touched her stomach, spread across her skin and back. Her other hand crept in to cup a breast. What was the world doing, savaging itself to death? Would it ever be the same, even if Shiva were deflected? Her hand moved down, her fingers reaching into the moistness.

What was it like, she wondered, having an erection? To feel that hot throb of blood, that driving lust. Sometimes it changed men so . . . or perhaps revealed them truly.

Her fingers moved in a circular fashion, pressing down, pressing in. What was left? A few last moments of pleasure, then the final void? Could that be true? Nothing beyond but nothingness? Were the Dancers of

Shiva and all the rest right? There is only the moment, and those moments are measured. Days, hours, finite and numbered.

Shiva.

It dominated everything, even her pleasuring.

Shiva, whose symbol is the linga, that phallic emblem. They worshipped him as the creative energy of the universe. But it wasn't really *Shiva,* it was just an asteroid.

The warmth spread and grew.

The world *will* be created anew, whether Shiva comes or passes. It will never be the same. But perhaps that is not all bad. We know the priorities, were forced to discover them—each person, each race, each nation.

She moaned and arched her back. Her rehearsed fingertips knew just what to do. They always had, better than anyone. Like the fingers of a virtuoso, they stroked the music from her.

Shiva.

A god descending.

Commanding. Taking. Using. Pleasuring.

. . . rising warmth, speckled with silken explosions of light . . .

Her moan was loud in the empty room.

Smooth skin, moist warmth, tense and lean, a tightening . . .

"Ahhh . . ."

Release.

Expanding outward, a wave of pleasure and heat, rippling, conquering, moving through trembling flesh and pulsing blood.

She gasped, sighing back.

Empty room.

Empty life, filled with fear and nothingness.

Weakness, trembling, flowing juices, contracting warmth, coming back. To the empty room. To the fear. To the now.

One day before the Alpha launch from Vandenberg NASA announced the results of the final systems analysis of the Alpha mission plan. Boost system reliability was eighty-seven percent. Guidance system reliability was ninety-two percent. These were the controllable inputs, the harvest of decades in space. But working in new conditions, after a ten-day voyage, necessarily lowered personnel reliability, which was estimated at sixty-four percent. This, added to the inherent errors in the astronomical data—Shiva's exact velocity, position, mass, composition, and shape—summed up to a total systems reliability of seventy-two percent.

"We could fine it better," one of the scientists said to Chuck Bradshaw, "but the Russians still refuse to give us the full dossiers on their people." He shrugged. "So we use guesswork and what we know of how they have performed since they arrived here."

The Omega group's probability of success was more difficult to compute. To calculate at all meant assuming that Alpha had already failed. If so, everything depended on precisely *how* Alpha had failed, and why. Without knowing this, Systems Group refused to release even a guesstimate. But scuttlebutt inside the organization said the rough chances for success were thirty-eight percent to forty-four percent, depending upon whom you talked to. Chuck Bradshaw decided to tell the Omega team their chances were good but incalculable. This decision was made only after considerable thought. Bradshaw had, in fact, ordered a study done. The results were so secret that they never appeared in ordinary rumor and gossip. The most optimistic estimates gave Omega a probability of success in doing what Alpha would have failed to do of eighteen percent. Omega's stated cleanup assignment, after the success of Alpha, was rated at sixty-five percent, but no one cared all that much about that aspect.

7 May: Collision minus 19 days

"Brothers, you are in the hands of God! He shall bring you to him! Mere mortals cannot change the will of God! The great asteroid from space is our destiny! One cannot change destiny! Welcome it! Put the sins of the flesh behind you! Meet the final destiny with dignity, with purity! Purge yourself of sin!"

The crowd roared its approval, shouting up at the bearded figure high above them. Brother Gabriel stood in the bucket of an immense fire truck extension, a great red arm that towered over them. Loudspeakers were wired to the metal pipes and his voice carried far up and down the wide road before the main gate to the Kennedy Space Center. The road was invisible, covered with people. Brother Gabriel's throng spilled out into the palmetto-studded sand all along the road, but there was a clear space between them and the electric fence.

"To change the will of God is impossible! These unbelievers cannot succeed! They can only succeed in angering Jehovah! Attempts to thwart the will of the Father will end in disaster for us all! Not in disaster of the flesh, but disaster of the soul! We must prevent this, for their sake as well as ours! They must be stopped! They cannot go on building their devil-machines! Stop them!"

"Stop them!" the crowd echoed.

"Stop them!"

The sound was like a tidal wave, a tsunami of voices, making the soldiers on the other side of the fence tremble. "Steady," came the rough voice of Sergeant Cooper, over a speaker. "Thompson, back in line, unless you were going to the john."

The soldier sheepishly turned back, his face red. Hands took steadier grips on their weapons. The men in tanks double-checked their gauges. Captain Saperstein, in a show of confidence, walked out into a cleared space, hands behind his back, and turned toward the gate. A helicopter thumped in from the south, did a banking turn, and flew away toward the gantry.

Saperstein followed the flight of the machine, then his eyes dropped toward the wrecks of the two kamikaze planes shot down earlier in the day. One was still burning, sending up a thick boiling cone of black smoke.

"Stop them! Stop them!" There was a chanting quality in the repetition, as if the crowd were psyching itself up to war.

And war it would be, Saperstein knew. He looked at the gas squad, then spoke in a steady voice to Sergeant Cooper. "Masks, Sergeant."

"Sir." The noncom bellowed down the line in each direction. "Masks! Masks!" The soldiers pulled their gray-green masks from the pouches and held their helmets between their legs while they tugged on the rubbery devices. Then helmets plopped back in place, straps secured, and weapons were gripped again with sweaty hands.

Sergeant Cooper sauntered over to Captain Saperstein. "Sir."

"Yes, Sergeant?"

"Do you think this will be the main attack, or down toward Gate Seven, where they tried before?"

"I don't know, Sergeant. We are not fighting an enemy with much military training. They aren't always playing by logical rules."

The burly sergeant nodded. "Wish I had a beer, sir, don't you?"

Saperstein smiled. "Wine is my drink, Sergeant. A light sauterne on a day like this I think."

"Never saw much in wine, sir. Too fancy. Too much to learn. Take a beer now. One, two sips, and ya know, ya know if its your kinda brew, get me? Don't have to know too many labels. Ya can get it anywhere. Hell, even on the base. I remember over in I-ran. They shipped beer, but no wine. Least for us grunts. Maybe you officers, now . . ." He smiled at Saperstein, who was about half his age.

"After this, Sergeant, I will buy you a beer. Imported."

"Thank you, sir. I'll remind you, come sundown."

Saperstein looked up at the sun. Sundown was an aeon away . . . and the worse could come then, even with the powerful searchlights patrolling the fence.

There was a gunshot far down the line, then another. Handgun. No answering fire from the troops.

"Stop them! Stop them!"

"Sir . . ."

"Yes, Sergeant, I feel it, too."

"Sir, I could borrow a scoped rifle from Henderson back there and the next time they shoot at us I could take out Brother Gabriel. He's an easy target up there."

"No, Sergeant. That's more of a political solution. You had better caution the men. Leave Gabriel alone. We don't want him a martyr. They are the worse kind of enemy. They can't be killed, they only grow legends. Whatever you do, see that Gabriel stays alive."

"Yes, sir. If you say so, sir."

"Simple solutions, Sergeant, are not always simple."

The sergeant shrugged and walked off, speaking to men up and down the line. The Gabriels still chanted. The helicopter came back and set down behind the sand-bagged line, spraying sand over the ambulances. Saperstein trotted back and met Colonel Morgan between a Bradley-C tank and an ambulance.

"Sir!"

Colonel Morgan saluted casually, his eyes going past Saperstein to the mob beyond the fence. "Any minute now, huh, Captain?"

"Yes, sir. But we're ready."

"Are you? Very difficult decision for these young men. Those are Americans out there. Many friends, maybe family."

"I know, sir."

Morgan nodded. His gray hair was trimmed short around the ears and tight on his head. His age was indeterminate. There was a small scar on his jawline and Saperstein had heard that a lot of his guts were plastic or transplants. He wore paratroopers wings and a combat infantryman's badge but no other ribbons.

"When it starts I'll make a sweep along the road. I'll be using Tri-C-Twelve. That'll knock them out for a few hours. If I were you, I'd send out patrols to search for weapons." He hesitated. "And . . . maybe bring in Brother Gabriel, too. Maybe we can talk to him. But be careful with him."

"Yes, sir."

The colonel returned Saperstein's salute and trotted back to his copter, which had not stopped its rotors. The chopper lifted and banked away in a great circle. Saperstein walked back toward the fence. He felt better. Someone up the line had authorized a more powerful gas than the Di-H-Ten they had. It wasn't going to be so bad after all.

"Sergeant Cooper!"

"Sir!" The noncom trotted over to Saperstein, who told him about the Tri-C-Twelve. "Ah, good, sir. I haven't decided between Heineken or Tuborg, sir, but I've got it narrowed down."

Saperstein smiled, but the smile died quickly. People were going to get hurt. There was nothing he could do about that, but it still bothered him.

"Stop them! *Stop* them! *Stop them!*"

"Ready, Sergeant."

"Ready, sir. Lieutenant Moser, too, sir." Cooper looked back at the big battle tanks. The commanders were dropping down, buttoning up. No one had to tell them.

190

"Stop them! Stop them! Stop them!"

"Now!" roared Brother Gabriel. "Stop this folly!"

"Are you *sure*, sir?" Sergeant Cooper said over the noise. "It'd only take a moment, Captain."

Saperstein shook his head. The fence was flashing as people threw themselves upon it. Others clambered up their bodies, touched the wire, stiffened in a flash of light, and fell back. But there were so many. A tidal wave of flesh.

It kept coming.

Saperstein called out, "Ready, men!"

"Ready!" bellowed Cooper.

The helicopter came in from the gantry area and began banking at the far end of the line. Saperstein tugged off his helmet and pulled on his mask. The helicopter leveled and Saperstein could see a faint mist coming down. Almost a mile away people began to fall.

Then the helicopter exploded.

Saperstein winced in the bright flash and on the retinal afterimage he saw the streak of fire coming up out of the palmettos. Some renegade army man with a heat-seeking infantry rocket.

The captain did not see the pieces of the helicopter fall into the crowd. He shouted a muffled command to Cooper, to give the order to fire when he thought best. "I've got to get another chopper in here with that gas!"

Saperstein ducked a bottle thrown over the fence. It exploded in a ball of flame and singed the hair on his hands as he dodged into the guardpost. He snatched a battlephone from the hands of a corporal and shouted for headquarters.

The human wave surged up against the fence, all along a four-kilometer line. Their unconscious bodies toppled back, or were smashed against the burning wires, where they were killed by the continued electricity or the feet of their brothers and sisters. Some made it over the top. Cooper shouted the order and gas grenades arced through the air. Dense clouds of white gas obliterated the fence. A few people staggered out of the cloud and fell.

Then others came through, leaping, their faces masked, guns in their hands. Surprised, the soldiers did not fire for a few seconds and the invaders opened up. The sound of gunshots brought the others awake and they returned the fire. Blood spurted. Men and women fell. The gas dissipated and there were waves of frozen bodies along the fence. Saperstein ran out of the guardhouse, his .45 in his hand. Cooper pointed down the line.

"Moser!" Saperstein shouted, pointing. Two tanks backed up and spun toward Gate Seven, spewing sand. They rumbled past and Saperstein looked around. A hundred or so people . . . and a few children . . . lay inside the fence. Thousands were stacked in silent and obscene piles along the fence, which still sputtered and flashed. A body fell, tumbling down, sprawling obscenely. It was a young woman.

The gunfire continued down the line. Saperstein froze his emotions and jumped up on a jeep hood to look around, staring through the big plastic window of the gas mask.

Brother Gabriel slumped in his high crane, an arm hanging down between loudspeakers. There was movement out in the palmettos as some of those still conscious ran away. Bodies littered the road. Some would not wake up.

"Sergeant, take a squad and fetch in Brother Gabriel. But bring him in alive, understand?"

"Yes, sir, if you really want it that way. And I think Heineken, sir."

"A six-pack, Sergeant. Get on with it."

"Sir."

Saperstein got down, as weary as an old man. He fell into the jeep seat and pulled off his mask. It was a hell of a day so far and it was only half over.

"He's here? Gabriel is here on the base?" Bradshaw frowned at the screen. "Uh, your name is, um . . ."

"*Saperstein, sir. Yes, sir, we gassed them when they attacked. Luckily they were massed up, or our grenades wouldn't have done much to them. They got the chopper with Colonel Morgan. He was going to use Tri-C-Twelve and—*"

"Yes, yes. Where is Gabriel now?"

"*I sent him in with Sergeant Cooper, sir. To the Provost Marshal's office. I think we can charge him with inciting a riot, trespassing on government property, failure to obey a lawful order, the—*"

"Thank you, Captain. I understand. Good work. But

192

we don't want any Brother Gabriel *inside* for those fanatics to try and rescue, understand. But I admit I'd like a good talk with him."

"*Yes, sir. If you'll excuse me, sir. I have burial detail. And, uh, Colonel Morgan and his pilot to bring in before too many of them wake up. The gas we used isn't as powerful as I'd like. It's just for riots, to break things up. I want patrols out getting whatever weapons they may have.*"

"Yes, Captain, I understand. Don't let me hold you up."

"*Sir.*"

The screen blanked and Bradshaw stared at his faint reflection in it. Brother Gabriel. The High Muckymuck of the Lunatic Fringe. Destiny's Tot. Chuck Bradshaw stood up and strode out of the office. Maybe they could turn Gabriel around.

"My men have him," Mankowski said. "They'll be along in a minute." Chuck Bradshaw nodded. The cinderblock room was cold, and a bit damp. The air-conditioning was relentless.

"You know," Mankowski said conversationally, as they waited, "we've had a team on this fruitcake ever since his movement got vocal enough and big enough to get our attention."

Bradshaw looked at the FBI Special Agent. "What do you do if they stay quiet?"

Mankowski shrugged. "Infiltrate, like always. Did it myself once, in the eighties. The Greenspace Movement, remember them?" Chuck nodded. He'd been one, when he was a kid. But then, Mankowski would know that. Or at least the FBI would. They kept dossiers for decades. "Of course, that never turned out to be anything subversive, but it was quite a trip, hanging out with those nuts."

Bradshaw looked at the door, then at his watch. Is he trying to provoke me, he wondered.

One of the other agents held a tiny box to his ear, then said, "Coming in now."

Mankowski got up and walked around to put one cheek on the front of the desk facing the door. He picked up a file and opened it. There was a knock on the door.

Bradshaw looked at the FBI man, who winked, then said, "Come in."

The door swung open and the armed Marine stepped in and saluted. Mankowski didn't return the salute. He just kept looking at the file. Bradshaw could see one of the FBI men outside, holding an arm.

"Sir, detail here with the prisoner."

"Yeah, okay, bring him in."

Abruptly a big figure loomed in the doorway. He was wearing one of the white jumpsuits used by the shuttle assembly personnel but Bradshaw recognized the beaming face of Brother Gabriel from the news programs. He raised an eyebrow at Mankowski.

"We put him in the jumper ourselves," Mankowski explained. "He was a mess when they brought him in."

"A mess, sir, as you put it, because of your own actions." Brother Gabriel's voice was full and resonant, the bass tones filling the room. Bradshaw recognized a powerful public speaker, and felt a twinge of envy. He'd never had that effortless charisma himself, a most useful tool of persuasion, whether it be with appropriation committees or mobs. The media had failed to give him the full feel of the man. Brother Gabriel exuded certainty, presence, warmth, and most of all, power.

"We were defending our facility," Bradshaw said mildly.

"Pointlessly, sir," Gabriel said heavily. He crossed the room in four quick strides, leaving the two FBI agents behind. He sat down in a folding chair without being asked, or asking, and his eyes inspected them all in an imperious sweep.

The two FBI agents came into the room, their faces inadequately masking their irritation. They closed the door and flanked it, regaining the professional inert control of their faces. They neither moved nor fidgeted and looked at no one but Brother Gabriel.

"Do sit down, Mister Kress," Mankowski said, with a hint of derision in his voice.

Brother Gabriel fixed him with an eagle's stare and said, "I prefer my title."

"But Kress is your name? Douglas Arthur Kress?"

"A man of another life."

"A better life than the one you're in now."

"In the eyes of the blind." Gabriel didn't blink and

194

Bradshaw found that faintly unsettling, but it didn't seem to bother Mankowski.

"An accountant who belonged to various fundamentalist churches for two decades before this," Mankowski said. "Family man. Respectable conservative. Paid his taxes and didn't cheat on them. Then chucked it all away for some high-profile Bible-thumping six months before Shiva strikes. You were all set up for this, weren't you? What I don't understand is how you could turn against your country this way."

"I wouldn't expect that you could, Mister Mankowski."

Mankowski blinked just once and Bradshaw saw he was surprised that Gabriel knew his name.

"I know you, of course," Gabriel said, his chin high, his eyes still piercing unblinkingly. "I have spoken to your men before, and others of our brethren have learned enough of your methods to identify you." He smiled warmly, disarmingly, with a sudden shift of manner. "We are not simpletons, as you well know."

"Yes, we do," Bradshaw broke in. "You've hamstrung this whole launch facility. You have made it very difficult and expensive to supply and operate. You've made your point quite thoroughly. What we want to know is when you'll stop."

"When the job is done, Mister Bradshaw."

"Stopping the launches?"

"Yes. We know these are the important ones."

"How do you know that?" Mankowski asked quickly.

"There are many with us," Gabriel said casually.

"Not as many as a few hours ago," Mankowski said harshly.

Brother Gabriel made a thin smile and his eyes seemed to laugh at them. "On the contrary. The followers you have slaughtered have had their places filled by ten times as many. We grow by the hour."

"You won't succeed," Bradshaw said earnestly. "We have heavy armor. We can call in air strikes if we have to. Those men out there don't like killing other Americans, but they will. I assure you they will. They understand their priorities."

"The next air strikes may not be gas," Mankowski said and Gabriel looked at him soberly.

"You will not do anything so foolish, sir. Jet fighters

making dives within the launch area, as the countdown proceeds? I am no technical man myself, but that seems fanciful."

Bradshaw knew it was, too, but he didn't want this fanatic to see that. The fixed, waxy look Brother Gabriel was now giving them was more disturbing than Bradshaw had anticipated. He had hoped that Gabriel could be talked to, reasoned with, especially now that they had him on clear incitement-to-riot charges. But that hope was fading. The man spoke as if he were looking out over a vast stretch of space between him and everyone else, as though he were speaking from a mountaintop.

"For *what?*" Bradshaw said suddenly. "Why keep this up? Don't you know . . ." He let his voice trail off because clearly Brother Gabriel had to know and didn't give a damn. Fanatics scared him. Only lunatics scared him more. They were unpredictable, dangerous, destructive.

"Mister Bradshaw," Brother Gabriel said softly, "you surely see that it is you who persist against all that is human?"

"You're a murderer," Mankowski said. "A *mass* murderer. How human is that?"

"It is you and your kind who pull the triggers."

"Look—" Mankowski halted as Bradshaw held up a hand. The FBI man closed his mouth with a snap, glaring pugnaciously.

"No point in going into that," Bradshaw said. "What I want to know is why you think, Brother, uh, Brother Gabriel, that we should let Shiva wipe us from the Earth."

"It won't."

"You think it's all a fake, do you?"

"Oh, no. Shiva will come."

"Then . . ."

"We shall all surely die. All of us here in this room, at least. But somewhere in the jungles and forests, in the mountains and caves and sheltered valleys of this good green Earth, men and women will live on. They shall inherit a world free of our excesses. They shall be given the Garden once more. The fearful immanence of God shall begin its mysterious work again. The failed

196

experiment you and I represent, Mister Bradshaw, will be erased."

"Ah. I see." There was a serene self-assurance in Brother Gabriel's sentences that gave him a certain hypnotic quality. Once he began, Bradshaw realized, an audience would lean forward in their seats to hear the next phrase. Brother Gabriel was that good.

"Do you think Shiva's arrival near the time of the end of the second millennium is purely accidental, gentlemen?" Gabriel asked, looking around, even at the two statuelike Marines and the door-flanking FBI agents. "Think. Shiva has been tilting down toward Earth for perhaps a hundred million years, two hundred million, a *billion* years. Is it likely that its terrible end would come just at the divine time of accounting?"

"Why not at the first millennium, one thousand A.D.?" Bradshaw asked.

"We were not so corrupt then," Brother Gabriel replied simply.

"A convenient theory," Bradshaw said, frowning.

"We do not have a theory, Mister Bradshaw. We have the word of God."

"As heard by you."

"As heard by us all. I am not the cause of this, sir. People do not follow me because of what I am, but because of what I see—of what they see."

"Jesus," Bradshaw said under his breath.

Gabriel stood up suddenly. His hand rose in the air, his voice boomed out. "You are an abomination before the Lord! You shall be struck down!"

"Get him out of here," Mankowski snapped.

Legally they had Brother Gabriel nailed firmly. He had violated a dozen laws. They had videotape on him by the kilometer. He could be held on general restraint order because of President Knowles's martial law declaration three days before the riot. But as the hours mounted it became clear that the followers of Gabriel outside the launch facility perimeter could not be stopped as long as they knew Brother Gabriel was being held prisoner within.

Already the attacks on the fences were being carried forward with devastating ferocity, if not military precision. The four shuttle launches had to be staged and re-

197

staged because of small systems errors. No sabotage, this time. Instead, the steady pressure from outside was causing human error among the tired and frightened staff. The long surging masses of people could easily be seen from even the lower levels of the gantries and the low growling and occasional burst of gunfire could be heard even within the bunkers. Helicopters swarmed overhead in a constant swirling dance; from time to time the choppers darted low, dropping gas grenades. All of the airships were punctured with bullet holes.

In a meeting among NASA, the FBI, Army, and presidential representatives the Brother Gabriel problem caused sharp division. If they kept him, some argued, the mass of Gabriel supporters might get worked up into such a frenzy to liberate their leader that they might break through the Army lines. If the Army released him, others argued back, Brother Gabriel might be just enough of a catalyst to set off a final massive assault. No one wanted a massacre. Even gassing the crowds produced deaths as people fell beneath boots and were asphyxiated under other fallen bodies.

While the discussion went on the Gabriel forces breeched the army defenses in two places. The breaks were quickly reinforced, the invaders contained, arrested, or turned back, and the perimeter once again secured. But the signs were clear. The troops were tired and unnerved by the suicidal assaults they had to withstand. Reinforcements from outlying bases were having their own difficulties with the rising riots in other cities, and might not arrive in time.

In the end the committee recommended to the president that Brother Gabriel be released. President Knowles acknowledged their message with a three-word reply. He ordered Gabriel released, and although it was done in a manner calculated to cast doubt on his cause and sanity, Gabriel returned to his followers a hero.

Within two hours the attacks escalated all along the long fence. The Army continued to repel them, but with increasing bloodshed and with more difficulty. The shuttle launches went forward, hampered by multiple holds. The ragged screaming from the perimeter made a buzzing hum in the background as the ground crews worked on. The Army sent trained snipers into the red towers and they settled in behind sandbagged revetments and sighted in their weapons. Then they waited.

"Never mind what they did, just get them out of here!" Chuck spoke loudly, his throat raw. The Provost Marshal on the screen looked back impassively. "Major, just dump them outside the gate, damn it! I don't have time to get tied up in prosecuting saboteurs or nuts or anything else. Kick 'em out, and let me fix up the damage."

"Yes, sir. I'll have an order cut for your signature and then these six will be transported to the Main Gate."

"Yeah, yeah, fine," Chuck said wearily. He snapped the connection and sank back in his chair. He wrinkled his nose. "Who stinks in here?"

"You do," Lisa said, smiling. "When was the last time you stopped to shower? Much less *sleep?*"

"I'll sleep *after,*" he growled. "Okay, what do you have for me?"

"Omega is ready. We might even be overtrained." She tried on a smile, but it couldn't hold on and slipped away. The nagging fear they all had was what was coming to be called the horseshoe nail. One tiny fact, one bit of information, a single piece of equipment that might somehow be overlooked, then turn out to be vital. Already they were almost ridiculously redundant in backup systems, in training, in computer simulations. Almost everyone could do almost everyone else's job, and that included the Russians, who had the hardest job—that of learning all the American equipment.

"No horseshoe nails missing?"

Lisa shrugged. "Who can tell? Maybe when we get there we'll find we need a hairpin or a rubber band . . ." The light tone of her voice died as she saw the expression on Bradshaw's face. "Sorry . . ."

"It's getting tougher to get things in here all the time, you know. We're in a goddamn state of siege. The Army had to push back perimeters ten kilometers ever since that renegade National Guard unit knocked down the chopper bringing in the wounded from the Orlando airport. That goddamn Gabriel is stirring up another riot. He's saying he'll have half a million here within three or four days. How the hell are we going to stop half a *million?*"

Lisa said nothing. The heat-seeking bazooka teams from the National Guard unit had damaged the gantry on Pad Thirty-seven, knocked a piece out of the old Vertical Assembly Building, and bagged three helicopters. Sniper fire had accounted for over sixty deaths and eighty wounded. The Army had been very rough in pushing the mob outside back to new and distant perimeters. They had used tanks, planes, choppers, gas, and bayonets . . . and lost another twenty-two men and women.

The defections had continued, both from the Army and from NASA, though there had been none in the last four days. Evidently those who were going to run had done so. In a way it was a relief. Maybe they could count on those that remained.

The Coast Guard had been almost totally free of desertions and their heavy offshore patrols had bagged everything from powerboats filled with armed Gabriels to frogmen coming in with plastic explosives. They had even captured ten Shiva Dancers who wanted to freak out on the launchpads. The Air Force had knocked down four kamikaze planes and one hijacked airliner. The last was a most regrettable incident as eighty-four innocents had perished with the four hijackers who had tried to crash into the control center at Mach One. Now a three-hundred-kilometer perimeter was maintained in the air at immense cost of men, fuel, and machines. Two tunnels had been discovered near the western fence; one had collapsed, burying four people in sand, and the other had been abandoned. A famous motion picture actor had led a group in support of the Alpha and Omega effort and had been killed in Orlando when they clashed with Gabriels. Terrorists had knocked out a NASA tracking station in Australia. Another group of unidentified guerillas had destroyed an Italian government backup computer facility in Milan. Martial law had been declared in forty-one of the fifty-four states. A presidental motorcade had been attacked by terrorists in Arlington, Virginia; but the cars had been a diversion. The president was traveling by helicopter; however, four Treasury men were killed.

"We're going to make it, aren't we, Chuck?"

"Of course we're going to make it. Jesus." He shuffled papers on his desk, his manner snappish and irritable.

"Where the hell is that security report on Station One? Ah. Look at this." He handed her a file marked *Top Secret*.

It was a report on the loyalty of personnel aboard Station One, the main assembly point for all extraterrestrial programming. Lisa quickly scanned the tersely worded report. "You mean you're replacing Gerald Camarillo?"

"Yes. He is being temporarily assigned to Station Two as systems analyst."

"For *disloyalty?*"

"No, for *suspected* disloyalty . . . no, damn it, make that . . . make that, Christ, reevaluation. That's it. Reevaluation."

"By any other name it would smell as bad. My god, Chuck, he's been on One for nine *years*. He knows every rivet and tank and nondiagrammed alteration. You can't shift him!"

"I *have* shifted him. He went over this morning. Did you read what it said, what he said? He said he wasn't sure the plan would work."

"Hell, *I'm* not sure it will work! And neither are you!" She glared at him. "For *that* you deep-six our best station commander?"

"It was out of my hands. Security, they shifted him. Actually, they wanted to drop him back here for a deep-probe hypnosis, but I . . . I couldn't see doing that to Gerry."

Lisa stared at him. "This gets worse all the time, Chuck. Not only have we tigers at the gate and defectors inside, but we have *security* men shooting down our best people! Is that what happened to Blaine Brennan?"

"Uh-huh. Blaine got drunk and spilled his guts to an undercover cop, who told Security. Seems he dreams about Satan and cannonballs and breaking open the Earth like an egg."

"My god, Chuck, who *doesn't* dream about the Earth breaking open? I want him back, damnit!"

"Lisa, he's been out of it for months."

"He's still better than most. Doing something will fix the dreams." She chewed on her lip and looked at Bradshaw's impassive face. He just sat slumped, staring back at her. Then he gave a sigh.

"Oh, shit." His voice was infinitely weary. He looked at her from under his brows. "Now listen to me. Brennan's out. He blew it with all that garbage. Tom Schumacher's in. That's it. There are no appeals."

"But—" She stopped under his look. She breathed heavily for a few moments, then blew out her breath in a lip-flapping sigh. "The powers that be, huh?" He nodded.

Lisa tilted her head at Bradshaw and smiled very faintly. "Why don't you go home and get some rest?"

"The family's moved to the base. In one of those terrible emergency shelters they put up."

"And which you took to set an example. Christ. Go home. You think this whole shebang will fall apart in eight hours?"

"It might." He smiled weakly at her. "Mother hen."

"Move your ass, Bradshaw. That's an order."

"Yes, Colonel, ma'am."

Neither of them moved for some time, then Chuck pushed down on his knees and got up. He walked out without a word. Lisa's eyes followed him.

The ghetto of Philadelphia was burning furiously. The streets were clotted with looters. The police were shooting on sight. A black man fell, his clothes expensive, his pockets filled with cash, his neck hung with cameras. No one noticed.

Seattle took a beating from micrometeorites. So did the countryside around Leipzig, Germany, and Arnhem, in the Netherlands.

Near Salisbury, Wiltshire, in southern England, more than a thousand self-confessed witches and warlocks gathered at the ancient megalithic posts of Stonehenge to "wish away" the threat of Shiva.

Beauregard Boyce Lee, the preacher who wanted to be part of the Alpha team, became a media event when he dared Shiva to take him in place of the rest of mankind.

Astronaut Susan Robinson found she was pregnant.

Blaine Brennan committed suicide, quietly and unnoticed.

Carl Jagens secured himself magnetically to the shiny aluminum skin. "Aft collar okay," he called automatically to Station One, a distant silvery double pinwheel turning behind him. He moved spider fashion across the reinforced cylindrical shell. Inside was the *Bolshoi*, riding in an aluminum and a steel trapezoidal corrugation for added support. This was the whole point, right here under his hands, and he had to be certain he knew every flange and clip.

Jagens stopped at the extruded aluminum alloy ring that formed the boundary of the warhead subsystem. He popped the external readout cover and studied the interior. The cluster of electronics, hastily sandwiched in among the manual components, glittered in the sunlight that slanted in and moved across as they turned.

He frowned. He had seen this a dozen times but every fresh look brought the same irritation. The design was cumbersome and confusing. Here and there were bundles of actual wiring, not printed circuits as there should have been. But there hadn't been time for last-minute systems integration with printed circuits, so the technical types had done the troubleshooting right on the workbenches in Station One, and this was the result. Jagens had spent his career in well-designed spacecraft, at the leading edge of the world's technology, following routines thought through far in advance and tested again and again. This last-minute patchwork business rankled him. But he knew things had to be that way. There wasn't time. There had barely been time to stencil in important instructions in Russian or English, so everything could be understood by both parties.

"Repping sequence A-48," he said, and began inserting his probe into portions of the electronic tangle in front of him. This was the last stage in checking out the *Bolshoi* subsystems and he would be damned glad to get rid of it. The last three weeks in orbit had been grueling beyond anything he remembered. There were plenty of tech people to assist, sure. But he and Calderon and Issindo had had to carry the brunt of it. They had to know these multiple-integration systems instinctively, to react to failures without hesitation. And on top of it all, they had to maintain the facade of certainty, of competence, of determination before the world. They had successfully fought to get the video news cameras out of their hair, but they felt the pressure even among the trained NASA technicians; the astronauts and cosmonauts *had* to appear superhuman or all around them were likely to lose their heads.

And even Carl Jagens knew he was no superman.

He called out coordinates and system parameters mechanically. The two techs in Station One answered quickly, briskly. They were right on top of everything. There were eight technicians for every astronaut or cosmonaut in the Alpha team, giving every kind of assist they knew how. But there was only so much they could do. Take this manifold he was working on, for instance. *Bolshoi's* target ranging was conventional radar. The actual power source and radiating antennas were in Command Module One, where he and Menshov would be riding. Even that had been a last-minute decision. The original plan had been to cut weight requirements by eliminating the radar power source entirely. Instead, the radar waves would be broadcast directly from Earth itself. Then both *Alpha* and *Omega* needed only to carry receivers to monitor the signals reflected back by the oncoming mass of Shiva. The whole damned project had gone forward on that plan for three months, until the final calculation of Shiva's orbit came in. Then the geniuses in Central Design found there was a fourteen percent chance that the Earth-based system wouldn't be able to operate correctly during the crucial last ten minutes before hitting Shiva. The reason was that the Earth systems would be nearly over the horizon with respect to Shiva in the last hour of encounter. Some of the radar dishes would be unable to crank down and broadcast that close to the horizon. The lunar dishes had been badly damaged during the early strikes and would not have been in the correct position in any case. These facts added in with another: some of the Shiva debris cloud would block the incoming radar waves, weakening the reflected signals. So at the last possible moment Central Design switched over and stuck radar transmitting equipment onboard Command Module One, cramming it into an already crowded tangle.

Everything seemed to be all right. *Bolshoi's* targeting depended crucially on her receiving antennae, and they were the best anybody could make. Jagens glanced up at the dishes ten meters farther along the shiny aluminum cowling. They all swept to the left, locked on, then swept right, as he tapped in the commands. Normal function, on the dot. He turned and looked in the opposite direction. Earth was a smear of color beneath him. The immense propulsion module for *Bolshoi* filled a quarter of his sky. A huge nuclear rocket rode within, linked to multiple boosters. Silhouetted against the sleek silvery rocket skin were the black webbing of the backup radars. He punched through instructions, muttering to the techs. The backup radars obediently swayed this way, then that, sighting on imaginary targets fed them by Station One. Lights under Carl's hand winked from amber to green. All normal. If the forward radars went out, the backups would cut in automatically and instantly.

Funny word, *instantly*. When people said that ordinarily, it just meant fast, a second or so. For Shiva that wasn't nearly fast enough. *Alpha's* redundant systems had to come on in microseconds. If the forward radars blew near Shiva, there wouldn't be time for either him or Menshov to respond. A little package of silicone and copper had to decide the primary system was kaput, and cut in the secondaries. Carl shook his head and smiled to himself. This Gordian knot of electronics might be able to do that, but he sure as hell wished they could have tried a couple of convincing complete simulations to check it out. The whole thing worked fine when they had it on the bench in Station One. But what did that mean, really?

Carl knew he was a perfectionist, but he could conceive of no other way. Most astronauts had traditionally been selected from combat or test pilots, and that tradition was mostly still adhered to, whenever possible, and Carl had been a fearsome commander to his ground crews when he had been flying atmospheric craft. Proper maintenance had saved him and his ship—not to mention his mission in the two "brushfire" wars he had flown in—on more than one occasion. He was not about to cut corners now, or change his way of doing things.

"*Ajax Four is jittering some,*" a technician called to him. Carl blinked and in an instant was back on top of what he was doing, no more daydreaming.

"Got it," he said. He dropped the sequence into the backup manually, saw the lights near his suited palm wink green, and relaxed. It really was a marvel of a system, he had to admit. It reminded him of the old joke, "Look at what God could do if he had money." To put this stuff together in a matter of months—command, payload, propulsion and service modules, all new and interlocked, with redundancy systems—was a miracle.

"*Sir,*" a tech broke in. "*We're getting an emergency*

hold from Vandenberg. I thought you'd want to know."

"What?" he growled.

"They're going into hold. They say their whole launch sequence is aborted."

"We haven't got any more Alpha equipment to come up, have we?"

"No sir, but there's some Omega stuff to come. And the rest of your team, sir. Nissen and Menshov are—"

"Patch me through," Carl said savagely. "Right to the top." He grabbed at a handhold on *Bolshoi's* shiny skin and jerked at it, pumping himself back and forth as his feet rotated free, feeling the surge of adrenaline. He looked down and located the West Coast of the United States, wisped by white, and glared at it.

12 May: Collision minus 13 days

"Mister President?"

Caleb Knowles looked up from his note-taking. Sometimes it straightened out his thinking to put the main points down in some sort of order, just to see if they looked any better in print, annotated with arrows, boxes, stars, and other doodling. Knowles feared some psychiatrist examining his jottings and had always destroyed them. "More from Vandenberg?"

"Yes, sir," the military aide said. "The fuel depot fire is under control now."

Knowles smiled. "Good. Good." He looked across the alcove of the White House situation room at the Secretary of Defense.

Sam Rogers sat with a cradled phone in his hand. "But the gantry system is derailed, they say." He tapped one foot nervously and it made a hollow little sound in the carpeted alcove.

The President looked past him at the uniformed men and women around the maps and machines in the main room. "They're sure the Gabriels outside couldn't have done it?"

Rogers nodded. "The fuel depot, yes, that could have been a small incendiary rocket. But not the gantry."

There was a short silence while they all looked at the President. Woods from the CIA, McNellis from State, Dr. Kinney, Mathison, the Senate majority leader, Hopkins from the House, a nervous light colonel from the Signal Corps. They all looked fresh out of advice.

The buck stops here, Knowles thought for the thousandth time. And they expect change.

There was a curiously cold and wet feel to the air, which had little to do with the air-conditioning. It was intangible. Strained. Like the faces that looked at him with concern. Nobody seemed ready to say anything.

"Did they track down that voltage overload?" the President asked.

"So far, no," Sam Rogers said evenly.

"Those subsystems are vital in the next few launches, aren't they?"

"Yes, sir, they are."

"The shuttle on the gantry right now—can it lift?"

"Yes, but—"

"I order them to launch."

"Sir . . ." Rogers leaned forward. "Sir, I should advise you that the Vandenberg commander believes that the Gabriels might have other incendiary rockets. They are sweeping the country around there but it's pretty rugged and empty. Plenty of places to hide. There are reports that an Army unit abandoned equipment in that class three days ago in San Pedro, and there was a theft at the Alameda base . . . if the Gabriels got something from either, and the fuel depot was a test by them—"

"That's all supposition, Sam."

"Yes, sir, it is," the pudgy Secretary of Defense said. He had a voice that got higher the longer he talked, the President noted. He thought it odd he hadn't noticed that before. It would almost be comical, if anybody felt like laughing. Rogers took a deep breath and went on. "But . . . the last few backup systems for the Omega team are on that shuttle. If the Gabriels catch it with a heat-seeker, no matter how small, we'll lose those components . . . not to mention the, uh, the personnel."

"Those are secondary systems."

"True, sir. But—"

"We can risk them."

"The components—well, perhaps, sir. But if the shuttle launch vehicle crashes on Vandenberg, we could lose everything."

"Vandenberg may not be much use from now on, anyway."

Sam Rogers didn't change expression. He stared at the President, whom he had known since college days when they had both dated the same Smith sophomore. Then, after a moment, when no one said anything more, he lifted the telephone to his ear and spoke rapidly, issuing orders. In a moment he put the telephone in his lap, keeping the line open, and looked wearily at the rug.

President Knowles turned to Willard Woods. "The CIA have anything on this?"

"Only what we get from the Bureau." He smiled faintly. The President had inherited the FBI Director from the previous administration and they had never gotten on. Knowles preferred using the CIA, even when he sometimes skirted legal difficulties by doing so.

"And what's that?" the President asked.

"Enough staff have turned up missing from Vandenberg to slow the launches. But the Air Force replaced them. Trouble is, we can't be sure some of them aren't Gabriels or any one of a dozen obstructionist groups."

"Why should they be?" the President asked urgently. "They're solid technical people, feet on the ground. Should be reliable."

Woods nodded and grimaced. "We've already had first-class personnel go off the deep end on this, Mister President. Nobody really knows why. They just lose interest or say they want to be with their families or that Shiva's going to hit us anyway, so what's the point . . . and they bug out."

"Like Anna," Sam Rogers said. Knowles and everyone else looked at him. His voice was hollow, defeated.

"Anna?" the President asked softly.

"My daughter, Caleb, you remember her? You spoke at her graduation." Knowles nodded, putting his thumb and forefinger to his lower lip and frowning at McNellis, who had moved toward Sam Rogers.

"Beautiful girl. She really was. Phi Beta Kappa, the whole thing. She got cancer three years ago. Inoperable. She spent the last two years of her life . . ." His voice trailed off, then he spoke again, loudly. "Like the Hedonists, like the Dancers of Shiva. She wanted to taste everything, try everything before . . . before . . ." He looked at the President, his eyes wet. "That's what they're doing at Vandenberg, sir. There's so much they all . . . they all haven't done . . ."

"Yes," Knowles said, turning back to Woods, embarrassed but disturbingly sympathetic. He knew how the young woman must have felt. He felt it himself, but he had responsibilities.

"And if one or two that are left are Gabriels . . . ?"

"Sabotage," Woods said with a shrug. "Deliberate."

"Only takes a few," Speaker of the House Hopkins said into the drawn silence of the room. In the corner an interface outlet went *ping* and began displaying written messages in yellow on a green screen. The Signal Corps officer pressed a button to log it in and then began reading it. Sam Rogers lifted the receiver to his ear when it began murmuring, but he sat there without expression, staring into space. Senator Mathison excused himself to go have an illegal cigarette.

"The bird is off," Rogers said, after a few moments. "Climbing." He blinked and wet his lips. "Climbing. Out of tactical weapons range now. On course." He put the telephone receiver down with a sigh.

The room relaxed, the President noted, but not very much. "I meant what I said about Vandenberg," he said mildly.

Sam Rogers had begun to smile. He stopped and said, "Sir?"

"We can't use it anymore if this goes on."

"Well, sir, I'm certain the Air Force is taking every measure it can to—"

"Yes, that's why I'm glad I didn't ask the Joint Chiefs to our little party here. The Air Force would never admit failure in front of the others. This way they'll just have to swallow what we say."

"The operation at Vandenberg is as tight as anybody can make it, Mister President, but there's miles of open country around there."

"But the Gabriels know what we're doing—and where. They've seen all the press releases—the ones everyone was so happily putting out six months ago, when we set up these mission launch schedules, to show everyone we were really doing something constructive. Back before we knew the Gabriels would—or could—get this bad." Knowles stopped and glared around the room. "We sold them on it pretty good, didn't we?"

"We can hold the Gabriels at Vandenberg, sir," Rogers said. "The California National Guard is being called up,

I've ordered in the Third Army and Breckenridge's paratroopers from Fort Riley."

"You weren't so sure a few minutes ago. You advised me not to launch."

"I . . . I was recommending keeping the temporary hold."

"We can't afford indefinite holds anymore, Sam." Knowles hunched forward in his chair and stared hard at Sam Rogers. He liked this man, they had campaigned together and for each other. In the Senate they had fought together, but when you were working with people you had to remember that they instinctively protected the people under them, the piece of government or business they knew and ran. It was second nature to any good executive, in or out of uniform. The fact that it sometimes distorted their picture of things beyond recognition was just a side product.

"I'll admit sabotage is a new term in the equation," Sam Rogers said, "but I don't think it changes things all that much. We can root them out."

"No."

Some of the others shook off their silence and began to murmur disagreement. Knowles held up his hand. "We've got a new problem now. The hardware is in orbit. Most of the teams have been up there for weeks putting it together." The President pinned the Signal Corps lieutenant colonel with his hard gaze. "What does Chuck Bradshaw say is the latest situation?"

"Running a little ahead, sir. As of eleven hundred hours today."

"Good." Knowles smiled. "Very good. What comes next?"

"Getting the rest of the crews into orbit. A few more launches. Then some backup hardware, sir, if we want it. If anything goes out of operational status in the next few days . . ."

"Let's hope it doesn't," the President said. "Get me Bradshaw direct."

"Sir."

Knowles slapped his hand down on the hardwood table in front of him and looked at the others in the room. "Let us hope it doesn't, yes . . . but if it *does*, we need *certainty*." Knowles leaned back in his leather chair. "And Vandenberg isn't certain. It could blow any time.

210

But we are going to put it out to the media that Vandenberg is under control, despite everything." He looked slowly around, trying to read all the faces. Mathison came back in, trailing smoke, and listened intently.

The President felt pretty good. It came from knowing what to do after so much indecision. "We'll even lift the control cordon on civilian aircraft. Let the networks get in some choppers for a squint."

"But that's *absurd—*" Sam Rogers began. He had dropped the telephone receiver without noticing it. It clattered off the table and bobbed wildly on the end of its cord.

"Mister Bradshaw, sir, on two six."

President Knowles punched the lighted studs on his desk-top set and Chuck Bradshaw appeared on the screen.

"Mister President?"

"Chuck, your backup plan is still on the back burner?" Bradshaw nodded. "Then all the crews are going out of Kennedy," Knowles said. "Along with their personal gear." Bradshaw nodded, unsurprised.

But Rogers looked stunned. "The Air Force understood—"

"The Air Force takes orders," Knowles said abruptly. "And I'm giving them."

As the President rode up in the small special elevator he felt the energy seep out of him. He was certain he had done the correct thing, but he was just as sure it had cost him a certain fine edge in his judgment. You couldn't take too many fast moves like that before you let the game run away with you, before you began to think everything could be solved by a quick finesse, by a grandstand play, something dramatic. So a prudent man had to use that kind of stuff with care.

Still, it had gone over. It was a myth that a President, any President, just told people to do things and they got done. Oh, sure, something vaguely like what you meant did happen. But full cooperation was what you wanted, and a man who feels put upon can't do as well as you want him to. Old habits died hard. So you had to coax your own staff along, spelling out things for them so they didn't hedge their bets on you and screw up the execution somewhere down the line, so that they didn't second-guess and try to figure out what you *really* meant. Even in this crisis something like that could happen. Hell, it had happened often enough in the middle of a war. Roosevelt could probably have written a whole goddamn book about that one point.

The elevator door opened with a soft hiss and Barbara Carr was waiting there for him. She smiled, said hello, and handed him a cup of hot tea. This was getting to be a regular ritual with them and one he liked. The President could let himself drink liquor in the evenings, but anything earlier might backfire.

"You were down there a long time," she said mildly.

"We were playing poker."

"What were the stakes?"

"Pretty high," he replied, and let some of it come into his face. Barbara's expression changed. He drained his cup of tea and handed it back to her.

"You need more tea and more rest," she said.

"Right." Knowles suddenly remembered that he had given up his cherished practice of an afternoon rest—often just reading something he didn't *have* to read, or taking a walk, or listening to music—almost a year before. Maybe that explained why all this was getting to him the way it was.

"So come along," Barbara said. She led the way into the private part of the White House, through tall doors, stopping only at a small brass food cart to refill the teacup. She made a comment about the weather and he responded with some obligatory talk. When he realized he was puffing up some short steps it dawned on him that he was awfully tired. Something had taken a lot out of him today.

Barbara led him to his bedroom and then stopped outside, smiling softly, and handed him the cup of tea again. He looked at her and then without thinking, waved a finger slightly toward the door. He turned, opened it, and went inside. She followed. He stood against a maple chest of drawers and sipped the tea and looked out at the wan Washington afternoon. A cloud deck made everything pale, diffusing the light, and the bulletproof glass in the windows further softened it. The lawn was green with the promise of spring, but that, too, was deceptive, as they replaced brown or worn patches with rolls of grass on an instant's notice. People got replaced the same way, he thought, when they failed or didn't live up to expectations. Politicians learned the lesson early.

Barbara Carr looked at him for a while, her face thoughtful, then she closed the door to his bedroom. She caught the eye of the lieutenant colonel who had come quietly up behind them, carrying the red phone case. He sat down in the hall, expressionless, and watched her close the heavy, carved door.

Barbara sat down on the bed. It was old-fashioned and high, with dark wood and a deep blue coverlet. She sat with her hands on her knees, as though waiting for a bus to arrive from somewhere, and then deliberately tucked one toe against the heel of her other shoe. Knowles turned toward her at that moment, the cup to his lips.

They were nice shoes, he noted, very nice. Black with the mid-length heel that looked better than the flat-footed things women were wearing these days, or at least the women he saw. She pried one shoe off with her toe and then repeated the gesture with the other foot. The shoes made little noise on the thick carpet. In the room there was only the faint hum of traffic noise.

She didn't look up at him, she just kept sitting there with her hands on her knees. Knowles began to think about what was happening. He thought about Catherine and the last time she had sat on that bed two years ago and tried to remember if she had done the same thing, taken her shoes off. No, it had been just the opposite. She had put on a pair of those low-heeled practical things, and then her coat, and then had marched down to the side entrance where the limousine was waiting, sure she would come back from a week in the hospital and everything would be all right. But as he thought about that the image slipped away and all he could see was Barbara Carr and her black shoes now lying on their sides on the thick tan rug, a very pretty combination, and then he looked at her eyes, so deep and dark, as they looked up at him, and he knew what was going to happen and for the first time in years he wanted it.

Carl Jagens stood in a small, private conference room and watched the earth turn on its side with majestic slowness. Up and around and down, the browns and blues and whites cycling forever. He had been up in space long enough that it didn't bother him anymore. Standing in a rotating reference frame had no visceral impact on him. All that mattered was local acceleration and "local vertical," the unconscious habit the mind has of assigning a specific direction as "up" and then coordinating every motion with that. It was all a mix of primordial instincts, but you had to be calm to let them work. At the moment, though, he was not particularly calm.

"What do you mean, you can't find him?" Carl barked into the comm mike in his hand.

The White House switchboard said something equivocal and Carl demanded to talk to Grace Price. A click. Another click. She answered cheerily and he forced his voice to be charming. "Hiya, Lovely. Trying to reach the old man."

"Well, I think he's resting, Carl."

"Can you slip me through to him? This is really important."

"Well, I'll buzz his private line, the one in his bedroom. But only once, understand?"

"Bless you."

"I'm buzzing."

"Yeah, I feel that way sometimes myself."

"Oh, I didn't mean—" She giggled, and the giggling embarrassed her. *"Carl, I thought you people were in orbit by now."*

"We are."

"You're calling from out there? How exciting. I never get used to . . . Oh, the President is coming on the line."

Carl smiled to himself. "G'bye, Lovely."

"Knowles here."

"This is Carl Jagens, Mister President. I'm wondering what's going on down there. The Vandenberg hold."

"Why not ask Chuck Bradshaw?" The President's voice was harsh.

"I . . . didn't reach him, Mister President," Carl replied. It wasn't precisely a lie because he hadn't tried.

Knowles sighed. *"Okay. Is this line secure? Where are you?"* Carl gave him the proper code designation. *"Here's the story then."* In a few words Knowles filled in the strategy. There had to be at least four launches from Kennedy Space Center. The NASA people would

214

act as though Kennedy was a backup, getting set for later missions if they were required, and that Vandenberg was still the site of the last crew launches. The Air Force was arranging for doubles who looked like Bander, Menshov, and the rest, to remain at Vandenberg and look busy while the real astronauts assembled at Kennedy.

"I see," Carl said slowly when the President was finished. "It's that bad then? It seems chancy, sir."

"*Everything's chancy,*" Knowles sighed.

"If the Under Secretary for the Air Force believes he can hold Vandenberg together long enough . . ."

"*Him?*" the President said, perking up. "*He used to be in the House, from Massachusetts. We used to say they named a town after him—Marblehead.*"

"Well, sir—" Carl stopped. He was certain he heard a woman's laughter in the background, a light and sparkling tone that seemed somewhat familiar. He frowned and went on. "Still, I wonder—"

"*Don't wonder. Just finish your job up there and don't tell anybody—repeat, anybody—about this.*"

"Of course not, sir. But if there are saboteurs at Vandenberg, I should think some strong measures are in order."

"*Such as?*"

"Sabotage is treason, sir."

"*Rogers says they have suspects. That's all.*" He seemed to want to end the conversation.

"Saboteurs should be shot. This is—"

"*I don't want more on my hands. Shiva is enough.*"

"I don't understand the delay, sir. This sandwiches the ground effort into a smaller time frame."

"*It has to be done.*"

Carl felt the words coming out of him before he could stop. "But you're jeopardizing everything! I can't believe these fanatics could force Bradshaw to change the mission plan. This is *your* decision, isn't it, Mister President?"

"*I arrived at this decision after—*"

"Don't give me that!" Carl exploded, interrupting rudely. "Something's changed, something's *wrong*. Bradshaw—"

"*Look, Carl,*" the President snapped, a hard edge to his voice. "*I know a switch like this upsets you guys in*

215

*orbit. I know you've been under a lot of pressure. But
you don't understand the situation on the ground. I—*"

"Mister President, it's not the pressure up here, it's
the screwups down *there* I'm talking about!"

"*Cut it, Carl.*" The even tougher edge to the President's voice made Carl stop, his mouth open. He
breathed deeply and stared wide-eyed at the wall for a
moment as he recalculated.

"Ah . . . very good, sir," he said finally, in a controlled
voice. "Sorry. Sorry to have disturbed you."

"*Take it easy, Carl. You're all tightened up. Goodbye.*" The line was suddenly static as Knowles hung up
abruptly.

Carl carefully replaced the comm mike. *I know
you've been under a lot of pressure.* What did that
mean? How could Knowles know that, for certain, unless
somebody told him? Unless *Bradshaw* told him. Something like that wouldn't come up unless it was important
—they didn't have time for gossip and idle talk. So
Bradshaw was concerned about him, and had been talking about him. Now this change. A switch at the last moment, with doubles for the astronauts? Was the B team
alerted? Was all this to conceal the fact that they were
sending up *more* than the rest of the Alpha and Omega
teams?

A replacement?

Somebody had to take the strain off Jagens, who was
showing the pressure too much?

But everyone—*everyone*—was under extraordinary pressure, every man, woman, and child in the world!

Carl leaned back against the bulkhead, suddenly
somewhat dizzy. The earth tumbled with stately slowness outside.

Was that it? Were they stalling? They'd have to do
some training, sure—unless they used somebody in the
present teams. Diego, maybe. Sure, bring him up to
speed on Alpha's job, make him commander. They
could do that in a few days. In the hubbub surrounding
the switchover from Vandenberg, few outside NASA
would notice. They'd put it down to pressure, loss of
courage. They'd "understand."

Then, when Diego reached orbit, there'd be a last-minute set of orders. Carl would be out, relieved of command, flying in the backup team, stuck with Omega, manning a scope or something.

They never came at you right out, they never did. You got kicked upstairs. Maybe they'd put him in command of Ground Control or attached to the goddamn President's Special Advisory Board.

Carl slammed a balled fist against the bulkhead. It was all going by so goddamn fast. *Was* that what the President meant? Was he covering for Bradshaw?

Earth, blue and tan, blurred by clouds, continued to spin while Carl breathed deeply, blinking in slow rhythm.

No. No, it was too much of a long shot. He wouldn't put something like that past Bradshaw, or past that politician in the White House—but at this late hour, the risks were too high. Bradshaw wouldn't have the courage to try something that risky.

Carl smiled slowly to himself. He had had a bad moment there, but now he was feeling better. He should keep in mind that these guys, Knowles and Bradshaw and the rest, were fundamentally weak. They were flawed. They were trained to be compromisers. They made deals; deals with people, countries, races, deals with themselves. That's how they had gotten where they were. No, the real explanation for this switch to Canaveral was what they said: Knowles wasn't willing to knock a few heads together, even if he did talk tough. If *he* were down there, as President, he'd have those saboteurs lined up and shot on live television. That would sew up the problem fast.

Still, he should stay on his guard. He was nearly home now. In a little while he'd be out in space, beyond any control by Knowles or Bradshaw and the others who preferred compromise to courage. Then this thing would go *right*.

Carl Jagens snorted derisively to himself and turned away from the sight of the revolving, mottled Earth.

13 May: Collision minus 12 days, 19 hours

Lisa felt drained, not of emotion, but of a capacity for emotion. She sat listlessly in the seat of the clattering helicopter that was flying her and Nino Solari up the main complex to the easternmost launching pad. They

217

flew past Canaveral's historic Pad thirty-nine, where they were readying the rocket that would take up Zaborovskii, Short, and Schumacher only hours away. The copter swerved and she lolled listlessly against the seat belt, her eyes half-closed.

Lisa was tired, not physically, but mentally. She had worked so hard, concentrating on the task at hand, that she only dimly realized that she had locked away most of her human responses. Her only feeling was relief that Diego had gotten off all right and had docked at Station One.

"Jesus, look at that!" Nino Solari leaned forward, between the seats, to point through the plastic dome. Lisa glanced at him, then down.

The distant horizon was marked with the smudges of fires and the wheeling dragonflies of helicopters. The tent cities were smashed and burning. Hundreds of thousands of people swarmed across the reclaimed swamp, fighting among themselves, falling in untidy clusters of gassed bodies, but still, by sheer numbers, overwhelming the Army. Thousands lay unmoving along the fence. Here and there attacks had succeeded, the fence breached by screaming Gabriels—to be met by gas-masked soldiers and clouds of knock-out mist. And sometimes by bullets. In quieter sections men tossed limp bodies into trucks for hauling away to detention camps.

But at several points serious major attacks had begun. Trucks, campers, several buses, a U.S. mail truck, and a bulky gelled gas carrier had been used to knock down the electric fence. Bodies were strewn all over the vehicles, but still the Gabriels came on, squashing bodies beneath their muddy boots, screaming, shooting. Lisa could hear the sharp bursts of machine gun fire that met them.

They were taking the helicopter because the launch had been advanced three hours. Their suits were in the mobile white rooms near the base of the giant red gantry. Most of the normal NASA procedures had been scrapped, drastically altered, or bent out of shape.

"They're breaking through!" Nino said loudly.

"The Army will hold them," the pilot shouted back, but there was more hope than confidence in his voice.

There was the sound like the strums of a giant guitar

and the helicopter shuddered. The pilot swore and veered sharply to the east. "What was that?" Nino Solari yelled.

"Bullets. We were hit," the pilot said. He looked grim and his eyes raced over the control panel. He threw a switch and the shuddering stopped but the craft slanted sharply toward the ground. "Gotta set it down," he cried.

The chopper swept low over a tank battalion, buttoned up and puffing blue smoke, then between a Military Police temporary barracks and a black column of smoke from a burning truck. It set down with a bump. The pilot brushed at them with his fingers. "Move! *Move!* Jump, damn it!"

Lisa and Nino tumbled out of the aircraft and ran, bent over, under the whumping blades and toward the barracks. The pilot passed them at a lope. "Hit the deck!" he shouted. They slid into shelter behind the barracks just as the helicopter whoofed into a ball of fire.

"What the hell happened?" Nino demanded indignantly. "Shouldn't you have been out over the ocean?"

"Thought I was out of rifle range," the pilot shrugged. "Guess they have something good."

"Never mind fixing blame," Lisa snapped. "We've got to get to Forty-one—and fast!"

They looked around the corner of the barracks and saw the mob disconcertingly close. Shouting, chanting Gabriels had broken through, overrunning the Army, trampling their own dead and unconscious. A nearby tank thundered and the ground shook. An explosion in the crowd threw bodies into the air. And parts of bodies. Lisa was splattered and looked down to see that it was blood. She shivered and stood up, grabbing at Nino's shoulder. "Move!"

They ran, followed by the pilot. A tank whumped, then another. Dust, blood, and screams filled the air as the huge tanks fired pointblank into the crowd. The mob didn't stop. Those behind ran up over the barricades of twisted fencing and dead bodies, throwing themselves between the crash vehicles and joining the slaughtered soldiers. Machine guns chattered. An olive-drab helicopter swept in and the soldiers ran back as the nerve gas was dumped. The Gabriels fell limply into the wreckage.

There was a momentary lull as those in the front ranks

fell, gasping and swearing. But the screams of those beyond were still to be heard. A soldier broke and ran. Lisa saw a sergeant turn and without haste shoot the soldier in the back. She felt like vomiting but she ran, breathlessly. An Army captain intercepted her, staring.

"You're . . . you're Colonel Bander and . . ." He looked back at the mob as a grenade went off. "What the hell are you doing here? Oh, the chopper that came down. What can we do for you?"

"Pad Forty-one—*now!*" Lisa's heart was pounding. She heard the screams rising beyond the mound of still bodies. A truck tilted against the fence exploded with a loud *whump.*

"Right," the officer said crisply. "Cooper!"

The sergeant that had shot the deserter ran over, saluted, his eyes checking out the astronauts. "Sir!"

"Get these people to Pad Forty-one on the double!"

"Yes, sir!" The sergeant took only a moment, his head swiveling around. "This way!" He started running toward a jeep with a top-mounted .50-caliber machine gun. "Out!" he yelled at the driver while he was still twenty meters away. He kept shouting until the driver heard him and responded. But his reaction was not fast enough for Cooper, who dragged the luckless private from the seat. The gunner standing in the back looked frightened, but she held on as Cooper started up the machine.

Lisa and Nino jumped in. The chopper pilot waved at them and ran toward the east. The jeep gunned around a tank, just missing the flare from its main gun as it fired over the heads of the mob into the advancing thousands beyond.

The screams and gunfire died behind them as Cooper raced along the concrete roads. He sometimes took shortcuts, which shook up the passengers. Lisa looked up at the gunner, pale and thin beneath her big steel helmet. They exchanged wan smiles and the gunner gave her a thumbs-up gesture, which was aborted by a two-wheel drift around an oncoming Cobra tank destroyer column.

Pad Forty-one rose red and spidery before them and Lisa pointed at the mobile white room parked at the base. "Anything else I can do?" the sergeant yelled as they sped across the hard-packed sand toward the massive bus.

Lisa shook her head. "Nothing except make certain

they don't get here until after we get off and Pad Thirty-nine launches."

"Yes, sir," Sergeant Cooper grinned. "And good luck."

"Thank you, Sergeant," Lisa said as the jeep slid to a halt and they jumped out. Cooper waved at them as he watched the two astronauts trot toward the big vehicle. The door opened and they climbed in.

"Well . . ." Cooper said, looking around at the gunner for the first time. "Listen, I thought going back we might swing along the fence and you can use that piece of yours."

"Uh, yeah, okay, sarge."

Cooper grinned. "Yeah, I know. Look at it this way. If they stop the launch, *none* of us may survive."

"Sure, right." The slim gunner gulped.

"Just do it, soldier. Think about it later." He put the jeep into gear and spun it around toward the distant fenceline.

Waiting for Lisa and Nino were the suit technicians, the complete professionals that seemed to ignore totally the faint explosions heard through the suiting room walls. Lisa greeted them with a smile, then began the complicated ritual.

Suiting up had often been compared to the ceremony of the matador donning his "suit of lights." But no matador's suit, no suit of armor, no uniform was ever more elegant, more complex, or more essential. Only a few coronation robes, bedecked with jewels, were more expensive. At one hundred forty thousand dollars each, they were the end product of decades of research and development.

Lisa saw the suit techs doing the last bit of lubrication on moving parts and a last-last check in total functions. Each astronaut was assigned a technician, with assistants as needed. Lisa, then Nino, excused themselves and went to the toilet for one final visit. Within the small white room Lisa inserted the tube, fitted it carefully, then fastened up her tight-fitting inner suit. A connection to a urine bag would be made later. The solid waste problem would be handled in the weightlessness of space, by a complicated procedure with self-adhering waste-disposal bags.

The count was moving well when Lisa returned. Despite the chaos the mission was not scrubbed. At least not yet. It couldn't be, really, not even if it endangered the lives of the astronauts. Too much was riding on it.

Technicians attached and methodically checked out the biomedical harness. There were five EKG sensors, signal conditioners, and a myriad of other electronic devices. Communications were checked. Helmets locked in place. Lisa began breathing the O_2 oxygen at 14 PSI. Just before takeoff the changeover would be made to one hundred percent O_2, with the pressure dropping gradually from 14 PSI to 5 PSI. This would wash the nitrogen from their blood and lessen the likelihood of bends in the remote event that the cabin did not hold its pressure during its greatest moment of stress, the boost.

Lisa paid attention to every single detail. While there was a complete spacesuit hanging in a sealed locker, in case anything failed or was even uncertain, she did not want to take the time to switch or retest the new suit. She had logged over a hundred hours in the suit she had on and had confidence in it. The pressure points were familiar. Undiscovered pressure points, in a new suit or a suit rarely used, could become maddening after four or five cruel hours on a flight couch.

Every flight crew had an air of preoccupation at this time. Not even the dramatic events taking place outside could penetrate; controlling that was the job of other professionals. The minds of the flight crew were on the critical events in the countdown. With so much hanging on this particular set of launches there was more stress than ever upon the astronauts. Nino had to be reminded to step into his suit, then to be prompted on suiting procedures he had gone through dozens of times. Even Lisa had to be nudged a couple of times.

But eventually they were suited up, breathing on an independent system. The suiting crew leader gave a thumbs-up signal and spoke into a mike. Lisa and Nino started toward the door to get into the crew transfer van and everyone around them broke into applause.

Lisa flushed with surprise and pride. In the early days of the manned space program it had been common enough to applaud, but in the day-to-day shuttle program such little touches had been abandoned. No one applauded the breadwinner going off to the office.

She looked at Nino in time to see his flashing grin

222

fade away. He looked nervously at her, rekindled his smile, and lifted a hand.

"Hey, how about that?" he grinned, speaking over the suit radio.

They waved awkwardly at the suiting crew, then at the applauding people outside, and sat down gratefully within the transfer van. The big white truck rumbled off, with swaying technicians monitoring the telemetry on a panel. Nino stood up for a moment to look out of the window. Then he sat down again, his face tight.

"Some smoke," he said. "To the south. Can't see much."

The van stopped at Pad Forty-one and Nino gestured for Lisa to get out first. She stopped on the steps, surprised at the number of people still around. They, too, were applauding. She waved at them, but was looking over their heads. Merritt Island, where the Kennedy Space Center was located, had not changed all that much since the historic sixties and seventies. The Indian River still moved sluggishly to the west and the Banana River to the east. Eighty-four thousand acres of tropical vegetation, sand, and some of the most expensive machinery and structures in the world. A short distance away was the blockhouse, a two-story structure of twelve-foot-thick reinforced concrete, with only a dome protruding above the ground. Lisa smiled faintly, thinking what she often thought at that moment, that all that concrete and steel was there for the protection of the launch crew and VIPs, while she and other astronauts sat high in the air with a million or more pounds of fuel under their butts. It was one of the reasons everyone in the world didn't want their job, no matter what they said.

Lisa waved in the direction of the blockhouse periscopes and again at a nearby blackbox television camera. Hi, folks. Just your average everyday world-saver going off to work. Clutching the briefcase-sized portable ventilator with its supply of pure oxygen, Lisa went slowly down the steps, awkward in the fifty-two-pound suit. No one was really comfortable in the suits until the law of gravity was suspended.

She looked up at the tapering tower, spectacular in its bright orange corrosion-resistant trappings. It cost one hundred forty-seven million dollars in the sixties and that much again for maintenance and additions over the years. The elevator was cramped with sandbags stacked and wired against the outside walls. They stared out through the steel openwork, over the sandbags. Something pinged off the framework and flecks of paint drifted down as they rose. Another shot thumped into the sandbags and everyone but the astronauts ducked; they were too bulky and had not heard the shot inside their helmets. Lisa saw dents and scratches all over the usually immaculate gantry.

She pointed her thumb at them and asked Nino a question. "What if they put one into the ship?" she said over the suit radios.

He ran his tongue over dry lips and shrugged. *"The gantry is between the nearest bunch and the ship. Those north and south are too far to do any damage. Or much damage,"* he amended with a wry grin.

In thirty seconds the gantry elevator had delivered them to the White Room, at the three-hundred-sixty-foot level.

Smoke on the horizon. Choppers circled everywhere. Lisa saw a flash, then two more, bigger and farther off, somewhere near the main gate, but then nothing else.

The White Room was a tiny, enclosed cubicle at the end of the swing arm which provided protected entry into the spacecraft. The preferred crew-escape route for critical emergencies, after strapping in, was across the swing-arm, into the elevator, and down to the white-painted ground rescue vehicle—an armored personnel carrier, staffed by a four-man crew, which would whisk them away to safety. The rescue crew had just one responsibility: to charge in, toss the astronauts into their vehicle, hang breathing systems around their necks, and drive like hell for safety. They were seldom needed, but their rehearsals often scared the astronauts more than the takeoffs.

There was another way out, via a long slanting cable and a safety loop, but that was even more dangerous. You hit the ground pretty hard.

"Hi, Gunter," Lisa said to the White Room "commandant." He had been the majordomo of the White Room for almost twenty years, since the beginning of the space shuttle program, and had the confidence of every generation of astronauts. He tolerated no nonsense, from the flight crews themselves, right on down to the military guards, and including the highest NASA officials. He had once refused a Vice-President of the United States admittance and made the politician smile and like it. His authority was nearly absolute and Lisa felt better at once.

Nino was put into the module first, which gave Lisa a chance for another look at the horizon. More smoke, more helicopters, some distant moving figures. A mist erupting here and there, stilling some doll-like creatures. Very little sound.

The wind was getting stronger. A gull limped across the sky. Lisa could feel the swing-arm sway slightly and felt momentarily nervous that the wind might increase to the point where they'd scrub the launch. But another look at the horizon and she knew they wouldn't. The bird would fly today and all the other birds with it. They had to. The safety factors would be stretched, refigured, possibly even ignored. No one had to say it; it was simply taken for granted.

Lisa looked down at the booster venting off excess pressure in clouds of liquid oxygen, and saw the American flag painted big and bold on the white side of the ship. Yes, it was America, but it was Russia, too, and humanity. But why did it take a global disaster to make nations cooperate? We could be putting up domes on Mars and sending probes down into Jupiter's atmosphere from orbiting stations now, if only the world could get together. A few pennies a year from each person. They'd never miss it. Skip a lunch once a year and NASA, or some global space team, could have colonies in space, research stations on the planets, probes going to the stars. Skip that lunch and a drink or two and mankind could have cryogenic ships going to other stars. Give us one percent of the welfare budget and we could do *all* those things, she thought.

"Lisa."

"Yes, Gunter, I'm ready."

Lisa grasped the bar and swung in deftly, in a well-rehearsed movement. She exchanged looks with Nino as she strapped down. They had been selected, certified, delivered, and sealed. It was going to be up to them now. The checkout began.

T minus thirty minutes and counting. One by one

those who were not needed left the White Room and descended. The room itself was swung away. Lisa listened to the complicated cross-chatter carefully. Wind conditions remained the only questionable factor in the countdown, and it was not too serious. Decades of launches had smoothed out the procedures. No one wanted to scrub. The immense Saturn 12-B was going to fly, come hell or . . . Gabriel's legions of fanatics.

T minus ten minutes and counting. "How they doing with the unauthorized visitors?" Nino Solari asked the blockhouse.

"*Holding*," was the laconic reply. He looked at Lisa and shrugged.

T minus eight minutes and counting. Lisa concerned herself with the complexities of the countdown procedure, but soon that was mostly done and she had time to think.

Think about what? The task ahead? No, that was dangerous. Think about the routine tasks. Concentrate. The routine, the known and rehearsed. The orderly and sane. The accepted, tested procedures. But the thoughts surfaced, unasked: Did anyone have the right to kill as she had seen?

But if they had not? If the soldiers had not fired and gassed and beaten back the invaders, what then? No Omega, no backup, no options. What of the millions—billions!—that were counting on them, praying for them, hoping? Did the majority always have the right? But this was a case of racial life and death! Surely even Brother Gabriel should see that! She pressed her lips together firmly. She herself was not indispensable, for there were other astronauts, but she *had* been selected as one of the best astronauts. It was a deadly, final game. Mankind needed the best players.

She noted that the switch to one hundred percent oxygen was occurring, with the pressure beginning to drop from fourteen to five pounds per square inch. With all the air usable a human did not need so much pressure.

Lisa shook her head, forcing her thoughts back to the here-and-now. "Control, how is *Omega Two* doing?"

"*Fifteen minutes behind you*, Omega One."

"And *Alpha*?"

"*Left Station One about an hour ago*, Omega One."

"Thank you, control."

Nino Solari spoke up. "Control, how are the unauthorized visitors coming along?"

"*Omega One, ready for interlock.*"

"Roger . . . but what are they doing?"

"*Omega One, ten seconds on my mark . . . five . . . four . . . three . . . two . . . one . . . mark!*"

"*T minus seven minutes,*" another voice stated.

"But the Gabriels," Nino complained. "What about them?"

"*Contained,*" another voice said in their radios. "*Don't worry about them, just stick to the launch procedures.*"

"Chuck?" Lisa asked. "That you? Listen, Chuck, what's happening down there?"

"*Never mind,*" Bradshaw snapped.

They lapsed into the tense jargon of their trade, repeating back numbers and checking constantly. Lisa's mind forgot everything but the launch. It had to be good . . . the first time. Minimum holds, no failures.

As Lisa's eyes ran again over the many dials she was reminded of the Englishman who said that astronauts were more like bus drivers than adventurers.

T minus one minute. Everything was *go.* The terminal count was on. Lisa looked at the green lights. No red. Escape module rocket ready.

T minus fifty seconds and holding. A minor problem while the inner chamber of the second stage engine cooled to prescribed limits. The delay of two minutes fifteen seconds affected both astronauts all out of proportion to the time lost.

"Damn it," Lisa snapped.

"*Hey, Beauty, you're on global teevee!*"

"Dink?"

"*The very same, Lovely. Your anchorperson for this historic flight. Hey, here we go. The count is continuing.*"

"*T minus forty-nine seconds and counting.*"

"*Colonel Bander? Major Solari? This is John Caleb Knowles.*"

Not now, thought Lisa. "Yes, Mister President?"

"*The hopes of America—and the world—go with you. Good luck . . . and good hunting.*"

"Thank you, sir."

"*Thank you, Mister President.*"

"T minus thirty-two seconds and counting."

"We'll be watching." .

"Thank you, sir, yes, sir." *Get out of the way!* Her eyes quickly scanned the board again. The second stage destruct system was activated, the automatic sequencer was on. There was little chatter on the circuits. The key checks of the navigation and guidance systems had been completed while the President had been making points with the world.

The last ten seconds seemed like an hour.

The booster was switched to full internal power. The power transfer was complete. In a few seconds they would have 1.9 million pounds of thrust up their tails.

"Eight."

Were they really going to do it or was this another cruel rehearsal?

"Seven."

Diego . . .

"Six."

Helium pressure down a point but still fine.

"Five."

The abort advisory system was fully activated.

"Four."

Nino had his fingers crossed, she noted.

"Three."

Would they be able to do the job?

"Two."

Could they do the job—could anyone?

"One . . . we have ignition . . ."

The roar was deep, the vibrations quivering through them like a bass note, deep and penetrating.

"We have lift-off."

The rocket rose from the pad slowly, almost ponderously, reluctantly. It hardly seemed to move at all, but the acceleration was building. Painstakingly the rocket climbed, trailing a fiery tail as bright as the sun. Lisa was pressed back into the couch, a giant's hand clenched down on her body.

"The tower is cleared." The control switched in that instant to Houston. But the vibrations, the noise, the shock waves of sound continued relentlessly. The Saturn 12-B rose like a star, a soaring fireball brighter than anything else in the Florida sky.

Lisa's sense of time was meshed with the spacecraft

clock, ticking off elapsed time. The altimeter reading rose. The computer flashed the trajectory parameters. The environmental and electrical systems were all in the green; the cabin pressure was bleeding down according to the schedule to prevent any blowup in the vacuum of space. The launch escape tower ejected; Nino could see out of his window.

"Omega One, *you are looking good.*"

Both Lisa and Nino were just along for the ride at that stage of the trip. Everything was automatic and predetermined. Changes would be taken care of within certain parameters. They could just gawk if they wanted. The first stage dropped away.

Both astronauts were old hands at shuttle launches; they were hardly tourists. But they were also human. The earth was a vast blue white marble outside their windows. Space was black until their eyes adjusted, and they saw stars. The second stage disconnected.

"*Insertion checklist,*" Houston said.

Lisa sighed and began the checking out. *Omega One* was in space.

The awful g-force lessened and they went through the routine quickly, reporting back by rote. Everything was fine. Then someone slipped.

"*The Gabriels learned a lesson,*" someone chuckled.

"*Get off the line,*" Bradshaw snapped.

"Hey, wait!" Lisa said.

"Omega One, *give us your pressure reading on tank two and—*"

"Chuck, cut the scam! What did he mean, the Gabriels learned a lesson?" There was a long silence. Only the sound of static. "Chuck?"

She heard him sigh. "*All right. They broke through. Several thousand of them. They were climbing the gantry as it pulled back. They . . . were were all over the firepit . . .*"

"You mean—oh, my God!"

Cremated. Seared. The great washing flame of the rocket engines crisping bodies like bugs. *Thousands.* Human beings. Americans like her. Believers. *People.* She felt her gorge rise and fought it. "Chuck . . . uh . . . we . . ."

"*There was nothing else to do, Lisa. You know that. They were counting on us stopping, but . . . but we couldn't. You* know *we couldn't, don't you? You* had *to get off."*

"Wha—what about *Omega Two?"*

"No problem. No one got near. They lifted about . . . um . . . a minute or so ago. No problems."

"Just us . . . how . . . how many were there?"

"I don't know. It doesn't matter. I mean, it's done."

"Chuck, how many?"

"Don't know, Colonel Bander. Several hundred. Maybe a couple thousand. We'll never know."

Lisa knew what that meant. The firepit burnt clean, the gantry washed with flame, leaving only anonymous crisps and blackened parts. A couple of thousand. Another few thousand along the fences. Millions more dead in riots all over the world. The suicides and murders. The triggering of insanity in hundreds of thousands of psychotics. Shiva *was* a destroyer, even if it never got to Earth.

"Chuck, I—"

"Hold it, Lisa . . ." She heard a mumble of conversation, then Chuck said, *"Yes, all right, that's it, then. Omega One, this is Launch Control, we are evacuating the Cape. From now all, everything will come out of Houston. Repeat, we are evacuating the Cape—"*

"Chuck! Launch Control! What in blazes is going on?"

Another voice came on. *"Omega One, we are closing down operation at this site. Repeat, we are transferring control to Houston. Do you read me?"*

"Chuck!"

He came back on the line. *"They're overrunning everything, Lisa, wrecking, destroying. We . . . we won't be able to—good God!"* Lisa heard an explosion, muffled but potent.

"Chuck, what's going *on?"*

"They blew Pad Thirty-nine! The VAB is on fire! They're everywhere! The Army can't hold them! Jesus!" Lisa heard another explosion. *"Why are they doing it? We've launched everything! They blew their last chance when the birds flew. Are they* crazy?"

Lisa heard another voice urging Bradshaw to leave. He called out to her over the increasing noise. *"Omega! It's up to you now! We won't be able to lift any more birds from here! It's your baby! Good luck! Tell—"*

There was an explosion and an abrupt silence. Not even a carrier wave. Lisa stared at the radio. She looked at Nino Solari who was also staring, his jaw muscles knotting.

"Omega One, *this is Houston. We are assuming control. Please inform us what your—*"

"Houston, what the hell is going on?" demanded Nino.

"Omega One, *we do not have that information. We will transmit as soon as we are informed. Please recheck your telemetry and phase with us.*"

Lisa looked at Nino with hollow eyes. "There's nothing behind us now," he said. His tongue touched his lips and then retreated, as if shamed. He blinked and took a deep breath. "Well, Colonel?"

Lisa also took a deep breath. "Start transmitting to Houston, Major Solari. They must match up on their computers."

"Yes, sir."

New York City suffered a minor meteorite strike, but the main damage had come long before from the rioting. The city was a dead hulk, burning itself out, its streets littered with bodies. The people that were left lived in high-rise fortresses without power or water. The city stank.

The Legion of Destiny held a great rally in Kansas City. A reporter covered it for CBS and was beaten and mutilated, her crew shot.

Chuck Bradshaw slept on a cot, only seconds away from the banks of computer terminals and communications equipment. He had leg burns, the Army had gotten him out. A lot of launch crew hadn't made it.

Colonel Mezieres, of the French Air Force, attached to backup on Alpha, rescued Dr. George Canfield from an angry mob in Houston. Canfield promptly went back to work on an analysis of Shiva data and moved into a barracks within the guarded perimeter.

Barbara Carr talked to the White House doctor and received a bottle of sleeping pills. She said the constant death, destruction, and depression had made her sleepless.

A group of Gabriel's followers took legal action and brought the government of the United States into federal

231

court in an attempt to stop the Shiva mission. Wearily, the federal judge put the case over until May twenty-seventh, one day after the expected intersection with Shiva.

A relatively unknown television comic became a big hit by appearing on numerous programs, wearing gray robes and a patently false beard, carrying placards announcing *The End of the World* and treating it like a fire sale.

Michael Potter, the Secretary of Space, announced to the world via global communications satellites that Station Three had seceded from the international cartel that had created it and, with Brazilian president Juscelino Belchior de Alencar, had formed the independent nation of Apollo. No immigration would be accepted and after Shiva struck they would build a Terran empire. The new nation lasted twenty-six hours before internal strife ended it.

Py Rudd of NBC reported that nineteen babies born at the Hollywood Presbyterian Hospital during that month had been named Shiva.

Wade Dennis came in and dropped his clipboard onto Caroline Weinberg's console. She made a face and shoved it to one side as the lanky man leaned a hip against her desk.

"Why do you carry that thing, anyway?" she asked. "You look like a stock clerk with it. You don't *use* it."

He smiled at her. "Sure, I do." He flipped open the thin metal cover and ruffled pages with his fingers. "A place to carry my doodle paper."

"Your doodle paper?" She made a face. "I hate it when you get me asking dumb questions."

"It isn't a dumb question. My doodle paper is what I doodle on. I think while I'm doodling. There have been plenty of psychological studies about doodling. *Some Aspects of Subconscious Random Artistic Expression.* You should read it sometime. Your doodles, for example—"

"I don't doodle."

"Yes, you do. They are very small and precise and you do them when you are on the phone. I gave some to Nick Dietrich. He thought they were marvelous. He blueprinted you like a readout."

"Who is Nick Dietrich? One of your games buddies?"

"Don't knock it. I get four thousand a year from that Trojan Horse game Quince and I sold to Videosport. Or I did," he muttered.

"Who is Dietrich and—"

"Oh, he's the author of that paper. *Some Aspects of Subconscious Random—*"

"Yeah, yeah."

"He read you like a book, just from your doodles. Told me how compulsively neat you were, how you think—"

"I'm not *compulsive—*"

"—like with your crotch *and* your higher logic centers, in a kind of synthetic committee, and—"

"Your Nick is a nano-mind nullskull!"

"Read you like a book. Paperback, of course. Publication date uncertain. In danger of being remaindered soon after."

"Huh," she snorted and then sat up as her screen began to print. "Here we go."

"Omega One?"

"And *Omega Two*. Got that info?"

Wade pulled a cassette out of a pocket and handed it to her. She slapped it into a slot and previewed the contents on a secondary screen, then backed it to the touch-point and stopped. Her fingers drummed on the console as she watched the information being fed in from Houston. She picked up a pen and put a border of circles and squares around the word *Boston* on the NASA stationery.

"Can I have that?" Wade said, straight-faced, pointing.

"What? Oh." She looked at the doodle, then abruptly crumpled the paper. "I'll never be able to do that again," she complained. "I'll have visions of shrinks poring over my trash basket, chuckling to themselves."

Wade grinned. "Want to see mine? Nick says I'm a closet van Gogh."

"Van Gogh was crazy."

"He *went* crazy because he wasn't appreciated. Want to see?"

"No. I might learn more about you than I care to know."

"Don't want to probe my random unconscious?"

"It's pretty random, all right."

Wade started to answer but the screen blipped. Caroline punched in the cassette program and the information

233

mixed in an electronic stew for two full seconds. Then the screen wiped and a new set of figures began building.

"*Omega* is going well," Caroline said. "Maybe . . . just *maybe* it will all work . . ."

"Maybe," conceded Wade. He picked up his clipboard and began drawing arrows sticking into spheres.

14 May: Collision minus 11 days, 7 hours

Captain Saperstein lay in the shade of a gutted tank. The smoke cleared in a gust of tropical wind and he could see across the littered area to the wreckage of Pad Thirty-nine. They had dynamited one corner; the immense red structure stood, but there was a slight tilt to it. Beneath were charred black blobs; bodies melted together in death. The slim young officer winced as he eased his position. The bandage around his arm was soaked in blood, his shoulder stiff and awkward.

Near Saperstein, with his feet sticking out into the sunlight, was a young soldier. He was dead. His last words had been, "Why me?" A good question, Saperstein thought. Why any of us? What a stupid waste! Of people, of material, of time. Was mankind really so incredibly stupid as to sabotage its only hope? Looking around at the wreckage and the bodies, he thought maybe it was.

Sergeant Cooper trotted up and knelt down, his chest heaving with exertion. He blew out his breath with an apologetic grin. "Getting too old . . . for this . . . sir! Whew!" He caught his breath with a fist to his chest, gulped, and gave his report. "Colonel Gregg says we might as well form up south of here. No use losing more people."

The noncom gestured to the west and north. "The Gabriels are drifting back. They failed, but I don't think they know it. They think they've screwed up all the pads." He pointed to the south, still breathing with difficulty. "They went through here and down that way. They did some kind of damage at every pad, damn their eyes."

"It can be fixed . . . somehow."

Cooper nodded. "Yes, sir. Colonel Gregg wants us to join up with him farther on down."

"Abandon this area? They might come back and *really* blow things up."

Cooper shrugged. "Dunno about that, Captain. The colonel, he said move our asses. Maybe they want to beef up the protection of the main complex, I dunno."

"Okay, give me a hand up." The sergeant helped Saperstein to his feet. He pointed at the dead soldier. "See if he still has a medix." The sergeant put a hand on the soldier's chest, shook his head sadly, and then lifted the soldier up enough to tug at the medix kit on his belt. He tore out the sealed bandage, and used it to rebandage Saperstein's arm. Another sergeant had come up, looking very tired, and leaned against the tank.

"Valentine, I want you to get a burial detail together and clean up this mess."

The sergeant, a lean Southerner, spat downwind and squinted into the glare. "Jesus, Cap'n, they're a heap of them."

"There's a bulldozer about three, four hundred meters down that way. Use that. Get the dogtags, if you can, and put them in a mass grave." A brief mental picture flashed into Saperstein's mind: an old newsreel clip of a bulldozer pushing up heaps of corpses at Dachau or one of those concentration camps just liberated. He shook his head doggedly, wincing.

"Hey, you okay, sir?" the sergeant asked.

"Yes. Do it now and catch up. Find someone with a strong stomach to drive the dozer. Keep five men with you. Do what you can."

"Yes, sir," Sergeant Valentine said, spitting carefully into the sunlight. He walked away, calling out to various soldiers, some of them wearing bandages.

"There," Sergeant Cooper said, sealing the bandage on Saperstein's arm. He looked around at the battlefield, his eyes bleak. "Never thought I'd be fighting Americans, sir."

"Me, either, Sergeant. Get 'em together and let's move out."

"Uh, sir?"

"Yes, Cooper?"

"One problem, sir." He indicated the southern route with his head. "Some crazy loon threw some Civol-7 into the canal . . ."

"Oh, sweet Christ." Civol-7 was a heavier-than-air gas,

a knockout gas to healthy humans, but often deadly to wounded or tired people. It sat in pools until strong winds or the ultraviolet of the sun destroyed it. The canal bisected the island, a way of controlling the water after the intrusion of so many buildings and security blocks. Filled with Civol-7, it would be impassable. They'd have to go around. "All right, Sergeant, we'll go around. Get 'em on their feet."

"Sir."

14 May: Collision minus 11 days, 3 hours

The docking went smoothly. Lisa's ship, officially *Omega One*, but already called *Last Chance* by many, drifted slowly into position, spinning at the exact rate of the vast double wheel that was Station One. The complex linkage of tubes and struts seemed to have stopped turning as the *Omega One* matched up. Lisa relinquished control to Station One's expert dockers and everything went on automatic.

With the tiny cabin pinging with the sound of readouts and the muttering of dockers Lisa took the opportunity to look at Station One. She'd seen it dozens of times before, on dozens of approaches in her capacity as shuttle pilot, a position in which all astronauts were obliged to serve. It had seemed vast, too spidery to be safe, too bulky to be secure in the sky: two thin doughnuts, one "above" the other, with tubes connecting them and tubes extending to the thick cylinder that ran down through the center of each "doughnut hole."

Will I ever see it again? she thought. She had no great emotional attachment to it. It was a marvelous piece of engineering, damned handy, with a fantastic record of service to mankind, but it gave her no more thrill than the landing field at Vandenberg. It was man's first spaceport, a way station to better things.

There had been a time when she looked upon it with awe, but that time had passed. She'd been many times to Luna, though not yet to Mars. She'd docked at all the stations, and while One was impressive, it was no longer awesome. Familiarity breeds indifference.

"*Station One to* Omega One, *twenty seconds to mag-lock.*"

"Roger, Station One," Lisa said automatically. She scanned the control panel. Briefly her eyes stopped on the large panel, its dials dark, intruding upon the cramped quarters. The guidance controls for the atomic missiles now riding quietly in orbit in band four, nineteen deadly bombs, mindless and potent.

"Fifteen seconds."

Nino Solari looked over, his dark eyes unreadable as he searched Lisa's face. He saw what she was looking at, but made no comment. The power they controlled was enough to devastate Earth, but none of them had been picked because they were unstable enough to entertain such thoughts. Besides, the destruction of Earth was pretty imminent, anyway.

"Ten seconds."

The rectangular maw of Station One's landing hangar was growing swiftly. It always seemed to come at you too fast, Lisa thought. The forward rockets flamed, sending them forward in their seats, pushing against the straps. The metal walls swallowed them. Lights along the inner surfaces were bright. The Omega One's hull clanged as the maglocks reached out and made contact. The slender white ship quivered slightly, then was pulled toward one surface. That surface became, psychologically, "down," even though there was still no gravity. They stopped with a cushioned shiver.

"Omega One, you are docked. Transport tube will engage in a moment. Welcome aboard."

"Thank you, Station One. We want refueling to begin at once."

"Roger, Omega One. Refueling in progress."

Lisa leaned forward and looked out of the port. Spacesuited figures in bright orange were coming up out of a hatch. They popped a small hatch and began snaking out the thick fuel line tubes. One of them looked up and waved at Lisa, who waved back automatically.

"Want to go in?" Nino asked, his hands on his belt release.

"No. Yes. All right." She sat there as Nino disengaged and floated up, twisting and wiggling back toward the airlock.

What is the matter with me? she wondered. I feel detached, vague, remote. I'm going through the motions. I felt this way before we lifted. Only the sight of those bleeding bodies, the fanaticism of the Gabriels, only that brought me awake. What is the matter?

She pressed her belt release and shoved up, weightless in the cabin's cramped space. It was easier to maneuver within the capsule in space. Volume forbidden to her by gravity was now available. She snaked back toward the lock, saw Nino waiting.

"You go ahead," she waved. He looked at her, then swung his helmet into position and locked it down.

"*Okay*," he said over the radio.

They heard the tube connecting, then saw the green light. Nino wedged himself into the tiny lock and thumbed the closing button. Lisa saw him looking at her, but a light reflection made a bright bar across the plastic and she couldn't see his expression. The hatch thumped shut and the cycling began.

Lisa floated, turning easily with each breath. The weightlessness had never given her trouble, unlike a few of the astronauts who never got used to it and took pills, or gritted it through. That wasn't bothering her, but what *was*?

Am I overwhelmed by the responsibility? All of them counting on me. Generations yet unborn. Life—*all* life, practically—depends on what we do. If Jagens fails, or doesn't get through, or doesn't do it quite right—it all falls on me.

Maybe it was good they gave command to Jagens, she thought. He's always so confident, so secure, so positive. Not because of blindness, but because he stops to think, he gathers facts, he *organizes* facts and theories, he . . .

Lisa shook her head. The airlock was recycling. She'd have to go aboard now.

Have to?

Why am I afraid? *Am* I afraid? I've probably met all of them before, and often. They are all on my side, our side, the side of Alpha and Omega and survival. Why am I hesitating?

Lisa firmed up her mouth and squeezed into the airlock. The hatch hissed closed. She opened the outer lock. A transparent tube, a series of bulbous sausages, extended from the hatch to the station wall. Standard procedure; no neophytes could get lost or let something float away. But she was no amateur. Don't take it personally, she told herself. S.O.P. Carl Jagens went through it, Diego did, she would.

Lisa launched herself toward the metal wall, guiding herself by fingertip control, expertly flipping over to catch herself on the hatch, feet first. She pressed the button and the big airlock opened. Nino was waiting for her. They clung silently to handholds until the outer hatch closed and the inner opened. There were two cameras on them.

Am I getting paranoid? Lisa asked herself.

Five people were waiting. One was a cameraman, recording, sending the image throughout the ship, probably throughout the world. She managed a smile, tight and forced, and waved. Without seeming to do it deliberately, she managed to put her back to the cameraman and greeted the station commander.

"Eddie."

"Lisa, Lisa," he said grinning. "So they picked you. Well, they couldn't have done better."

"Thanks. Steve. Diane. Hi, Kim." She nodded at the cameraman, anonymous behind his machine. "How much time do we have?"

"Sixty-five minutes," the commander said. "Want to get out of those suits?"

"No, just give us a floor for a while."

"This way."

The small party shoved off, using handholds to brake and push against. They turned into a tube ten meters in diameter, sailed through several "fast-locks," which would slam closed at emergencies, and Lisa felt gravity coming slowly back to her. She was beginning to feel she was falling, something like skydiving.

Everyone kept carefully clear of both her and Nino, she noticed, as if they didn't want to be responsible for the slightest hindrance or injury. They were as valuable as the warheads now. Irreplaceable units.

"Captain Jagens get through all right?" she asked into the silence.

"Oh, yes, no problems," the commander said. "We got them out of here in record time."

Steve Megan spoke over the suit radio. "Omega Two is fifteen minutes behind you. We'll park them awhile, of course. We've never had so much traffic all at once before."

"Had to," Lisa said. "The Gabriels were . . ." She hesitated and Diane spoke up.

"*We saw . . .*"

More silence. They started flip-flopping as Eddie Manx, the commander, turned over. They all landed softly, but with far greater impact than at the central hub. Lisa could feel some kind of tug. There was an "up" and a "down" now.

They went through another lock and in a few minutes Eddie Manx signaled it was all right for them to open up. With a sigh Lisa unlatched her helmet and took it off. Kim took her helmet and carefully held it, possessively. The cameraman moved in for a close shot and Lisa gave him a frown before she remembered herself.

It would be a lot easier if everyone in the world—probably literally—weren't watching my every move, every expression, she thought. Would all those billions rooting for Alpha and Omega really help?

There was an awkwardness that Lisa felt obliged to dissipate. "Well, uh, Eddie, the old place looks the same."

"Yes, yes," he said gravely, his eye flicking sideways at the cameraman. He, too, Lisa suddenly realized; we are all playing roles. Heroes and heroines. Spear carriers and bit parts. I only hope there are no buffoons or tragedians.

"They ever going to give you a third doughnut?" she asked. Eddie Manx flashed her a grateful smile. That third ring was a sore bone of contention. NASA said they needed it to keep up with increased traffic, as space for goods in transit, for increased personnel living space, for more space sciences facilities, for a hundred things. She was giving Eddie Manx a chance at worldwide exposure. He launched confidently into what was probably a well-rehearsed speech, outlining the need and the necessity. Lisa smiled and nodded, but her thoughts were far away.

Diego. Shiva. Fear.

She had pointedly not asked about her lover, hoping it would make her seem cool and professional. No one had offered information. *Alpha* had docked, refueled, and left. Routine.

Eddie Manx asked her a question, mostly rhetorical, and she responded with the standard NASA line: space

240

was the future, space had the answers, look at all the good to come of it. That, too, was routine. There were a hundred questions to which every astronaut had pat, NASA-formed answers. And all the answers were true. Mankind did need the expansion into space. If nothing else, Shiva proved that.

Steve Megan was ready when his commander ran down. "This Russian, Zaborovskii, do you get along with him well?"

Lisa looked at him a moment before she spoke. She and the Russian had not spoken a dozen words outside of work-oriented or polite conversation. "Colonel Zaborovskii is the consummate professional," she replied. "He has given us total cooperation in all phases of this operation.

It's a play, she thought. Some kind of play where the players have only a faint idea of their lines. But then all life was an improvisation. You never get to practice the important things at all. My life is first-draft, she thought. Maybe the history books will clean it up, make it neat, sanitize the whole thing. If there *are* history books.

"And Carl Jagens, what do you think of him?" the cameraman called out. Lisa ignored the question, turning toward Eddie Manx.

"Eddie, how long now?"

The short, stocky Manx looked at his watch. "Plenty of time yet, Lisa, don't worry. Say, how about a drink?"

"No, thanks, not that kind, anyway. Water?" She was feeling the light gravity and it made her feel slightly queasy. She looked toward the outer wall. There, beyond the thick plastic port, were the spinning stars. As she looked Earth came into view. It was a black disk against the stars, with a bright crescent along one edge. She could see tiny dots of light, smudges really, against the velvety dark.

Cities. Tokyo, where thousands had committed suicide. Peking, where the riots had been ruthlessly suppressed. Bombay, where millions dying was nothing new. The United Nations had even flown in bulldozers to help with the cleanup. Chicago, where Gabriels had all but destroyed the aging Sears tower as a symbol of technology. Jakarta, where Indonesians had five governments in six weeks. Rio, Tehran, Karachi, São Paulo, Seoul, and Madrid, where millions rutted in the streets between praying fatalists. Cairo, where ancient religions had flourished again. Tientsin, where a group called the Technocrats fought with the Last Men for control of vital facilities. Leningrad, where the Gabriels had secured an unexpected foothold. Rome, where the Pope issued warnings and prayers and televised high masses. Caracas, where the Virgin of the Apocalypse was reported. Harbin, where a million Chinese died in a mysterious plague.

The world was going to hell, she thought, long before Shiva arrived. But it was not all madness and hedonism, she reminded herself. Millions—*billions!*—were acting sanely, or as sanely as such mad times would permit. They hoped and prayed, they kept vital services functioning under great difficulties, they kept calm, they went about their business. She thought of the water-purification plant at Leavenworth, Kansas, that had been abandoned because the workmen had joined the Gabriels. The water reclamation had gone awry, poisoning hundreds in Kansas City. One of them had been an aerospace engineer who failed to complete a vital test because of his illness. The test delay had cost NASA four vital days at the Palmdale facility in California. The jet pilot rushing the quickly tested valves to Cape Canaveral had been delayed because someone in Flight Operations had decided it was no use and walked off without telling anyone, to go home and seduce his next-door neighbor. The jet had arrived late at the Cape, causing stress among the ground crew. One of the crew had fumbled and dropped a fuel line, starting a dangerous fire that caused Operations to move *Omega One* to Pad Forty-one.

It was going on and on, an endless interconnected linkage. The NASA facility at Perth, Australia, had been partially destroyed by an electrical fire caused by a convert to the Last Men. This had transferred Southern Operations to Hawaii, which was not properly equipped. This in turn pushed the missiles lifted from Vandenberg to take a slightly different orbit than planned.

The cult known as the Monkey Wrenches did their damage in gleeful secret; the Last Men rioted, demanding, demanding, mindlessly demanding, but never satisfied; the Gabriels, larger and better organized than the others, had done their best. Millions had died. *Millions.* Newsmen estimated a billion people would die *before* Shiva arrived, just in riots, in revolts, by starvation and disease because the necessities had not been provided.

"Pardon me . . ."

The weight on her shoulders was immense. But I must not crack, *I must not crack*, she thought.

"Colonel Bander—?"

The Earth spun out of sight. The moving stars returned. "What? Oh, yes, Kim?"

"Time to go back, sir. *Omega Two* is parked."

"Um, thank you." She took her helmet, looking toward Eddie Manx. He was acting as straight man for Nino Solari, who was rather enjoying his time in the sun before billions of earthbound well-wishers.

They aren't *all* well-wishers, Lisa thought. Most, yes, but there were many who thought what they were doing was against God's will, or insane, or that the whole thing was a fraud. The blatant prospace propaganda they had been getting for the past hour must have convinced them.

"—and we'll do the cleanup, which is very vital, of course," Nino was saying. "All those *little* asteroids are big enough to wipe out London or New York or Tokyo," he smiled. "Can't have that."

"Nino."

He looked around and the dark shining camera lens swung toward her. "Let's go," she said.

"Any last words?" Steve Megan asked.

"Sure," Lisa said with a tight smile. "When they make a movie of all this, and they will, I *do* hope they don't have Shiva whistling through space, flaming and smoking."

She turned away at Steve's blank face, just seeing him begin to break into a smile. "And you, Major Solari?"

Nino stopped as he was about to lower his helmet into place. He looked at Lisa, then smiled a confident Italian smile. "Just one word of caution . . ."

"Yes?"

"Remember that when you look out into space you see a lot of Was." The helmet clicked into place and he turned with Lisa. Behind them, everyone was suiting up rapidly. No one wanted to miss anything.

In the airlock Lisa looked at Nino with raised eyebrows. He grinned at her. *"Well, what I really wanted to* say was that you always told me never to leave my fly open in my space suit."

"Thank you, faithful companion."

"You're welcome, chieftess."

Back in *Omega One*, they strapped down and were all business as the ship was sent on through the central cylinder by magnetic impulses. Behind them *Omega Two* was coming in.

"*Omega Two*, this is *Omega One*. Do you read me?"

"*Omega One, this is* Omega Two. *We read you five by five.*"

It was Zaborovskii. "*Omega Two*, switch to Tac Three, please."

"*Roger*, Omega One." There was a click and the Russian said, "*Something confidential, Colonel Bander?*"

"Nothing much, Colonel Zaborovskii. Just remember they have an eye there. All Earth is watching."

"*Understand*, Omega One." He chuckled briefly. "*I am Russian, Colonel, I understand about these things.*"

"I bet you do, Aleksandr." It was the first time she had used his name like that. "Well, uh . . . good luck."

"*Luck, Colonel Bander . . . Lisa? With all this training all this magnificent equipment? Aren't you being a bit superstitious, Colonel Lisa? Skill, Colonel, skill and training and opportunity.*"

Lisa laughed. "Oh, there's lots of opportunity, Aleksandr, more than enough for everyone."

"*Perhaps.*" He sounded grumpy. "*But we are redundant, Colonel.*"

"Let us hope we stay that way, Colonel Zaborovskii. Once Omega becomes the prime functionary we are *all* in trouble."

"*Ah, it is as you say. We are firemen, I believe you call them?*"

"Insurance, Aleksandr. You hope you never need it."

"*Yes, that is so.*" The Russian paused. "*We are docking, Colonel Bander, if you will forgive me—?*"

"Of course . . . and . . . still . . . good luck."

"*Well, I must admit Lady Fortune is a factor at times. So I take your good wishes. And good luck to you, Colonel . . . Lisa.*"

"Omega One, out."

"Omega Two, *out.*"

Lisa stared a moment at the stars. They were out of

the tube, the automatic pilot swinging the ship around for the next leg of their flight: the acquisition of the nineteen missiles.

Then Shiva.

In her temperature-controlled suit Lisa Bander shivered.

The bodies of gassed Gabriels littered the wide road that ran along the western edge of Cape Canaveral. Someone had panicked, Saperstein guessed, and substituted Civol-7 or some other potent gas for the usual riot control gas. He lowered his field glasses and sighed wearily. "We'd better swing farther west, Sergeant. There's still too much Civol-7 around."

"We could wait it out, sir." He squinted at the lowering sun. "What's it take, ten, twelve hours of UV? It's had maybe five now."

Saperstein shook his head. "It'll be night before it breaks it down. The evening breezes will move it around and . . ." He winced and felt his arm. "Damn. No, we'd better form up with headquarters as soon as possible."

"What happened to the helicopters, for Christ's sake?" the sergeant muttered.

"He would have sent them if he had them, Sergeant," Saperstein said. "Leave some kind of message for Valentine, one he can't miss, and get the troops moving west."

"Sir." Cooper turned toward the rag-tag remnants of Saperstein's guard detail: forty-one battered survivors, including some strays, a civilian NASA employee and a pair of Navy technicians.

Saperstein looked west. They'd have to cross the Banana River, maybe all the way across Merritt Island, but probably not, then south to the town of Merritt Island. Get a boat there, he thought, and turn east, to Cocoa Beach or up to Cape Canaveral direct.

He sighed. West was Disney World, a national institution. A perfect world, untouched by time or death. All the presidents lived there, and spoke. Sleeping Beauty walked and talked. No one was tired. Everyone was happy. No one bled in Disney World. It was a swell place.

The Alpha ships flew in a V formation. Between the widespread arms of the V was *Bolshoi,* but it was steadily falling behind. Unable to attain the velocity of the Alpha personnel ships, or even that of the twenty-megatonners, the immense Russian bomb lagged behind. It was boosting steadily under the constant thrust of its nuclear engine. The power plant rode on shock absorbers, to avoid sudden, damaging jolts to the explosive mechanism if it should strike debris near Shiva. The payload shell structure was buffered and electromagnetically impenetrable, except through its external antenna system.

The widening gap between the Alpha ships and *Bolshoi* was planned. This was so that the Alpha team could scout ahead, plot a course, then get into position behind the nickel-iron mass of Shiva before *Bolshoi* came plowing in. The twenty-megatonners would be decelerated and they would arrive after the main blast, aimed toward any wayward shard.

For nearly the entire journey toward Shiva the V would remain intact, a routine to dull their nervousness and provide the best communication with the nuclear bomb spacecraft.

Jagens switched to a rear camera, getting a glimpse of the rapidly receding space station. He glowered at the double-doughnut.

"Comrade Jagens—"

"Don't call me comrade, General," Jagens snapped, giving Menshov a dark look.

"Excuse. Habit. *Captain* Jagens?"

"Yes, General, what is it?" Jagens's eyes rescanned the control panel. Everything was jury-rigged, mostly untested, inadequate for the job—a kind of spaceborne *Santa Maria.*

"We test the bomb-arming circuits now, no?"

"In a little bit," Jagens snapped, his voice harsh. I'm in charge, he thought. I'll say when we do things. Goddamned Red. A general, for Christ's sake! Well, I shouldn't complain. I'm a volunteer. No one made me do this. No one but Carl Jagens.

General Dmitrii Menshov watched Carl Jagens from

under sleepy eyelids. The Russian had a way of not moving, just breathing, with his long-lashed eyelids drooped and shadowed by his bushy brows. His very stillness was a kind of motion-to-be, as though he would at any time burst into action. It disconcerted most people. Menshov had been observing the effect of his presence on the attitude of Captain Carl Jagens, United States Navy. The tall American seemed to ignore the Russian—and everyone—except in line of duty, in which case his attention was intense. Those under him soon learned to be functioning at peak efficiency.

But there was something gnawing at the American. It had to be, Menshov thought. There was something beyond the incredible pressure on them in the days ahead. With only a tenuous radio link with Earth, the responsibility rested solely on the shoulders of one man: Carl Jagens.

Menshov wondered: just what kind of man was this Jagens? He had read the dossiers on all of the astronauts, then had reviewed them when the final selection was made. They were much alike, not too different from his fellow cosmonauts. Intelligent, tested, confident, highly motivated, with fast reactions and good judgment. None of them had come from exalted backgrounds. There were scholarships, but most had worked to get through school, helped by their parents. None were brilliant, all were dedicated. They knew the value of cooperation, but were still relatively innocent in the larger values of world opinion. They showed glimmerings of it by including a black, a woman, and ethnic minorities in their final team selection. But they had passed over one or two who were better astronauts to achieve the politically balanced team. What had the discredited Khrushchev said? No matter how humble a man's beginnings, he achieves the stature of the office to which he is elected. Menshov wondered: but does he ever forget those beginnings? A man carries that history with him, within, sometimes like precious cargo, other times like empty suitcases.

Jagens and Menshov were the only team members in *Alpha One*. The Mexican-American Calderon, the Japanese-American Issindo, and his own Olga were in *Alpha Two*. Americans were so ambivalent, so filled with hyphenates. The Italian-American Solari, the African-American Short, the German-American Schumacher.

And the *Omega* commander: English, Irish, a touch of French and Swiss, a dash of German and Czech. The mongrel Americans. But from this genetic stew new forms had been created. Menshov was Georgian for a hundred generations, which meant Turkish and Iranian invaders, Mongols and Tartars, Syrians and Kurds. Perhaps a mongrel himself, he thought. Only my people stayed put and let the genetic infusion come to them, instead of going to a neutral ground where the genetic mix could take place.

Menshov automatically read the missile control panel. The special panel for the four-hundred-megaton bomb, riding in an American spacecraft a hundred kilometers to their port, was dark, as were the lights of the twenty-two twenty-megaton missiles flying on their starboard. Such power, more power in one place, under one command, than had ever been assembled before in the history of man.

Menshov had no worries about himself, or Major Nissen. But the Americans were enough of an unknown quantity to keep him alert. Good men had broken under pressure before, and no one in the history of mankind had *ever* had such pressure before. Every man had a breaking point. What was the American's?

The burly Russian handled the responsibility as he handled all such conscientious trust: by treating it as just another factor, along with what was upcoming for lunch and double-checking airlock pressures. Phlegmatic, perhaps, but Menshov knew he would never break from a too-active imagination. What was the saying? Those with too much imagination are never heroes? Perhaps. It was best to be moderate in all things.

But how would the American commander handle it? He seemed too tense, too quick, too much aware of the public as well as private pressures. But there was no knowing what his American masters had ordered him in secret. Menshov would have to handle those eventualities when they happened.

"Commander, message coming in," he said. Jagens nodded and pressed the stud that slowed the info-flash transmission to normal time. It was all trajectory information from Boston, funneled through Houston. Shiva's exact position and course. Closer observations on the elements of the swarm, given in three-dimensional projection in the small holowell.

"Message received, Houston. *Alpha One,* out." Menshov stared at the holographic image. It was not complete, but each computer-directed set was getting a clearer image. It was going to be an even more difficult penetration than they had thought. They couldn't use one of their twenty-tonners to blast a clearer path through the dust and minor chunks, as had been suggested. There was no way really to determine where the pieces would go. They might merely create a larger volume of unlogged pieces, with no time for a better holographic reconnaissance or course plot. They would have to feel their way in, taking their chances with unlogged meteorites, trusting to skills never truly tested except in simulators.

Shiva was not going to be easy.

Menshov permitted himself a faint smile. If it was easy, no one would have gotten upset. He might not even have been sent. Someone like Zaborovskii probably, but perhaps even Agabalaogly or Vitver. They were good enough for anything below the utmost importance to the state. And the planet, he reminded himself.

No, Shiva was going to demand the best, the very best.

16 May: Collision minus 9 days, 18 hours

One of the plain metal letters of *The Thales Center* sign was missing. Paint was splashed over the NASA logo. Someone else had tried to pickax the cement wall in some futile rage. The broken ax lay in the shrubbery. Trash littered the sidewalks and was caught in the dying shrubs. A cold wind tugged at Wade Dennis' coat as he jumped out of the National Guard personnel carrier and strode across the stained concrete entrywalk to the door. The security guard opened the door as he approached, but Wade held up his special pass anyway.

"Keith, is Miss Weinberg in yet?"

"Yes, sir. One of them Army fellas brought her."

"Thanks." Wade smiled briefly at the National Guard sergeant and his troop of six men lounging in the lobby. The noncom just looked at him. None of the soldiers even looked up from their card game.

Wade found Dr. Bogartus in the hall, outside the computation room. "Jesus, Jesus," the short, pot-bellied man said, wiping his balding head with a pudgy hand.

Wade stopped abruptly. "All right, what's the matter, Don?"

"Jesus, Jesus, you don't know, you don't know."

"And I never will, unless you tell me. What is it now?"

"People. They aren't showing up. Jesus, Jesus. I don't know what I'm going to do. Raferson's dead—they found her in her apartment last night. Signorelli's missing. O'Keeffe skipped out—he told me he would and I didn't believe him. Morris Dreyfuss, Lou Ghiberti, Rhoda Davidson—all quit. Just walked out."

"Scared?"

Bogartus shrugged. "Who isn't? No, they just gave up."

"Gave up? Gave up?" Wade Dennis balled his fists and struck at the wall. "What's the matter with them? We haven't even come up to bat yet! *Alpha* isn't even within strike range! What's the matter with those clowns?"

"Hung-hsi's here, but depressed as hell. Bert Palma was talking of suicide yesterday, but he's here. Bahadur Amhed is—"

"Who's that?" Wade interrupted.

"University of Bombay, that hotshot the U.N.—"

"Oh, yeah. He all right?"

"All in the hands of the benevolent Buddha, he says. Jesus, Wade, this whole place is falling *apart!* Janitors, security people, the fucking secretaries, that New Zealander—whatshisface, Fergusson—skipped out. Quit. Went home. Didn't report. Jesus, *Jesus*, man, if we can't do the goddamn job we'll—"

"All right, easy, Don, easy. Get that kid from Berlin, that Miller, Mueller, get him in to replace Raferson."

"He's never done anything like—"

"Get him, Don. Move up Eleanor to replace Signorelli, Eleanor Walker. Forget replacing Ghiberti now, but ask MIT for Ray Rosenblum to fill Dreyfuss's place. Rhoda's gone, too, huh? Damn. Who can we get to—"

"How about Yorimichi? He's here from Japan, you know, just in case. Or Emile Hupp? He just arrived."

"Fine—either one. What else is falling apart?"

"Everything. We've had to go on emergency power twice in the last two days. Bombings over at the power station. The world is going *crazy*, Wade! Jesus, what's the matter with people? They should be doing everything they can to *help,* not hinder."

"Not everyone reacts to stress the same way, Don." He started through the door. "I'll be in here—but try to stay off my back, huh?"

"Sure, sure." He waved, walking away. "Jesus, Jesus . . ."

Caroline looked up and smiled. "Hi. Got here okay?"

Wade nodded. "U.S. Army Delivery Service." He picked up the readout sheets and scanned them quickly, slipping them through his hands back into their neatly folded pile. What he read was all triangulation input from Palomar, Kitt Peak, and the biggest Russian telescope. They would all soon be useless. Only the space station telescope, still manned by Dr. Zakir Shastri, would give them any sort of accurate information. One-point information. But the big earthbound scopes could not depress below ten degrees above the horizon, the angle required at sunset. The sunrise sightings were a little better. In the last ten days of its approach Shiva would be ten to fifteen degrees above the horizon then. That meant the best information would come late, at the last minute, which meant that the course corrections would be vital right up until the last minute, up until the actual radar fixes from *Alpha* could take over.

He grunted and let the paper slither back into the tray. Caroline was bent over a console, her fingers tapping out a code and her eyes on the readout screen. Her tongue was caught between her lips, barely peeking out. She looked leaner, he thought, almost gaunt. But she was here and working.

Without disturbing her, Wade left the room and walked to his office. He sat down, looked sadly at the piles of work that had been left undone, his entire "Objects in Near Space" atlas. There were thousands of devices, parts of modules, machines, space stations, flotsam and jetsam, weather and communication satellites, and a hundred categories of miscellaneous items, from a lost Hasselblad going back to Apollo to the frozen carcass in a Russian manned module, all floating around up there. Someone had to log them, determine if they were where they should be, compute the reentry dates, recheck, add new entries, recheck and re-recheck. A massive project much too late in coming, but growing more and more necessary. They had lost one shuttle on a collision with space debris—not a meteorite as the press insisted—and that had only contributed more garbage to the skies. It all would reenter at some time and most—but not all—would burn up. But they had to be kept track of, and with even greater accuracy than NORAD or the Russian or Chinese military did. Pinpoint accuracy. Complete inventory.

But that was all postponed now. Later, he had been planning to expand into listing all the nonplanetary objects within the orbit of Mars. Pinpointing every asteroid, ship, comet, and space pebble big enough to cause damage. Then every object in the whole solar system. It was all possible, given time and money, and observations. But now the "space atlas" was academic, at least until the Shiva problem was resolved. The tapes and folders and dossiers were getting dusty.

And if Shiva *was* blown up—there would be still *more* space debris! And if it wasn't . . . then the whole project was pointless.

Wade sighed and pulled the videophone toward him, punching out the familiar numbers deftly. He had positions to fill, work to get done, a strike force to direct, a world to save.

"Colonel Dunnigan, please. This is Wade Dennis, at the Thales Center." Wade drummed his fingers on the desk top until the screen blinked and he saw the bland, lined face of the officer appear.

"Dunnigan here, Doctor Dennis."

"Colonel, I think we need extra troops here and—"

"No chance, Doctor. We've got riots in every section of the city . . . looting . . . a lot of important people to guard, places that—"

"Colonel," Wade's voice cut through harshly. "Maybe you don't understand what we do here. This isn't just another NASA outfielder station. We do the *computation* for the Alpha team here, sir, *and* Omega, and if we can't do our job, they can't do theirs. And I don't think I need add what happens if they can't do theirs."

The colonel stared at him for a long moment. "What are you asking for, precisely?"

"More troops . . . and *better* troops. I'm getting dopers and goldbricks. I want professionals, Colonel. I know you are National Guard and last week these troops were office workers, bikers, mechanics, and housewives and what all. But they are in uniform and I want extra troops, I want them *now*, and I want them *screened!* I don't want any defectors to the Dancers of Shiva, any Gabriel trash, anything like that."

"I . . . I think we can supply that. I was about to give up on the south side, anyway. We'll draw back and—"

"I don't care where or how you get the men, Colonel, but I want them. And another thing; there's a hotel three blocks from here, a Hilton Inn. I want you to take it over and seal it up. I am going to move all of my people in there, from myself down to the maintenance men. Plus their families, dogs, goldfish, children, everything."

The colonel narrowed his eyes at Wade. "Internment camp?"

"In a way. I want guards for them, going and coming. Make certain no one gets hurt or strays."

"Or runs," the colonel said grimly.

"Yes, or runs. We've lost some of our best people in the last few days. No more. I'm stopping the drain." He glanced at his watch. "I want that hotel empty and secure by five o'clock. At *four* o'clock I will have a complete list of everyone I want moved. You will supply transport and security. There will be approximately ninety people, plus whatever families they have. Can you make that deadline?"

The colonel glanced offscreen, then held his hand over the pickup mike for a moment while he spoke. Then he looked back at Wade. "I'll have an aide of mine there within the hour, Doctor Dennis. We will require a written order, authorizing this entire project."

"Fine, Colonel, I don't care how you cover your ass. I'll have the paper, thumbprinted and everything."

"Then, sir, we will meet your deadline. Will that be all?"

"For now, Colonel. And thank you." Wade's screen blanked out and he stared at himself in the dark gray reflective surface. *Jesus,* he thought, *Jesus.*

"Ladies and gentlemen, the President of the United States."

John Caleb Knowles looked up from the papers, sitting behind the Lincoln desk, and stared right into the camera with a solemn expression.

253

"Fellow Americans." He paused slightly. "Fellow human beings everywhere. The best effort that we have been able to launch has left Station One to intercept Shiva and destroy or divert it. It is a joint task of many countries, not just one. Important links in this effort remain here, on Earth, but everyone and everything in this tremendous undertaking is important, whether that link be one of the astronauts or technical personnel still here on Earth. Our prayers, our hopes go with them all."

Knowles glanced down, as if to read his speech, which was unnecessary since it was being displayed on a tele-prompter over the camera lens. But Knowles knew his timing and his dramatics. He felt numb, empty, a husk. But he also knew his job.

"There is still much to do here, much to accomplish and much to prevent. There is no reason for panic. There is no reason for the looting and destruction. Shiva *will* be stopped. Our lives—so disastrously interrupted—will soon be able to resume their normal paths. I ask you to coop-erate—with each other, with the police and authorities, with plain common sense."

He forced a weak smile to his lips. "Perhaps things will never be quite the same again. Perhaps we have changed, living, all of us, so close to death, a death both personal and racial. But it shall not happen. Shiva *will* be stopped. Within just a few short days it will be over." *One way or another,* he thought. "And then we can pick up the pieces of our shattered and scattered lives, return to our homes, and begin again to rebuild.

The smile faded quickly. "I want to thank the thou-sands who helped launch this magnificent effort, who built and supplied and created a unique force in the his-tory of man. I hope we have learned from it, from the international cooperation, from the now-obvious need for an adequate space force. Yes, even the need to put our eggs in other baskets, to put man out into the stars, onto other planets in our own system, into colonies in space where never again can one menace threaten to destroy the entire human race."

Knowles sighed and smiled. "Thank you, ladies and gentlemen. I will continue to keep you aware of develop-ing events. Thank you."

The cameras switched to an exterior night shot of the White House, carefully avoiding the massed lines of parked tanks. An announcer, in the communications center in the White House basement, spoke in his beautiful voice, "This has been President John Caleb Knowles, speaking from the White House, in Washington. We will now return you to our regularly scheduled broadcasting."

Knowles got up as the lights dimmed. He scooped up the papers on his desk, squared them neatly, bouncing them up and down on the leather pad, then put them down. His eyes had adjusted to the dimmer regular light and he walked out of the Oval Office with dignity, ignoring the dignitaries who were trying to get his attention. Myron Murray blocked them, saying, "Gentlemen, please, the President will see you in a few moments."

In the small bathroom Knowles looked at his tired face in the mirror. The bathroom light was pitiless. It showed every line, every bag. He thought about getting those soft pink bulbs in there, the kind they had in bars and women's restrooms. He'd look better then. The man in the mirror grinned crookedly at him. Right, sure. Cosmetic light. Cover it up and it isn't there. The lines would smooth out, the bags would go away, that trapped look in his eyes would disappear.

Sure. Right.

He straightened his suit coat, flushed the toilet, and walked out and down the hall. Myron Murray got to him just as he was going into the little office. "Sir, there's quite a few who want to see you. Senator Mathison, Secretary Rogers, Powell Hopkins—"

Knowles waved his hand in a negative gesture. "No, no. You take care of them." He went on into the small office and let himself down carefully into an overstuffed chair and closed his eyes, leaning back.

"Sir, Secretary Rogers wants to move you and the staff to Colorado within the next two days. It's all been prepared and—"

"No."

"Sir, the Secretary of State advises it, the Joint Chiefs—"

"No. How would it look? I run for cover when a couple of hundred million can't."

"Mister President, no one would blame you, sir. Someone has to run things. You were elected. It's your responsibility to go, sir, and—"

"Myron." Knowles opened his eyes and looked at Murray. "You go. Take whoever wants to go with you."

Murray swallowed. "No, sir, I'll stay here with you. But the Cabinet wants you to—"

"They want me to go so *they* can go. No. I'm staying."

"Sir, the Department of Defense has prepared some estimates of damage to the eastern seaboard if Shiva—"

"No." His voice was weak, listless. Knowles felt everything run out of him, like a boil bursting, draining. "No," he repeated, eyes closed, barely breathing.

Murray stood uncertainly, looking at the President. They had been together a long time. Master and vassal. Murray's wagon to Knowles' star. He couldn't leave him now. Maybe tomorrow he'd listen to reason. It only made sense. That was why the Department of Defense had hollowed out that mountain. There'd be no radiation to guard against, its defenses constructed against a different kind of assault, but it was the safest place on the globe right now.

Tomorrow. He'd talk to him tomorrow. Murray began to leave, quietly, and was at the door when Knowles spoke again. "Sir?"

"I said, ask Miz Carr to come see me, will you?"

"Miz Carr, sir?"

"Barbara Carr."

"Yes, sir, I know. Uh, yes, sir. At once, sir. If she's still in the White House."

"She's here."

Murray closed the door and went back to the Oval Office. He stopped just outside the closed doors and thought. No, better to keep this as quiet as possible. He turned, stepped down the hall a few feet, and opened an inconspicuous panel in the white wall. Within the niche was a phone and a tiny screen. He punched the main operator. "Get me Miz Carr, Barbara Carr, please. I think she's still in."

The operators found her in seconds. Not for nothing were they considered the best operators in the world. The record had been getting Carnaris in the middle of the Gobi in four hours by dropping him a radiophone by air, when the President wanted to tell him personally about the Nobel prize.

"Miz Carr?"

"Yes, Mister Murray?"

"The President would like to see you at once, ma'am. He's in the little office. By the Oval Office, not in the Executive Office Building," he added unnecessarily. He became annoyed with himself. He hated to be redundant.

"Thank you, Mister Murray, I'll be right there."

No hint in her voice, he thought. They *were* having some sort of affair, weren't they? If they weren't, they should be. She was a handsome woman, and the President was not past the age, by any means. But be discreet, Miz Carr, be *very* discreet! Even with people rutting in the street, be careful. Once this thing is over and everything back to normal, it won't do any good to have it known that John Caleb Knowles was fucking around. The sexual activities of presidents were bound to come out sometime. They always had.

"Thank you, Miz Carr." He hung up. What will you call your memoirs, he wondered. *Knowles Rising As Shiva Descended?* Murray made a grim face and snapped his fingers at a presidential aide that came into view.

"Higby!"

"Yes, sir?" The young man, clean-cut and ambitious, was a little surprised at being singled out by the powerful Murray.

"Contact General Sutherland and Colonel . . . oh, what's his name, the one that's on loan from the Air Force—?"

"Graham, sir?"

"Yes, Graham. Have them report to me as soon as possible. Have Sutherland bring every contingency plan for executive evacuation with him."

Higby licked his lips, then hurried away. Murray watched him go, thinking.

The presidency must be preserved even more than the President. Maybe the Vice-President should go right away, instead of waiting. He turned again to the phone, asked for immediate contact with Vice-President Gorman Reed.

"He's in Minnesota, sir."

"I don't care, get him."

Murray drummed his fingers on the wall, staring at the gray screen as it flickered slightly. With Reed in the Colorado hole the presidency was safe. Continuity was preserved. Nothing could harm them there. His mind went unbidden to Barbara Carr. Maybe through her he could get the President to move. Get her scared, afraid for her life. She'd jump at the chance to get into the safest place in the world. Well, one of the safest, he amended; the Russians had their two boltholes and probably the Chinese hierarchy did, too.

Get her to Colorado and the President would follow. Neat. Safe. Ready to go back to work once it was over. Murray's fingers stopped drumming as he became aware of them. He hated it when he revealed himself that way. But these were extraordinary times. He smiled without humor. Weren't they all?

Barbara came out of the Usher's office on the first floor, finished with checking the dinner guest list. Outside the windows of the North Portico there were two pools of bright light where television correspondents were taping remotes. The thick blue carpet of the North Entrance Hall was soft under her shoes as she went around to the wide stairway and trotted down to the ground floor. Her smile was perfunctory as she acknowledged the presence of Senator Buford Dunn and the Undersecretary of Defense, Theotis Dudley, who were talking with fierce seriousness by the tall doors of the Vermeil Room. They stopped, watching her walk away toward the West Wing. Dunn said something and Dudley grinned, but Barbara pretended not to hear. Both men were unreconstructed chauvinists.

A small crowd came out of the Diplomatic Reception Room as she passed and she had to wend her way through excited dignitaries. She smiled at Senator Rauchenberg, who had helped her husband in the early days, but he was too involved with a near-hysterical Indian ambassador to do more than acknowledge her passing.

The White House was more filled with VIPs than usual, most of whom had rather distraught expressions. She skirted a young and pretty secretary whose eyes were unnaturally bright, laughing up at a tall British diplomat, whose face was flushed with a careless ingestion of free champagne. She passed the closed doors of the Map Room, noted several people lined up at the doctor's office with minor cuts and bruises, probably from getting through the demonstrators outside, then stopped to let some white-coated waiters from the immense kitchen come out with trays of hors d'oeuvres.

Eat, drink, and be merry. Even in the White House.

Barbara walked quickly past the Housekeeper's Office and held her badge toward the guards. An immaculately uniformed Marine held a portable electronic analyzer to it and it clicked satisfyingly. Barbara nodded pleasantly to the two men in civilian clothes in the hall beyond. They were members of the Executive Protection Service and although they knew her well, she sensed their X-raylike eyes probing her.

What did he want?

The thought she had been suppressing surfaced as she walked toward the Oval Office area. Her steps slowed and she took a moment to sip some cold water at a fountain.

You know what he wants, she told herself. What he's always wanted and what you've wanted. Don't lie to yourself, Barbara. At first the thought had been strange, forbidden, then oddly exciting. First it had been the thought of the President, *a* president, making love to you. It had been exciting, stimulating, erotic. She blushed faintly as she turned toward the Oval Office, remembering how she had reacted, how she had touched herself, thinking about it.

Then it had become, not the President, not even President Knowles, but John Caleb Knowles making love to her in her mind. A man, not an image, a creature of politics, a media monster. Then closer still, more intimate still: Caleb.

That afternoon they had had together had been awkward and marvelous, she thought. She had taken control gently but firmly, and he let her. It had been a sudden and unplanned gesture on her part, yet, in her heart, she knew it was more than that. It had been an expression, almost, of everything she was and wanted to be: wife, mistress, lover, power groupie, courtesan, nymphomaniac —she quickly amended it in her head—*apprentice* nympho.

They had not spoken of it since, though looks had passed between them. It was obviously painful for Knowles to bring it up, and Barbara did not think it her place to. She was satisfied to be behind the scenes, to help in a time where the kind of help she could offer might be very, very important.

She thought briefly about that afternoon, extending on into the night. He had been swift at first, demanding, exploding within her in an almost embarrassingly brief coupling. But then, with the pressure off, the mood and relationship established, they had gone about pleasing each other with loving care, with deliberate speed, and with rising respect.

It shamed her, the memory of some of the thoughts that she had formed during that time, the egotistical, self-centered images: *I, Barbara Ellen Carr, am in bed with the President of the United States.* But she couldn't help it. The "accolade" came unbidden. It was a heady kind of power.

And power is an aphrodisiac, she admitted. She saw it expressed every day. Rogers, the nondescript Secretary of Defense, had quite a reputation with women, second only to Senator Tucker of a few years back and Kissinger of a generation previous. But her attraction for Knowles had gone beyond that. She did not deny she was aware of it, but now she thought it more balanced. Barbara and Caleb, Caleb and Barbara, a man and a woman.

She turned down the passage toward the small office. An Air Force colonel she did not know sat outside, with the radiophone on his lap. He looked at her without expression. The Marines flanking the door came to attention, and the sergeant knocked discreetly. At a sound she could not make out, the impeccable Marine opened the door and ushered her in. Lang, the President's butler, inherited from the previous occupant of the White House, was pouring coffee. He raised his eyebrows to her and she nodded, and he poured a cup for her, then quietly withdrew as Barbara stood waiting.

The President looked up, smiled, and asked her to sit down. She did, watchful, trying to read his face. The Washington game, she thought, trying to read the Real Thoughts, the actual meaning. She picked up her coffee, added a sugar-substitute, and sat back, waiting. Caleb Knowles would get to it, whatever it was, in his own good time.

The silence deepened. Barbara could not hear the traffic, not even the strident yells of the protestors that seemed always to be outside these days. The police kept them across Pennsylvania Avenue and the grass had been worn away long ago, giving an unaccustomed shabby look to the street.

She stared into the small wood fire, quietly sipping the

coffee. She was getting used to these little quiet times with the President, though she did not take them for granted. Sometimes he asked her over to the office in the Executive Office Building, which he often used, and other times to the Oval Office, but most often to this small, unpretentious room. A Remington on one wall, a Wyeth on another, pure Americana, yet a vivid Goldstone abstraction hung like some rainbow mandala on another. It would be a shame if all this vanished, she thought, then smiled wryly at herself for the presumption. If this room was destroyed, more than likely millions, if not *billions*, of people would be destroyed, too.

Knowles stirred and cleared his throat. "Well. Um." He looked away from the fire and grinned shyly at her. "Well, Barbara, how are you today?"

"Fine, Mister President." She smiled back. Those hours in bed seem dreamlike, one of her frequent sexual fantasies, a memory imperfectly recalled. "Just fine, all considering. How are *you*, sir?"

"Same. Considering." He shifted his bulk and straightened up. "Barbara . . ." He seemed reluctant to go on She primed him.

"Yes, sir?"

"Do you think . . . um . . . do you think you could call me something else? Instead of Mister President? In private, I mean." Before she could respond, he hurried on. "You get awfully tired of that isolation, you know. Take Senator Clayberg. We were freshmen congressmen together. His wife and my wife, they . . . um . . . they knew each other well. We got drunk together, fought for the whales and dolphins together, we took on Exxon, too, can you believe that? Fought 'em to a draw and they've hated me ever since. Jim Clayberg and me, we were the young turks, y'know. The Clayberg-Knowles Bill brought the icebergs up from Antarctica, we bulled through the legislation that got the solar collectors out into space, we . . ." He stopped, nodding, his eyes sad.

Barbara waited patiently. The cup was cold in her hand and she put it down, rattling the saucer and making Knowles blink. "Ah. Yes. Young turks. Well. You know what he calls me now?" He peered at Barbara intently.

"Well, I've heard him say, uh, Mister President."

"Yes, Mister President. Oh, yes, it's the office, not me, and all that. But you know something? I used to think you were old when there was no one around anymore to call you by your first name. Now I can add one: when you are elected to this office. No more Caleb, no more J.C., no more Knowles even. All formal now. You understand?"

"I, I think so, sir."

"Caleb. For God's sake, let there be *someone* that will call me *Caleb*."

Barbara broke suddenly into a brilliant grin. "All right . . . Caleb."

He smiled warmly at her. "Better. Much better." He shifted again, looking younger as he smiled. "Ever wonder about the Pope?"

"The Pope, sir, uh, Caleb?"

"The Pope. Who ever calls him by *any* name? The names they use aren't really their own, they assume them." He sighed. "Well, maybe by the time they work up to *Your Holiness* they've had all those years of *Your Eminence* and *Your Grace* and *Most Reverend* that they've forgotten their name, anyway." He made a noise with his lips, a popping sound. "Aw, hell, what's in a name? Barbara, you play the banjo?"

"Uh, no, sir."

"Always wanted to play the banjo. Sounds really terrific when someone who really knows goes at it. Crystal clear. Sharp. Like a harp, only faster, more . . . um . . . crystalline. Fun, too, don't you think?"

"Yes, sir." She looked at him as he resumed staring into the fireplace. But now he was smiling.

"Got every Jimmy Clyde Brackett album, you know that? And Wayne Avery, too. Flatt and Scruggs, Pete Whistler, the whole bunch. Doesn't go well with being the President though, does it?"

Barbara shrugged. "Why not? Kennedy liked sailing, Lincoln told jokes, Truman played the piano . . ."

"Different, different," Knowles said, waving his hand in dismissal. "Eisenhower, Ford, Brown, they liked golf. Sailing was fancy eastern establishment stuff. Now Jefferson played the violin a little; Tyler, too. Coolidge played the harmonica, but I don't think they advertised that much. Warren Harding, when he was young, played the cornet and the alto horn. No, not many in this office had any musical ability.

"Now Teddy Roosevelt, he liked boxing and wrestling,

shooting and hunting, of course; jujitsu, would you believe it? And riding, tennis. An active man.

"Coolidge was an odd one. Know what he liked? Golf and fishing, of course. Standard American stuff. But pitching hay he liked, and Indians clubs, the mechanical horse, and . . ." He stopped abruptly and looked at Barbara a little sheepishly. "Aw, hell." She thought he looked like a little boy and dimpled a smile back at him.

"Go on."

"No. No." He shook his head, returning to stare into the fire. "Still . . ." He took a big breath and let it out noisily. "The banjo. A Vega Wyte Lydie with deluxe machine heads," he said proudly. "Scruggs pegs, adjustable fifth-string tack. Five strings, of course. Finish by Frank Selinger.

"That's, that's a good one?"

"Best, the best. Just don't . . . just don't get much chance to play. Miz Carr, would you consent to become my mistress?"

Barbara blinked in surprise. "Sir?"

His smile had gone. "Can't marry you right now. That's a big operation, protocol, that whole thing. Can't even promise I *will* marry you, if you want the truth. But I . . . I need the love of a woman like you." His eyes came around to her and she saw the silent pleading in them, the pain and embarrassment. "I'm not much good at this sort of thing. My wife and I . . . it's been so long, that . . ." He smiled shyly. "Well, I don't really know how to ask a woman anymore, I guess. I feel I have to start negotiating or something, like in the Congress. That time, you know, it, it meant something to me . . ."

"Please, Caleb, don't."

"Don't what? Don't go on, don't say it, don't think it?"

"No, Caleb . . . there's no need. Yes, I would be most honored to become your, your mistress."

"Funny damn word, isn't it? Still don't have one that fits. Maybe we should run a contest. Girl friend just doesn't seem right. Woman I'm seeing . . ." He shook his head. "Freemate sounds okay." He laughed, a short bark followed by a rumbling chuckle. "Contest, that's what. Decide what to call a woman instead of a mistress, which is a sexist word. And a man in the same situation. Then there's the crack of the ass." She raised her eyebrows at him, frowning.

"The division back there, between the buttocks. No name for it. Asked Admiral Begelman one time. Big navy doctor. He didn't know. They have names for every damn little muscle and vein in the body, but not for the gluteal cleft. That's what he suggested. Gluteal cleft. Dumb name. No one'll use it." He grinned at Barbara. "Back of the knee. What do you call it?"

"Uh, back of the knee, I guess."

"Knee-pit?"

"Oh, Caleb!" She pretended to be disgusted, but her head was still spinning. *The president's mistress!*

Knowles chuckled and said, "Well, what about it?"

They both knew what he meant. She smiled as she said it, but her words were faintly accusing. "Not exactly the most romantic proposal I've had."

He waved his hand in the air in a presumptive way. "Yes, yes, I'm certain of that. Not my way, though, I'm sorry." He made a face. "Got me in a lot of trouble, that way. People like to edge around things a bit, sniff at them, poke, think. Not me. Certainly not with Shiva and all." He looked at her and that pained expression was back and it tore into Barbara's heart.

"Yes. Yes, Caleb."

He let out a big sigh. Then he looked shrewdly at her again. "No demands or assurances?"

"Caleb, you knew what kind of person I am before you asked. Now stop second-guessing and backing off."

"I am not backing off." She just smiled, tilting her head to one side. "Well . . . well, I guess I expected *something* else.

"It *has* been a long time since you dealt with women on . . . on this level. We are, I think, different than when you were a young man courting the girls."

" 'September Song.' Oh, I love that one."

"What?"

"A young man courting the girls. No good for a banjo, though." He looked at her and laughed. "Damn, you know, I feel pretty good." Unconsciously he felt his stomache. "What do you have to do this afternoon?"

She shrugged. "Nothing I can't put off."

He stood up and she uncrossed her ankles and stood up, too. They were both smiling, but both very awkward. She didn't know if she should kiss him or not. "I've got

264

about an hour's work," he said. "Maybe by then you'll, you know, be free."

"I will be. I'll . . . I'll be in the private quarters."

"Yes. Um." It was an increasingly awkward moment. Abruptly, Knowles leaned forward and kissed her on the cheek, near her mouth, holding her by the shoulders. She felt very touched by the awkward, impulsive gesture. He moved away, still obviously awkward, but his face beaming. "Yes. Well. In an hour, then."

"In an hour."

He went out, closing the door behind him softly. Barbara sat down again, a lot of her collapsing inside. Yet it was not a panic or a distressing feeling. Well, she said to herself, you came here because you like Washington, because you like power and the heady feeling near the top. Now you've really gotten into it. But in a way you would never have imagined, not in a thousand years. Not really, not *really* really, only silly fantasies.

She took a deep breath, held it, then let it out. *Get to it, girl,* she said to herself.

Caleb Knowles worked quickly, his mind elsewhere. He delayed ordering a national martial law, but imposed it in Los Angeles, Honolulu, New York, Chicago, St. Paul, Dallas, and Atlanta. It was regretfully necessary, and added to the burden assumed by the federal government. He signed papers, thumbprinted others, dictated a policy statement about the Canadian situation, instructed the Department of Defense to assume responsibility for the Alaskan and Mexican pipelines, signed the Disaster Relief Bill, and replaced the ambassador to China, who had committed suicide.

But he was thinking about Barbara Carr, as eager as a boy on his first date. Disgusting, not suitable for a man of my age and position, demeaning, he thought. But the excitement rose and he could not help himself. Not just sex, though that was part of it. He saw Barbara as an escape, not some shoddy sexual thing. He remembered the story about Kennedy, who allegedly had greeted two of his Cabinet officers, Bundy and McNamara, in his bedroom, getting out of bed naked and casually walking over to put on a bathrobe—with a woman not his wife in the bed. In the White House, sex was nothing new, but it was to John Caleb Knowles.

Maybe, after, maybe I could play her something.

Bach's "Bourrée for Lute, Number Two." "Salty Dog Rag."

"Foggy Mountain Chimes" might be just right.

17 May: Collision minus 8 days, 21 hours

In the command module of *Omega One* Nino Solari pulled out a checkout list and began going over the procedure necessary to gain optical acquisition of Shiva. He was early, but there was nothing much else to do, as Lisa seemed wrapped in her own thoughts and uncommunicative.

The onboard optical telescope was quite small but they hoped it would be adequate. Solari frowned as he read through the list. At apparition—first sighting—he was to measure the diameter of Shiva and its albedo. In other words, its size and its reflectivity and absorption of light. He would be using a liquid-helium-cooled bolometer for this, fitted with a 1.6 micrometer filter. By comparing Shiva with a standard star—in this case Alpha Ori had been selected—the scientists back on Earth could compare the thermal flux from each in the infrared portion of the electromagnetic spectrum. They would get a relation giving the surface albedo of the asteroid, by measuring how much radiation it was reflecting—reemitting—of the flux originally falling on it from the sun. Then photometry experiments at the other wavelengths would give the spectral reflectivity. That would nail down just how iron rich Shiva was. Knowing that, they could get Shiva's mass to two decimal places.

Solari sighed and let the list rest on his lap. He had always been thankful that as a shuttle pilot he had not had to learn a lot of the scientific stuff his predecessors had. He had been trained in milk-run stuff: Earth to station, station to moon base. Simple, routine, few real dangers. He had always been able to relax and enjoy space and the stars. He'd gotten very good at it. He *was* a very good pilot. But not such a good scientist. He hesitated to reveal his ignorance to Lisa. She had enough on her mind, and, after all, the optical system *was* within his capability to operate. He just had to rehearse a little, to be certain.

Solari stole a glance at Lisa. She had just returned to her seat from the rather complicated and embarrassing procedure of defecation. Astronauts generally just pretended it wasn't happening, which Solari had always thought was quite oriental. The Japanese had a saying, he remembered, about nudity: it is often seen but never looked at. Same with onboard biological functions. Doing such things in zero gravity, or under the light gravity of a spinning ship, had a comic aspect, but most astronauts soon tired of finding humor in that. He picked up the checkout list again.

Additional notes said that the Orbiting Astronomical Observatory on Station Three was also tracking Shiva, using the star Capella as a reference point, since it was bright and had some proximity to the line-of-sight. In the final briefing session they had been told again that the Terran observatories would be only marginally helpful. Much depended on the link between the ships, the OAO, and the NASA processing center. Nino let the list drop again. He looked out the window at the stars, remembering.

On his fifth shuttle flight the onboard radar had gone out, and everyone wanted to just go into a parking orbit. But there had been VIPs aboard, plus replacement parts for Station One's solar power transmitter. Not exactly the most urgent cargo in the world, but important enough. Micrometeorites had ruined the main solar collector and transmitter. It had been expected to go out hours before. If it went, millions of people would be without power until the North American Grid could adjust. People might die. So Captain Nino Solari had taken the ship in, on manual, eyeballing, closing his ears to the frantic radioed commands. He'd done it perfectly, without a jolt, docking expertly. That had been flying. Real flying. Just like atmospheric combat, out there in the outermost layers of the biosphere, outthinking, outguessing, outfighting the enemy.

Solari sighed. The only war he'd ever been in had been short, a political war of pride and unreason, but he'd gotten two of the enemy himself, one-on-one, a record matched by only one other pilot, and that pilot had been an enemy. He rattled the checkout sheet and tried again to concentrate. He had to learn it.

Lisa stirred, brought from her distant thoughts by the

rustling of the paper. She glanced at Solari, seeing his dark frown and the fierce look he got when he was concentrating. *You were born almost a hundred years too late, Nino. You should have been in World War I, in the cockpit of a French Spad or a German Jagdstaffel 2, with no more instruments than a compass.* She smiled, but the smile quickly faded as her thoughts returned to Diego.

She loved him, yet the thought of loving one person and on others seemed unreasonable. *We just aren't that way, or at least I'm not. Why do people become upset if you say you love more than one? We have more than one friend, why not more than one person to love, really love? Surely that is more realistic.*

Lisa's eyes ran automatically across the console, checking, monitoring. *Is it all a genetic thing,* she wondered? *Maybe something started by men, so that they would "know" their children were theirs? Something very caveman about that, as were so many of the things we did or didn't do. If a man's children were his blood, then they would back him up, protect him, help him. But if they were the progeny of another man, how could he trust them?*

She sighed. *Was that wrong? What she couldn't understand was why lines of descent had, in most cultures, descended through the male. Through the female was the obvious way. It is easy to know that this child came from that womb, but not so easy to be certain that the seed came from those genitals.*

Abruptly she shook her head to clear it. *What thoughts! If I don't keep a clear head, there might not be any children for me or anyone.* She leaned forward, turned the radio on and spoke.

"*Omega One* to *Alpha Two,* come in, please." She paused, then repeated herself. "*Omega One* to *Alpha Two—*"

"*Omega One, this is* Alpha Two, *over.*"

"Colonel Calderon, I believe."

"*Hiya, Lisa. Howya doing?*"

"On course, of course. How's *Bolshoi?*"

"*Trackin' fine. We just said 'Heel!' and it's coming right along.*"

"Diego . . ." Both knew everything was being overheard, taped, possibly even rebroadcast to the world. They had to say it all between the lines. "We're getting

268

pretty far out for a bunch of milk-run jockeys, aren't we?"

"Hey," said Nino Solari, "we'll get it done."

"Lisa, I—"

"All right, let's cut the chatter." It was Jagens, from the command module. "You know the bit. Route everything through NASA channels. Any information you have might be useful groundside. Anything else is just gossip, got me?" Lisa stared at the console with a set face. "All Alpha-Omega transmissions, from now on, must be okayed by me. Or by General Menshov," he added quickly. "Use the down-link only."

"Hey, listen, Carl," Diego said, "who made you house mother? Is it after lights-out or something? Nothing wrong with me talking to Lisa."

"Colonel Calderon," Jagens said in an icy voice, "please observe proper communication procedures."

There was a slight pause and Lisa opened her mouth to speak, but Diego spoke first. "Alpha Two switching to S-band frequency one."

Lisa reached out and switched to the main "down-link" band, the talk-line to Earth in the complex of telemetry that conveyed spacecraft parameters to Earth satellites, and from there to the designated bases. The "up-link" telemetry lines debriefed inboard electronics, diagnosed expected systems failures, and conveyed "up-data" on Shiva from other sources.

"—Omega One, come in. Alpha Two to Omega One, come in."

"Colonel Calderon, you have not followed procedures," Jagens snapped.

"What the hell are we maintaining radio silence for, Carl? So the enemy won't know we're here? This isn't brush war flying, Jagens. Shiva doesn't have ears. Omega One—"

"All right, put a lid on it." It was Chuck Bradshaw's voice, the one with the edge on it, the no-nonsense voice they all hated.

"I started it, Chuck," Lisa said, "and I—"

"Serious up, folks," Chuck said. "Let's cut the traffic to a minimum, shall we?"

"Exactly," Carl Jagens said, smugly.

"Carl . . ." began Chuck, then he paused. "Captain Jagens, you are in command." There was a hidden warning in Chuck's words, but they brought a sudden realization to Lisa. What could Chuck do, if Carl or anyone disobeyed, or veered from the suggested operational plan? If either Alpha or Omega failed, they'd be dead and probably NASA and most of the world, too. If they succeeded, it didn't matter; it would be the success, under whatever conditions, that counted. They'd be heroes and heroines unlike any that had existed before. Literally world-savers. With those kinds of stakes, reprimands were almost meaningless. Bradshaw could only count on everyone obeying in the common interest. But he couldn't *make* anyone obey. No threat was big enough.

Jagens said, "*Resume normal routine. Alpha Two, you have permission to communicate with Omega One.*"

"*Alpha One, this is Alpha Two, request withdrawn.*"

Lisa looked bleakly at the console as she heard Jagens acknowledge the transmission. She felt more alone and set her face in an expression of blankness, a protective shield against revealing her emotions. They always expected the female astronauts to be more emotional, and even after all these years, the cliché persisted. Lisa had learned early to mind her tongue and face.

She listened with only slight attention as a flurry of transmission came up between Earth and the two teams. Words and phrases flew by her. Phased-array radar antennas. A check on the Reaction Control System, which provided attitude stabilization during entry into the Shiva swarm. The deploying boom for directional antennas on *Omega Three* was twenty percent down. The family of intercept trajectories was being sorted. Minimax analysis on angle of entry. Latest information from Thales Center.

Diego, she thought. What were you trying to say? What was *I* trying to say? Touching across space. Reassurance. Memory. Love. But maybe Carl was right, she thought. Stick to the plan. Don't think about anything else. Do your job.

"Houston, this is *Omega One*, requesting information on possibility of ionization within the Shiva swarm. Over."

"*Omega One, we are on that. We expect some, and if it comes we know it will hamper communications. There'll be attenuation, of course, but we hope . . .*"

We hope. It was always *We Hope. We Estimate. We*

Believe. We Compute That. Blind men sailing over the edge of the world. How little we know, she thought. Intuition. Guesswork. Estimations. Approximations. Guesstimates. Scientific witchcraft. How very little we know. Ants trying to stop the descending foot. But stinging ants, she grinned suddenly.

"—so keep us informed, Omega One. *Over.*"

"*Right, Houston. Out.*"

Lisa looked out at the stars. The darkness beyond the firelight.

17 May: Collision minus 8 days

Lisa watched the clock move toward the seven. Listlessly, she lay limply on the couch, her eyes hooded, watching the clock. In seconds it would be four days. Four days of weightlessness, of tension and boredom—the worst possible combination—four days of acceleration and then coasting, a handful of metal objects thrown at an intruder.

Click. Four days. Hooray.

Nino Solari was curled up, his face turned away. Without the usual experiments, mission objectives, and duties, flying through space in a metal box about the size of a couple of phone booths was no fun at all. There was no tension or difficulty between her and Nino; they were too professional, too well-trained and experienced. But neither was there anything exciting about it, either.

There should be music, some kind of musical score that reflected the mood, she thought. When they make the movie of all this there will be. They'll just dissolve from takeoff to arrival at Shiva. Cut out the dull stuff. Wouldn't life be nice if you could just dissolve through the dull, dumb, repetitious times? Music in the air to warn you about the bad stuff coming, of an impending love scene, when the really critical things were about to explode. Just like when they showed shuttle flights. If they showed any procedure at all, it was wonderfully abbreviated, without any of the long checklists, the holds, the boring hours. Just jump in, fire up, cut to the long shot of the rising ship, maybe a quickie showing the pilots looking tense, then a voice-over saying they had achieved orbit and a nice space shot coming into a station, or heading out to the stars on a special mission. Well, this was certainly a special mission.

A screen blipped and she looked at it. The radar fix on Shiva was messy, fuzzy and dangerously erratic. They were still navigating on input from Thales Center, which computed from the various optical telescopes. The core—the big rock—was still unresolved. Alpha was ahead, but in not much better a position; its radar, too, was still fuzzy. But the Alpha ships had started to decelerate, to slow down and match up with Shiva.

The tension continued without resolution, a raw nerve in the midst of the blob of oatmeal that was their boredom. They flew on, uncertain, afraid, feeling the responsibility heavily.

She felt very inadequate.

18 May: Collision minus 7 days, 22 hours

"Miz Carr, you must persuade the President to move to Colorado." Myron Murray's eyes bored into hers intently.

"I mentioned it, Mister Murray, but . . ." She shrugged and smiled. "He's stubborn."

"You're the only one." He stepped closer. They were near the entrance to the State Dining Room. President Knowles was farther down the hall, outside the oval Blue Room, talking to the Indian ambassador, who had not heard from his country in three days, and was near panic. "If you go, he'll go."

"But I wish to be near him." She looked Murray right in the eyes, her gaze level. "He needs me."

"The country needs him, Barbara." Murray moved smoothly into the use of her first name, establishing a shaky intimacy. "You don't want Reed to take over, do you? He was a compromise candidate, you know that." Murray cast a look down the hall toward the chief executive. "No, we need someone with the prestige and the experience of Caleb Knowles. If this country goes . . . is so devastated that . . . if it comes that we have to pull this country back together, perhaps even all of North America, we'll need a Caleb Knowles."

"He says he's staying."

"It's his duty to go. It's his duty to survive."

Barbara narrowed her eyes. "*You* want to go."

Murray nodded. "Of course I wish to survive, Miz, uh, Barbara. That's only natural. But my survival is unimportant; *your* survival is unimportant. His *is* important."

"You're frank, Mister Murray."

"We have no time. I've already authorized transportation for key personnel. Almost half of Congress has already gone. The Pentagon, vital services . . ." He shrugged. "It makes sense. Staying here is a needless act."

"The captain of his ship . . ."

"What? Oh, I see, yes. The analogy is incorrect. We *need* President Knowles and—"

"You need *a* President Knowles. A leader, a charismatic figure."

"Which Reed is not, nor is the Speaker of the House. Perfectly good politicians, but they know their limits. That is, Powell Hopkins does." He touched her arm. "Barbara, if you *ever* wanted to serve your country, this is the time!"

She did not reply. She was watching Knowles. He didn't much like the Indian ambassador. "He's a sanctimonious hypocrite," she remembered him saying. "Millions of his countrymen starving and he blackmails you with the thought as he stuffs his face at the embassy buffets. Whole damn country is royally screwed up. They absolutely refuse to understand effective birth control though they give lip service to it. Only a fraction can farm worth a damn and don't seem to care. They're so damned righteous, like being a holy man gives you the right to leech off others! Political poison, the lot of them!"

When Barbara had asked what he meant, Knowles had said, "How can an American politician say to a nation of fouled-up starving people, 'Get out of it yourself, you got yourself into it.' Those starving children haunt us . . . and they know it, the bastards. But we have our own millions to feed with our own food. But you can't say that publically, and those sonsabitches blackmail us, morally."

India was like the relative of someone rich and famous, who knows that person will pay his debts just to keep the scandal quiet. Knowles often grew angry at the arrogance of the self-styled Indian intellectuals who loved to harangue Americans about what was wrong with them, yet

273

their own country was corrupt, diseased, pretentious, and prone to senseless revolutions and riots.

"Miz Carr?"

"Oh, excuse me, Mister Murray. Look, Mister Murray, the President makes up his own mind and—"

"No one makes up his own mind. Excuse me, Barbara, but no one, especially a president, really makes up his own mind. There are always considerations, pressures, commitments, policies . . . it narrows down the options, limits the choices. Sometimes, despite everything, there is only one choice, only one 'right' answer." He shrugged and spread his hands. "Every leader, every president, every *person* takes advice. You can advise him. There's no shame in it, in going out to Colorado. There's duty in it, responsibility and common sense. *You* can help him make that right decision."

"I heard you, Mister Murray. I . . . I will speak to him again, but if he is adamant, that will be it."

"Do you want to die, Miz Carr?"

She looked at him. "No, of course not. But I don't expect to live forever, either."

"A life as a sheep or a moment as a lion—?"

"If you wish." She turned away, annoyed. Of course she wanted to live. She wanted very badly to live. She'd found something. Something and someone she wanted very much. Yes, she'd love it if Caleb packed up and took the helicopter that awaited them to Andrews Air Force Base and Air Force One. He'd be safe, and alive, and they could . . .

Barbara firmly put the thoughts aside. She would do what he wanted. She had made that commitment secretly, to herself in the middle of the night, with his head on her arm. Old-fashioned, yes; sensible, probably not; satisfying, very much so.

My man.

My man is the leader of the world. Who am I? An overeducated widow, still attractive but for how long? Soon, only too soon, they will love me only for my wit and charm. Let me live these last days . . . perhaps even last hours . . . wildly and foolishly. Mistress to the king. Not Pompadour or du Barry. I have no desire to run kingdoms, or secure jewels and honors and riches. I just want . . .

What?

What *do* I want?

Angrily she squared her shoulders and started walking toward Knowles. "I will do as I said," she said to Murray over her shoulder. He didn't say anything.

Knowles had gotten away from the Indian ambassador, who was fretting under the bored gaze of a State Department man. Knowles broke into a grin as he saw Barbara. "Come on," he said, taking her arm and turning her around. "Let's get the hell out of here! Goddamn bastard! Wanted to go with me to Colorado. When I said I wasn't going he said I was insane!"

Barbara smiled. "Are you?"

"Sure, but I'd never admit it to that poltroon! Come on, let's go upstairs."

"Why, Mister President!" Barbara said in a bad Southern accent, putting her fingertips to her bosom.

"Take the elevator," he ordered, knowing that if he went back toward the stairs he'd be again snared by the ambassador. "Got to keep those bastards out of here, the whole lot of them. Declare a state of emergency. Only United States citizens and not many of them."

The elevator door whispered open and Knowles ushered her into the small, but plush-lined chamber. He kissed her, passionately but with a smile, and the door whispered open again. They came out in the first family's private quarters. But only Knowles lived there, with Lang, his butler, and Lang's wife, Adele, who was assistant Housekeeper.

The President made himself a drink, then poured some white wine for Barbara. "I've been working on a new tune," he said. "'The Kentucky Ramble.' I'll just get my—"

"Caleb . . ."

He stopped, squinting at her, waiting, smiling.

"Caleb, maybe you *should* go to Colorado, to that Air Force mountain thing."

"I saw Murray talking to you."

"He makes sense. You *are* the President."

"That's right, and that's why I'm staying. Captain of the ship of state and all that garbage."

She took a deep breath. "Are you, are you committing suicide?"

"Hell, who knows?" He went across the high-ceilinged room and picked up his banjo, giving it a few happy

275

strums. "None of us are getting out of this life alive, m'dear. One of those space rocks could plunk down in the Potomac just as well as Kansas or Karachi." He ran his fingers across the strings in an agile chord, then slapped the instrument loudly. He swung it by the neck and set it neatly in a couch. He looked at the painting on the wall nearby. The Maine coast, a watercolor by Jamie Wyeth, crisp and wet, with the feeling of sand and wind.

"Goddamnit," he muttered, "I hate what that damn Shiva is doing to this country, to this world!" Abruptly he turned to her. "Tell you what. I'll send everyone to Colorado. Murray, Reed, Hopkins and Mathison, the Supreme Court—"

"They've already gone."

"The generals and the admirals and the captains of the president's nayvee. The lot of them. We'll have this place to ourselves. Just you and me and the ghosts. Run naked in the halls and skinny-dip . . ."

She just smiled at him. "You and the Dancers of Shiva."

"We'll invite them in. Big affair in the East Room. I'll play the banjo and everyone will take off their clothes—"

"Oh, Caleb." She laughed at him, warmly. "You closet hedonist. All that you missed, huh?"

He grinned and shrugged, looking younger than she had ever seen him. With Alpha and Omega in space he had done what he could. It was out of his hands now. Later, if there was a later, he could go back to being leader of the free world and all that other stuff.

"Come here," she said.

He hung back, grinning, looking at her. "You're going to try and talk me into Colorado."

"No, into making love with me."

"With, not to, huh?"

"Yes. That's the best way."

He took her in his arms, suddenly very sober. "Yes, it is, isn't it?"

In Brazil, the disastrous religious fever that had swept through it in the eighties came again, triggered by the self-crucifixion of ninety-nine "saints" in Rio de Janeiro. In Brasilia more than two hundred allowed themselves to be nailed to crude crosses on the grounds of the remote capital. Several of them were fairly high government officials. In Natal, another "miracle": three young convent girls reported seeing what came to be called "Our Lady of the Shining Star," and hundreds of thousands gathered there to pray. The self-crucifixions increased, as did the deaths resulting from loss of blood, infection, and exposure. In São Paulo, over ten thousand people died in a riot trying to see the "Young Virgin of Sorocaba," who had confessed to being visited by Christ, who had worn a robe dripping with blood. Brazil was in the frenetic grip of a religious craze that killed hundreds of thousands, many of them suicides.

In Lebanon a rich banker, for fifty years a miser and "goldbug," had cast a solid gold statue of the goddess Astarte. It weighed eight hundred kilograms and hundreds worshipped it daily. Their hastily written rules of worship changed daily, and always toward the bizarre and cruel.

In Munich a "strong man" rose to sudden power, denouncing the West as a panic-monger, the Russians as decadent and cynical power-players, the Chinese as godless freaks, the black nations as upstart monkeys, the Jews as the Cause, and the efforts in space a fraud and a sham. Millions came to his red and black banner, marched on the government buildings, seized them, and proclaimed themselves the Free Sovereignty of Bavaria with a harsh new set of laws.

In Manchester, England, Lord Birkenhead, a life peer and former waste products czar, had himself and his protesting twenty-four-year-old wife, a former Miss Liverpool, placed in a cryogenic vault for "the duration of the emergency." Sabotage of a power plant by a splinter group of followers of the principles of Brother Gabriel, caused a premature defrosting under less than ideal conditions.

In Akron, Ohio, survivors of the Cleveland meteorite strike were considered unlucky and were shunned. In Bogotá, Colombia, twenty-eight thousand people crawled on their hands and knees, over broken glass, two miles to the cathedral. In Melbourne, Australia, a riot that started when the breweries ran dry destroyed great sections of the city. In Tanzania, President-for-life Amani Nero proclaimed himself Lord of Africa, Rising Star of the World, and Master of Magic. To celebrate his ascendancy he had every prisoner in every prison beheaded.

The Taiyuan nuclear plant four hundred kilometers southwest of Tientsin, China, exploded. No cause was announced. In Copenhagen, the street orgy that had been going on for eight days ended in a mysterious mass poisoning. Suicides and major crimes were up everywhere, as were rapes. A father in Union Furnace, Ohio, shot his entire family as a "sacrifice" to Shiva.

Businesses stumbled to a halt as the money dried up and people stopped buying and stopped coming to work. Some continued on, just to pass the time, or because they didn't believe any of it. Barter regained its popularity. So did the fulfillment of vendettas.

Women still became pregnant. Some by accident, but many by determination and on purpose. It was a good sign. People were still hopeful. Or still stupid. But a baby holds promise for the future.

19 May: Collision minus 6 days, 10 hours

Saperstein and Cooper lay in the saltgrass and stared at the bonfire. The figures danced around it, the firelight glistening on exposed flesh. "Those aren't Dancers," Cooper whispered.

"I know," Saperstein replied. He twisted in the hard-packed sand. His right arm was all but useless, supported by some webbing belts, and throbbed endlessly. "Gabriels maybe."

"Didn't know they carried on like that."

"Maybe they are mutating."

"Huh?" Cooper looked with surprise at his commander.

"Mutating as the pressures change, like a virus. They think they've stopped Omega, or at least crippled the effort. There's nothing more they can do at the Cape. Down in Houston, maybe. So they are mutating, changing, becoming . . . God only knows what."

"Looks like, well, they look like Shiva Dancers to me, except they have their clothes on."

"We'll swing around them, Sergeant. Southeast. We'll be at Merritt Island by dawn."

"Sir."

They crept back and got up to move away at a crouch. Nearby, to the west, there was a long line of dark houses. Some were abandoned, a few burnt out, and others very quiet. Saperstein figured them to be fortresses of silence, hoping events would pass them by. Good luck, he said to the dark rectangles.

20 May: Collision minus 5 days, 20 hours

The building shook like a giant rattling a box. The front windows exploded inward, killing a National Guardsman and wounding others. The entire Thales Center complex shivered. The electricity went out and within the windowless rooms there was chaos and confusion. Men screamed, women cursed, people fell, spilled papers made the floor slippery, and broken plastic shards from the ceiling fixtures cut hands and knees.

Caroline Weinberg groped for Wade Dennis in the darkness, gasping with effort as she threw aside a chair that had crashed into her. "Wade! *Wade!*" Her hands found him and she heard him groan.

Quickly she felt over his body, encountered his hands trying to feel his head, and then felt blood on the back of his head, matting the hair and oozing over her fingers. "Are you all right?" she asked over the cries and noise.

"What the hell happened?" he grunted.

"Explosion or . . . or another meteor hit."

"Are the lights out or am I blind?"

"The lights are out, darling," she said, holding him. "What happened to your head?"

"Hit it on the desk, I think." Someone flashed a light across the computer room and someone shouted for help. "Where the blazes is the auxiliary power?"

"It'll come on in a minute, hang in there."

But it didn't come on in a moment. National Guard soldiers found flashlights and led the people out. Wade hung an arm over Caroline's shoulder and held his head with the other, swearing softly the whole time. Outside, the early evening sky to the west was crimson, but not with the setting sun.

Fire.

Fire, smoke, dust. The National Guard officer at his jeep radio announced that "something from space" hit in the Boston suburbs. Fire engine sirens made speech almost impossible for a few moments. Caroline took a first aid kit from a passing medic and sat Wade down to bandage his head. It was bloody but not too serious, at least not compared to some around them.

"We've got to get that auxiliary power on," Wade said. "Houston needs the info and, oh, God, the temperature will go up, those damn chips will heat up . . . oww!"

"Sorry. There, that's it. I'll staple your head on later." Caroline tried to smile, but couldn't.

"Help me up."

"Stay here," she said, pushing down at him. "*I'll* go check the auxiliary . . ."

He clawed at her clothes and dragged himself up, almost undressing her on the sidewalk. There were bodies and moaning injured all around. Looking west he could see rubble in the streets from collapsed buildings, wrecked cars, fires starting, fires billowing out, people running. He turned with a strickened, blood-streaked face toward the north, where the basement entry was. Caroline went with him, reaching for him as he careened suddenly toward the wall. He caught himself, gasping, wide-eyed, swaying. He cursed and shoved off from the wall. A police car with a smashed fender went by, siren screeching. Wade shook off her hands and they went along the wall to the basement entrance. The four Guard soldiers stood uncertainly around the buckled door, and let Caroline and Wade in without a word.

The ceiling had collapsed. A pipe had impaled the more fragile parts of the diesel generator and a broken concrete column had half-buried it. Oil leaked out into a rising pool, thick and dark.

"Oh, God," Wade said wearily. He turned to the corporal in charge of the detail. "Keep people out. I'll get some people here to help, but stop that oil leak or we'll have an explosion. Try to get the engine free. Any of you know diesels?"

The young, beardless corporal shook his head. "No, but there's Lounsberry, Sergeant Lounsberry, over in the motor pool."

"Get him. This is top priority, you understand?"

"Y-yes, s-sir."

"We need the power for the computers, for lights, for . . ." Wade coughed and swayed. Caroline grabbed his shoulders, but he shook free. "Top priority. Alpha and Omega, God save us, need what we have here."

"I, I understand." The young noncom turned and began barking orders. "Rivers, go get the captain! Lebow-sky, get that leak stopped. Sagasta, you help Lebowsky." He turned back to Wade. "Can I help you, sir?"

"No. No. I . . . I have to find power. Does the Guard have portable units?"

"Yes, sir, but I dunno where they are. Probably out at Logan, after that Gabriel mess Wednesday. Maybe some at the Boston Army Base, though."

"All right, thank you." Wade started back along the sidewalk, and was met by the captain in charge, whose name Wade could not remember. He explained the problem and stressed the importance of restoring power. The captain excused himself a moment, checked the damage himself, then came back along to Wade and Caroline.

"A mess, a blessed mess," he said. "Whole damned city's a mess. All right, what's our deadline here?"

"Deadline?" Caroline asked.

"How long before it's too late? Before getting power to your machines won't do those space fellas any good?"

"Ah . . ." Wade tried to think, but the throbbing in his head was getting worse.

"Three days. They are about four days or so out," Caroline said, frowning. "I'd say seventy to eighty hours, more to collision."

"All right," the captain said briskly. A line of soldiers trotted by, led by a gray-haired sergeant, and they stepped toward the curb. The red in the west getting worse. Ash was beginning to fall. "Wonder where it hit?" the officer said. "Watertown? Belmont maybe? Some-where on this edge of Middlesex county, though. Blessed Jesus." He shook his head. "What a mess. I'm in in-surance. Massachusetts and Lunar Life. Thank Jesus we don't hold much paper out that way." Somewhere a wall collapsed in a grinding noise. A fire engine, followed by a red automobile, blared its way through the intersec-tion down the street.

"I'll do what I can," the captain said to Wade and Caroline. "I'll talk to Colonel Dunnigan about it. He'll understand. He went to Harvard," he added proudly.

"Fine," groaned Wade, who was getting dizzier by the second, "get him. Do what you have to do, but we need power *quickly*. Not three days . . . sooner . . . the sili-con chips will warm up . . . the balance will get off . . ."

"Ohh," groaned Caroline. She had become so used to the stable computers she had forgotten they existed in tanks of helium kept well below zero. "We only have a few hours . . ."

"Blessed Jesus," the officer muttered, sighing. "All right," he said with sudden decision. He broke into a run back toward his jeep radio.

Caroline and Wade limped along behind. He had to lean against the wall for a moment to get the weakness out of his legs. He smiled apologetically at her. "Sorry," he said. He hated being weak, hated being at less than full functional level.

She made small sounds of sympathy and when he was ready she went with him to the front of the Thales Center. The captain turned from the radio, stepped over some prostrate bodies, and came quickly to them.

"No dice. The colonel says every one of their portables is hooked up to a hospital, or to vital communications."

"There's *nothing*—" Wade groaned as his savage snarl made him wince. "There's nothing more important than Thales right now, Captain!"

"But the people in the hospitals, Mr. Dennis—!" He waved down the street. "The operating rooms are overflowing! They're doing meatball surgery down there like it was a combat zone. The burn wards are clogged! The hit was near Watertown. There *is* no Watertown and the fires are coming this way!"

"I don't *care*, Captain! If we don't get back into operation there'll be no Boston. No Massachusetts. No New England. No godforsaken United States! Maybe no fucking *world!*" Wade swayed and Caroline grabbed him. His eyes rolled up and he fell limply. She only barely managed to prevent his head from striking the sidewalk.

Caroline stared up at the officer. "He was not exaggerating, Captain, uh, Captain—?"

"Hennessey, ma'am."

"Captain Hennessey, what he said is absolutely true. We *must* restore the power to the computers. We can use candles, flashlights, whatever, to *see* . . . but the machines need power!"

Hennessey chewed at his upper lip. "Blessed Jesus," he said softly.

20 May: Collision minus 5 days, 1 hour

"Alpha One, *this is Houston.*"

"Houston Control, this is *Alpha One,* go ahead."

"*Carl, this is Chuck Bradshaw.*" Jagens glanced at General Menshov, who looked back impassively.

"Yes, Chuck?"

"*Bad news, I'm afraid. We're taking some hits down here, you know. Minor stuff mostly. Bloomington, the one in Indiana, got a hit. Northern Chile got a couple, Hokkaido is in bad shape. . . . Yemen, Libya, one in the Balkans somewhere, one near Antwerp—*"

"Yes, yes," Carl said impatiently. "Get to it. Please," he added diplomatically.

"*Boston. Near Boston, actually. Knocked out the power to the Thales Center. The computers are down. They're trying to get them up again before they heat up, but the whole area's a mess. We're flying stuff in but Logan's out, totally, for some time to come. We're trying to find some little commercial airport we can set down in, but the communications are completely fouled up.*"

"No Thales, no accuracy," Jagens muttered. He looked at Menshov. "Do you have anything we can route through, maybe something we don't know about?"

Menshov's wide Slavic expression didn't change. "How much time do we have?"

Jagens repeated the question to Bradshaw. "*About four or five hours. By then the elements will be too warm,*" Bradshaw said. "*They'll have to recalibrate and God only knows what all.*" They waited, all of them, for Menshov's answer.

The Russian was quite aware that his own countrymen, both in Houston and back in Moscow, were listening to him. Should he reveal *Mosk 8,* at Saratov? Or the Prastrånstvo Institute? Was there time to make the necessary hookups? Could it be done through the satellites in time? Was this some kind of trick, to get them to reveal super-secret computer bases? They could hardly fake a meteor impact on Boston, but perhaps they were only taking advantage of the situation? At Leningrad they had something, he wasn't certain just what, but he had heard rumors. Was he supposed to know about that one? Or the others, for that matter?

"I do not know, Mister Bradshaw. Contact my superiors in Moscow, please."

Jagens snorted in disgust, but Bradshaw was more diplomatic. "*General Menshov, we don't have time—to contact, get the right people, get permission, make the changes. I . . . oh, never mind, we'll do it ourselves. Somehow.*"

"Keep us informed," Jagens said.

"*Right. Houston, out.*"

Menshov perceived a new coldness from the already frosty Jagens. "We will need more raw information from the optical sightings," the Russian said. Jagens nodded, deep in thought. "All the changes in trajectory. Both *Alpha* and *Omega.*" Jagens did not acknowledge. Menshov sat quietly, breathing shallowly. He looked out the port. *Was I wrong? We have shown them so much already. Bolshoi. Enough bits and pieces that later, when things calm down, they will put together and build up a newer picture of where we are. The new molecular impressions, for example. I saw their faces when they realized what we had in the Bolshoi controls. They don't need any more from us. They'll all be debriefed, as we will. But we've learned more about them than they have about us,* he thought. *The stream of information going back in the diplomatic pouches had turned into a river. Much would be salvaged from this disaster.*

Jagens stoically made a status check. Everything was correct. *Boringly correct,* he thought. He took a chip from a pouch and slipped it into the onboard computer and punched up the screen. The chess board appeared in color. It was a Schultz program, without the time lapse put in. Jagens was scornful of players who needed the ego-boosting salve of having the computer take a human length of time to decide its move. But on the other hand, it *was* a beatable program, with the ingeniously designed Schultz program. You were really playing Michel Schultz, not the computer.

Carl switched the mike to the proper circuit. "King's pawn to King Four."

"*Queen's Bishop pawn to Queen's Bishop Four,*" the computer said at once, the image blinking its change.

"Knight to King's Bishop Three."

"Pawn to King Three."

The speed of response *was* disconcerting. Jagens furrowed his brow. The trap to avoid was the temptation to show the damned computer and respond just as swiftly. "Pawn to Queen Four."

"Pawn takes pawn."

Jagens took a deep breath and settled in. Schultz had a good end game. He smiled, remembering a favorite college trick of playing one computer program against another, with programming ability a big factor in the designed options. "Knight takes pawn."

"Pawn to Queen's Rook Three."

"Bastard," he said aloud. But it passed the time. People were like chess pieces, he thought. Only the rules were far less precise.

"Caleb?"

"Mum?"

"Wake up."

"No."

"Come on, darling, there are important people who want to tell you important things."

The President of the United States opened one eye and stared resentfully ahead. The one eye swiveled around until it came to rest on Barbara Carr. Then the expression changed.

"Come back to bed."

"No, now they say it's important."

"It's *always* important," he grumbled, settling the blankets around him again.

"No, this really is."

"Then you tell me."

She sighed and sat on the edge of the bed. "Listen, I don't *know* what it is, but they act as if it's important, so . . ." She shrugged. He made a sound that wasn't actually a word. "Come *on!*"

"Ohhh—!" He twisted around and flipped back the covers. He was wearing a baggy T-shirt and nothing else. He pulled off the shirt and threw it away as he stomped toward the bathroom. "Coffee!"

She sighed and picked up the phone. "The President would like his coffee. And please tell General Whatshisname and the Secretary he will be with them in a few minutes."

She hung up and went over to push open the bathroom door. Caleb Knowles was standing there urinating with his head back and his eyes closed. "You better look where you're aiming," she said.

"You come act as director," he muttered sleepily.

"Oh, no," she said. "Do you know you are getting worse every day? Everyone knows we're sleeping together. You invite that Murray into our bedroom and—"

"Oh, hell, Barbara, sure they know. This place has more ears than a corral full of donkeys." He leaned toward the mirror and made a face at himself. Yawning, he stepped into the shower and closed the door. She heard him gasp as the water started, then sigh as it was adjusted to his approval. He started singing "Sweet Betsy from Pike" with great enthusiasm.

She leaned against the doorjamb and crossed her arms under her breasts. "They are not very happy with you these days."

"What?" he shouted.

She shouted back. "They're not very happy with you these days. The party biggies. The majority leader."

Knowles laughed. "Screw the party. If I save Earth from Shiva, I won't even have to campaign next time."

"If *you* save Earth."

"What?"

"Nothing." She sighed and stepped into the bathroom to look at herself in the mirror. God, she was getting to look terrible. Too many pills, too many long hours, too much . . . too much what? Too much living? You weren't living before, she told her frowning reflection, you were only existing.

Is this living?

Yes, it's living.

It's living and loving and doing some good in the world.

She touched her face, watched her hands touching her face, and felt her fingers. Without me, he'd be over the edge. You are holding him together. Admit it. Don't be modest with me, Bobbie Summers Carr. I know you. You are a born self-sacrificer.

With a start she realized she had not thought of her dead husband since this whole crazy thing had begun. She looked at her hollow eyes, her lips parted, but her mind was frozen. The water stopped and the door clicked open. Knowles reached out for a towel, his hair curled and dripping. The water beaded up on his hairy body, reflecting the lights. She looked at him in the mirror, vigorously rubbing the towel over himself. He caught her eye in the misted mirror.

"Voyeur," he said with a grin.

"Uh-huh. Wanton woman, too," she said and made a playful grab for his crotch. He jerked back with a laugh, then seized her arm and pulled her close.

"You're wet!"

"Right!" He kissed her hard, dropping the towel. The mood changed. She felt him grow hard against her stomach and she gasped. Barbara's hands slid between them and she seized him.

Knowles laughed, deep in his chest, his eyes sparkling at her. Barbara felt a weakness in her knees and tightened her grip on him, making him wince, then laugh. "Watch it!"

"Undress me," she said.

"I thought you had General Whosis out there and the Secretary of Space Stuff waiting?"

"Let 'em wait."

"And eat cake?"

"Undress me?"

He tugged at her clothes and she kept at least one hand wrapped around his penis the whole time. Then, naked, she came back to him. He put both hands over her breasts and she sighed.

"I like 'em like yours," he said hoarsely, kissing her on the neck. Her hands stroked him passionately. She realized she was panting and it embarrassed her, but she couldn't stop.

"Oh, Caleb . . ."

She saw them together, in the misted mirror. He moved one hand down to her buttocks and squeezed and she saw the flesh billow and redden. Hurt me, she thought.

Then he pressed on her shoulders and she knelt, her eyes locked with his. Her mouth opened and she guided him to her and took him in. She looked up at him, saw his half-lidded expression of pleasure, felt her own moist warmth. Her red warm mouth moved on him, back and forth. She closed her eyes and devoted her entire attention to pleasing him.

After a few moments she heard him growl, felt his

287

hands lifting her up, pulling her toward the bedroom. "No," she said, her voice husky, "let's do it here."

Knowles didn't care. They had made love all over the White House, in the center of the Great Seal woven into the rug of the Oval Office, in the Lincoln Bedroom, behind the closed door of a linen room, and once against the wall of the State Dining Room. He lifted her up, set her on the sink and she spread her legs, her arms around his neck, guided himself into her, his face intent. He entered her and they both let out a long sigh. She locked her arms around him, then her legs, clinging with a frenetic desperation. Her breath was short and she moaned raggedly. He seemed to go into her and into her and *into* her, impaling her from crotch to mouth. She was panting now, ragged sounds, raw sounds, but it was the only way she could breathe.

Her climax came quickly, much too quickly, a shuddering ripple that left her weak and helpless. But still he drove into her, hard and demanding, like a nation demands, like a whole screaming race demands. Her muscles tensed, her mouth opened in a long, shivering gasp. She had a sudden flash: the Secret Service agents outside, listening, grinning. The image faded, unimportant—she didn't care what *anyone* thought.

He drove into her and drove into her. He never seemed to come out, only go in. Deeper and deeper. She was limp, a ragdoll that clung to him by static electricity. Another orgasm built up in her and she quailed before it, afraid, frightened. She balled her fists and tried to cry out but he filled her. A searing feather of flame passed over her as she cried out. He grunted, then roared, his hands digging into her hips, holding her, pumping his rigid organ into her in a relentless thrusting.

She screamed out again as he rammed into her and froze, face contorted, body rigid. She felt him pulse, then felt the loosening, the spurting, the finale. Her throat was raw as she gasped again. She felt the hot jet of his semen in her, turning her inside to melted butter, to lava, to flame. Her whole pelvis spasmed and to her astonishment she felt herself going into another orgasm.

"Oh, God, God!" she cried. Then it was over, and they clung together, limp, swaying, the tile sticky beneath her buttocks. She saw them indistinctly in the misted mirror.

Bodies. Flesh. Joined.

"Oh, damn, damn, that was good," he sighed.

"Yes," she said, sighing. Her heart was pounding. He pulled away, still damp, smiling weakly. He swayed and laughed and caught himself.

"Damn, damn . . . thank you, thank you . . ."

After he had wandered off into the other room she sat there, looking at her imperfect image in the mirror. Naked wench. Wanton. A President's seed lies in your womb, she said to herself, her lips barely moving.

She was so weak, so tired. It took a lot of effort to get down from the sink. A quick shower, she thought, then one of those pink-and-blue pills, and a red, and maybe a striped green-and-brown. She'd feel better then. They helped her forget. Only she couldn't forget too much. She had to help. It was important that she help.

21 May: Collision minus 4 days, 23 hours

Wade Dennis sat in the wrecked lobby on a stack of rations, his back against the scratched wall. His head hurt badly, but he tried to go over in his mind what the Alpha team would be doing in the next few days.

One day from intercept, at approximately minus twenty-two to twenty-five hours, Thales Center would have to provide the final information. From then on it would be too late. Events would be happening too rapidly.

At minus twenty-one hours, with Shiva a glowing gray crescent against the blazing face of the sun, the unmanned bomb-carrying vessels would flip head for tail and begin to decelerate. Only the two command modules, *Alpha One* and *Two*, would race ahead, leaving the V formation. They would enter the Shiva cloud well ahead of the following fleet of missiles. Inboard systems would carry out the last reconnaissance of Shiva's debris. Then the two command modules would decelerate further and come to rest with respect to Shiva. The dark, rocky face on the night side of Shiva would be their only refuge from the raw energy of *Bolshoi*. Signals from the command modules would guide *Bolshoi* through the Shiva swarm at high velocity, bringing it within a few hundred meters of the sunward face. Proximity sensors were to detonate *Bolshoi* within fifty meters of Shiva. The mass of the great asteroid would block the lethal radiation before it reached the command modules.

But all this depended upon exact targeting. An error of five hundred meters was intolerable. The X-ray and particle radiation from a near miss would fry the *Alpha* crew within seconds. Estimated probability for survival in the command modules was forty-three percent, taking into account targeting errors and irregularities in Shiva's slowly turning profile. Up until onboard radar could be used effectively, the major navigation would have to be done by Thales, which collected data from all the sighting sources and computed it, then sent it out via Houston by the proper transmission station on the side of Earth facing *Alpha*.

In the meantime the *Alpha* and *Omega* crews were just passengers, waiting and thinking. It was the thinking that was going to be the hardest for them, Wade knew. But he still had things to do. Impossible things. The Hilton Inn didn't have an intact window facing west. Several of their technicians had been hurt. Captain Hennessey was doing his best, but there were people bleeding all over Boston.

Wade sighed and opened his eyes. A young tech was lying near him, the side of her face covered with a bloody bandage. Beyond, a bare-chested black man was carefully applying a salve to the burns of one of the National Guardsmen injured in putting out the fire across the street. Captain Hennessey came in, hip-twisting through the people and wreckage lying on the lobby floor. His face was sweaty and grim.

"Doctor. No dice on the Kennedy Hospital power plant. They are knee deep in casualties and all ORs are filled. A young nurse threatened to give me an amateur vasectomy if I tried to take it."

"Captain, we—"

"I know, I know." The weary officer dropped down on the ration boxes and fell back against the wall. His helmet clanged, making him wince. "I'll think of something." He sighed. "Three and a half hours left, huh?"

"Yes." The headache was blinding. He probably had a concussion. What the hell were the signs? Focusing the eyes? He looked out through the glassless windows, blinking. Okay, not bad. Wasn't there something about dilation of the eyes or motor reflexes? Damn, it hurt to think. "Got to do something . . . fast . . ." he said softly.

"Yeah, yeah. Okay. Look. We . . . we *take* one."

"From where?"

"Nearest hospital. No, not take, uh, run lines. No, they could cut those, uh . . . no, that would work . . . maybe . . ." He turned toward Wade, his helmet scratching on the wall. "Do you need power *all* the time?"

"Well, uh, no. *Got* to cool the chips down, then . . . uh . . . make the transmissions, no, uh, first the computations and uh, the transmissions. No, wait—we have input from . . . God, I can't think very well." He felt weak, but not as weak as he had earlier. Very tired. "Maybe we could set up . . . uh . . . five-minute shifts . . . power here for five, in the hospital for five, or . . . Christ, I dunno."

The officer heaved himself up with a grunt and stuck out his hand. "C'mon. I'll need your help."

Caroline came out of the interior of the building carrying some files. "What's going on?"

Wade took Hennessey's hand and let him do most of the work of lifting him to his feet. "I'm going with . . . with Hennessey . . . to, uh, to the hospital."

"Wade! You can't, you're hurt!"

"Who isn't?"

"I'm not." She tried to shove him back, but he shook his head doggedly.

"Got to, got to . . ."

"Captain, make him—"

"Need him, ma'am. Really do. Those jokers down there wouldn't give me a bandaid on time. Can't say I blame them, but I need the doc here to pull some rank."

"I'll go with you." Wade tried to protest, but Caroline was adamant. They went out into the street and climbed into the jeep. Hennessey called over a sergeant. "Gifford, take some men and go down that way three, four blocks and over one. I think there's an electrical supply store there somewhere. Bring me back enough cable to run from here over to Kennedy Memorial."

"Mother of Mary, Cap'n! That's a quarter mile!"

"Get on it. Top priority. Garrity!" A young lieutenant turned and trotted over from helping the medics.

"Sir!"

"You're in charge. Gifford's going for some cable. We're going to lay a line from Kennedy Memorial to here. Round up every stray soldier or sailor you see. We're going to need guards along the whole quarter mile."

Garrity didn't blink. "Sir!"

Hennessey climbed into the jeep and started the motor. They crunched over glass and sped away down the street.

"It is out of the question. You people are insane!" The man in the white coat tried to shove the door closed. Captain Hennessey put his shoulder to the door and kept it open. He looked very apologetic.

"If you'd just listen to these people, Doctor Curzon, please."

"I have listened," the slight, moustached man answered angrily. "I've given you my answer." He looked at Caroline and Wade with icy fury, outraged that his wishes were not carried out at once.

"Doctor, there's a greater matter at stake here—" Wade began.

"I've heard your case, *Doctor* Dennis. I sympathize with your problem. But surely an organization as large as NASA could take care of its own? There's no more to say." He attempted again to close the door of his office, but Hennessey kept it open, looking even more uncomfortable. Curzon impaled him with a look. "Captain, I hope you never need surgical help."

"So do I, doc, but these people have a point. There *is* something greater at stake here."

"I am sworn to help. I am a doctor." He waved his hand at the crowded corridors. "This is the greatest emergency in the history of Boston! You must excuse me, I am needed elsewhere."

He shouldered passed Hennessey and Caroline caught at his jacket. He glared at her, his face red with anger. "Miss . . . Miss whoever you are, take your hands off me! People are *dying!*"

"The *world* may die, Doctor Curzon, can't you see that? Are you *that* blind?"

Dr. Curzon held himself under tight control. "Yes, I think I understand and I sympathize. I've *said* that. But I can't help you. These people need me *now*. I can't let them die because of a *maybe,* somewhere in outer space."

"It isn't very much out," Wade said heavily. "It's damned near *in.* And it isn't a maybe, it's a matter of celestial ballistics. Shiva *will* hit us. If we had the center going we could probably tell you right now *where* each chunk of that swarm will strike. Given the right observations. I—"

"I can't help you." Curzon pulled loose from Caroline and went quickly down the hall. He pulled off his blood-splattered jacket and went into the operating room scrub area.

Hennessey sighed and leaned against the wall. "Well, what do we do now?"

Wade looked with tired, pain-reddened eyes after the departed Curzon. "We take the power."

Hennessey sighed softly. "I was afraid you were going to say that. Look, doc, I don't know if I could get my boys to do that. They . . . they aren't regular troops, you know, they're Guard. They . . . maybe they have people here . . ." He waved his hand around vaguely. He wiped the sweat from his face.

Wade's face was a tragic mask. "I know. But we've got to do it." He turned to Hennessey and his feverish eyes bore into him. "Look, you believe what we're doing is right, don't you?"

"Blessed Jesus, doc, I . . ." He looked around, trapped. "You're asking me to, Jesus, to fight a hospital full of . . . of . . ."

"That's right—a hospital full of sick and dying, fighting the doctors and nurses and everybody that is here to save them. I know what I'm asking, Hennessey."

The captain sighed and pushed himself off the wall, his hand wiping his face again. "Blessed Jesus . . ." he sighed. He looked at Caroline for help, but saw none in her face. "I . . . I know it's the right thing to do for, you know, the big picture but, Christ . . ." He bit at his lip and looked at the ceiling. A woman screamed down the corridor and threw herself on the still small form of a child lying on a gurney table. Hennessey looked at her with bleak eyes.

"It will be like this everywhere," Caroline said. "If there are hospitals left standing. Everywhere, Captain."

"Yes, ma'am. Look, I'm just an insurance salesman, and—"

"Want to bankrupt your firm?" she asked quietly. "A callous way to put it, but if we don't get the power *Alpha* won't get the—"

"Yes, I know!" snapped Hennessey in sudden irritation. "Stop blackmailing me, will you?" He glared down the hall where the mother was fighting with two attendants who were taking the boy's body away. "Look . . . all right, but . . . we gotta do this in a way . . . in a way that no one . . . or, uh, as few as possible, are hurt, okay?"

Caroline and Wade nodded, but Wade blinked and felt dizzy. "Let's go take a look at the plant, if we can," Caroline suggested.

"Yeah, save time that way. And scout the defenses."

They took the stairway to the basement. The emergency power plant rumbled away in a separate concrete room. A huge oil supply tank was in the next room, enough for several days of power. An overalled technician looked at them curiously, then walked away to answer a phone below a blinking light. It was too noisy for them to talk very much but they saw the attendant look at them suddenly. From a door at the far end of the room a group of security men and city police suddenly burst through. They saw Hennessey and his companions and came quickly at them with drawn weapons.

"Sir," the leading policeman said, "you'll have to leave. There is a report of a saboteur down here."

"Of course, officer," Hennessey said smoothly. "We were just inspecting the emergency equipment ourselves. This is Dr. Weinberg and Dr. Dennis, by the way."

The policeman nodded, but no one holstered weapons. "You hospital staff?" the officer asked.

"No, we're from Thales Center," Caroline began, but the officer cut her off with a wave of his hand. His gun remained steady.

"No unauthorized visitors. Connolly, post a detail here." He turned to the security man with him. "We'll take turns, O'Hara. If you'll . . ." He broke off to look back at the three intruders. "Robbins!" One of the officers stepped forward, his eyes wary. "Take these, uh, visitors outside, please."

"Right, Sergeant." He gestured toward the stairs and

Wade followed Caroline and Hennessey out. He looked back, memorizing the layout again.

Back in the street Hennessey sighed. "Curzon didn't waste time. Actually, of course, there should have been a guard there anyway." He sighed, looking at the encroaching darkness. "Well, we're spread pretty thin. Okay, come on. We have a blitzkrieg to plan."

They hurried down the street to the jeep, jumped in and crunched over more glass to turn around in midstreet. They quickly pulled over to the curb as an ambulance came screeching along, followed by two cars and a steaming pickup filled with pale, frightened people with homemade bandages, or none. A little farther on a dusty city bus lumbered by, all its windows smashed out, and filled with moaning wounded.

Hennessey tried to remember a prayer, then gave up as they turned down the street toward Thales Center.

Wade Dennis shoved back his sleeve and looked at his watch. The tiny red numbers told him they had less than two hours to get hooked up. He looked at the preparations Hennessey had made. The city bus had given him the idea. They found one abandoned and made up some realistic-looking bandages. Those actually wounded were loaded last, to be the first off and give them a "cover." Guns were stashed under seats, concealed in bandages and clothing.

Most of the soldiers were reluctant and suspicious. All were scared. Corporal Thatcher, the one who had been guarding the Thales power plant, was sent after the two men who had deserted. He returned before the last men were loaded into the bus. He nodded to Hennessey and accepted a bloody head bandage from one of the secretaries.

He looked chillingly efficient.

Wade had taken precious minutes to convince Caroline to stay behind, to be ready to start the cooling and checking of the silicone-mag chips in the liquid helium tanks. Hennessey's men had laid cable from the Center to within a block of the hospital. Everything was ready to go. But no one wanted to be the one to order it.

Hennessey stepped up into the bus, held on to one of the slippery chrome bars and shouted down the vehicle. "I know you don't want to do this. Neither do I. It's

295

shitty work. But you must believe that unless this here computer place gets power Alpha will fail and Omega will fail and the whole blessed world will go down the tubes." He grinned suddenly, a wide Irish smile that sparkled. "You'll talk of it when you're a bunch of old bastards, how you saved the blessed world." Some of the men laughed and a redheaded woman with corporal's stripes called out to him.

"Let's get on with it, Captain! I'd like to get even with that place for the bills I've been getting!"

There were strained laughs. Hennessey spoke quietly to his noncoms; the ones that would bring up the rest of the company once the firing started. Then he swung into a seat, put his arm in a sling and gestured for the door to close. The bus fired up and the driver, an overweight motor pool sergeant, pulled the long vehicle out from the curb.

Caroline watched it chug away, turn the corner and disappear. Suddenly she realized she hadn't said goodbye to Wade. She took a step, then stopped. Not goodbye, but be seeing you. *Au revoir, auf Wiedersehen, sayonara* . . .

She turned and strode briskly into the Thales lobby, looking straight ahead.

The bus slowed, allowing another ambulance ahead of it. There were cars parked all around. Several policemen were directing two tow-trucks in clearing up the tangle. The bus edged through. No one paid any attention to them. Hennessey spoke quietly to several soldiers about how to get rid of the policemen at their back.

The bus stopped short of the emergency entrance and tired-looking attendants, many of them volunteers in blood-smeared civilian clothes, came forth to take the wounded. No one seemed surprised that some of the soldiers had weapons hung on slings from their shoulders.

Hennessey got out. He directed several men with his thumb, and five of them stumbled away, pretending dizziness, and moved back toward the policemen at the tow-trucks. Hennessey was counting on the fact they had moved too quickly for Curzon to get any reinforcements in from a police force spread thinly through the city. He put his arm over the shoulder of a young soldier and put his face down and allowed the private to help him along.

Behind Hennessey, Wade grinned. To be an insurance saleman maybe you have to be an actor, he thought, moving along with a hand held to his bandaged head, ready to cover his face if he spotted Curzon or any of the medical personnel he had seen earlier.

Hennessey was hamming it up, groaning and limping extravagantly, but the entire force got into the hospital quickly. They avoided the interns who moved quickly among them, assigning priority, always saying, "Take care of my buddy first, sir," and referring them to the genuinely wounded. Wade felt proud of the real wounded. They knew what they were getting into, that they were placing themselves in a very dangerous position from a number of standpoints.

Hennessey stopped his men outside a door to the basement. They slumped against the wall, putting the actually wounded on the perimeter. Then one by one they slipped through the door into the basement stairwell. There were fifteen soldiers there when Wade arrived. About a third were women, part of the new combat army.

Another man came in behind Wade and Hennessey motioned them down. The concrete shaft seemed to echo every step, every rustle. At the first landing the red-headed woman from the bus grabbed at Hennessey's sleeve and whispered, "Sir, are we just going to barge in there . . . uh . . . shooting?"

"It's going to be pretty hard to surprise them, O'Flynn." He turned away in irritation, but she pulled him back, pulled his head down to hers and whispered fiercely. Hennessey looked surprised, then asked her, "Are you *sure?*"

"Better'n gettin' shot at, Captain," she grinned. She had a rather weak grip on the grin, but it held.

"Okay, move to the front."

They went down as quietly as they could, massing up on the last steps. Hennessey kept everyone back off the landing, then he crept forward and opened the door a little, peering in. He looked for a few seconds then straightened and whispered to his small assault force, holding up three fingers. "By the door to the right. One across, with his back to us." He looked at the redhead. "If you're ready, O'Flynn."

To everyone's astonishment the woman handed the nearest soldier her rifle and started to undress. One of the soldiers looked startled, blinked, and started to stop her. She glared at him and his hand dropped. In moments she was naked, red marks from her bra and belt on her pale skin. She rubbed at them in annoyance, not looking at her fellow soldiers, but not appearing to be uncomfortable. The concrete floor was cold and her nipples puckered up and came erect almost at once. She moved to the door, put her hand on the knob, and looked back at Hennessey. He waved the men against the wall and nodded.

The redheaded O'Flynn threw open the door and ran out into the power room screaming. "Oh, my God, my God! Look out! Oh, God, don't let it get me!" She ran across the room, drawing everyone's attention, and threw herself on the single officer. "Save me! Oh, my God, my God!"

"What is it? What's going on up there?" The three officers by the emergency power room stepped toward her. She twisted around, giving them a good look at her lush, freckled, pale figure.

"It's terrible, terrible! They . . . oh, my *God!* What's happened is, oh, God, God!"

"What's going *on!*" The officer she had grasped was trying to fight free, but she pinned him tightly. Her leg had entwined with his and she was staring at the back entrance with wide eyes.

"They're . . . they're—oh, no, no!"

Hennessey waved and the soldiers poured through. One of the officers turned toward them, gun in hand. He fired and the soldier next to Hennessey spun away and fell. Another of the National Guardsmen fired a machine gun burst over his head, spattering off the concrete ceiling and whining away.

"Blessed Jesus, watch out!" snapped Hennessey. The policeman that O'Flynn had grabbed tried to draw his service revolver but her adroitly placed leg was the pivot upon which the startled cop spun, crashing into the floor with bone-crushing force. He groaned and lay still. The other members of Boston's finest raised their hands.

Hennessey tossed O'Flynn her clothes. "Nicely done!" he called. He posted a guard at both entrances, then led Wade back up toward the emergency entrance. They found outraged interns and moaning patients under the guns of his second section of nervous but determined soldiers. "Get the cables in here!" he commanded.

Sergeant Gifford came in, throwing off loops of thick cable as he came. He dropped the end of his line and motioned one of his squad forward. "Hook up and take it on downstairs. I want it rigged in one minute!"

Hennessey dug out his radio. "Prometheus One to Prometheus Two, come in."

"Are you all right?" Caroline asked.

"Damn, doc, use the radio procedure. And after I thought up that dandy code name." But he was grinning at Wade. "Hell, yes, we're fine. One cop with a busted head, one private with a .38 slug through his hip. Not bad. Over."

"Thank God! When will we be hooked up?"

"Gifford says one minute. I'll call."

"Right. Is . . . is Wade there?"

Hennessey handed the radio to Dennis. "I'm all right. Maybe by the time they, they get some people in to counterattack, we'll have a chance to convince them."

"Speak with silver tongue."

"Uh, right." He handed the radio back to Hennessey, who told her they were going to speak to the hospital staff now.

Hennessey ordered up a guard of ten men and moved with Wade through the crowded corridors toward the operating rooms. Everything was as before—crowded, bloody, with the stink of death and disaster.

Curzon came out of the operating room with blazing eyes, stripping off bloody gloves and throwing them away abruptly. "How *dare* you come in here and—"

Hennessey raised a .45 Colt automatic and pointed it at the surgeon. "Doc, shut up, will ya? Really, I'm sorry as hell, but you wouldn't listen. Now we got the power plant, we got a line strung, and right about now . . ." The lights went off. There were screams and noise but almost at once someone switched on a battery-powered light, a bright camper's lantern.

"As I was saying, we're taking your power for a bit."

"You *can't!*" In the wavering light of the lantern the surgeon's face was stricken. "I can't operate in *this* kind of light! I don't know how! I, I *can't!*"

Hennessey looked very pained and embarrassed. "Listen, doc, my soul is gonna burn in hell for this day, but not as long as it would if I *didn't* do this. Dennis, how long before we can switch back?"

"Seventy to ninety minutes. Once we reduce the temperature to something like normal we can start signaling for the input and . . ." He shrugged. "Once we have that, we, uh . . ." He stopped as a woman cried out. He could hear people, men as well as children and women, crying and groaning. "We'll do our computations and shoot off a signal . . . then, uh, we can—"

Another scream and a scuffle as someone in the darkness fought. The light swung away, then came back. Other lights appeared, all battery-powered camper's lights, and a few flashlights. "Go on," Hennessey said.

"We can give the power back to the hospital for a while . . ."

"How long?" snapped Curzon.

"An hour and a half to, uh, maybe two hours." Wade felt dizzy. He leaned against the wall, suddenly breathless. "Then, uh, then we'll have to take some of it back about every five hours. Maybe every six. For about, oh, twenty minutes. Maybe thirty." He looked at Curzon, vainly hoping for understanding.

The surgeon nodded briskly. "Very well. You are all responsible for every life in this hospital, the lot of you. Every death makes you more of a murderer. I hope you understand that."

Hennessey nodded wearily. Curzon glared at them, then turned away. He shouted over the noise. "Quiet down. This is Doctor Curzon. The power will be restored in approximately two hours." There was a concerted groan but he shouted them down. "Quiet! Quiet! The *soldiers*—" his voice was sarcastic, "are not to be interfered with. I want no heroes, do you understand me? At the end of two hours we will have power for about another five. I want the nurses and interns to organize their surgical cases for that time. Quiet! There will be another break in power about every five or six hours, for approximately one half hour." He turned to Hennessey and Wade. "You will provide us with some sort of warning, both for the restoration of power and the cessation?"

"Yes, sir," Hennessey said miserably.

"See that you keep your bargain. Give us as much warning as you can so that we might best utilize the time periods." He turned away abruptly. "Ryan! Casey! Round up the lanterns for surgery! Flashlights can be used elsewhere. Put two lanterns in receiving, for preliminary diagnoses. Move!"

Curzon looked at Hennessey. "Get out of here. You are in the way." Without another word the surgeon returned to the operating room. Hennessey shrugged and motioned for his men to leave. They went back to the emergency entrance. Hennessey rechecked the power room, gave orders for the guards, and started walking out. Wade caught up with him on the sidewalk.

"Blessed Jesus," the officer muttered angrily. "I'll be saying Hail Marys from now till doomsday."

"We had to do it."

"Yeah, yeah." They walked over to the bus and got in. "Get us the hell out of here," he growled. The door hissed closed and they crunched out over the glass and trash and went back toward Thales Center.

"Who the hell is this Thales, anyway?" Hennessey grumbled as they neared the Center. He had been watching the guards along the sidewalk where the cable ran.

"He was one of the Seven Wise Men, or sages, of Greece. About the sixth century before Christ. He was the first to understand that the myths no longer satisfied man's curiosity about the origin of the world."

Hennessey grunted, peering out the shattered windows. "In other words," he said as they ground to a stop, brakes hissing, "this Thales guy was the first to start thinking scientifically."

Wade shrugged. "I suppose so. Or the first to stop taking things for granted."

Hennessey got up and shouldered his way out of the bus. He motioned over a sergeant. "Take some men and go back down the cable. Get those things off the street. String 'em up, on poles or something. It'll take extra cable, so dig some up. Go ask Gifford where he got his. I don't want vehicles running over the lines."

"How about putting some two-bys on each side, Captain?" the sergeant asked. "Nail some cleats, hold that cable right snug between."

"Better yet, Murphy, excellent, excellent. Faster, too. Do it."

"Yes, sir." He saluted and hurried off.

Hennessey waved Wade in, but his own eyes were on the flickering red glow across the western horizon. "Blessed Jesus, will ya look at that? Fire storm, do ya think?"

"Big, whatever it is. Let's hope it doesn't get here before . . . before we do our job."

"Yeah," sighed Hennessey. "Look, you go on in. I'll stay out here awhile, okay?"

Wade nodded and limped on in. He looked back from the shattered lobby. Hennessey was looking up, his face reddened by the western fires. He seemed to be praying.

21 May: Collision minus 4 days, 18 hours

Secretary of Defense Sam Rogers drummed his fingers impatiently on the conference table, looking around the situation room in annoyance. He had a slight touch of claustrophobia, and being this far underground always bothered him. He looked at his watch, then compared it to the big clock on the wall labeled for their time zone. The middle-aged Cabinet member looked across at Gilbert McNellis, the Secretary of State. He envied McNellis's outward calm, even knowing it was a facade, the professional mask necessary in his game.

Rogers twisted around in the other direction to glare at one of the many presidential aides that still infested the White House. "Higby, where is the President?"

The young man was holding an open line. Acknowledging the question with a look, he whispered into the mouthpiece, then listened. "On his way, sir."

"On his way, on his way," grumbled Rogers. He looked around at McNellis and General Sutherland. "Vacuum at the top, gentlemen. He sits around playing the goddamn banjo all day, and at night—"

McNellis looked at him blandly. "That's hardly an impeachable offense, Sam. As for Miz Carr, I think it's an excellent situation. Bound to relieve tension."

Sutherland cleared his throat and shifted stiffly in his seat. His fundamentalist views on sex, politics, and morals were well known. Both Secretaries ignored him; four stars or not, he was a hired hand.

"But the *banjo*, for Christ's sake?" complained Rogers. "I've supported him through thick and thin, but this—!

If the news of him and that widow got out—sufferin'
Christ!"

"Senator Leland is the only one who would have the
nerve to use it," McNellis said smoothly. "With half the
nation praying and the other half fornicating, I don't
think it would harm him all that much."

"Just the same," began Rogers, but Higby broke in.

"Excuse me, gentlemen, the President is coming down."

The three men turned toward the door. General Sutherland shoved back his chair to make it easier to rise. It
was the presidency he honored, not the man. They heard
the elevator open and a few moments later the advance
guard of the Secret Service came into the room. A few
moments later the President entered. Rogers look beyond him for Barbara Carr, but she was not there. The
Secret Service men left, to take position outside the
doors. The three presidential aides tried to look alert
and dependable.

Knowles sat down slowly and put his hands flat on
the tabletop. "All right, let's get it over with."

Myron Murray entered, holding several files, and
stood respectfully near the door. Knowles looked at Rogers. "Sam?"

"Here's the situation. Mister President. *Alpha* is almost there. Two days, about. *Omega* right behind them.
But the Cape is a mess. We wouldn't be able to launch
for six days, minimum, should we have to. Vandenberg
is ready but doesn't have anything. We're committed."

"Nothing new there," Knowles said and looked at Mc-
Nellis.

The Secretary of State cleared his throat. "Sir, the entire world is in turmoil. The damages are in the billions,
the deaths in the millions. We're luckier than most, I
guess. But people like this Brother Gabriel, like Simon
Buckler, like the Predestiners or the Afterworlders,
they're causing real damage. The Dancers of Shiva, and
others like them, they are just raising final hell, but the
ones like Gabriel are actively destroying our civilization.
It is going to be a bitch to get things going again, afterward."

"If there is one," Knowles muttered. "General?"

The officer sat stiffly. He patted a thick briefcase sitting on the polished table. "The Primary Evacuation
Plan has yet to be activated, sir. However, a number of

303

key personnel have been deployed to their proper posts. The Vice-President is in the Colorado facility, as are approximately two-thirds of the Senate and House. The others have returned to their homes, or . . ." He seemed a little embarrassed and hesitant to continue.

Knowles nodded. "Yes, or rutting away in hotels with government secretaries, I know. Go on."

"We are only awaiting your signal, sir, to activate this plan. The communications center has been—"

"Let those who want to go, go," Knowles said. "I've said that before. I'm staying. Murray, what do you have?" The abruptness of the President kept them all off base. Murray took a moment to react.

"Mister President, there's one high priority matter. The Thales Center—that's the NASA computation facility in Boston—was damaged by the Boston strike. Lost their power and they, uh, they took emergency power from a hospital nearby."

Knowles narrowed his eyes at his assistant. "How?"

"With the, uh, aid of a National Guard unit, sir. There are numerous complaints, accusations, and so on, and they are totally justified, but . . ."

"Go on, Myron."

"Well, sir, without power that facility could not supply *Alpha* with the proper navigational information. The fact that a number of deaths are said to have occurred because of—"

"All right, what is being done to get power in there?"

"NASA is flying in emergency power, but you must understand the city is a mess. The Army has its hands full, the Guard is strung out all over the place."

"You mean, with an Army and Air Force, not to mention everything else we have, we can't get some emergency power in there?" the President growled.

"They're trying, sir," Murray said. "But with the fires, the mess . . . well, uh, we have a report that an Army helicopter crashed and the second couldn't even find the Center. The city is practically ablaze. The winds are moving the fire toward downtown Boston . . ."

"All right, do whatever you have to do," Knowles said, standing up. "Spare no expense and all that. If this whatever-it-is is that vital a link, we must get it operational."

304

He started to leave but General Sutherland snapped out a rather impertinent, "Sir!"

"Yes, what is it?" Knowles looked at the Army officer from under dark brows.

"Sir, the plan . . ."

"I *told* you, General, weren't you listening?"

"The general was hoping you'd reconsider," Murray said quickly.

"The general is a pain in the ass," Knowles said, still looking at the uniformed man. "Look, General Sutherland, in just a few hours *Alpha* will contact Shiva and either destroy that damned rock or not. My going to Colorado won't help that."

"Sir, that was not, is not, the intent of the evacuation plan. It is to preserve the presidency, conserve the leadership, and—"

"Yes, yes," Knowles interrupted. "Let's not go over this again and again. Myron has been enough of a nag about it and he has even infected . . . other members of the staff. You go, General. You take whoever wants to go. I just hope a cook stays, but if no one does, that's all right, too. I used to make pretty good omelettes and stews and I can do it again."

Knowles jerked a thumb upward. "That building up there is the home of the President of the United States. I intend to be at home if we have guests, wanted or unwanted. Now let us hear no more about it." Knowles looked past Sutherland at Higby. "Higby, you staying?"

"Uh, yes, sir."

"Good. If Mister Murray here goes, you can take his position."

"I'm not going, Mister President," Murray said.

"Sure, go. Reed can use your expertise. Who else can keep that hack straight? Well, gentlemen, it has been nice." Knowles turned and walked out quickly, collecting his bodyguard as he went.

Left alone in the room the men all sat down. "The captain of the *Titanic*," Rogers said. "He thinks he's the captain of the blasted *Titanic*."

"His option," McNellis muttered.

"Well, gentlemen, my options are limited, but clear," General Sutherland stated. "There will be an official evacuation as of sixteen hundred today. Helicopters will land at three-minute intervals on the south lawn for transport to Edwards. Luggage and files should be kept to a minimum. I will have trucks here by fifteen hundred for that. There are twenty-two CN-5s ready at Edwards now. They will ferry everything and everyone to Ent Air Force Base for transshipment to the Teller facility." He stood up and put the briefcase under his arm. "Gentlemen." He walked out briskly.

For several moments after he had gone there was quiet in the situation room. They could see and faintly hear the activity in the main map room. Myron Murray looked at Higby, who seemed to be lost in thought. "You going?" he asked McNellis and Rogers.

"Dumb not to," Rogers said. "I want out of here."

"No reason to think Colorado is going to be safer," McNellis said.

"Teller is a *fortress*," snapped Rogers. "Designed to stand up under *atomic attack—!*"

McNellis shrugged. "I believe I shall stay."

Rogers shrugged and got up, shaking his head. "Always thought State was strange in the head." He left without another word.

"You?" McNellis asked Murray.

"I'm staying." He looked at Higby, who didn't change expression. "I'm sorry, Bruce."

"That's all right, Mister Murray," Higby said. "I better get the general's word around." He got up, then paused at the door. "Um, there will be a lot of people glad to go."

"Yes," Murray said. Higby hesitated, then left.

Murray and McNellis sat together a moment, glancing up as the two silent aides walked slowly out. Murray sighed. He'd have to go have another talk with Barbara Carr, he thought. There was still a chance.

"Are the cherry trees blooming?" McNellis asked.

Murray looked up in mild surprise. "Damned if I know. I've been, uh, busy."

McNellis sighed wearily. "Drove right by them yesterday and didn't notice, can you beat that? Can't remember if it was yesterday or last year I saw them bloom. They certainly are nice to look at when they are, huh?" Murray nodded. "We ought to have a day for viewing the blossoms, the way the Japanese do, don't you think?"

Murray nodded, not hearing. Why didn't the President

listen to reason, he thought. It was insane to stay, knowing what could happen.

21 May: Collision minus 4 days, 13 hours

Jagens sat staring out the port. The cabin lights were out and the only illumination came from a number of colored control lights and one small readout screen with its constant monologue of words and numbers. I feel like talking to someone, he thought, but certainly not General Menshov. Damned Russian. I see him looking at everything, listening, analyzing, soaking up everything we know. Maybe I should arrange a little accident for the Red general, Carl thought. Better in the long run. But we'd have to get rid of the others, too. Be damned risky.

But this whole thing was risky. Could they *really* stop what amounted to a flying mountain, even with the biggest damned bomb ever built? So many things could go wrong. They were operating on such a slim reel of information. The OAO and Thales and any number of others could be wrong. A percentage point here, another there, and *so sorry*, excuse, please, bad mistake.

Carl wondered what Lisa Bander was doing. Sleeping like the rest, he supposed. Or maybe sleepless like him, staring out at the stars, trying to pick the swarm out of the background of stars. She wasn't a bad sort. Good as a man in almost everything, he thought. But, in the end, he knew he couldn't trust her. All the women in his life, his personal or professional life, had betrayed him one way or another. Why should Bander be any different, just because she was a fellow astronaut?

Mother had been the first, but not the last, Carl thought grimly. Running off like that, leaving him with a tyrant of a father, becoming little more than a trollop, she'd shamed him. But she'd helped him, too, though she didn't mean to. She'd made him strong, independent, unafraid to act alone, to *be* alone. The tyrant father had made him strong, too. He'd had to be strong, to preserve his personality against the insensitive onslaughts of a man who was always right, would never admit being wrong. I forged myself, Carl thought, on the fire of the conflict between us.

His mother had been a weak woman. He knew that.

Her reaction to the strong father was to run, to change, to hide. His own reaction had been to fight, to grow armor, to become better than anything his father could ever be. And I've done it, he thought with grim exaltation. I lead the team that will literally save the world. Or die trying. Yet even in failure there would be grandeur.

But we shall not fail. I shall not fail. I *cannot* fail. They are all looking to me, hoping, praying. It is my chance, it is my *only* chance. Nothing before has tested me. Afterward, everything will be an anticlimax, no matter what they give me to do. And I could have anything: a Mars mission will be easy, a Jupiter mission certainly, maybe even a starship. After we save the Earth they'll be grateful, deliriously grateful. They'll build a fleet of spaceships! And I'll take them out.

Carl smiled thinly. Such dreams men had! After Shiva the world will be hard put to pull itself together, to rebuild the shattered cities, bury the dead, start living again . . . there will be no money for space, much less a fleet of starships. He sighed, his eyes drooping. First things first. Stop Shiva. *Then* dream of starships and new planets and great glory.

We all had such dreams, though, he thought. When we were young trainees, sitting in simulators, bringing a shuttlecraft into docking position. Testing oneself against the others, against the system, against the greats of previous times. How simple Armstrong, Aldrin, and Collins seemed now! What a simple milk run that was! Just a trip to the moon. One generation back, yet it seemed closer to canvas-winged biplanes than the true beginning of the space age. Primitive ships clogged with crude devices, ancient procedures, inadequate materials and safeguards.

Yet not so different. Because the blind fools had given them so little money, they were flying only slightly updated versions of *Saturn Vs*, in spacesuits not much different from the days of Apollo. True, they made milk runs to Luna, and there were a lot of skylabs and space stations—far more sophisticated, but not much different in degree.

What we need is a quantum leap or two. A stardrive. When Armstrong stepped onto the moon, Carl was a little boy, infected by the space age. Carl had expected him to say, "Today the moon, tomorrow the stars," but he hadn't. With the moon a regular landing spot, even the flights to Mars and Venus hadn't been all that different. It would all be more of the same, until we go to another *star*. And if he was successful—*when* he was successful—he'd have the juice to make it happen. "Today Shiva, tomorrow the stars!"

It would happen.

It *must* happen.

Carl Jagens had to show them all. He had to get even. The mother who had run off—she'd know, if she was still alive. Maybe even now, in some sleazy bar, she was slurring her words and trying to make everyone believe that the man in *Alpha* was her son. He'd show his father, too, wherever he was. He'd be alive. He'd always be alive, if only to annoy him. Always critical, sneering, contemptuous. Nothing was ever done well enough for him, nothing, even if it was perfect. But he'd show the old man.

What had Chang Chao said? "A small injustice can be drowned by a cup of wine; a great injustice can only be drowned by the sword." Revenge is a necessity, he thought, a dreadful and terrible necessity. You cannot live unbalanced, compensating all your life for the unfulfilled revenge so avidly sought. Never mind that once the revenge is consummated you will have grown so used to the imbalance you will not ever be normal. It doesn't matter. There are always those you should revenge yourself on.

Carl glanced at the console. He felt faintly shameful for having thought of calling Lisa Bander. What could he say to her? He could not say the things that mattered. You do not give your enemy a sword, you do not show them chinks in your carefully constructed life-time armor. That would be madness. And if there is one thing I am not, Carl thought, it is insane.

Zakir Shastri fell ill and was returned to Earth in the last shuttle flight, which made a tour of the manned satellites. He left Radhakrishnan in charge. They never expected to see each other again.

Astronaut Mort Smith's drinking had become such a problem he was removed from active duty and put into a Navy hospital.

Nikolai Menshikov, assistant to the former premier, defected to London, where he mysteriously died, almost at once. Kirov, the new head of Russia, issued statements saying that the Soviet cosmonauts were going to save the world.

Igor Fedynsky, the atomic physicist, discovered after years of dismissing Mozart as trivial, that he actually liked the Austrian's work. He listened to almost nothing else, including his wife.

Veracruz Llave was devastated by a impact-caused tidal wave in the Bay of Campeche. The same wave damaged Merida, in Yucatán, and lapped at the base of the Mayan structures at Uxmal, where the scouring waters uncovered a number of new buildings in the jungle mounds.

In the rockcut tunnels of Teller Air Force Base an aging senator named Leland drank sour mash and plotted the overthrow of President Knowles.

On the island of Hispaniola, in the country of Haiti, voodoo rites to remove Shiva from the sky were conducted almost nonstop. So were the orgies.

22 May: Collision minus 3 days, 10 hours

Barbara Carr closed the bathroom door after herself and put her handbag on the toilet. She bent, fumbling through the purse, and found the plastic cylinder. She drew a glass of water and thumbed out four pills. They went down with a swallow of bitter-tasting water and only then did she allow herself to lean against the wall and sink into the upwelling of emotions.

The depressions came more often now, particularly at night. The staff was no help anymore. Everywhere she went in the White House, people looked away. They answered her in short, curt sentences or with overly polite exactness, as if they had to handle her with very special care. Domino theory. If she went, the President went.

Nonsense, she thought, looking at herself. He was strong. He *had* to be strong, and he knew it. That very fact increased the pressure on him. He had no place to go and relax, to let the steam off, to set down the public mask.

No place but bed. There and there alone he could forget himself. There and there alone she made her contribution. She held him, soothed him, gave him pleasure, and asked nothing in return.

The man she held at night was a different man from the man the world or even the White House staff saw. A President was supposed to be a leader, set an example, be a standard-bearer. When a leader wasn't like that, the people became afraid. But she could see the cracks in Fortress Knowles.

He went to his Cabinet meetings and made his decisions, but more and more he relied on the advice and recommendations of his subordinates, of experts and generals and power brokers. But there was something in the way he clung to her at night, in the way he buried himself in her bosom, in the warm pleasures of her flesh, that chilled her. There was a desperation in him, a strangeness, and every day it grew stronger.

She couldn't sleep, there was no one to talk to, at least not to talk to with an honest give-and-take. She was separate from the others, all others, and even separate from Knowles. God only knows where her family was, and she had not been very close in any case. Her friends treated her oddly, with a careful kind of exactness that made her draw back from them.

The news of Shiva was everywhere, impossible to escape. Messengers arrived constantly, all bearing ill tidings: a city in flames, a power system down, a riot, the death of a friend or the suicide of someone in power somewhere. Death became a dreary, monotonous ritual, but never lost its impact to sicken and to debilitate.

Knowles had his moods and she tried to cater to them. There was the sharp, crisply speaking executive making life-and-death decisions without hesitation. There was the rutting goat who couldn't get enough. There was the quiet, sad-faced man with eyes focused on some distant, unseen horizon. But the mood that frightened Barbara Carr the most was the entertainer.

He sat on the bed, playing the banjo, talking about the old and better days, of early political triumphs, bygone pleasures, dead friends. He smiled a lot, often talking with great excitement, and they almost always ended up making love like two randy teenagers. But those moods frightened her, perhaps because she responded to them. She, too, would like to escape to Never-never-land, even to Never-was-land, where the good things happened and life did not change every day, where the sword of Damocles was not in the sky.

She could not sleep, but when exhaustion dragged her down, she dreamt, and her dreams were nightmares. The terrors came rushing up from the depths, smothering her in symbols and blood. She awoke in sweaty sheets, her pulse racing, eyes staring in blind panic. Only the pills from the understanding White House doctor kept that under reasonable control. Other pills smoothed her out for the time she had to spend with Knowles.

She knew what she did was important. It had to be. Without her she was certain the President of the United States would crumble under the pressure. At an even swifter rate than he was. Her job *was* important. She told herself that several times a day. She believed it for hours at a time, especially when they were in bed together. He was like a teenager discovering sex. He couldn't get enough, delighting in each new act, each new novelty. She opened herself totally to him, denying him nothing, perfecting her not-thinking state with each bizarre request.

She put the pill bottle away and picked up her handbag, snapping it closed. She opened the bathroom door and stepped out into the tall, vaulted corridor. There hadn't been time to check her face, but she thought she probably looked all right. He saw pretty much what he wanted to see anyway.

Down the corridor came the President, flanked by two Secret Service men. Barbara smiled at him and he smiled back, a sudden brightness in his face. She put out a hand to the doorjamb to keep her balance and kept smiling. Maybe today would be better. There wasn't all that much time left, anyway. Then the whole matter would be decided. She could hold on. She was going to like it then, when it was over. It would be just fine.

A rifle shot screeched off the concrete wall, ricocheting viciously through the Thales Center lobby. Begrimed Guardsmen jumped for cover, swearing lustily as they grabbed their weapons. Bent low, Captain Hennessey came out of his commandeered office as more shots came in through the shattered windows.

"Thatcher! What the hell's going on?"

The lean corporal turned from his niche in the sand-bagged barricade. "People up the street, sir."

"People? What people? Uniformed? Rioters?" He fell

against the sandbags and twisted to peer out the slot. More shots thumped into the bags around them and someone on the roof let out a long stream of machine-gun fire that temporarily silenced those in the street. But it was dark and they could be hiding almost anywhere.

"They looked like civilians, sir," Thatcher said.

"Oh, great," Hennessey muttered. He dug out his radio control and switched to headquarters frequency. "Red Dragon One, this is Tiger Charlie, come in, please."

"Tiger Charlie, this is Red Dragon One."

"Red Dragon One, advise Colonel Dunnigan we are under fire from civilians attacking from the southern quadrant."

"Tiger Charlie, this is—"

"I'll take it." Hennessey recognized Dunnigan's voice. *"Is that you, Hennessey?"*

"Yes, sir!" He grimaced as more shots dusted off his sandbags. "We're under fire from civilians, sir! Shall we return fire?"

"Of course, Captain! You have a vital facility there. Protect it at all costs."

"Yes, sir." A sergeant dropped to his knees near Hennessey and the officer made a pistol shape with his hand and fired it several times at the street. The sergeant nodded and crept away. Hennessey spoke into the command channel. "Sir, have you *any* idea what's happening out west of here?"

"Big fires, Hennessey. We've given up trying to stop them. They are drawing up plans to dynamite a fire break."

"Oh, shit," Hennessey said aloud. He had property to the west. His next words were drowned out by a long volley of shots from the Guardsmen. There were screams from the street.

"They're people from the hospital, sir," Thatcher whispered loudly, an ache in his voice.

"Colonel, I'll call you back. Tiger Charlie Out."

"Hang in there, Hennessey."

"Uh-huh. You sure about that?" he asked the corporal. Thatcher nodded, pointing. A body lay face down in the littered street. She was wearing hospital green. Her blood was vivid red.

"Why? Why are they hitting at us?" Hennessey complained angrily. "They can't win."

Thatcher shrugged. "Maybe they don't know that. They gotta be ticked off 'cause of the power thing, sir."

"Fire over their heads!" Hennessey shouted, but his words were covered by the racket from the roof's fifty-caliber weapon, which ripped gouges from the street and building facades. "God damn it! Thatcher, you go up there and tell that gunner to stop that!"

"Sir!" The corporal crept away into the hall, then ran lithely up the stairs to the roof. From there he could see the street better. And the city bus coming, plates of metal hastily welded to its front. He turned and ran downstairs as fast as he could.

"Oh, no!" Hennessey said, hearing the news. "Well, stop it! Where's Daily? He's got the fucking flame-thrower, doesn't he?"

"Uh, Daily's gone. I dunno where, sir. Maybe he ran scared, maybe we lost him somewhere." Thatcher shrugged.

"Sergeant Vayne!" Hennessey crooked his finger at a slightly built noncom. "Find that goddamn flame-thrower and stop that bus! Thatcher! Get back on the roof! They're probably going to ram! Or maybe it's full of gas-oline!"

Hennessey's communications noncom waved at him. "Sir! We lost contact with the unit deployed along the cable! No, wait, he's . . ." He stopped, frowning, while Hennessey waited impatiently. "Sir, it's Private Shanks! He said they were knocked out by some trick . . . can't hear him good . . . he's . . ." The noncom's face fell. He shook his head at Hennessey.

"Awright," Hennessey snarled loudly. "First things first! Stop that bus! Then we restore the cable!" He ducked and blinked as more shots slammed off the concrete walls. He saw Wade Dennis crouching by the elevators and ran over to him. "What the hell are you doing out here?"

"What's going on?"

"We're under attack, apparently by—" He ducked as a slug careened off the marble walls, spraying them with dust. "By your friendly neighborhood hospital."

"The power's off."

"I know the power is off." Hennessey wheeled in his crouch and squinted out into the street. There was sporadic fire, then a sudden long burst from the heavy ma-

314

chine gun on the roof. The two men hunkered down, grimacing, as some snipers fired back.

"We're going to have to transmit in twenty minutes or so. I've got people doing the math on battery calculators, for Christ's sake!"

"First things first, Dennis! We'll—"

The roof machine gun chattered again, a long gun-warping burst that made Hennessey curse. Then they heard the slugs whining off metal and the bus was thundering down the street at them. It ran over a squirming body and headed toward the lobby in a suicide drive. There was a *whoom* from the opposite side of the street and the inside of the bus blossomed into flame. The front exploded out, then the roof. The long vehicle lost speed, angled toward the side of the street, rammed a burnt-out car, and stopped.

"Got 'em with a bazooka, by God!"

Then the bus exploded. Flame billowed out, shredding the bus, breaking windows for blocks, sending metal shards flying in every direction. The shock wave knocked over some of the sandbags. The noise was deafening. Shards of hot metal flew through the lobby, ricocheting off walls and people. A shapeless piece of smoking iron pinned a young soldier to the lobby wall, gutting him efficiently. He stared down at the gory mess, rolled up his eyes, and died.

Hennessey swore, blinking away the painful dust of ground glass and dirt. The remains of the bus burned furiously. Fires had been started in several nearby buildings. Men were moaning. A young female soldier lay half-naked in the middle of the lobby, most of her exposed flesh blackened and seared.

"Those crazy bastards!" Hennessey snarled. "We gotta get those cables back in operation! They must have ambushed the guards at the other end and—" Turning toward Dennis, he stopped. A bright strip of aluminum protruded from the side of his neck.

Hennessey caught him as Dennis started to fall sideways. Blood spurted massively. Hennessey lay Dennis back as gently as he could, swearing under his breath. Wade's face was white. His eyes were staring and his lips moved slightly. Blood spilled out over the pale lips. Hennessey ripped the tourniquet from his own medix pack and applied it to the wound. Before he could get it around it was soaked in blood. The aluminum strip protruded still, no longer shiny bright.

"Medic!" A young woman hopped from the burnt soldier to Dennis. She took over efficiently, with swift and sure moves. "The one that's burnt?" Hennessey asked, his eyes on Dennis's face.

"Dead. Three all told. Four unless we get this one to the hospital fast."

"But—!" Hennessey felt trapped. It was the hospital people that had caused the deaths. They'd never take Dennis. He stood up, anger making his face flush. "The hell they won't!" He began calling for officers and noncoms.

The damage report showed that the attack by the hospital people had killed eleven soldiers, with fifteen wounded, nine of them very seriously. Plus Dennis.

Within five minutes Hennessey was leading one pincer of the attack, his senior lieutenant the other. They were making their way through side streets, through alleys and even through basements.

Hennessey stuck his head up from the basement entrance of an apartment house across the alley from the hospital. He saw a neat row of bodies along the alley. Most of them were soldiers. He recognized Ellenby, the pretty young brunette with the great rear who worked in his bank. She had no right leg. She'd never make sergeant now, he thought bitterly.

His men crowded in behind him. Hennessey quickly gave orders. There were bound to be some guards on the roof, so he sent five soldiers up to the top, after instructing them to talk in code, as the hospital people probably were listening on captured helmet radios.

After a few minutes he heard, "Top deck secure." There had been no shots. He waited. A minute dragged by. "Got 'em spotted." That meant that the rooftop patrol had sighted in on the snipers on the hospital roof. Hennessey motioned and Thatcher led the first group up the steps and across the alley in long leaps. One of the soldiers stepped on a pale hand protruding from under a bloody ground sheet, reacted violently, and fell against the brick wall with a clatter. The patrol flattened against the wall and edged up the dark alley.

Hennessey motioned the next group up and joined them. "Hit it!" he muttered into the microphone. He

316

heard firing begin on the other side of the hospital. Then there were shots from the roofs over their head as they ran up the alley toward the ambulance entrance. Bullets careened off the brick and off the cobblestones. One man fell, tripping two more. They scrambled to their feet as the firing overhead ceased.

Then Hennessey's gun bucked in his hand as he fired at the armed men who appeared at the entrance. There was noise and flame all around, long chattering spurts from machine guns. Someone threw a concussion grenade and the bodies at the entrance fell over.

"Crazy, *crazy!*" swore Hennessey. He jumped up on the platform, slipped in blood, and caught himself. He sent a concussion grenade rolling down the hall. It exploded, sending out a blizzard of paper. The burning paper had not settled to the ground before Thatcher had led his patrol in. Hennessey stomped over to the house phone and peered at the list taped to the wall. He dialed 452, Admin.

"*H-hello?*"

"This is Captain Hennessey of the Massachusetts National Guard. I demand your surrender at once!"

"*But, uh—*"

"Where's the boss?" God, he was tired, bitter that he had to do it all over again, going against sense and decency. He'd be courtmartialed, he knew that. Inquiry. State of emergency. Martial law. Duty. Rules of War. He leaned against the wall. His men ran in past him, loud and jingling with equipment.

The little redheaded O'Flynn trotted past, giving him a quick grin. Didn't need her this time. Or maybe I do, Hennessey thought. Fine body. Does war make you horny? Does that explain the rape and pillage? Does anything? Should I take a stim-pill? Pay for it later, but—

"*Doctor Curzon here.*" His voice had a snap to it and Hennessey resented him at once.

"Captain Hennessey here, you goddamned murderer!"

"*See here, Captain, it was not my idea to attack you. One of the patients . . . his wife was in surgery and—*"

"You were in charge, you should *know* these things!"

"*I've been in the operating room for—*"

"Then you should have given tactical command to someone who could give it his or her complete attention!"

Curzon started to speak but Hennessey cut him off. "This whole thing has been a needless waste! We need your power and we intend to have it, Doctor! There's a bigger issue at hand here than just one hospital!"

"*Captain Hennessey, we—*"

"Shut up! I've got wounded coming in and you *will* take care of them! I'll give you all the medics I can spare, but you *will* take care of them!"

"*Yes, of course, but—*"

"No buts, Doctor!" He slammed the phone down. He began snapping orders through his helmet radio, obtaining information, securing posts. He broke off when the wounded started coming in. Some were on stretchers, some were limping but on their feet. Others were helped by friends, bloodied and dazed, their eyes staring, in shock. Hennessey saw Caroline Weinberg at the side of a stretcher bearing a very pale Wade Dennis. The end of the aluminum fragment protruded from the hastily wrapped bandage.

Caroline looked up at Hennessey with tear-filled eyes. Her mouth was slack and shapeless. Hennessey had to ask his question twice before she responded.

"What?"

"How much time do we have before you *must* send the next transmission?"

"Uh. Oh." She looked at her watch, blinked away the tears and tried again. "Uh, ten minutes."

"You ready on your end?"

"Yes. But there's no power . . ."

"There will be. I've put every man on it I can spare. They only broke the line at the power plant. It'll be fixed in a minute. You'd better get back to the Center."

"But—"

"Nothing you can do for him. I'll see he goes into the operating room as soon as I can."

"Uh . . . all, all right." She looked down at the unconscious Wade and touched his blood-flecked cheek. Then she turned on her heel and walked rapidly toward the exit. She jumped down from the loading platform and began running.

Hennessey told the stretcher-bearers, "Take him to the operating area. Put him at the head of the line and don't take any crap from anyone."

"Yes, sir." They picked up Wade and went down the

318

hall. Hennessey leaned against the wall. The place was so goddamn noisy. Moans, screams, crying, orders. Another fucking siren. Hennessey limped out toward the alley, noting that somewhere he had twisted his ankle a little. He sat down on an overturned trash can and leaned back against the wall. The air smelled of brick dust, blood, and spoiled garbage. He closed his eyes.

What happened to that horniness? he asked himself. All gone. Gone away. The world melted around him in slow motion. He opened his eyes lazily, seeing a detail carrying in wounded. Everything seemed far away and unimportant. He closed his eyes. In a moment he was snoring.

The stretcher-bearers put Wade Dennis down against the wall, just one stretcher away from the entrance. The first stretcher was a pregnant woman with a bullet in her side. They looked at each other, the stretcher-bearers and the pregnant woman.

"Am I going to die?" she asked.

One of the stretcher-bearers knelt down, forcing a smile. "No, hey, of course not. You're next in line here. They got great doctors here, you know. My sister had her baby here, four, five years ago. A piece of cake."

"Is there a priest?"

"Uh, I dunno." He looked up at his companion, who shrugged. "Find out, will you?" The man nodded and looked around, wandering off. "Just a few more minutes," the woman was told.

"Hold my hand?"

He took it. "Where's your husband?" He knew he shouldn't have said it the moment he spoke.

"Dead. Someone knifed him day before yesterday. All we had in the place were candy bars. We sell cards and paper and things. Just a few candy bars."

The stretcher-bearer patted her hand. "Yeah, yeah. It'll be all right. Don't you worry. Just a few—"

The lights went out.

There was a crash as someone dropped some bottles and a lot of cursing. In the dark the stretcher-bearer held on to the woman's hand tightly, muttering assurances.

In the darkness no one saw or heard Wade Dennis regain consciousness. He tried to speak, but couldn't. There was something wrong with his neck. Something in it. He felt the bandage and felt the end of something metal and sharp. He tugged weakly at it, but nausea swept over him. Why was it black? Was he dead? He could hear people, but he couldn't see anything. No, there was light, streaks of light. Maybe they'd help. He tried to call out, but there was still something in his throat. He reached up, feeling for the metal, his whole body in pain and very weak.

Just get that thing out of his throat. He had to tell them. He had to get the word to *Alpha*. He pulled at the metal, but it was caught in the bandages. Why didn't someone help him?

He felt so weak. So cold. Why was it so cold and dark?

When the lights came on the stretcher-bearer grinned at the woman. "See? Look, they're going to take you next, okay?" He stood up, moved his feet, felt the stickiness, and looked down. He was standing in a pool of bright red blood.

He turned toward Wade Dennis and stopped. The blood was his. He had bled to death in the darkness, while the power was sending the message to the guys in space.

"Thank you," the woman muttered weakly. The stretcher-bearer watched them lift her and he smiled, a ghastly wreck of a smile.

"They got a priest," the other stretcher-bearer said, coming back, stepping over Wade. "Goddamn," he swore softly as he stepped in the blood. He looked down dumbly. "The priest, he's coming."

"We better get him out of the way." The other man agreed and they picked up Wade and took him back through the corridors and out into the alley. They put him down next to a corporal they remembered and took some newspapers to clean off the stretcher as well as they could.

Then they went back, looking for more wounded.

25 May: Collision minus 23 hours

"Houston, this is *Alpha One*, how do you read me?"

"*Alpha One, this is Houston. We read you at four. Must be interference.*"

"Roger, Houston, but we'll make do. Are you prepared to give us backup mode on illuminating Shiva with ground radar?"

"*Roger, Carl.*" It was a different voice, which Jagens recognized as Dink Lowell's. "*But the time factor may foul us up.*"

Carl nodded, glancing at the Russian. The disadvantage to the ground-based system was that it limited operating range and time, since the earthbound antenna system was only visible half the time.

"Understand, Houston, but will use only as a backup. We will rely on inboard power. We are on our final approach."

There was a pause. "*Good luck, Alpha One.*"

Jagens wanted to reply that luck had little to do with it. He hadn't studied and worked for all these years to rely on luck. "Understood, Houston. *Alpha One* out."

Menshov was silent and for that Jagens was grateful. He needed his full concentration on the task ahead. Quickly, he reviewed the situation. If they hadn't diverted Shiva in a couple of hours, it wouldn't matter. There would be a collision, even if only a glancing blow, but a blow on a titanic scale. Earth simply would not be out of the way. What they did in the next couple of hours would determine the fate of mankind.

The diagnostic subsystems were tuned, acutely radiation sensitive. He turned his thoughts to the actual method they were going to use.

About eighty percent of the total energy in a nuclear explosion appeared first as radiation. After explosion, the weapon material had a temperature of several tens of millions degrees; pressures were many millions of atmospheres. Within a hundredth of a microsecond, a hundredth of one-millionth of a second, the fireball would be completely stripped atoms—ions plus electrons. Most of the radiation would come out as soft X rays.

The energy would be conveyed to Shiva by radiation,

321

whereupon the asteroid material itself would emit radiation. A shock wave would form. The weapons material would accelerate outward, forming a rather thin shell of high density called the "hydrodynamic front." This front would act like a piston. A compressional wave would become a steep-fronted shock wave.

Jagens made a memory scan of the figures so long computed. For near-surface bursts, crater depth would be about half the crater radius. Such a crater, formed from a shock wave, would rip apart the near zone of the asteroid. For a sure kill, Jagens thought, we should require a crater radius equal to Shiva's diameter. But if Shiva *is* solid rock, a kilometer in radius, it would be "killed" only by a bomb of ten thousand megatons. Clearly, that was impossible. They could not "kill" the asteroid.

Deflection, then, was the best hope with one weapon, one pinpoint strike. Jagens furrowed his brows as he reviewed the "guesstimates" bracketed by the scientific study teams. The crucial help was that the heated material near the burst would eject from the hot crater, becoming a "rocket exhaust" and pushing at the asteroid. Thus, once you heated it, Shiva would push itself.

It was crucial to get a very near burst. Within fifty meters, if possible. Jagens smiled thinly. A hole in one from far beyond the moon. *Fifty* meters! But such a close explosion would yield a velocity change of about forty meters per second. Carl shook his head. So inefficient! Compared with simply converting the burst energy into a change in Shiva's kinetic energy, the huge Soviet bomb was only about three percent efficient.

Jagens ran through the *Bolshoi* package in his mind, searching and probing for possible goofs. The package included the shock and thermal insulation. The nuclear device had its end plates bolted to the booster head. That fixed it to the stainless steel longitudinal mounting flange in the payload stage shell structure. Final jacketing and housing were buffered and electromagnetically impenetrable, except through the external antenna system. The antennas were deployed at the rear of the booster to avoid the possibility of being sheared off by meteor collision.

Carl repped and verified the warhead systems, flipping switches. Fusing, safe-arm, destruct subsystems, plus their packaging. If Bolshoi were to hit Shiva before detonation, the whole thing would go to pieces in 0.01 milliseconds. The triggering time for the uranium assembly, which touched off the hydrogen—thermonuclear—shell, was one whole millisecond. Given the uncertainties, the weapon had to blow higher than twenty meters to be safe, and effective.

So they had to be certain *Bolshoi* didn't trigger from some random circuit noise. Even a few milliseconds of error was too much. To stop a premature detonation, the safe-arm system had to work beautifully. Carl grimaced. They could defy the law of gravity but never escape Murphy's Law.

The heart of the safe-arm system was a rotatable disc, or gate, which put a barrier in a cylinder, stopping a burst of fulminate of mercury, which would be ignited by an exploding bridge wire. Redundancy in all systems was imperative. But it was still new, and untried.

"Incoming message," Menshov said. Jagens glanced at the burst-transmission dial, but the microsecond transmission had been completed. It was the final directions for the approach. Jagens checked them, then punched them into the guidance system.

They were committed.

With the sun behind it, the dust cloud that was Shiva shimmered. Within it were streaks and bars of darkness, shadows thrown forward from the larger pieces. Slanting through was one dominant band of darkness: the shadow of Shiva.

By running up the telescope to maximum Carl Jagens was able to get a faint outline. The flying mountain of rock was turning slowly and he caught glints and flashes off the irregular surface. But the face of Shiva could not yet be seen.

Jagens edged over and let General Menshov take a look, watching his face for reaction. He was disappointed. The Russian did not change expression. He sat back and looked at the American astronaut. "It will be difficult to penetrate through that. It is not just dust. There are all sizes of rocks."

Jagens nodded. "Must have been a collision in the past, shattering one or more pieces. But you're right, we cannot just bore right in." He flicked open the channel to Earth.

"Houston Control, this is *Alpha One.*"

"*Go ahead,* Alpha One."

"We've seen the cloud—and it's a cloud, all right. Very dense. We'll have to swing around and match up, then edge in."

There was reluctance in Dink Lowell's voice as he answered. "*That'll use up a lot of time, Carl, and time is something we don't have much of.*"

The man thinks in clichés, Carl thought. It's a good thing they phased him out when they did. "We must, Houston. There's everything from dust on up in that swarm. Unless we match velocities we'll get peeled going in."

"*Let us get back to you on this, Carl.*"

"No time, Houston. This is a decision of the man in command in the field."

"*Carl, you aren't on a naval ship out there—*"

"The principle is exactly the same!" Carl looked at Menshov, mildly surprised to see him nodding encouragingly. "We are in agreement here. We are moving to match up with the swarm. *Alpha One* out."

"*Now, damn it, Carl, this is too important a decision for one man to—*" Carl cut him off. The call light blinked almost at once but Jagens ignored it.

"Plot us a match-up," he said to Menshov, who just nodded as he began punching buttons. Jagens hesitated, then opened the S-band frequency to Omega. "*Omega One,* this is *Alpha One.*"

"*Alpha One, this is* Omega One, go ahead."

"*Omega One,* we are moving into a position to match up with Shiva and will penetrate on that basis."

"*Alpha One, we were monitoring your transmission to Houston.*" Jagens smiled very slightly, waiting for the rebuff he was certain Bander would give him. When nothing was said he raised his eyebrows.

"*Omega One,* are you in concurrence?"

"*Alpha One, naturally. We lose time but gain in reliability.*"

Jagens's assessment of Lisa Bander went up a notch. Very sensible of her to see the situation so quickly. He had been prepared for an argument and a test of wills. "We will transmit our course data to you as soon as completed. You have even more time to make your corrections."

324

"*Roger.*"

Another voice crackled on the line. It was Colonel Aleksandr Zaborovskii, the second in command of *Omega*. "Alpha One, *this* is Omega Two."

"Go ahead, *Omega Two.*"

"*Captain Jagens, may I speak to General Menshov?*"

Frowning slightly, Jagens said, "Just a moment, *Omega Two. Omega One*, have you any other questions?"

"*No questions.* Omega One *out.*"

Jagens glanced at Menshov, saw him trigger his microphone, and nodded. "Go ahead, *Omega Two.*"

"*General Menshov?*"

"*Da.*"

There was a stream of fast Russian, well-mixed with what Jagens thought was slang, code, or both. He turned to frown at Menshov, who remained blank-faced as he cut off Zaborovskii curtly. In clearly spoken English Menshov said, "You need have no fear, Comrade Colonel. Captain Jagens is a competent officer and has made the proper decision."

Zaborovskii said something else, something about a chain of command and checking first with headquarters. Jagens smiled his thin, cold smile. That was the trouble with the Ruskies. They always had to check with Big Brother. Hive-mind. Jumped-up peasants. He wondered what Schumacher, the Navy man in the same capsule, and Short, the black Marine, thought about their Russian friend.

Menshov closed off his compatriot and returned to his calculations without comment. Jagens looked ahead. Even with the naked eye he could see parts of the swarm now, flickering against the glare of the sun.

In *Omega One* Lisa looked at Nino Solari. "We'll lose time his way," she said with a sigh.

"But we knew that would be one of the possibilities," Nino said. He shrugged expressively. "Why are they getting so upset down there? Jagens simply picked one of the options."

"They're the ones getting hit right now," Lisa reminded him. "And they are probably getting punch-drunk."

"Yeah, and they are second-guessing us," Nino grumbled.

"They don't want any mistakes, that's all," Lisa said defensively. "We have only one shot at this."

"Two," Nino said. "*Alpha* and *Omega*. But *only* two."

"Button up," Carl Jagens said, locking down his helmet. The dust cloud was clearer now, bright flecks winking and flashing as they tumbled through space. General Menshov said nothing, his eyes on the telemetry dials.

Shiva was visible only as a bar of shadow through the dust and chunks. *Alpha One* had successfully swung to match the speed of the flying mountain. Side jets were bringing the capsule in through the swarm and Jagens was on an adrenaline high.

"*Two degrees starboard, one up,*" Menshov said into his suit radio.

Behind them and above was *Alpha Two*, Diego commanding, with Ikko Issindo and the Russian, Olga Nissen. They were monitoring *Alpha One*'s entry and would quickly follow. There was not a lot of time remaining. Shiva was approaching Earth and *Bolshoi* was coming right in at Shiva. The *Alpha* ships had to be behind the bulk of Shiva itself to have any chance at all of surviving. As it was, in the minds of many, the entire mission had become suicidal, with only two chances: slim and none. That included both their immediate survival and the successful deflection of Shiva.

Pinnng!

A nubbin of rock, traveling slightly faster than the rest, struck *Alpha One* a glancing blow. Menshov's eyes flicked to the air-pressure gauge. All was well. Dented, but not hulled.

"*Bolshoi* coming in," reported Issindo, from *Alpha Two*. He quickly added the pertinent technical information of direction and speed, relative to the mass of Shiva.

"*One degree descent, one east,*" Menshov said.

"*We've been hit,*" reported Diego Calderon calmly. "*Air pressure dropping. Holding steady. Major Nissen is patching it.*"

Fast work, thought Jagens. The Russians were good. Or the hole was a small one. All the ships had sticky plasters for minor holes; peel off the backing, slap the dish-sized circle over the hole, and in a few seconds it had completed a chemical change and turned very hard and stiff.

Ping! Pinnng!

Two more slight hits on *Alpha One*. They were deep into the swarm, with *Alpha Two* coming in behind.

Bump.

They nudged a rock out of the way. Jagens saw it tumbling off, disturbing the stream of particles, creating a bow wave through the dust, which had been undisturbed for a long, long time.

Time stretched out for all of them. Houston attempted to talk to them, but they ignored the patchy voice, distorted by the swarm. Golden streamers of light flickered in the cabin.

Jagens said, "All right, we're just about in position. Report, *Alpha Two.*"

"*Snuggling up behind you, Carl,*" Diego said. "*About two hundred meters to your stern and fifty above.*"

"Remind me to correct your radio procedure, Colonel Calderon," Carl said calmly. "Where's *Bolshoi*, General?"

"*The signal is harder to read in here than we anticipated,*" the Russian said, his voice harsh. "*We never thought there would be so much dust.*"

Jagens looked out of the viewport. The dust was like a thick soup, glinting and swirling. The larger rocks cast broad blades of shadow through the banks of shimmering dust particles: Jagens thought of fish moving through ocean deep. Only a hundred meters away something vast blocked out all light. Shiva.

A black rock wall filling half the universe. Against this silent face they sought fragile shelter. *Bolshoi* was to explode on the other side of Shiva. This spot was best protected from radiation. For a brief moment Jagens let a fear surface in his disciplined mind, a fear all the astronauts had, yet none had voiced: that it was a suicide mission, that Shiva would not protect them from the swirling turmoil created in the dust and rocks around Shiva. They had all denied the thought to themselves; they had to, or they could probably not have gone on.

The study team calculations showed that even *Bolshoi* couldn't shatter Shiva, so *Alpha* wouldn't be pelted with debris. At least not directly. But who knew what would happen when the exploding force disrupted the centuries-long flow of the swarm?

But even success was a big risk. The deflection *Bolshoi*

caused was enough to ram Shiva into the *Alpha* craft within seconds. To avoid collision, the onboard navigation and thrusters had been programmed to compensate instantly for Shiva's new vector, and to do it far faster than any pilot's comprehension and reaction time.

A fly dodging a boulder, Jagens thought. And they had to do it without a good visual fix. Nothing was very clear in all this dust. Navigational stars were obscured or erratically sighted.

"*I thought the astronomers said we could see in here,*" the Russian said in his heavy voice.

"Nothing ever is just like you think. Are we in control, or not, General?"

"*Yes, Captain, we are.*"

"And the other missiles?"

"*On the periphery, and ready.*"

"And yours, *Alpha Two?*"

"*Same, Captain Jagens,*" answered Colonel Issindo.

"*Omega One,* do you read me?" Carl said.

"*Alpha One, this is* Omega One, *we read you, but it's scratchy, Carl.*"

"Stand by. *Bolshoi* is coming in, in . . . seventy seconds."

No one answered. There was nothing to say. General Menshov watched closely the blip on his screen that was *Bolshoi.* On the next screen was the programmed flight and detonation pattern, with the superimposition of the actual flight. So far they were identical.

There was silence in the cramped *Alpha One* capsule. Mechanical subsystems murmured and clicked. These were not heard by the helmeted men, though they were aware of the slight vibrations.

Ping! Ping! Bits of Shiva's swarm bounced off the ship. *Bonk! Tink!* They went unnoticed by the men. Their eyes kept going to the dark surface of the flying mountain of rock and iron, only a few hundred meters away. They paced it, slightly behind and to one side, directly opposite the designated strike zone.

Jagens was aware he was holding his breath. He sucked in more air, then held it, unconsciously, waiting.

From the time *Bolshoi* entered the outer edge of the Shiva swarm until it exploded was less than a second. No human could possibly achieve a proper detonation. Only carefully programmed onboard computers could.

328

Menshov gave *Bolshoi* the last command, feeding it the final navigation figures. It was now on its own. The crews of the two ships prepared for a dangerous battering. Those that were so inclined said prayers.

Jagens looked across Menshov at the green screen with the dotted yellow line crossing it. A red dot moved along the line.

"Call it, General," he ordered.

"Twelve . . . eleven . . . ten . . ."

Was their flight path the proper one? Carl wondered. There was plenty of dust, but no rocks of any serious size, yet . . .

"Seven . . . six . . . five . . ."

So many things could go wrong. Murphy's Law was still in effect, even this far from Earth.

"Two . . . one—!"

Bolshoi flashed through the swarm like a shark through minnows. A rock no bigger than a baby's fist sheered away a vital part of the rear navigation disk. Another rock, not any bigger than the baby itself, was, for a whole fateful second, directly in the path of the bow radar disk. The onboard computers decided in a conversation milliseconds long that Shiva was fractionally closer than previously recorded. An order was sent to the detonation circuit, which blindly followed its programming.

The light was first. A sudden brilliance leaped into a shimmering presence, filling space, reflecting off billions of particles. *Bolshoi* disintegrated into a white-hot point of light, directly in front of Shiva. The shock wave plowed through the thick banks of dust, scattering fist-sized rocks and shards of stone. Shiva shuddered for a fraction of a second, stripped naked of its gritty mantle of dust and rocks. The larger companion stones spun away, chipped and ruptured.

The shock wave rippled through Shiva, wrenching it. An ear pressed to the burnished surface would have heard a deep ringing that lasted for minutes, an acoustic tremor like the voice of an angry god. But the massive iron mountain did not shatter.

A vast spherical shock wave rolled onward. It spread around the rim of Shiva, driving dust and rock shards before it. The two Alpha capsules would have been shielded, if *Bolshoi* had exploded as planned, on the other side of Shiva. When the massive Russian warhead exploded, detonated early, directly in front of the asteroid, the *Alpha* craft were only a few thousand meters below the horizon of Shiva. The shock wave spread around Shiva and struck the fragile capsules.

First light, then sound.

Without their helmets sealed, all aboard would have been instantly deafened. The impact was a force, driving them into their padded couches, slapping their heads to the side.

The ships tumbled. Gyros and stabilizing subsystems cut in. Each ship corrected differently, riding on the fluid currents in the wake of the shock wave. Each fought to correct for spin about all three axes.

Both *Alpha One* and *Two* were pitted and battered. External sensors went blind. Components were ripped away or damaged. The shock wave roiled through the swarm.

Ikko Issindo swayed unconscious in his harness, his face bloody, his arm floating limply in the null-gravity. Droplets of blood filled the air like a fine mist. Diego Calderon shook his head to clear it and twisted to look at the Russian cosmonaut.

Her head lolled inside her helmet. Her eyes were open and staring. Her neck was broken.

Diego checked the air pressure. It had dropped and was still dropping fast. He looked around, following the droplets of blood as they floated out of Issindo's smashed helmet. A pinhole above and behind his head. Diego slapped free of his harness, grabbed a "band-aid" and peeled off the backing. He floated to the hole, slapped the sealer over it, then pushed himself back.

Peering into Issindo's helmet, Diego winced. Dead, or dying. There was nothing for Diego to do. He pulled himself into his seat, snapped on the air conditioner to suck the droplets of blood from the air, and reached for the radio switch.

"*Alpha One,* this is *Alpha Two,* come in."

He waited, then repeated himself. There was no answer. "*Omega One,* this is *Alpha Two,* come in." No answer. Desperately, he tried Houston. No answer from anyone. His radio had to be out.

Peering out the small port, Diego could see Shiva. It was still there, still tumbling slowly. Had they deflected

330

it? They certainly hadn't destroyed it. He had to contact someone and find out what was going on!

He quickly pulled out the radio circuits and examined them as well as he could. There was nothing wrong with them, all just strips of plastic with impregnated chips. The trouble had to be with the various exterior antennae. He switched to the stand-by antenna, but there was still no response. Either *Alpha One* and both of the *Omega* ships were gone, and the swarm interfered with transmission to Earth, or both his antennae were gone.

Diego took another look out the port. He wasn't getting any closer to Shiva. If anything, he was slightly farther away. He bent over and started to dig into the underside of the control panel.

In southern California, standing on a brown, bare hillside, Diego's mother watched the pale dawn turning crimson. It would be toward the sun, they said. Her son was out there, near the awful thing. She wondered if that meant he was close to the sun as well, near its searing flames. She hoped not. Your children never told you what they did. They lived in a different world.

She shuffled her feet on the cold ground, rustling the dry grasses. The eastern sky grew lighter, into eggshell blue, the familiar color of her youth. With so many factories stopped and the cars and trucks almost gone, the sky was better again. She waited, watching.

Then, at once, there it was. A flash so bright she flinched from it, making a sound of pain in her dry throat. A hard white glare. She looked away, her eyes carrying the image of it. Out of the corner of her vision she sensed the thing fade into redness and then die. But it still pulsed on in her retinas.

With the flare and the fading went her last hope. Her son had brought into the heavens a small, quick sun. How could a mere man take fire into the sky and live? No one could survive such a thing. Not even her Diego.

No, to do such a thing meant a sure death. When Diego had been with her last she had seen that he had tried not to talk of this thing. She had seen then that he knew he would die. And now the thing had come. In the chill spring morning she had watched the starfire bloom above and had seen her son die. She crossed herself, feeling the shriveling commence, feeling the loneliness creep in. She knelt. To pray for the dead.

Kingsley Martin finished his solitary lunch and walked out into the yellow London sunshine. Virtually no businesses were open any longer, but he had known that the Gay Hussar would be; they were an old-line restaurant and nothing would perturb their schedule. Today, the Bulgarian beef had been perfect. He had traded the owner the last six tapes in the Strauss series for the meal; the first six had been bartered the evening before.

He walked down through Soho Square, past the red brick buildings that still carried the tinge of seedy Soho reputation, now preserved and almost institutionalized. He had elected to spend the last few hours here, in central London, where so much of his life had been focused. Now it was time to watch the main event.

He found the streets virtually empty on the walk down to Trafalgar. Apparently most people were out in the countryside, where perhaps they felt safer. Certainly if food deliveries slackened any further, city living would become impossible. Or perhaps they were in church, or before their television screens, listening to the endless commentary by the network reporters.

As he approached Charing Cross Road he heard the distant murmur of a crowd. More people were on the street, too, and some were walking quickly, their boots crunching on the broken glass from the last looting spree. He checked his watch as he made his way along the side of the National Gallery: there was plenty of time.

When he looked up he stopped abruptly. Trafalgar Square was jammed with people, all kinds of people from all classes. They were waving banners and crosses. At the center, just under the tall column which supported the Nelson statue, a huge wooden cross burned. The wind shifted, bringing him the oily smell, then he had to squint into the smoke that coiled upward from it.

Was there a man tied up there? He couldn't quite make it out and moved on. Someone brushed past him, bumping his shoulder and hurrying eagerly.

Kingsley began to edge around the crowd, debating whether he should stay. He didn't much like crowds and those radiating hostile vibrations were his least favorite. Public gatherings in Trafalgar were an old tradition, so he shouldn't have been surprised that the religious types were here in strength. He worked his way through the thickening mass toward one of his favorite buildings in London, the church of St. Martin-in-the-Fields.

The front had been splashed with red paint.

Or was it paint?

Kingsley pressed closer but the crowd noise grew and the bodies surged against him. He retreated rather clumsily toward the National Gallery. An Anglican priest elbowed him rudely, then muttered a quick apology through clenched teeth.

He saw that the two fountains in the square were not operating; people wearing soiled gray robes swarmed over them, their long sleeves flapping. As he looked toward the south he could make out more mobs choking the Strand.

Then he saw the immense banners. They were tied to the roof of the National Gallery, hanging down and covering most of the front, billowing out in the slight breeze, bright blue stripes with a big white circle on each. Within the circle, huge faces: Jagens, Menshov, and Lisa Bander.

Kingsley stared at her looming face. It wasn't a good likeness, but somehow the artist had caught the hint of a smile at the corners of her mouth. He studied it, then looked away. He found the banner unnerving; it seemed as though she were staring directly at him.

The crowd's pitch rose. He glanced at the sky. It was almost time. Here, in England, *Bolshoi* would explode in midafternoon. People in the western United States would see it at dawn, and to the Soviets, their Armageddon weapon would light up a distant twilight.

Kingsley edged away from the square, slipping between people who were shouting things, and moved toward the National Gallery. A sudden quiet came, dying down, a hissing as thousands inhaled at once.

Then, high in the bowl of the sky, a small yellow flare burst. An answering roar exploded from the mob. The fireball grew wan, pale, and was gone. The cheers of the mob were ragged. Some were elated, others angry. The mood was mercurial. Those with portable radios were the centers of clusters of listeners. The crowd muttered, then surged violently. "It didn't work!" people yelled. More cheered, many groaned. Fistfights started, a man was

333

gutted with a rusty bayonet, spilling his guts in a gray-green tangle. People fought blindly, angrily. The mob surged back and forth, pulling down and trampling its members. Men cursed, women cried out. Kingsley felt something under his shoes and found he was standing on someone's arm. He was almost knocked over by the backward press of a yelling group. A low, threatening murmur swept across the square. Kingsley decided to get the hell out, and began a vigorous pushing campaign of his own. He felt something soft under his feet but did not look down.

Blocked for a moment, he saw a man climbing, but it took a few moments before he realized what was happening. A small band of men and women were gathered at the foot of the National Gallery. One of them had scaled the first story and was unfastening one of the guide ropes that held the enormous blue banners in place. As Kingsley watched, the man freed the rope and it uncoiled limply, reaching very nearly to the pavement. One of the men grabbed it, tested it with a tug, then started pulling himself up. He put his feet against the granite of the structure and hauled himself up with astonishing rapidity. When he had cleared the crowd he could be seen to be wearing a sweat shirt stenciled with the insigne of the Armageddonite sect. At his waist, hanging from a thong, was a bottle.

Kingsley looked around, wondering where the bobbies were, and listening for the shrill cadence of their sirens. He couldn't see a one, not even on nearby rooftops. Perhaps the rumors were true, that the police were on strike. Everyone else was.

He looked back, concerned, and saw that the man was making his way up the rope directly under the banner of Lisa. Sudden alarm filled him. He knew it was unreasonable alarm: the banner was not the territory, the cloth was not Lisa. But it was still alarm.

The mob had seen the men now; the shouting increased. The first man waved, then leaned down to encourage the second, before edging along the balustrade. The second man had almost reached the top now, his biceps bulging. He reached the top of Lisa's banner and hauled himself over the lip of stone. He waved to those below and did a little dance; the crowd responded with a roar.

Unhooking the bottle from his belt the man brandished it to more cheers. Kingsley suddenly realized what was going to happen. The bottle contained something that would burn easily. The man would ignite the banner. The first man had disappeared while the rope-climber basked in the attention of the mob.

Firing Lisa's banner would touch off the others and in short order the entire front of the National Gallery would go up in flames. The Gallery was well-crafted stonework, but the supporting structure could burn, as well as possible damage to the Gallery's contents.

This lot doesn't know or care about that, though. They wanted only to destroy the image of the astronauts.

Kingsley grunted and shoved forward. Others pushed back, or passively resisted. He slipped by some, bullied others, shoved more, ignoring protests and an occasional weak punch. The crowd seemed to thin and part before him and he was suddenly in the clear, at the base of the Gallery. The last few people had slapped him on the back, shouting encouragement. Almost everyone was looking up, their faces distorted, their mouths open.

A robed man came at him, unshaven and hard-faced, saying something savage which was unheard in the growing noise. He grabbed Kingsley's arm. Kingsley pulled free and pushed the man, roughly, toppling him over. The man had been carrying a rough walking staff of natural, unfinished wood, probably thinking it fit in with the biblical image. Bloody convenient, Kingsley thought, and snatched it up

Two men came at him at once, hands out, their faces distorted with rage. The crowd noise blotted out everything else. Kingsley took the staff in both hands and struck out at the first one with sudden viciousness, catching him cleanly in the head. The second man hesitated, looking at his companion with horror, then rushed at Kingsley with renewed fervor. Kingsley lunged to the side and brought the other end of the pseudo-biblical staff up in a blow that hit his attacker in the stomach. The man stumbled, taking both of them down in a tangle.

Kingsley looked up. The man on the lip was splattering Lisa's banner with petrol. He could smell it. The crowd cheered and clapped hands. A few nearby cursed Kingsley, shaking fists, as Kingsley kicked himself free and stood up. The man who had carried the staff got to his feet but backed off as Kingsley advanced, holding the staff at port arms. The crowd jeered and the robed figure straightened, cried out, and rushed Kingsley.

Darting in, looking for a new angle of attack, he met the hard-driven end of the staff in his gut. The man sucked in air, bending over, looking green. Kingsley swung the staff again, clipping him in the skull, and the robed man fell.

The others, getting unsteadily to their feet, stopped. Something guarded in their faces told Kingsley he could look upward again. The man was still spraying.

The mob could easily have overrun Kingsley, and he knew it, but they lacked a leader, or someone to instigate the attack. They hung back, swearing, but their attention kept going up to the man on the high lip of the Gallery.

Kingsley faced each person who looked at him, staring at them, as if confronting each individually. When he did this, they always glanced away, or looked up, refusing the confrontation. Turning, Kingsley walked over to the rope which dangled down from the man's high perch. The Armageddonite was concentrating on his work, but taking his time under the approving noise of the vast crowd.

Kingsley saw that the man had his feet entwined in the rope as he stood on the narrow ledge, bending over to spill down the petrol. Kingsley seized the rope and jerked it to one side. The man saw what was happening and tried to kick free, but he was too entangled. He grabbed at the ornate coping, dropping the bottle, which fell into the crowd and smashed, spreading fumes.

Kingsley yanked again, then started trotting along the steps, pulling the rope as tight as possible. The man's hands scrabbled at inadequate handholds. He lost his grip on the ledge, his eyes bulging. Kingsley saw his mouth widen in a yell, but the scream was buried in a great roar from the crowd.

They liked death, especially dramatic deaths. Even now, after the world was soaked in blood, they liked death. Mobs always liked death.

They got it. The man came, tumbling, pinwheeling to the pavement, hitting with a smack that Kingsley could hear above the noise.

Kingsley dropped the limp rope and studied the crowd. Only a few moments before this mob had been angry and powerful. The orange burst in the sky had enraged them. But now, without even knowing whether the great bomb had been effective, they were changed.

He peered into their faces and saw them as children. Maybe they saw themselves that way, too. The noise abated. People began moving off. They had shaken their fists against the astronauts and engineers who labored to stop Shiva. But now that *Bolshoi* had gone off there was a growing stillness in Trafalgar Square. He could sense the mood change; it was as palpable as sunlight or rain. Once the arsonist had fallen, the wind had gone from their sails.

Children. A pack of unruly kids, faces smeared with stolen chocolate, all silent and numbed after the raucous party was over.

God help us, he thought. I wasn't all that much different from them, months ago. Fear takes strange forms.

He looked around, peering upward for the first man, who could still come out and spoil his victory. There was no sign. He saw a bobbie on the edge of the crowd. "Move along now, please."

He felt a curious new certainty fill him. Whether *Bolshoi* had worked or not, the people here had at least begun to come to their senses. Perhaps there was hope for them all, now.

He sighed, and turned to help the man who had fallen.

More than a billion people watched the drama on their televisions. More would have, but there was no power. So they clung to each other and watched the dot growing in the sky.

Deep in the cold tunnels of Teller Air Force Base, deep within a Colorado mountain, the Secretary of Health, Education, and Welfare, Monica Alice Ashby, Junior, sat and stared at a hypodermic syringe of Morphine-8, trying to get up the courage to pick it up. It was pure stuff, more than enough to do the job. She didn't want to be alive when Shiva arrived.

Besides, her ulcer was killing her.

The Pope blessed the faithful from his balcony.

337

Secretary of State Gilbert McNellis lay in a pool of h
own blood in a Georgetown house. A Smith and Wesso
revolver, all its cartridges fired, lay next to him. On h
stoop lay two of the three invaders he had hit. His famil
had just enough time to get out the back door, throug
the garden of Senator Dunn and to an Army reserve un
coming along Wisconsin Avenue. The Secret Servic
guards had been gone for hours.

On N Street, not far from the house where John Kenned
had lived, Under Secretary of Defense Theotis Dudle
crouched behind a great mound of uncollected trash. H
had exchanged his Savile Row suit for denims and an un
marked army fatigue jacket. His pockets were stuffe
with money and jewelry, all of it his, and a Ruger Blac
hawk .44 was in his belt. He was waiting until the Arm
had gone on up Wisconsin, then he'd make a break t
the east, then south on Pennsylvania Avenue to th
White House. He had his pass and identification; they'
let him in. They had to. It was one of the few place
left that would be safe.

Of course they'd let him in.

Senator Buford Dunn stood in the Statuary Hall of th
Capitol. The light was dim, the recesses shadowed, th
noises amplified. It was here, in this spot where h
planted his feet, that John Quincy Adams had found yo
could hear everything being whispered across the room
It had been used by the House of Representatives then
back before 1857. Now it was filled with statues on grea
pedestals, one from each state, depicting that state's se
lection of a great man or woman. Dunn had always bee
a little annoyed at that. They rarely took one of the stat
ues away, to replace it with, presumably, a still greate
person. He felt closed off, unable to achieve the greatnes
he felt he deserved. He had accepted that he woul
never become president, and he didn't want the gelde
position of the vice-presidency, either.

But he'd been a good senator, maybe the best his stat
had ever sent to Washington, that city Kennedy had de
scribed as having Southern efficiency and Norther
charm. He had thought maybe, just maybe, he'd ge
more than a dam and a high school named after him
Somehow, he had fixed on a statue in the Capitol Build

ing. Right there, between Will Rogers and Ralph Nader. Nothing too modern, but in his best suit, holding a book, an old-fashioned book, and looking north toward the Senate chamber.

He sighed and looked around for a seat. There weren't any. The room whispered and echoed. It sounded like paper slipping in a breeze, like distant crowds, like silk rustling. He waited, and nothing happened. He wasn't certain just what was supposed to happen, then he turned and walked to the rotunda, then out through the pillars to the steps of the East Front. He paused, testing the air. It was a nice evening, except for the fires to the south. There was the smell of pine on the wind.

Maybe he'd walk over and sit in the Lincoln Memorial. It wasn't too far. He wasn't that old. Even if he didn't think he'd get much older.

The Russian general unfastened his seat harness and came half up out of his chair to pull Carl Jagens back into his seat. The American commander had a bloody forehead and the inside of his helmet was smeared with blood. The cabin pressure was up, so Menshov unfastened Carl's helmet and took it off.

Carl lay in the couch limply as Menshov broke open the first-aid packets and put a bandage around the forehead wound. Head wounds were always bloody, but this one didn't look all that bad. They had been flung around rather roughly, after the explosion, and Jagens had somehow struck his head on the helmet.

The bandage completed, Menshov returned to a monitoring of the ship's functions. The radio was out. The starboard steering jet didn't work. The food-packet storage had popped its door and packets were strewn everywhere. The radio to the twenty-two twenty-megatonners was still intact and Menshov thought briefly how he might adapt that to a signal to Earth.

All that done, he looked out at Shiva. If they had done any damage, he couldn't see it on this side. He sat in his seat and ran a test on the onboard computers. They checked out, so he ran the sensor data through them both. Then he sat back, staring at the yellow letters on the dark green screen.

They had slowed Shiva, but the deflection had been minimal.

Bolshoi had exploded too soon.

Ping!

Menshov ducked automatically. There had been a few light touches earlier but he had ignored them. But this was a strong hit. He checked the air pressure: all right.

Ping! Bomp!

Frowning, Menshov ran a quick check. The swarm was moving ahead of Shiva, pulling away from the slowed asteroid. The explosion had also ejected much debris from the swarm, causing ripples in the long-established patterns.

They had to get in touch with Earth. This would require massive new calculations.

Ping! Bonk! Thud. *Pop!*

Menshov reached for the controls and eased the ship ahead. He didn't want to try to get out of the swarm. Instead, they should get in front of Shiva, to let the mountain of nickel-iron protect their stern for them. The capsule took a few more sideswipes before Menshov got the craft into the lee of the asteroid. There, in the shadow, he matched the velocity of the Earth-bound rock, and looked at Carl Jagens.

The American astronaut came around slowly, then blinked and was conscious. "What happened? Did we kill it?"

Menshov shook his head and explained the situation in a few plain sentences. Carl started to sit up, but an expression of great pain crossed his face, and he fell back, panting.

"Here," the cosmonaut said, handing Carl some painkillers and a flask of water to suck from. Carl took them, his hand shaking with weakness, and swallowed the pills with a grimace.

"Captain, I don't think you are fit," Menshov said. "I think I should—"

"No!" snarled Carl, his eyes glaring at the Russian. "I'm here, I'm alive, *I'm* in command!" But the effort weakened him, and his mouth sagged with pain. His eyes wavered out of focus, but he fought back, still glaring.

Menshov shrugged. "You are physically unable to continue your duties, Captain. I am formally assuming command under article nineteen, section three of the Mutual Assistance Pact signed by your president and our Secretariat only four weeks ago."

"Screw my president and your Secretariat, Red, *I'm* in command of this mission!"

"Captain, when you are well enough, I will return command to you and—"

"No, you won't! You're a glory-grabbing son of a bitch! I've had my eye on you from the first! You Russians are all alike! Claiming you invented the telephone or whatever! Well, you're not going to grab control of *this* one!"

"Captain Jagens, I am formally—"

Carl reached for him, his face a grimace of pain and anger. He caught Menshov by the metal rim of his spacesuit and, braced by his seat harness, pulled the startled Russian toward him. In the lack of gravity the Russian sailed up face-first into the video-transmission controls. He screamed just as he hit, but then was silenced. Growling like an animal, Carl pulled him back, ripping him loose from the controls that had stabbed into his face. Then he impaled the limp cosmonaut again, crashing him into the sharp corners and protruding instrumentation.

Carl flung the Russian aside with a snarl. Menshov floated away, bounced off the black boxes of the opposite bulkhead, and came back at Carl, arms waving limply, streaming droplets of blood. Carl grabbed Menshov and roughly stuffed him into his seat. He unbuckled, found the Russian's helmet, and jammed it over the bloody head, locking it down tightly. He fastened the seat harness around the body haphazardly, then dropped into his own couch with a grunt. His fingers gripped the arms until they turned white, and his eyes stared out the port unseeing.

Shiva was now so close to Earth that even a small backyard telescope could pick out details. *Bolshoi* had slowed Shiva and scattered the swarm. The swarm moved ahead of Shiva. Seen from Earth it was a silvery haze that thinned and grew and the fragments pushed outward by *Bolshoi* moved apart.

The swarm would reach Earth first, and now nothing could stop it. Luckily, some of the largest chunks had been kicked sideways by the explosion, and they would miss Earth. Many of the smaller pieces of rock, and all of the dust, would burn up in the atmosphere. But the swarm would continue to do much damage; that was unavoidable.

341

On its present course Shiva itself would soon rip through Earth's blanket of air and bury itself in the planet forever.

Dark and burnished from its voyages near the sun, the massive asteroid swept on.

The nausea came and went, as did the weakness. Carl did not look at the Russian again. He was a mutineer in the most important space flight in history. What Carl had done was only right. There was no time for proper legal procedure. None. There was only time to stop Shiva.

Jagens ran a feverish test on the radio. Only the frequency to the missiles was still functioning. Then Carl noticed the Geiger counter.

In the red.

He stared, suspended in time. He'd been exposed. When the ship had tumbled, it must have gotten out of Shiva's radiation shadow, into the bomb debris. Then Menshov had moved them in front, to protect them from the swarm coming up the stern, but had exposed them to further radiation.

He was probably dead.

For a long moment Carl Jagens felt nothing. Only a faint wonder. Then like a dam breaking, there appeared a crack. Then a trickle. Then a great rushing of joy.

He was free.

He realized his reaction to his death sentence was curious. A quiet, back-of-the-mind part of himself, the part that was always cold, always dreadfully logical and unemotional, looked upon all of it with satisfaction.

You wanted to be a hero, big shot. Here's your chance. Your last chance. No matter *what* you do, you are not going to live through it, so you have nothing to lose.

Only your reputation. Only your legend.

Legend.

They would talk of him through the generations of man. If he was successful. If he wasn't, it wouldn't matter. Either way he'd be dead.

There are different ways of dying. But not to Carl Jagens. To him there was only one way: after the mission was accomplished.

He need not even worry about death by radiation poisoning, a lingering and particularly horrifying end. He'd do what he had to do, then simply open the airlock. No, first, put the capsule in some kind of orbit, a burial site in space. Or head it into the sun? It didn't matter. That would just be frosting, like a plaque.

Nothing mattered, except stopping Shiva. If he didn't stop Shiva, then his death would be meaningless. He'd be forgotten and to be forgotten was never to have been.

First, he thought, survey the assets.

Alpha One, reasonably secure. Radioactive, but secure. Twenty-two missiles and the means to direct and control them.

Now, what about the others? No one answered, so they are either dead or rendered ineffective. He must do it alone.

Those in *Alpha Two* must be dead, or exposed, unless they had stayed within the shelter of Shiva. It didn't matter. It had always been up to him, anyway.

Quickly, he plotted a course for one of the missiles to come through the swarm. Then he moved to the side opposite the blast area. Most of the swarm had moved on ahead, but a radar check showed the tail of the swarm still coming up. He must work quickly.

The missile streaked in, exploding violently against the mountain of rock. It did nothing; it wasn't intended to do much. It was only a guide, a test, a pathfinder through the debris.

He began to program the remaining twenty-one missiles to strike Shiva at once. Twenty-one times twenty megatons. Something had to work.

The explosion of the first missile caught Diego unaware, catching him out of his acceleration couch and flinging him against the metal bulkhead. The capsule tumbled wildly as the shock wave struck it. Diego broke his arm against the missile control unit, switching nine of them to manual and disconnecting them from *Alpha One.* Blackness came swiftly, seared with the redness of pain.

Jagens blinked as nine of his lights went out. He swore at the computer, but nothing he did brought them back. It seemed impossible that nine of them could have been exploded or somehow destroyed all at once by the blast. They were too far out, too well swaddled in redundancy. They weren't destroyed, he thought, they were disconnected!

Someone is alive out here, someone else!

Alpha Two, that goddamn Calderon! *He* took my missiles away, Jagens thought angrily. "That bastard!" he snarled. "That Mex bastard!"

That left a dozen. Twelve times twenty-megatons. Maybe it would do it. He had no idea how much deflection might have been achieved in the first explosion, when *Bolshoi* was detonated. Some certainly, but not much. Maybe another push would do it.

He went back to the programming of twelve missiles, getting them to the target all at once, detonating within a millisecond or so of each other, at the right spot on the spinning asteroid. Catch the spin at the right point, hit it just right, and you could add the spin of the asteroid to the push.

A delicate touch was needed. If his head would only stop pounding. It was hard to see when your head pounded like that. But he could ignore it for as long as it took. Heroes never had it easy.

"Why did he explode the little one?" Nino Solari asked.

Lisa Bander shrugged, her face grave wth concern. "Maybe it was a last futile gesture, maybe he was making a path through, I don't know." She continued to call to the rest of the mission. "*Alpha One, Alpha Two,* this is *Omega One,* come in, please. *Alpha One,* do you read me? Come in, please."

"Give it up, babe," Nino said. "They are either dead or their radio went blooey."

She sighed. "*Alpha Two,* this is *Omega One.* Diego? Diego, this is Lisa. Come in, please."

"*Omega One, this is Houston Control, come in, please.*"

"Go away, Houston, we're busy."

"*Omega Two, this is Houston. Do you—*"

Another voice broke in. "*Lisa, this is Dink. What's happened? The OAO says you slowed Shiva but didn't deflect it worth shit.*"

Lisa smiled wanly. "We don't *know* what happened, Dink. I think their radios are out. Maybe they're dead. I . . ." She caught herself and closed her eyes for a moment. "I don't know. We have to go in now. We have nineteen missiles to hit that rock with and we're giving it everything."

"*Colonel Bander, if* Bolshoi *didn't effect a deflection. I*

344

don't think your missiles will." Lisa knew the voice, but couldn't place it. One of the scientists.

"Can't bring 'em home," she said, almost in a whisper. "Got to give it a try."

Dink Lowell came back on the line. *"Maybe if you could link up with Alpha's missiles, hit it all at once . . ."*

"Fine, except I can't contact *Alpha*. Either of them. I'm cutting off now. Going to go in closer."

"Omega One—"

She cut the line to Earth. It would be there if she needed it. "Let's move in," she said to Solari.

Pain.

Pain brought Diego back from the blackness. His first stirrings increased it and he cried out. He floated in the cramped cabin, a foot wedged between some equipment, anchoring him. His face was a hand's width away from the staring dead eyes of Olga Nissen.

A wave of nausea caused Diego to buckle and the pain of moving his arm almost threw him back into the pit of unconsciousness. It was his left arm. The break seemed to be in the forearm.

He twisted carefully around, keeping the injured limb floating out. At least the lack of gravity kept it from pulling. He broke the seal on the first-aid kit and pulled out one of the splints. Wincing, he wrapped it carefully around his arm, but did not inflate it. He took a deep breath, checked to see his foot was still wedged tightly, then took the limp fingers of his left hand in his right hand.

Diego inhaled, waited a beat, then pulled. He grunted as the pain swept over him again, bringing him to the edge of blackout, but he stayed conscious. He had not dared remove the spacesuit as he knew he might not get back into it, and there was every chance he would need it. He quickly fumbled at the tiny vial, releasing the compressed air that inflated the splint to rigidity. He grimaced with pain as the device held his forearm tightly.

Hoping there was no serious blood loss, Diego then set about to righting the ship and getting it back on course. Althought he was at the constant edge of blackout, he fought it. A painkiller would dull him too much. There would be time for that later.

He was moving away from Shiva, but not falling behind

it. In a few moments he had computed a course that would bring him back toward the massive rock. Only after he had punched the course into the navigation computer did he take a painkiller.

Now what? Through bleary eyes Diego watched the slowly turning rock. Every second brought it kilometers nearer Earth. What could he do? If *Bolshoi* hadn't stopped it, what could he *possibly* do?

Well, for one thing, Calderon, he told himself, find out what you *can't* do, find out your assets. He began a running status check.

The first thing he looked at was the Geiger counter. The ship had some exposure, but nowhere near the lethal dossage he feared. The invisible killing rays had been mostly blocked by Shiva's mass.

He continued the Recall Evaluation Program, repping the damaged craft as well as he could.

Carl Jagens stared at the mass of Shiva and felt a great exaltation. The ultimate challenge, he thought. I survived everything they threw at me to arrive at this moment: air combat, all the space training, that incident on the moon, the long Mars flight. I survived the final, most important selection. No! More than that—I was selected the *leader! Chosen* to lead! I survived the premature explosion of the faulty Russian bomb, the mutiny, everything!

Yes, true, I face death, but it is not the first time, only the last. But I went through all of it, all the years of friendlessness, of making it my way, of smiling and intrigue and work, all of it to do this one thing! My entire life has been aimed at this one lonely moment, this one final, climactic experience.

Only God could have directed me here, against all the odds, against the obstacles and imperfections. He must want me to do what I am doing, to do what I have done, no matter the cost. My life is forfeit, but it is small payment for eternal fame.

His fingers uncurled from the arms of the acceleration couch and he reached out to press the button that would activate the small fleet of missiles, bringing them in at Shiva in a deadly rain of power.

Light filled the cabin.

Lisa and Nino Solari were blinded, stunned by the sudden rippling flare of a string of explosions.

"What the hell is going on?" Nino said, rubbing at his eyes.

"Someone is firing the missiles at Shiva," Lisa said, trying again to contact the *Alpha* team. "*Alpha*, this is *Omega*, come in, please."

"*Omega One*, this is Houston. What's going on? Jesus, tell us, will you? We're beginning to get some hits here! A piece of that swarm hit off Uruguay an hour ago and a tidal wave knocked out Montevideo!"

"Dink? Damn it, I don't have time to chat!"

"Lisa, we just got word something cratered San Bernardino. There are earthquakes all along the San Andreas fault out there! Chengtu is gone, in the Szechwan province. There's a goddamn lake of hot glass in the Rub' al Khali desert!"

"Dink, leave us alone!"

"We're getting shotgunned down here, damnit! What are you people doing up there? Melbourne just got hit with a tidal wave, and there's—"

"Dink! We're doing what we *can!* I can't communicate with *Alpha.* I don't know who's alive and who isn't! Someone just hit Shiva with a mess of warheads. Look, let's forget deflection and think about deceleration. Never mind a damage report on spaceship Earth—there's nothing we can do about that up here, understand?"

Before they had a chance to answer Lisa continued. "I want quick, back-of-the-envelope stuff. Get the *percentages.* I think we are better off going for deceleration at this point. But get me some numbers, *pronto!*"

"Uh, yeah, Lisa . . . uh . . . listen, they're checking it through now. We've been having trouble with the Boston facility. Power down there, but we finally got a battalion in with some portable power and they'll be coming through with the readings shortly and—"

"God damn it, Houston, never mind the local news! I don't care how you do it, just do it. Get me numbers—and fast! Is it better to go for a slow-up and a miss than a deflection try? Hurry it up!"

"*Roger*, Omega One, we . . . oh, here's Chuck . . ."

"*Omega One*, this is Houston Control. Bradshaw here."

"Houston Control, this is *Omega One*. Got something for us?"

"Affirmative, Omega One, *Boston* says there has been just about half as much deflection as we need." Solari groaned. "Um, sixty-one percent, to be exact. Did you hit it with everything you had?"

"Negative, Houston, that was *Alpha* and we don't know what they did. All, part, we don't know. The radar images are still pretty fuzzy. Lots of garbage still up here."

"Well, whatever you have, you'd better punch it in as soon as possible. Every second makes it more difficult."

"Understand, Houston. We have been going in for some time now. As soon as we are in position behind Shiva we will target our missiles."

"Uh . . ." Bradshaw seemed to hesitate. "Um, good luck, Omega."

"Understood, Houston. *Omega One* out."

Lisa looked at Solari, but his eyes were on the radar screen, trying to separate wheat from chaff.

Ping! Ponnng!

Bits of rock from the last explosions careened off *Omega One*. Immediately, Lisa sought to warn *Omega Two* behind them. "*Omega Two*, this is *Omega One*. Incoming debris, repeat, incoming debris."

"*Acknowledged*," said Colonel Zaborovskii in his heavy voice.

"*Omega Two*, be prepared to—"

Another bright explosion made her wince. Someone had hit Shiva with another atomic bomb.

"Lisa, for Christ's sake, we can't go in there with those bombs going off! And we can't send in the missiles, either, not until we're certain a blast won't knock them out going in."

Lisa nodded. "*Omega Two*, hold your position. We've got to stop these explosions and coordinate our efforts." For a full minute Lisa attempted again to contact the Alpha ships, but there was no response.

Lisa blew out her cheeks and glanced at Nino. "Well, we've got to get in closer, my friend."

"Yeah," the astronaut answered dryly. "I knew this good part couldn't last."

"We must find out which ship survived and who is firing those rockets."

Nino looked at Lisa closely. "It, uh, it might be Jagens . . . in which case . . ."

348

"In which case Diego is probably dead." She shook her head and her short hair spread out in the null gravity before it settled down again. "I don't want to think about that right now." I'll think about it later, she told herself. Later. A private later.

"See if you can get any sort of telemetry fix. They have to be signaling the missiles."

"I'll get *Omega Two* to triangulate with me," Nino said, his fingers already busy.

Ping! Ponk! Lisa looked up. *Bonk!*

Ting!

Thud.

It was going to be big trouble going in, she thought.

Diego stirred again. The second blast caught him in his couch, but the pain of the wrenching around sent him into oblivion. His capsule tumbled again. The droplets of blood that had been floating in the cabin drifted toward a pinhole in the thin metal bulkhead. A faint hissing would have been heard, had any of the cabin's occupants been conscious.

"Look!" Lisa said, pointing out the port.

A long thin streamer of something was coming out of Shiva. As Solari stared, another joined it. They merged and created a long gaseous trail behind Shiva, backlit by the sun.

"Water and methane," he said. "The bomb blasts must have warmed up the whole damned rock. My God, look at that!"

The cometlike tail increased in intensity and became multicolored. More gases poured out of the heated rock, creating a long, colorful tail.

"I hate to say it," Nino said, "but it's beautiful."

"So's that," Lisa said, pointing at a picture screen.

Earth was a discernible blue-white disc.

Time was running out.

Carl swore at the nine dead lights. *Nine!* Nine would do it! Why had he been denied the nine? Was there significance in the number? A cardinal number. Nine muses. No, that was nothing! What had that fool, the one at the party, what had he said? The Nine Jewels, the culminating stage of spiritual development in the occult. Something in that perverted science, astrology? No, reject, unimportant, forget it. Nonsense. Wait, wasn't there something about Nine Mystic Names? Some kind of Satan-worship bullshit? But what if it isn't bullshit, what if—

Stop.

Get a hold on yourself.

Calmly.

You have been chosen.

What you do is the right thing to do.

Do not be swayed.

Decide.

Then do it.

Carl frowned at the unlit squares. They had failed. There were only a few possible reasons. Think. What is the rule of probability? Faulty electronics, maybe. The missiles had gone in with the rest, only the light hadn't lit. No, the ship's circuits were almost foolproof, all molecular construction. The single missile that had failed to respond in the first flight had been a programming error. He had sent it in later, fuming with anger and frustration.

Another answer was that the nine missiles had been destroyed. But what would have done it? They were too far out for any blast damage and it was unlikely debris could have knocked out all nine, all at once. They must then still exist.

Another possble answer: they were switched from the command circuit manually.

Calderon.

Calderon in *Alpha Two*. He did it.

But why? He had not been chosen. He was interfering. He was dooming Earth to destruction.

Carl swung the radar screen into its forward mount, as close as he could get it. Where *was* that bastard?

Consciousness returned slowly to Diego Calderon. The pain helped. It was something to cling to. A reality in a mist of uncertainty. There was pain, there would always be pain. Pain was something you could count on.

Something long and colorful streamed and rippled in the blackness. He focused his eyes and saw the comet that Shiva had become.

Going in with flags flying.

350

I should be doing something about that, he thought ha-
sily.

Missiles.

Hit it again.

He looked at the control panel. Nine green lights. Three
and three and three. There were no other lights on that
panel. The others were gone, dead, exploded.

Jagens had used them up against Shiva. But had they
done any good?

Diego felt frustrated. He was blinded and deafened.
Out of communication with both Earth and the other ships,
he had to proceed as best he could. Maybe he would do
the wrong thing. The entire operation needed coordination. He hoped the others were not cut off as he was.

But he had nine twenty-megaton missiles. If all the
other *Alpha* missiles hadn't diverted Shiva, what could
nine more do?

But he had to try.

He noticed the cluster of bright red droplets against the
bulkhead. Pinhole! He struggled up from the couch and
reached for a sealing patch from the kit.

Tink!

He winced as he held the patch to peel off the backing.
Already he was composing the program in his mind that
would bring in his nine missiles all at once.

Ping!

Pop!

He slapped the patch over the hole and pressed it
smooth, squeezing away the droplets of blood. He pulled
himself weakly into the couch again.

Ponk!

Nine at once. His Sunday punch. His only punch.

Pinnng!

"Got him," Solari said. "Got to be. See? The signal is
Carl's. He left on the operating telemetry for missiles he
doesn't have anymore."

"Could it be, uh, *Alpha Two?*"

Nino shook his head. "Nope. Each ship has a distinct
signal. That's *Alpha One.*"

"Lock on it and let's go in."

Ting!

Nino grinned. "When you duck in a spacesuit you look
like a turtle."

351

Lisa did not smile back. *Omega One* began to move. Ahead of them was the long bright tail of Shiva, easily visible and growing bigger all the time.

In Houston, an assistant handed Chuck Bradshaw a teletype message. He winced and passed it to Dink Lowell. Calcutta, Tientsin, and Hokkaido had suffered severe meteor damage. Ethiopia and the Saudi Arabian desert boiled under massive meteor strikes. All air traffic had been grounded throughout the world. Milan and Detroit were burning out of control. More "miracles" reported, more riots, more deaths.

Dink dropped the paper in the wastebasket. There was no need to tell the astronauts any of it. The advance part of the swarm was hitting Earth. It was only a matter of time before the end.

Unless a miracle happened.

A man at one of the consoles crossed himself, stood up, carefully shoved his chair into the desk, and walked out. His screen was left flickering. There was no replacement.

Carl Jagens stared hard at a particular blip on the screen. It was slightly brighter, though no bigger than the yellow images of the various rocks still escorting Shiva.

Metal.

Alpha Two. It had to be.

Without conscious effort Carl Jagens turned the ship toward the tiny blip.

Calderon.

He had the nine missiles. He'd go there, take command of the missiles from that fool and send them crashing against Shiva.

Then he'd . . .

Then he'd . . .

Carl could not think beyond that moment.

First things first. Go to *Alpha Two.* Take the missiles. If he had to, he would kill Calderon. It would serve him right. Poetic justice even. It would leave him, Captain Carl Jagens, United States Navy, alone. The ineffectual *Omega* team was unimportant. *He* would divert Shiva. Only he.

The ship streamed fire and began to move toward the tiny distant capsule of *Alpha Two.*

"Closing," Nino said. "Can you see him yet?"

"No. There's so damned much—"

Ping!

"—dust still. There's no—wait! No! Yes! There, that's
im! See the lights?"

"Uh-huh, right spot."

Deftly Lisa adjusted their flight path toward the distant
d and green running lights.

"—One, *this is . . . Control, come in, please. Omega
ne—*"

"What is it?" Lisa snapped. "We cannot read you very
ell. Too much interference from the dust and Shiva's
on, I guess."

"*—your signal. Your radar image has merged with
hiva's . . . and . . . NASA believes . . . you . . . Al-
ha . . . over.*"

"Houston, your transmission is breaking up. We cannot
ad you," Nino said.

"Never mind them," Lisa said, cutting off Houston once
gain. "Let's link up with *Alpha One.*"

"That'll be pretty tricky. He's moving off that way."

"They don't pay us for the easy stuff," Lisa muttered,
quinting at the tiny resolving dot of a ship.

Ping!

Tonk!

onk!

Carl Jagens ignored the tiny rocks hitting the ship, ex-
pt for the ritual check of the air pressure gauge. He'd
t hulled by a few but as soon as he turned and went
ith the swarm he'd be all right.

Ponk!

Ping!

The sounds echoed in the capsule, along with the
ratches and bumpings of others that hit at an oblique
ngle. Carl frowned as another signal appeared on his
dar.

Another ship?

Omega!

What were they doing here? This was *his* mission! He
ached for the radio switch before he remembered.
Vell, ignore them. They could not share this glory. It was
is. *He* would save Earth.

Wait!

353

They had missiles! Nineteen missiles!

His hands reached for the controls. The ship slowed. H[e] matched their flight path and watched as they dre[w] alongside. He even admired the way *Omega One* deftl[y] touched his ship.

Bump.

He didn't want them in his ship and he didn't want t[o] leave the command ship.

Physical contact, of course. Quickly, he patched the ra[-] dio's antenna outlet to the ship's hull.

"—One, *this is* Omega One. *Are you all right? Over?*"

"*Omega One*, this is *Alpha One*. Of course, I'm a[ll] right. The radio antenna is out, that's all."

"*Carl, where's Diego?*"

"*Omega One*, please observe correct radio discipline[.] I've warned you about this before."

"*Carl, where's Diego?*" Anger and fear were in Lisa['s] voice.

"Dead. They're all dead. The Russian, too. He trie[d] mutiny. Can you imagine that? Mutiny!"

There was a long silence from the other ship, then Lis[a] spoke again. "*Alpha One, how do you know Colone[l] Calderon is, is dead?*"

"He's dead. That is unimportant now. What *is* impor[-] tant is the missiles. Transfer control to me on, um, circui[t] one zero eight. I will assume control at—"

"*Carl, we can patch you through to Earth. Transmission is a mess, but they can give us the best plan.*"

"The best plan? There is no *best* plan, there is only one plan. Hit Shiva with everything we have!"

"*Yes, but at the right point, the proper spread of—*"

"I command you to surrender control to me!"

"*Captain Jagens,*" Nino Solari said, interrupting hur[-] riedly. "*Here's Houston, sir.*"

"I don't care if—"

"*—ton Control, how do you . . . if . . . Boston esti[-] mates . . .*"

"Give me control of those missiles, *Omega One!*"

"*—deflection attempt has been progressing and . . . only a twenty-seven percent cha . . . it . . . uncertain . . . work . . . warheads function at opti—*"

"No!" shouted Carl. "Only I! Only I can properly es[-] timate the system's reliability! My plan! This is *my* plan[!] It will work! I will take the missiles in! I will divert[

Shiva! My plan will work! It was the Russian's fault! Detonated too soon! It was the fault of that Red bomb! But I'll make it work! *Omega One!* You will transfer control of your missiles to me at once! That is an *order!*"

Lisa looked at Nino Solari. Carl Jagens was beyond all reason. She touched the controls. A jet of flame moved her away from *Alpha One,* breaking contact. Houston Control continued to talk, suggesting plans and options, but Lisa ignored them.

"Nino, set up a program to bring all our missiles in to just beyond the perimeter of the swarm."

"Time, Lisa, time. Maybe we should bring them straight in, bang."

She nodded. "I know. Every second brings it closer. But we must be *right.* You bring them in while I talk to Houston." She opened the line up again.

"Houston, this is *Omega One.* I want a program for bringing in all nineteen of my missiles for maximum deflection. Over."

"*Omega One, this is Bradshaw. Lisa, we . . . we just received word from the OAO. There's a sizable chunk heading right for here. It'll hit somewhere between Beaumont and here. Maybe as far south as Galveston. We're evacuating.*"

"Chuck—!"

"*JPL will pick it up. I'm flying out there right now. They've had a bitch of an earthquake there, but they're operational. We've got to run. Houston out!*"

"Chuck!" But the carrier wave was gone.

Her face white, Lisa looked at Nino, who was switching around on the frequencies. He flashed her a smile. "Got it!"

"*—this is the Jet Propulsion Laboratory, come in, please. Omega One, we are taking over ground control. Do you read me? We are transmitting . . . the . . . at Goldstone . . . where . . .*"

"Damn!" Nino said. "They were coming in pretty good, then, poop!" He fiddled with the dial a moment.

"*—we . . . through . . . Omega . . . the . . . Propulsion . . . in, please . . . One . . . ground control, over? Omega . . .*"

"JPL, this is *Omega One,* your transmission is erratic, but go ahead."

"—One . . . *read you . . .*"

"JPL, we need a program for bringing in all nineteen missiles for maximum deflection."

"*—monitored your . . . Houston, Omega . . . been working on . . . have in a few minutes. All hell breaking . . . around here and . . . power is . . . the quake . . . governor did . . .*"

"JPL, JPL, This is *Omega One.*"

"*—ahead*, Omega One."

"JPL, the Russian bomb slowed Shiva . . . maybe we can slow it further, rather than deflect it. Maybe it could miss Earth entirely. Can you give us an estimate on that? Which is our best option? Trying to deflect or slowing?"

"*—get back to you . . . few . . . moments, while beep . . . and . . .*"

"Sounds like a goddamn crystal set," muttered Nino.

Ping!

The isolated bits of space debris still took their toll of *Omega One.* Lisa contacted *Omega Two* and got their status report. Then the Jet Propulsion Lab called back.

"Omega One, *this is . . . and . . . have an option set for you to . . . your nineteen . . . do the job and . . .*"

"JPL, JPL, this is *Omega One*, repeat, please."

"Omega One, *this is JPL . . . an option set for you to evalu . . . estimate your nineteen will not . . . job . . . but analysis of radar . . . that there are remaining five . . . to eight are . . . possible control of . . .*"

"There are still some of *Alpha's* missiles here?" Nino said.

"*Affirmative*, Omega One. *Deep Space radar estimates . . . to eight are . . . possible control of . . .*"

"How can we get them?" Lisa grumbled. With Diego dead . . . with Diego dead . . . She shook herself.

Ping!
Ponk! Ping! Bonk!
Bump.
Ting!

A hissing. It rose in pitch and became a wail. Lisa's ears popped. She reached for a patch with one hand while the other scrabbled at her seat harness. Twisting, half out of her seat, she peeled the patch and slapped the sticky disk over the hole. It wasn't big enough; air still escaped through the rent. Frantically, but without wasted motion, she peeled and applied another patch. The hissing stopped. She sank back into the couch and blew out her cheeks.

"Omega One, *this is* Omega Two!"

"*Lisa, this is Julie Short. We've been hit . . . hulled several . . . Got most of the leaks patched, but our navigation computer is mostly a mess.*"

"Omega Two—what about the crew? Schumacher and Zaborovskii?"

"*Colonel Zaborovskii is hurt pretty bad. He got sprayed when the nav computer was hit. Tom's hurt, too. Broken wrist, couple of ribs, his eye. They're both out now.*"

"What about you, Julie?"

"*Semper fi, Lisa. I can't seem to move the lower half of me but I can reach most things from here. When we evacuated the air it froze whatever was bleeding, I guess.*"

"My god, Julius," Nino said huskily. "Can you patch in to navigation through Earth?"

"*Negative, Major Solari. The . . . and metal . . . gone.*"

"Say again, Major Short," Lisa said. "Omega Two, come in."

"Trouble," Nino said.

"*Omeg . . . un, this is . . . are you receiving muh . . . most of the radio is . . . and we can only con . . . you . . . to Earth?*"

"Affirmative, Omega Two," Nino said. "Patching your signal though now." To Lisa he said, "Hope they put it on redundancy, that dust is screwing up the transmissions good."

"Uh-huh. Omega Two, can you continue the mission?"

"*. . . One, this . . . uh and then . . . but do not think we can control the tumble at this time. Request per . . . to . . . subject to . . . over.*"

The image of a tumbled, hulled capsule crewed by three injured men was in Lisa's mind. She remembered the old tapes of *Apollo XIII*, with the exploded tank that sent that fragile craft tumbling through space. She remembered their "Houston, we have a problem," and how proud she had been of them. "Permission granted, Omega Two."

Almost at once she put them from her mind. There were more important things at hand and that other crew was made up of high-survival types.

". . . on . . . will do . . . NASA and . . . farther away from . . . Shiva . . . good luck, and . . ."

"Good luck, *Omega Two*," Lisa said quietly.

Ponk!

Ting! Tonk! Bomp!

Pinnng!

Diego Calderon swayed in the acceleration couch. The controls wavered before his eyes. The grids and graphs blipping across the readout screens were doubled, super-imposed, blurred.

Tonk!

Shiva blocked out a great ragged section of darkness ahead. It was turning slowly, reflecting bits of sunlight. Behind it, pouring from blasted holes and ancient vents were the multicolored streamers of gas, water vapor and methane.

Ping! Ponk!

Thump.

Scratch. *Ping!*

A green light went out. Number four, gone. Diego stared back at the panel. Probably taken out by some rock. Not even exploded, just rendered useless.

Eight punches left.

Pinnng!

Thump. *Bomp, ting, bing, wham!*

The air pressure started to drop again. Diego reached for a patch as he sought the hole. Overhead, easy to reach, only . . .

Only he couldn't move very well. His hand was shaking, his head throbbed, his arm a great dead weight.

The hiss got louder.

Tink! Pop, ting, thump!

Consciousness wavered. The patch hardened in his hand, turning useless.

Carl pulled back from the optical telescope with a grim smile on his face. The exhaust flames could be seen as the missiles jockeyed for position. They were *Omega's* "parked" missiles, traveling along with the swarm at zero relative speed, awaiting use, maintaining position. Carl Jagens started to move out toward the missiles.

"Stay there, don't go anywhere," he said softly.

* * *

Someone handed Chuck Bradshaw another teletype. He glanced at it, but didn't really read it. Something about Canada's eastern province, Newfoundland, Greenland. Great rush of melted ice drowning Angmagasalik, where-ever that was. Skyspies reported hits in Siberia, the Caucasus, eastern Turkey. Algeria got another one. The new African state of Kasongo hit. Floods, fires, riots.

He brushed the paper off onto the floor.

Carl matched up with the cruising twenty-megaton missile, a long gray-and-white shark. When he went out he pulled up the corpse of General Menshov with him, then thrust him away without a thought, letting him drift.

Jagens snapped a safety line to his ship and jumped over to the missile. The spurt of correcting fire made Carl hang on tightly, but he inched himself forward, pulled the special wrench from his kit and opened the access panel to the controls. One simple twist of a switch disconnected the deadly missile from anyone's control.

Then Carl repunched a code which put the missile under his own control. He jumped from the hijacked missile back to his own ship.

The capsule seemed larger now, with the body of the Russian gone. Bits of reddish crystal—frozen blood—were the only reminders. Carl slipped back into his couch, but did not bother to repressurize the cabin. He bent over the optical telescope, searching for the next missile.

"Lisa!" Nino Solari's tone of voice made Lisa twist around from her inspection of the black sky. "One of the missiles just went!"

"Exploded? Hit?"

He shook his head. "Can't tell. It just went dead. That signal just stopped, *pow*. Like it was turned off. But it *could* have been hit. Pretty far out, though, still."

"If we could get an optical fix, but there's so much stuff around still, it's hard to—"

A giant clapped his hands next to her ear.

The capsule flipped around, the stars and Shiva did a dance. Lisa clamped her helmet shut as she tried to stop the spinning. A quick glance showed her that Nino Solari was injured. There was blood pumping forth, bubbling out in a frothy foam from his side, being swept up and toward a ragged hole just over the starboard port. She reached back, slapped his helmet closed and locked it. Nino was white-faced and in shock, already gasping for air.

Lisa brought the injured ship under control, set the autopilot and struggled loose from her harness to get the repair kit. Once the entrance hole was plugged, Lisa turned in the cramped cabin and sought the exit hole.

The chunk of nickel-iron had punched through the cabin, through Major Solari and his couch, through a redundant telemetry system, melting and spraying itself into droplets that splattered everywhere. She found six small holes and one good-sized one. And a ruined flight control backup system.

Only after all the patchwork was done did Lisa struggle back through the floating bubbles of bloodfoam to help Nino. He was pale and unconscious. She tried to tear away his spacesuit and the layers of undergarments, but they were all too tough. She lost precious moments finding a scalpel in the medical kit and cutting through to Nino's injured side.

She couldn't tell what was wrong, except he was badly hurt. She got out their biggest bandage, and broke the inset capsule. It flooded the web of the bandage with antiseptic and coagulants. She pressed it across the wound. She gave him a shot of antishock, then another to keep him quiet for a while. He was going to be of no use for some time to come.

Then she used some of their patching tape to seal up the suit as best she could. All the time bits and pieces of dust and rock continued to strike the capsule.

She shivered as she climbed back into the acceleration couch. The players were getting fewer and fewer in this final great game.

Rocks pelted Myron Murray's limousine as it came through the White House gates, between the parked tanks and helmeted soldiers. He stared out at the mob dully, his eyes heavy with fatigue. He knew and felt their anger and frustration. They were scared and wanted someone to *do* something. In America that someone was always the President, the government. He understood, and was grateful for all those who stayed on, took orders, did their jobs, kept the thin fabric of civilization somewhat in order.

The entire perimeter of the White House grounds was lined with soldiers, armed and armored. Tanks stood at the corners and the entrances. More tanks and personnel carriers were parked along nearby streets. The mobs were kept at bay by patrols, and sometimes by canisters of gas. But the baseball players among them could lob stones quite a distance. Undercover police moved through the crowd, watching for grenades and weapons, radios in their ear plugs and watchful eyes restlessly roaming.

Murray felt the first effects of the pills he had taken. His eyes brightened as the limousine pulled up under the South Portico. Over his head, on the Truman balcony, there was a sight he thought he would never see: sandbags and machine guns. Rocket launchers, picked men with sniper rifles, and tactical communication equipment were on the roof. The White House was under siege.

Murray got out and walked quickly into the Diplomatic Reception Room, to be greeted by Steve Banning, the presidential press secretary. He, too, had the artificially bright-eyed look and abrupt movements of a man kept erect by stimulants.

"Myron, is it true?

Murray nodded. "Kalinin's disappeared. No one has heard or seen him for hours. The Pentagon is certain he's been deposed—he wouldn't be the first head of state to fall—but the CIA thinks he might have gone to some hideout in the Urals."

They started walking along the ground floor corridor to the elevators. "How's . . . ?"

Banning shrugged. "Still determined to stick it out here." He made a face. "Damn."

Murray grinned wearily. "Yeah, me, too. Getting out west would get *those* out of our hair." He made a gesture out toward the mob, which never seemed to go away, day or night, only change personnel. "I don't know what the hell they expect us to do. We're *doing* all we can."

Banning punched for the elevator. "This is Miracle House, Myron, you know that. All problems can be solved here. Even Shiva."

"Uh-huh. Howya doing?" he asked the Marine on guard.

"Fine, sir."

"Rather be somewhere else, son?"

The boy looked slightly shocked. "No, sir!" He gave Murray a frowning look. "This is where I'm needed." He indicated the outside with his chin. "They're getting pretty nasty, sir."

"And you'll be ready for them?" The elevator sighed open.

"Yes, sir, of course." He flashed a quick grin which made him look even younger. "The Marines are always ready, you know that."

Murray smiled sadly and patted the Marine on his blue shoulder and went into the cage. Banning punched a button. "He's still in the family quarters." They exchanged looks, and Banning shrugged. "Yeah, still."

The sound of banjo music was the first thing they heard when the doors opened on the top floor. Murray followed Banning toward the family area of the White House. There were a number of soldiers in the hall, along with the usual gray-suited Secret Service men. The security at the door was very tight, which both reassured Murray and saddened him. There had been seventeen assassination attempts since Knowles had announced the Shiva plan. A helicopter had been downed by a heat-seeking rocket fired from the roof of the Treasury Building, but the President had not been in it. Condolences had gone out to the family and government of the Prime Minister of Canada, who had been in it, but the turmoil in that country prevented prompt delivery.

The banjo music was louder inside the family quarters. Steve Banning indicated the family living room and Murray went in, while Banning stopped to speak to Grace Price.

John Caleb Knowles sat on a stool before the fireplace, one leg tucked back, his fingers flying over the strings of his banjo, his head back, eyes closed. He was smiling.

Barbara Carr looked up from the couch and smiled at Murray, then patted the seat beside her. She was wearing a bright caftan, which clung to her body. Murray noticed, for what was really the first time, how voluptuous she was. Or maybe it was the legs-tucked-under position, or the loosened hair. He sat down next to her and shook his head against her silent offer of a drink.

Knowles finished the tune with a flourish and opened

his eyes to look at Barbara. "There! My uncle Abraham taught me—oh, Myron!" He put the banjo down against a chair and leaned forward to shake his hand. He seemed genuinely glad to see his assistant, and Murray thought the president looked better than he had in some time.

"Are you well, Myron?"

"Yes, Mister President. But Premier Kalinin isn't." Knowles raised his eyebrows and Murray quickly repeated what the CIA and the Pentagon brass had told him. Knowles nodded, his smile momentarily dimming. "My guess is that when *Bolshoi* didn't do the trick, they used him as a scapegoat. And he's not had any other propaganda victory, either. It's our hardware up there, not theirs."

Knowles nodded, his attention wandering. He picked up the banjo again, but looked back at Murray. "Leave it up to the experts, Myron. And get yourself some sleep. That's an order." He smiled abruptly. "You ever hear 'Tennessee Mountain Rag,' Myron?" Without waiting, the chief executive started playing. His head went back and his eyes closed.

Murray got to his feet and looked at Barbara Carr. She smiled back brightly. Too brightly. There was that tight look around the unnaturally luminous eyes. Drugs. Everyone was taking them, in one form or other. Forgetfulness in a capsule. Happiness in a pill. He took Steve Banning's elbow, nodded to Barbara, and tugged the press secretary outside.

"Where is Reed?" he demanded.

"Out west," Banning shrugged. Gorman Reed was Vice-President of the United States, but few in Washington thought much of him. He was a frequent subject of jokes by late-night talk show hosts in their monologues, but Veeps frequently were. Nothing new there, except the desperation.

"Is he up on things?"

"He gets the standard daily briefings, why?"

Murray looked back at the guarded door to the residence section. "He might be needed," he said darkly.

Banning, too, gave a quick look. "You mean, uh . . ." He stopped, blinking, afraid to speak. Murray took his

arm and pulled him down the hall, almost to the Queen'
Bedroom.

"No one gives a damn if he's balling Barbara Carr o
not. He might even pick up a few votes if it were known
but he's never going to get a chance to run, Steve."

"Aw, Myron, you're—"

"I'm serious, Steve, listen to me. He's going into his own
little world. It's a very pleasant world. Music, sex, no
cares. He's not wandering around the halls talking to the
portraits like Nixon. He isn't drinking like Grant. He
hasn't become a religious zealot like Scott. But he'
cracking up."

"No one must know," Banning said quickly.

"Gorman Reed must know. Mathison and Hopkin
must know. If they don't already." He looked back at the
doors again, as Banning nodded. The Senate majority
leader and the Speaker of the House had powerful intel
ligence networks all through the bureaucracy of the
United States.

Banning looked hard at Murray, careful and suspicious
"Are you saying we should think about Article Two?"

"No, Article Twenty, section three, and Article Twenty-
five, section two."

Banning's face grew grave and troubled with each
word. "Are you suggesting that we—"

"No, of course not. We must just make the appropriate
parties aware that . . ." Murray glanced down the corridor and pulled Banning further away from the sentries.
". . . that such action may be necessary. We must advise
the Chief Justice, Reed, Hopkins, Mathison, the Secret
Service."

"Jesus Christ, Murray . . ." Banning wiped a meaty
hand across his face. "The media will crucify us, if they
think we're—"

"We're not. And forget your goddamn media, Steve!
You're not an anchorman anymore, you're White House
staff, with a loyalty to the presidency." He dug his fingers
into Banning's arm. "The presidency, Steve, not the
President."

Banning nodded uncomfortably. "Jesus Christ," he muttered, looking trapped. "But who the hell wants Reed
running things? He's a fucking cowboy!"

"A westerner, Steve, not a cowboy. There's a lot of difference, and I think you better start getting that straight right *now*."

Banning nodded uncomfortably, his eyes squirming around. "Jesus," he said again. "Jesus, Jesus."

"He's cracking, Steve. He has every sign. It's a wonder . . . it's a wonder he's stuck it out this long."

"You've been with him a long time, haven't you?" Banning asked.

Murray nodded, his face strained. "That's not important now. Only the country is, the world." He took a deep breath. "I'm going out to Teller."

Banning looked up at him, frowning. "You going to hole up in that mountain?"

"No. I'm going to brief that Vice-President myself."

"Getting in on the ground floor, Myron?" Banning said suspiciously.

"We don't have *time* to do it the full, legal way, like the first Johnson, or like they started to do with Nixon. I'm just doing my job, that's all."

"Your job is to get the things done the President wants done."

"If he weren't . . ." Murray broke off, and took another deep breath. "I'm doing what must be done."

"I'll read all about it in the history books," Banning said, moving off, shoulders hunched.

Murray nodded. He supposed it would end up there. If there were any history books.

"JPL, JPL, this is *Omega One*, over."

". . . One . . . *read you* . . . *and it* . . . *over* . . ."

"Your transmission is terrible, JPL. Maybe you can get the computers on this and pull something out, so I'll keep talking." Lisa gave Nino a quick look. "Major Solari is still unconscious. I am unable to contact *Alpha One* or *Alpha Two*. I have decided to make one more attempt to obtain the cooperation of *Alpha One*. I am going EVA, repeat, going EVA to rig the cutting laser as a signaling device. Repeat, going EVA in approximately three minutes for purposes of rigging a laser. Do you read me, JPL?"

". . . *Ell* . . . *drit* . . . *plan to* . . . *cooperation of* . . . *NASA will* . . . *Bradshaw contact* . . . *bleep* . . . *a laser as a* . . . *you as beep* . . ."

Lisa sighed. The transmission was almost incompre-

365

hensible now. They had computers programmed to extract a signal from the background, but they had never been designed for such a distance or such interference. "Your signal is garbled, JPL. I will execute plan as soon as I sign off here. *Omega One*, out."

" . . . *bleep* . . . ega One, *we* . . . *copy* . . . *drit*, *bleep* . . ."

Lisa checked Nino's helmet, then her own. In a few moments the air left the cramped cabin in a rush, turning to thin snow in the chill vacuum of space. She floated up, secured a line to her suit, and dug the cutting laser out of the locker. It had been included in case they had to implant warheads on the asteroid surface. She snaked out the cable connecting it to the capsule's power source and floated out into space.

She never tired of it. None of them ever did. It was something special. Scary, but special. This was the first time she had ever had extravehicular activity that she had not paused to look at the big blue marble, marveling at it. This time she only glanced at it to orient herself. It was still small but fractionally larger than the last time she had looked.

All around her was the glittering mantle of dust. Bars of shadow leaped ahead of the swarm, slanting away from the sun behind them. At the beginning of each bar of darkness was a rock. The biggest bar lead straight to Shiva itself. The great asteroid flashed and gleamed as it turned slowly, reflecting the sun from its irregular surface, but keeping its face in darkness.

Keeping an eye on the bits of rock that traveled along with their capsule, Lisa began rigging the laser. She felt a tremor and briefly saw a fist-size rock tumbling lazily away. The relative speed had been minor. It was little more than a bump, but all such encounters were potentially dangerous.

Using some of the chemical tape, Lisa fastened the base of the laser to the base of the telemetry mast. In that fashion she could turn and direct it to some extent from the inside.

She felt another tug and saw that a ragged hole had appeared in the radio disk. It was not big, but for a moment she saw the same hole in herself. She slipped quickly back into the capsule and locked the hatch. She began a Morse code message in the general direction of where she believed Carl Jagens's ship to be.

It was a chance in a thousand, but she had to try it.

Carl Jagens caught the winking red dot out of the corner of his eye and he frowned at it before he figured out what it was.

A laser, useless as a cutting tool at this distance, used as a signaling device. He caught a fragment of the message: NEED YOUR COOPERATION CARL WE MUST—

He stopped paying attention. There was nothing he *must* do, except save the Earth. He swung the ship toward the next twenty-megaton missile.

Ping! Ponk! Tick! Bonk.

Diego's mind swam back. Damn, he had passed out! He was in pain, but the first thing he did was check the clock. About eleven minutes had elapsed. He looked at the air pressure gauge. They still had integrity but were dropping slowly. He pulled himself around painfully to look at Ikko Issindo. From the white, frozen expression he knew the little colonel was dead. Two down in *Alpha Two*, but one to go.

Pinnng! The hull vibrated with the strike, making Diego wince. He pulled himself around and checked the missile board. He still had eight. Would that be enough? After *Bolshoi*, could *anything* be enough?

Diego leaned over to look out the port and orient himself to Shiva. He followed the thick band of darkness up to the big rock, then his eyes jumped back to something he had seen pass across that dark band, backlit and bright.

A ship!

Searching through the dust, Diego found the capsule and quickly identified it as *Alpha One*. What was Jagens doing? Then, even as he asked the question, Diego knew the answer.

I didn't lose a missile—Jagens took it! And he's after the others! He'll send them at Shiva one at a time and piss them away! He'll not accomplish anything!

Swiftly Diego located the missile toward which he thought Carl was flying and sent his own battered ship in that direction.

Ponk! Ping!

How can I stop him? He must be stopped. Or made to

listen to reason. Diego scratched at his unshaven face. He's an intelligent man, he'll listen to reason.

Jagens saw *Alpha Two* approaching. Damn fool Calderon must still be alive. Him or that Japanese bastard. The Russian woman? No, even Calderon would have taken care of her by now. Arrange a little accident, who'd know? No use letting them have any glory—or worse—a chance to screw things up.

Carl was irritated. That fool Bander woman on his tail, blinking away like some idiot traffic light, pleading, begging. Stupid person. Space was no place for women. Upsets their cycles. And now someone in *Alpha Two* was still operational.

Coolly, Jagens reviewed his options. He chose the best one and altered his course toward *Alpha Two*. Let's parley, Calderon. Uh-huh, let's do that, little brown brother. Let me into your cabin. Where the missile controls are.

He's going to talk, Diego thought. Good. He was a reasonable man. Sensible. We all want to get the job done. With communications out, he probably thought we were all dead and was doing his best. Sure, a few moments now and they could link up.

A light came blinking from the porthole of *Alpha One* and Diego squinted as he deciphered the message. ALPHA TWO GLAD TO SEE YOU ALIVE LET US TALK COMMUNICATIONS OUT HERE WILL PULL ALONGSIDE TIME IS SHORT. Then came the words JAGENS, COMMANDER, ALPHA TEAM.

A little reminder, Diego thought. All right, noble leader, come alongside.

The hatch secured and the air pressure restored, Jagens signaled for them to open their helmets. As his lifted Jagens said, "Never liked to talk over suit radios." He smiled thinly. "You never know who's listening." He gestured at Issindo and Major Nissen. "Why don't you dump those two? Give you more room in here."

"Carl, what's going on? Let's get together on this. I still have eight missiles. I accidentally cut them out of the circuit when, ah, when you set off that first missile. I was caught unawares and—"

"Yes, yes, Colonel Calderon," Carl said, making a ges-

...ure of dismissal, awkward in the space suit. "Now if ...ou'll return these missiles to my control we can get on ...ith it." He turned toward the control box, but Diego ...opped him.

"Wait a minute, Carl!" Diego pushed himself through ...air, twisted, and blocked Carl from the controls. On ...e periphery of his vision he saw he had nudged the ...ussian woman's body so that she hung out of her seat ...t a grotesque angle, her arms floating out.

"Calderon!" Jagens glared at him. "This is an *order,* ...olonel Calderon! Return these missiles to my control— ...t once!"

"Whoa, wait a minute—"

"Every minute brings Shiva closer to Earth, Calderon."

"Carl, I know that, but we have to talk. Your way isn't ...oing to work. We have to hit Shiva with everything, at ...st exactly the right spot."

"You are a traitor, Calderon! You one of them Gabri-...ls, huh? Yes, that's what it is, you're trying to delay un-...l it is too late!"

"Carl, don't be silly, I—"

"*Captain* Jagens to you, traitor! I am in command of ...is mission and I shall not fail!"

"Carl, you must—"

"You are under arrest, Colonel Calderon! You will ...nfine yourself to housekeeping duties aboard this ...pacecraft and I shall assume total operational com-...and."

Diego stared at Jagens. "Carl, you are out of your ...ourd! What you're saying is nonsense. Now, we've ...t to—"

"Calderon!"

"—we've got to get the info about just where to hit the ...rget and—"

Jagens hit him. Diego crashed back against the bulk-...ead, his helmet unhooking and spinning away, bouncing ...f equipment and dead bodies. The effort sent Carl back ...ward the hatch and he grabbed the interior struts to ...aintain his position. He saw Diego's helmet and ...ughed.

"Too bad, traitor," he said, reaching to swing his hel-...et into position and lock it down.

Diego saw what Carl was going to do and he threw ...imself across the small cabin at Jagens. But the an-

369

chored astronaut slammed Diego in the side of the hea
as he got within range, knocking him over the seats an
onto the control deck. Diego almost passed out from th
pain, but swam back through a red haze to grasp at hi
helmet.

Contemptuously Carl kicked the helmet away. It spu
through the air, struck the missile control panel and tum
bled off. Diego grabbed for it as Carl cracked the sea
on the hatch. The air screamed out in a great wrenchin;
hiss, almost carrying Diego with it. But he grabbed a
acceleration couch, hung on, feeling the cold and th
panic.

Carl clubbed him again, sending him spinning. With ;
gloved hand Carl snapped the remaining eight switches
restoring the missiles to his control in *Alpha One*. He
looked at Diego, gasping for air, and the helmet stuck
between black boxes the full length of the cabin away
then he smiled. With a practiced twist he sailed out
through the hatch, grasping his secured safety line, and
started across to *Alpha One*. Diego Calderon had beer
left to die.

Lisa swung the telescope into a different quadrant and
peered into it. Two ships, together. *Alpha One* and *Two*.
Someone was alive after all! Maybe Carl had found Diego! Found him alive!

The blackness was closing in around Diego. Pain shot up
his arm, like a tiger ripping at his flesh. But the greatest
pain was in his lungs. With the last of his strength Diego
pulled himself out of the well between the couches where
he had been knocked, and his gloved hand reached for
the helmet. He touched it, moving it, and the glassite
sphere drifted away.

Stars. Lights. Darkness. Everything was closing down.
It was confusing. His hand touched something, seized on
it, pulled it to him. He could hardly see. His whole chest
and head were pounding with pain, a great hollow empty
pain.

The helmet.
Put on the helmet.
Get it right the first time.
Over the head.
Around.

370

No, again.

Around.

There.

Lock it.

Now the air.

The valve was hard to get to.

The blackness was almost complete.

His fingers moved the valve. Just barely moved it.

The darkness came in. All the way in. The tide of space, and death.

He drifted.

Something.

A glittering something.

Blink.

Blink.

Blink.

His chest hurt.

Everything hurt.

He closed his eyes, tensed the muscles and looked again. The blink was a control light. Red. Red. Red. The seal on the hatch was broken. The hatch was open. Why was the hatch open?

Air.

Air gone.

Thin air in helmet. But air.

He reached for the valve, fumbling weakly, fighting the dense pain that flooded him. More air hissed in and he sucked it in gratefully.

Air!

Beautiful, invisible air!

His vision cleared, but his eyes hurt. His head hurt. His chest hurt. His arm ached. His stomach felt like heaving. But he was alive.

Weakly, Diego pulled himself to the hatch. He saw Carl Jagens opening the hatch on *Alpha One*.

Had so little time passed? It seemed like forever.

Diego reached down and opened the equipment locker. The cutting laser came out, its cable spilling out behind it. He turned, plugging the cable in, then looked back at *Alpha One*.

Carl was going into the hatch. Diego lifted the bulky laser and aimed it at *Alpha One*. The ruby red beam sprang ruler-straight at *Alpha One*, splashing off the port.

Carl reacted, turning in what seemed like slow motion to Diego.

Diego looked at him. He could not see Carl's face behind the dark protective faceplate.

"*Fool!*" Carl's voice came over the suit radio. "*Kill me, you insipid ass!*"

Diego's finger tightened on the trigger. He wanted to. The suit would be little or no protection at this range. The suit had no effective reflective surface, no shiny shield. A little pressure of his forefinger and the ruby beam would cut right through the suit, through Carl, and the air would rush out, the blood turn to red crystals floating in the swarm.

"*Kill me or I will kill you!*" Carl shouted. Then he laughed. "*But you can't, can you, you simple shit? No balls.*" Contemptuously Jagens turned and went into the ship. The hatch closed behind him. The ship moved off, swung away.

Suddenly Diego's mind slipped back into the real world. He let go of the laser to twist and push and jump toward the controls. He pulled himself into the seat and fired the rockets at once, unmindful of the swarm around him.

Ponk! Ping! Ping-pink-dink-pinng!

The flame jetted out from *Alpha One* and stabbed through space just where Diego had been.

Bannnng!

The ship vibrated to a hit and Diego looked around to see that the hatch had taken a hole. *So long hatch, so long airtight ship*. The minor rocks and pebbles continued to bounce off the ship as it cut through the swarm. Diego pushed himself away just long enough to cut the eight missiles free once again from Jagens's control. Only then did he bring the ship around and put it on a course with the swarm.

Reluctantly, he freed Olga Nissen and Ikko Issindo from their couches and helped them out into space. It was, after all, perhaps a more fitting burial ground than Earth.

If they ever returned.

Or if there was anything to return to.

Then Diego began to look for a way to communicate with Lisa Bander.

CARL PSYCHOTIC, Lisa read. HE HAS CONTROL OF ONE

372

MISSILE DANGEROUS NEED LINK WITH EARTH COMPUTE EXACT SPOT TIME TO HIT SHIVA WITH EVERYTHING. Lisa frowned, for that was going to be a difficult job. I WILL ATTEMPT TO NEUTRALIZE JAGENS.

"No!" Lisa grabbed at the controls to her own cutting laser, to send a message to Diego, but his message ending frustrated her: LOVE AND LUCK DIEGO.

"No, damn it, leave him *alone!*" she muttered, angry and frustrated. Then she took a deep breath and began a message to Earth. Maybe they could get through with burst-pulse messages, taped and compressed, then repeated and repeated. She flipped open the line to Earth.

Chuck Bradshaw was thrown across the room by the earthquake. Equipment toppled and people screamed. Chuck yelled across to Dink Lowell. "Never mind that! Keep that tie to *Omega!*"

"I'm trying," Dink yelled back, then fell himself as a second rippling wave ruptured the floor. The lights went out.

In the western end of the San Fernando Valley another advance member of the Shiva swarm weighing approximately forty tons struck, vaporizing a good part of Tarzana and triggering a major earthquake.

The Jet Propulsion Laboratory was temporarily out of business. Chuck Bradshaw staggered forth into the dusty day, hearing the sirens and the screams, and sat on the edge of a planter. He was very surprised to see tears falling into the dust of the patio.

It had been a very long time since he had cried. It was even rather novel. What did you do today, Daddy? I cried. How exciting! You're human after all.

Yes, he thought, very human. I cry every time the human race dies.

"Mister President?"

"Yes? Oh, Myron, come in. Care for a drink? Very good chablis."

"No, thank you, sir." Murray looked at Barbara Carr. She seemed to be asleep, her face turned away in the big bed. "Am I disturbing you?"

"Oh, no, Myron, not you. How are things?" John Caleb Knowles looked pleasantly at his assistant. "Everything going all right?"

"Yes, Mister President, as well as could be expected." He hesitated. How could he get her body out? The pill tube was still lying on the floor. A single red-and-yellow-striped killer was near the foot of the bed, next to a pink high-heeled shoe. Murray silently damned her for giving up, and for running and hiding into death. Without warning, too, giving him no time to make adjustments. Others had committed suicide, too, but none so close to the President, nor as personally involved.

"Sir, I wonder if you'd like to go down into the Emergency Room for just a few minutes. General McGahan is there, Secretary Warren, General Hornfield—"

"No, no, that's all right, Myron, I'll stay here." He strummed a few notes on his banjo, resting it on the coverlet. "I think Barbara and I will just play a little." He looked fondly over at her. "'Jug Band Music' or 'Jesu Joy of Man's Desiring,' my dear?"

Involuntarily, Murray looked at Barbara Carr, too. "Oh, all right," the President said. "Ah, 'Turkey in the Straw' it is."

Myron Murray was forgotten as the notes filled the room. Caleb Knowles wore an angelic expression as he played away. Murray backed out and closed the doors behind him.

"Well?" Grace Price asked impatiently.

Murray shrugged. "Give him something in his milk, then get her out when he goes to sleep."

"What'll we tell him?" the Marine captain asked.

Murray looked at him. The Marine was so young. He didn't know how they kept their uniforms so neat. "You'll tell the President that she's out for a drive, a walk, out shopping, out buying him a present, anything *pleasant*, you understand?"

"Yes, sir."

Murray looked at the President's secretary, who sniffed. "It's not right, you know, any of it," she said. "*Her* being in there, dead *or* alive. God will witness that I did my best to get along with her, even helped her, knowing how she was helping him . . . well . . . adjust. But it's still not right, a President of the United States carrying on like some—"

"Mrs. Price!" Murray's voice cut into her diatribe and she gasped. He leaned close to her, his face for once showing emotion, and it frightened her. "Mrs. Price,

John Caleb Knowles is a sick man. He has lived under pressures you cannot possibly imagine! You, Mrs. Price, will treat him with respect!"

Grace Price blinked, then rallied her dignity. The special assistant *was* correct. Even Nixon had been allowed dignity. She looked at Murray haughtily. Presidential assistants, however powerful, came and went. She had been there since the Carter administration, in one capacity or the other, doing her job no matter what party was in. *She* was a fixture, no matter *who* occupied the Oval Office. "Mister Murray?"

They looked at each other and she was the first to break her gaze, looking away from his burning, red-blotched eyes. "When will the new President arrive?"

"Not for some time, Mrs. Price."

"You mean President Reed is staying in that, in that mountain?"

"Yes. Until after Shiva . . . until the situation is resolved once and for all."

"But the President belongs here. This is the official residence."

"He'll get here." If it's still here, he thought. His mind was occupied with logistics, getting out to Teller, establishing himself with the new chief executive. Reed had his own man, Miller, but Murray could provide the transition, the "authority" of transfer. They could get it all straightened out later. The Supreme Court was all out there, except one of them, and they'd stamp approval of the whole mess.

Murray looked at the lieutenant colonel seated by the door, holding the self-contained radio link to the Joint Chiefs of Staff, the Pentagon, and two super-secret military command posts.

"That's not operational, is it, Colonel?"

The officer's face was professional, expressionless. "No, sir. It's strictly for show."

"All right. No use hurting him, letting him know."

"No, sir." The others nodded.

"Poor bastard," the Marine officer said. They all looked at him and he flushed. "Well, he is," he said defensively.

"We all are," Murray said wearily. He turned toward the elevators and the trip to the helicopter pad. He should be in Teller as soon as possible.

"We must get her out," Grace Price said. "It's not seemly."

The Marine nodded solemnly.

In Santa Barbara, California, where Zakir Shastri had been removed for medical help, an angry crowd of elderly people swept through the hospital and beat him to death. Their excuse to the police was that Shiva was his fault.

Corporal Thatcher, of the Massachusetts National Guard, was given a field commission to lieutenant. He did not get drunk. He was already drunk.

White House aide Bruce Higby slipped from the ground floor exit near dawn and ran for the helicopter, which was hovering just off the pad. He could see General Sutherland through the open door. The renegades in control of the Executive Office Building started firing. The chopper pilot didn't wait. She lifted swiftly, battering down the historic trees. A limb, torn from the tree planted by Andrew Jackson, flopped through the air and knocked the fleeing Higby to the ground. A shot fired by the renegades stilled him.

Chicago received a terrible battering from a shower of debris that spread across Lake Michigan and all the way to Aurora.

Ogallala, Nebraska, disappeared. The muddy South Platte River flowed sluggishly into the crater and turned to steam.

Secretary of Defense Sam Rogers sat at a green felt table with the senate majority leader, the Speaker of the House, the Director of the FBI, General McGahan, and Vice-President Gorman Reed. He was down three hundred forty thousand dollars, had a headache, and a tic. The Veep was the big winner. The room smelled of antiseptic; a congressperson had blown his brains out that morning.

"The jack bets," said Powell Hopkins.

Brother Gabriel knew it was his time to die. He felt it suddenly, not knowing why, just knowing. He had been speaking to a group of ragged wounded on a road near Orlando, Florida. Disney World was not far away. The faces were lifted up toward him, as he stood on the slanting bed of a pickup truck parked just off the road.

A state police car screamed past, stirring up shreds of banners and choking dust.

They were always looking at him and he couldn't let them down. They expected him to lead them, to save them, to return them to the New Eden.

He knew it was about to happen. He didn't even question how he knew, or how he could possibly know. But death was coming, coming from the skies, a bolt hurled by the Lord God himself.

Brother Gabriel turned toward the sky. It was cold, the sky stained with dust and smoke. His robe, no longer white, fluttered in the wind.

"Brother, save us, save us!"

"Lead us to the new land, the promised land!"

But Gabriel just looked up. The face and image of Brother Gabriel, but the mind of Douglas Arthur Kress.

It's time, Lord?

It's time, Douglas.

Did I do well, Lord? Did I do what you wanted?

You tried, Douglas. One can ask no more.

I failed you, then.

No.

But I did not succeed. They went out. They are trying to stop it, this blasphemous Shiva.

Yes.

How can I not fail and not succeed, Lord?

By doing your part.

I did my part, Lord?

Yes, Douglas.

A smile, serene and sweet, a smile of innocence and happiness crossed his bearded, begrimed features.

I did my part.

In the plans of the Lord.

To help them toward the New Eden.

He felt very happy.

It was not much of a meteorite. It came into the atmosphere over Liberia, going west, flaming and molten, one of a hundred knifing through the biosphere that hour. Most of it was vaporized over the North Atlantic. Over Bermuda it hit turbulence and its fiery path bent down.

It descended toward Florida. Toward Orlando. Toward a road near Disney World. The heat of its passing seared the hair of a bearded man standing by the road, looking skyward, his hands outstretched. But it did not kill him.

The fiery lump exploded in the musty swamp beyond, setting some trees on fire and splashing boiling mud in every direction. The bearded man swayed, blinking, his robe splattered. He turned and looked at the bubbling spot in the swamp.

Nothing happened.

There was no second meteorite. No death from the sky. At least not for Douglas Arthur Kress, not then.

"Hey, you're one lucky son of a bitch!"

Blinking, Kress turned, swaying unsteadily. "You okay?" the soldier asked. He was a middle-aged sergeant. A few feet behind limped a younger man, an officer, with his arm in a sling. "Maybe you'd better sit down, old man," the soldier said, taking his arm and helping him to sit down on the tail gate of the pickup.

Kress looked around. There was no one else there. "You got any water?" the officer asked. When Kress didn't answer the captain said, "Sergeant Cooper, look in the cab."

"Yessir." The officer leaned a hip on the edge of the pickup and rubbed his wounded arm, looking around, grimacing.

"Kill me," Kress said.

"Huh?" The captain looked down at Kress.

"I said, 'Kill me.'"

The officer looked at the man with disgust. "Jesus, mister, you just had the world's best opportunity. If you had just stood a step to the left—"

"Kill me!" There was residual power in Kress's voice and a snap to his look. But it died under the officer's calm stare.

"Wait a minute. You're that, that Gabriel nut."

"Kill me. You have a weapon. Kill me."

"Sir?" Cooper said, slamming the pickup door and lifting a canteen.

"Give him some," Saperstein said, motioning to Kress.

The bearded man looked at the sergeant. There was an edge to his pleading. "Kill me."

Cooper looked at his superior, raising his eyebrows. Saperstein shrugged and started to walk away. Cooper offered Kress a drink, but was refused. Cooper slung the canteen and adjusted his equipment belt, eying Kress critically.

"Sir, if you don't mind my saying so, why don't you go find a place to stay and get some rest. Things'll look better then." Kress just stared at him. Cooper made a face and started walking after his captain.

"Hey, sir, you wanna go over toward Disney World? I haven't been there in, Christ, twenty years!"

"Home, Sergeant Cooper, home."

"Yeah, well, okay." He looked back at Kress. "That guy's familiar, but I can't place him. We seen him before."

"Gabriel. Brother Gabriel."

"No, shit? Well, yeah, I see it now. Christ, he doesn't look so, uh, so important now, does he?"

"He isn't," Captain Saperstein said. They kept on walking down the road. The hollowed eyes of Douglas Arthur Kress followed them until they turned the distant corner and disappeared.

He slowly raised his eyes. He could see it with the naked eye. Shiva. See it in broad daylight. Shiva the Destroyer. It had destroyed him.

It just hadn't killed him.

Nashville. Karachi. Volgograd. Sardinia. Lyon. Exeter. Scranton. The village of Castellon de la Plana, Spain.

Hits. Fires, panic, rioting, death.

Tehran, Crete, central England, Cincinnati, tidal waves engulfing seacoast towns everywhere.

Shiva was sending ahead her calling cards.

"Eight? You only have eight, is that right?"

Chuck Bradshaw waited impatiently for the equipment to compress his message, send it to *Omega One* in a burst-pulse, wait for the transmission time, then for the computer to clear her answer through the background static.

"JPL, this is . . . ga One. *Eight, that's correct, eight, repeat eight.*"

"Roger your eight, Lisa. We are computing here and will have answer for you soon. Over."

He looked at Dink Lowell, who was sporting a bandage on his face and walking with a limp. Emergency lights had been strung and they cast stark shadows. Dink heaved a sigh and flicked a glance at the squad of scientists who were computing the final hit. One of them tore

379

off a piece of paper and read it over. With a speed that drove Bradshaw into clenching his jaws the woman walked over to a man and they conferred for several seconds. Only then did she bring the paper over to Bradshaw, who snatched at it impatiently.

"This is it?" The rawness in his throat made him cough and he glared at her. She nodded. He looked at the figures. They meant nothing to him. "Will she be able to understand this?"

The woman smiled faintly. "Her onboard computer will. All she has to do is feed in the pertinent local data —any changes in speed or distance, pitch, roll, yaw, that kind of thing. Then push the button." She shrugged as if it were the simplest thing in the world.

Bradshaw thrust it back to her. "Send it! And be certain she understands."

The woman walked away unhurriedly and coded it for the burst-pulse operator. Chuck Bradshaw paced away, then back, the dust and grit crunching under his feet. He scraped a sticky foot clean on a desk too heavy to set right again, and sat down abruptly. He glared at Dink Lowell. "What the hell are you grinning at?"

"I'm not grinning."

"Yes, you are!"

"It's my natural face. I'm a pleasant guy."

"Saying I'm not?"

Dink shrugged. Bradshaw took a deep breath. "I'm sorry, Dink." The astronaut dismissed the whole incident with a shrug. Bradshaw looked around the littered room, then back to Dink. "We are sure taking a beating, aren't we? Our industrial strength is zip right about now. No one's working. Everyone's praying or fucking or stealing."

"I'd rather be fucking."

Bradshaw nodded. "But not the terminal fuck."

"No," agreed Dink, "I figure my terminal fuck ought to come round about my ninety-fourth birthday, give or take a fortnight."

Bradshaw didn't answer. He saw the communications officer move and his eyes swung that way. The computer was processing an answer.

"*Information received and . . . stood. Will do our . . . est. And, Chuck? Listen, good luck down there. Omega One, out.*"

Good luck down there.

Good luck everywhere.

Bradshaw felt his shoulders slump and the grit behind his eyes was worse than ever. The pills made him jumpy and irritable. His job was done. But maybe, just maybe, there would be something else he could do, or should do. He had to stay. If it killed him.

The rest was up to Bander and Calderon.

And Carl Jagens.

Ponnnngg!

Diego ducked, hurting his nose on the microphone inside the helmet. He was angry with himself; no ducking was going to work. You'd probably never hear or see the one that got you. The vibrations came through the metal and plastic of the ship. Little rattlings, twitches, jerks, scrapings. The craft was being slowly scratched to death. Already one of the three rocket nozzles was operating erratically, having been struck repeatedly.

The brown-skinned astronaut looked grim. From what he had gathered about Vandenberg and Cape Canaveral they might not be able to launch any kind of rescue effort. There had been no news from the Baikonur Cosmodrome, but that was nothing new; they had always kept the tightest imaginable security.

Ping! Tonk! Thud.

Diego searched the sky ahead, both with his eyes and the radar, luckily still functioning fairly well. He had transferred control of his small fleet of missiles to Lisa and had received a laser signal of acceptance. Going in after Carl Jagens might mean he would not come out. Someone had to give Shiva its deathblow.

If, indeed, the hurtling mountain *could* be killed.

Tinnnggg! Pop, bang, bump, ping!

He looked at the clock. He had less than one hour to find Jagens, neutralize him and get into shelter behind Shiva, opposite the point where the missiles must hit. Every second counted. Lisa would be positioning them now, leading them carefully in through the swarm, flowing with it, trying to reduce any losses or damage.

There!

The beep on the radar, hard and clear, appeared from behind the larger, "softer" image of a tumbling rock.

Carl Jagens.

Diego headed toward him recklessly.

Ponk! Tink, bonk, bang, bump!

The smaller asteroids all around him might possibly burn up in the atmosphere of Earth, or—if the angle was right—be deflected by the blanket of air. But Shiva would, unless stopped or deflected, cut right through with only minimal deflection. Even a certain kind of near miss could still be completely destructive: as the mountain of nickel-iron was near the turnaround point of its elliptical orbit, it could easily be turned and return quickly to strike Earth solidly. There would be no time whatever for further deflection attempts, even if the capability lasted. If the deflection was not great enough this time the Destroyer was in a position where it could return shortly after. There was only *one* chance. The die was cast.

Pannng!

The capsule spun wildly. A hole appeared almost straight ahead of Diego, then another and another, shredding metal, slicing through a hydraulic line. The red fluid dribbled out, formed into crystalline spheres, and floated. Diego countered the spin, but at a perilous cost of fuel.

He lifted the laser, aimed it at Carl's ship, and began signaling. He stopped almost at once. His hands were trembling. He forced them into steadiness, took some deep breaths, and lifted the laser. His arm ached. He needed sleep.

Carl did not respond to his signal, so Diego started to send a message without waiting for acknowledgment.

CARL WE MUST MERGE FORCES STRIKE SHIVA AT POINT DESIGNATED BY NASA ASTRONOMERS RESPOND RESPOND DIEGO.

Nothing.

Another blip showed on the radar. Lisa Bander, moving into position behind Shiva.

CARL ABOUT TO DETONATE EIGHT MISSILES YOUR SIDE SHIVA PLEASE RESPOND CALDERON.

Again nothing.

Diego sighed and turned the capsule toward Shiva. His fuel was about gone. He watched Carl's ship as it spun slowly. He noticed a flash. A few seconds later another flash. He swung the telescope toward *Alpha One* and looked at it.

The hatch was open. Carl was out of the ship. But

where? Immediately Diego knew where. Hijacking missiles!

He swung the laser toward Lisa but she was out of sight behind the rock.

Where was Carl?

Diego looked at the fuel gauge. Enough to get behind Shiva and brake in its protective shadow. Or enough to go to *Alpha One*. But not both.

Diego swung the ship toward *Alpha One*.

Stop Carl Jagens.

Lisa Bander looked at the changing numbers on the clockface. There was not much time. She floated along next to the slowly turning mass of Shiva. The growing blue marble of Earth was hidden, as were Diego and Carl.

The missiles were programmed and ready, the target point precisely fixed by the NASA scientists and astronomers. It was going to be very close. She knew that when the time came she would detonate the warheads, whether Diego was protected or not. She had to.

She waited. The numbers blinked on.

Shiva was ahead of Diego, but the tail end of the swarm was still going by, roiled and writhing as it broke over the flinty surface. His radar was jumpy, creating great bright shapes from clusters of dust and rock.

Diego moved up close to Carl's ship. He could see the cabin was empty. But scanning the sky he did not see Jagens. They floated alone, amid the rocks and dust, pilot fish to the great whale of Shiva, only a few hundred meters behind them.

Then he saw Carl.

He saw the blip on the radar first: a missile. Then Carl, riding it like a horse, like Captain Ahab on Moby Dick. The edge of the access hatch gleamed: it was open. Carl had his hands inside it.

Without thinking, Diego turned the capsule toward Carl. The commander of the *Alpha* team looked up. For a second Diego could see the reflection of his control rockets in Carl's dark visor. Then Carl had something in his hand. It was blinking red. A laser.

At this range it was not a harmless signaling device, but

383

what it had been designed to be: a cutting laser of great power.

Diego's capsule was bathed in red. The front metal began to glow. The ragged edges of several holes began to glow even brighter. Diego cut the thrusters and swung the ship sharply to starboard south. When the main thrusters were close enough and aimed at Carl he intended to fire. The flame would possibly incinerate Carl; it might also explode the missile. If the missile exploded, he would be killed, but more importantly, it might disturb the balance and position of the other missiles around.

Diego stayed his hand. He had no strong objections to killing Carl. It simply had to be done. The man was mad and dangerous. But he could not afford to take the chance.

Besides, Lisa needed the missile.

Diego used almost the last of his fuel braking. The metal had ceased to glow, the heat rapidly dissipating into space. He twisted around, shoving himself toward the hatch. He grabbed the laser, disconnecting it, and switching to internal batteries. It would be somewhat less powerful and for less time, but it gained much in portability. He launched himself out the hatch, barely taking time to hook in a safety line.

The last thing Diego noted was the clock. He had only minutes left, and damn few of them.

Carl was closing the access panel on the missile. He looked around at Diego and fired at him in almost the same gesture, but the red beam went past Diego. Diego fired back, but in being careful not to hit the missile, he also missed Carl. Jagens floated away from the missile, grabbed at his flying jets and moved quickly toward his own ship, propelled by puffs of compressed air. Diego fired again and narrowly missed. He used his own compressed-air system to head toward the missile.

Carl did not fire at him again. He abandoned the laser and Diego realized it must be depleted. Carl wiggled into *Alpha One* and shut the hatch just as Diego got to the missile. He scrabbled along it awkwardly, searching for the access panel. It was one of the Russian rockets and he was not familiar with it. Carl's jets fired and the capsule moved off.

To hijack another missile, Diego guessed. He found the

panel and clawed at it. He had no tools. In his haste he had forgotten. For want of a nail . . .

He pulled the cutting laser around, aimed it at an angle and cut right through the side of the thin metal, taking out the panel in one scoop. He brushed aside the droplets of metal and reached in. His heart sank. Carl Jagens had reprogrammed the missile, then fused the controls with a light touch of the laser. There was no way Diego could get control of the missile.

The clock in his head said it was almost time.

Lisa Bander looked at the numbers flicking by. She looked out the port, then to the radar screen, then to the numbers again. It was almost time. Her heart beat faster and she was sick with fear.

Diego Calderon sat astride the missile, thinking. At any second he expected the rocket engines to burst into flame and send him against the rock cliff of Shiva.

He could not reprogram the Soviet missile. What *could* he do? He could cut it out of the circuit entirely, leaving it a dead hulk. That would take it out of Carl's control but also remove it from any usefulness. And it might be a case of not-quite-enough if all the missiles were not utilized. Even a near miss, with Shiva plowing through the atmosphere of Earth, would cause planetwide devastation from which civilization might take centuries to recover.

He hefted the laser, then lifted himself off the missile, floating nearby. He held on to remain in position, then fired the laser into the side of the missile, just below the hole he had carved. Something flashed. There was an explosion of metal and plastic. The missile rolled, taking Diego with it.

He clung on, then moved up the craft a bit. He used the laser once again to gain access to another part of the guidance system. He reached in, squinted, and touched the hardware within. The gyroscope was disturbed; the rockets blasted silently as the ship twisted violently to conform to the position set by the gyro.

It was now aimed at Shiva.

Diego peered at the turning rock. He knew the spot he intended to hit, and noted it. He reached again and the main thrusters fired. The Soviet missile moved toward Shiva.

But Diego Calderon had no intention of being a kamkaze rocket pilot. Not if he could help it.

Crudely he brought the rocket around, tail down in respect to Shiva. He couldn't land her, but he could bring it close. He cut the rocket by blasting into the controls with his laser. The last of the red beam fused the metal and he tossed away the weapon. The missile floated down, slowly descending in relationship to the mass of Shiva.

Then Diego shoved himself away from the missile. He didn't know if he was aiming at the right point on the turning mountain, but he had little choice. The Soviet missile would be close in when the other warheads exploded; it should add its power to the others.

As Diego sped toward Shiva he searched the sky for Carl. Jagens still had one missile under his control. There was no telling what he would do with it.

Lisa's fingers flexed, and she grabbed one hand with the other. Not yet. Almost, but not quite yet.

The luminous numbers flitted across the screen.

Diego hit Shiva hard. It was an awkward landing. He thought he was well away from the radioactive blast point created by *Bolshoi* and the other missiles, but he wasn't certain. Nothing was certain.

He grabbed at a ragged, sharp-edged protuberance and hung on. The stars spun overhead. The spin of Shiva was taking him away from the impact point.

He only hoped it was swift enough.

The radar went *bleep* and Lisa looked up, startled.

A missile was on its way toward her.

Carl's last spiteful gesture.

I die, you die, we all die.

Lisa Bander stared at the glowing dot, moving swiftly toward her. Her eyes went to the clock.

Not yet.

Not yet.

Soon. Hold on. It must be right. Don't panic.

Oh, my God . . .

Diego saw the exhaust flare against the glowing dots of

386

dust and rock, coming out of the outgassing streams of colorful vapor.

Oh, no—!

Carl Jagens was mad! If he couldn't save the world, no one would!

Lisa stared, hypnotized, her eyes moving from clock to radar blip and back. The numbers were wrong. It was going to get there too soon, before she should fire. She'd have to fire too soon. Shiva would not be in position, not be at the optimum point where they thought maximum deflection could happen.

The numbers were wrong, dead wrong.

Her finger reached for the button.

Microseconds.

Time stretched, slowed, became elastic. The glowing numbers changed, the luminous dot moved, the stars turned.

She had to act. Too soon was better than not at all. But wait until the last possible second. Play it safe. Better too soon than too late.

You are going to die.

Don't think about that. Everyone dies. Think about your job. Be a professional.

Microseconds.

Her finger stabbed toward the button.

Diego saw the missile explode. But it exploded in pieces, not in atomic detonation.

An asteroid. It had struck something, or something had struck it. It was traveling too fast, too recklessly. Something nature had put there aeons ago had taken it out.

Then the explosion came on the far side of Shiva.

The mountain shuddered, ripping Diego free from his protective perch. He was flung, unconscious and limp, into space.

Light.

A great wave of force cleaving through the dust, boiling the gases, twisting the rock.

But it plunged on.

Lisa was bleeding at the mouth. She didn't have time to figure out why Carl's missile had not reached her. She tried to swallow as much of the blood as possible, as the droplets were floating and sticking all over the inside of her helmet.

Air pressure: zero. She was hulled somewhere.

Shiva?

Her capsule had been knocked away and it took the navigation computer a moment to find the right stars and orient itself. Lisa's fingers moved stiffly across the console of the onboard computer.

Shiva had moved a fraction.

Slowed and moved. But ever so little!

Was it enough?

"JPL, JPL, this is *Omega One*, do you read me? Did we do it, repeat, did we do it? Confirm." We have nothing left, she thought. Confirm it, God damn it!

As she waited for the seconds to pass, before the computers and transmitters relayed her message, she had a brief flash: Diego.

No, don't think.

Do your job. Grieve later.

Answer, damn it.

Diego drifted, slowly turning, floating outward with the other objects ejected from the swarm. The vast comet-shaped swarm itself was pulling ahead of Shiva. Dust and rocks and minor asteroids caught up to it, coming in through the colorful tail of gases to strike the sunlit side, exploding into shards or scraping by, taking new paths. Other portions of the swarm sailed silently by, creating a turbulence in the dust, moving on, a vast shotgun blast from the beginning of time, heading straight for the home of man.

"Omega Two, *this is JPL, we read you three by three. The estimates are being made and we will have them for you in a moment. How are you, Lisa? This is Chuck Bradshaw. Over.*"

"I'm . . . I'm all right. I . . . I don't think the others made it. I've lost cabin pressure. Fuel is down to zip." I don't think I'm going to make it, she thought.

"Hang in there, Lisa. There's a ship coming out from Station One. Eddie Manx is in command. We estimate twelve hours until arrival, your area. Over."

What's the use? I'll be dead by then. There's not twelve hours worth of air left. Something plugged the aft tank and I didn't even notice. Maybe I should tell them not to bother.

No, wait. There could be others. *Omega Two*, maybe even . . . Diego.

"Anticipate arrival, JPL, and . . . thanks. *Omega One*, over."

"Can you give us a better status report, Lisa? We think that . . . wait a minute . . . Lisa! Here's the info! You did it, babe, you did it!"

A wave of nothingness went through Lisa.

Hollow, empty nothingness.

All that. All the effort and deaths and they were just even again.

"Congratulations, Lisa!" Lisa could hear yells and shouts, distant and filtered. *"The OAO, Boston, Palomar —they all agree! Shiva will not only miss Earth, it will almost certainly go into an orbit around us!"* There was more cheering and someone shouted something incomprehensible into the microphone. *"Far enough outside the orbit of the moon not to cause any serious dismay. A few moonquakes, they say, but we'll weather that. If we can take the Shiva swarm and live through it, we can live through anything!"*

Lisa felt small and cold and tired.

And lonely.

She hugged herself, her mind a ball of frozen splinters. And deep within, a tight screaming ball.

Diego . . .

"Lisa, it's spinning. And our long-time projections show us the orbit is stable. We've got a new moon! Lisa?"

She did not even turn her head to look out the port. Let it spin.

"The spin is along the long axis," the excited voice continued. *"That means we can use it! Lisa? You okay?"* The voice rattled on, but she could not concentrate on it. *"If we hollow out the interior we'll have a spinning cylinder. A space station, Lisa, as big as we'd ever want! The centrifugal force will be like a light gravity. We'll have more usable mass out there than a fleet of ships could lift in a lifetime!"* Lisa dimly heard what could have been laughter. Laughter seemed so strange, so distant and bizarre. It had been a long time since she had laughed. If she had ever laughed. *"We can cut a hole in the top to let in sunshine, stick solar cells all over it,*

grow crops, make our own air, even export *iron, righ*
down the gravity chute!"

Lisa nodded dumbly, distantly. A click. Another frequency. *"Lisa, I've got the President on the line."* There was a pause. *"Lisa? Omega One, come in, please."*

"Knowles, you mean?" She didn't feel in the mood for speeches. She remembered all the dumb stuff Nixon had said after the moon landing about it being the greatest day since Creation. But nobody had died back then. How much worse stuff would some politician gush out about Shiva? How much more media hype would there be? She sighed, suddenly weary and depressed.

"No, Reed, Gorman Reed. Knowles, ah, resigned. Listen . . . we're putting him through . . ."

Seconds passed. Lisa sat numbed, not thinking, staring at a patch that had oozed goop before fixing solid. The driblet looked like Baja a little. A faint nausea was slowly draining her face of color as the adrenaline seeped away.

"Colonel Bander? Hello."

She didn't answer. She heard Chuck Bradshaw's voice, a little faint. *"It takes several seconds for your voice to get there, sir, and hers to you, and ah, there's some computer augmentation of the signal."*

"I see. Well. Maybe you don't realize what you've done, Colonel Bander. That was a brilliant improvisation of yours. I've been thinking about this whole thing, about Shiva. I think you have done more than you imagine."

She felt a first stirring of interest, more to escape the pale boredom that had swallowed her than anything else. "Oh? Uh, what's that, Mister President?"

"Shiva is a vast mountain of iron and, I'm told, other valuable elements. Now they are all close to Earth. In orbit, where we can get at them. Near the orbital factories. New raw materials and a fantastic amount of them. Shiva itself can be hollowed out in the process of mining and made livable. Space colonies, Lisa—the real thing, with a potential for economic growth and self-sufficiency."

Lisa blinked, thinking, as the President went on. *"Shiva's metals will provide all the shielding we will need for cosmic rays, the high-energy protons, solar flares—the works. We won't have to bring the crews Earthside regularly to keep their exposure down. You've done*

*more than just to stop a terrible threat, you and the rest
of your group. You've given us a whole new way to
climb up, out of this well of gravity, to build a bridge to
the moon, then to the stars. And to stay.*"

"What . . . ?" She frowned. This guy, this unknown who
had been so eclipsed by Knowles for so long—how did
he think of that? Did he pick someone's brains? No,
there hadn't been time. Maybe he's right. Goddamn,
maybe he's *right!*

Beep.

Lisa blinked. Beep, what beep?

She struggled up and looked around. A single spot appeared on the locater panel, the frequency that reported
the spacesuit emergency channel.

Beep.

Lisa unceremoniously shut off the channel to Earth,
flipping the switch that sent the locater disk to hunt and
seek. She prayed the whole thing was still operational,
that it was not a loose bit of something, of—

Beep.

Diego?

Carl?

Beep.

Lisa swung the telescope around, glanced at the coordinates, and put her eye down close. Her helmet prevented her from getting close enough. With irritation she
switched the image to the main screen.

Something white floated amid the stars.

Diego.

Beep.

Her heart pumped wildly. She brought *Omega One*
around, then edged it toward the white blob. The suit radios didn't work very well from within the ship to another
spacesuit outside, not without a repeater antenna, which
she no longer had.

Beep.

It had to be Diego.

Or Diego's body.

Beep.

Tink. Ping.

The space debris still bounced lazily off the capsule,
but there was less of it now. Most of the swarm had
moved on ahead, leaving the slowed and diverted Shiva
behind.

Beep.

She looked at the screen. It *looked* like Diego's suit. It *was* Diego's suit!

She maneuvered the ship with careful jets, then matched the velocity of Diego's body. They were drawing rapidly away from Shiva. She balanced the ship in relation to him at about thirty meters. Then she unharnessed herself, checked her compressed jets, and drifted out of the ship, trailing a double length of safety line.

The darkness receded, but there was still pain. He heard a voice, tinny and distant.

"Diego! Diego, darling!"

He turned his head and tried to focus. Someone was close, a great dark eye, a single eye with the blurred reflection of the sun. Floating close, touching him. He wondered why that person was not using the radio. Always use the radio. Proper procedure.

"Diego! It's me, Lisa!"

Her helmet touched his. They floated in the blackness. He was alive. He hurt, but he was alive and she was alive!

"Did we do it?" he asked hoarsely, clearing his throat and asking it again. "Did we do it?"

"We did it! But we've got to get back to the ship! You're almost out of air!"

She swung him around and his head began to clear a little. Without her aid he used the jets to move toward the distant capsule. He saw through the hatch that Nino Solari was dead in his seat. When he saw Lisa about to take the body out he stopped her, shaking his head.

Diego tapped Solari's air supply. Lisa leaned over and uncoupled his radio and replaced it with one from Solari's suit. "Great . . ." he sighed, over the new connection. He drifted, breathing deeply.

"*Not much of that left,*" Lisa said. "*A few hours' worth.*"

"Yeah," he frowned. "Not enough to pull us through."

"*No,*" she agreed.

They stared at each other in silence. He reached out and touched her and she put a gloved hand over his.

"Hey," he said suddenly. "Something I remembered from the emergency backups . . . the LOX."

"*The liquid oxygen—yes!*" Her eyes opened wide.

"There's an external tank, for maneuvering. You mean to—"

"Yeah. Any left?"

Lisa turned and thumbed her board over to inventory readout. *"Still reading pressure,"* she said. *"Must be a fair amount."*

"Okay. We boil it, then."

"How?"

"Torch. Laser on wide scan, if we have to. Boil it off and bottle it and breathe it."

Lisa nodded slowly as she thought it out. *"I think we can do it. Risky, maybe, with the pressure that high. Have to be certain the couplings will take the pressure surges when we boil it."*

He smiled at her. "We can manage that."

She returned his smile. *"Of course we can. I'll start—"*

"No. Let's rest. We've got time."

"How are you feeling?" she asked.

"Pretty good . . . for a dead man."

An expression of sadness crossed her face. *"Carl?"*

Diego squinted off into space. Shiva turned in the distance, a vast mottled face spinning beneath a chorus of stars. "He bought it, for sure. He was out there when the missiles went off. I . . . I saw him launch one at you, his last one."

She nodded.

"A dumb bastard," Diego said simply. "But he was brave. He was brave right to the end. Shows you how much bravery is worth. He believed . . . too hard."

They sat in silence for a moment.

"They say Shiva's going into orbit," Lisa murmured.

"Goddamn," Diego said admiringly.

"Let me get an update." She thumbed on the channel switch.

"—ing Omega One. This is President Reed. Over."

"Reading you, sir," she said. *"I've got Colonel Calderon."*

She glanced at Diego and they smiled crookedly, waiting for the transmission.

"What? My God, that's good. We'd . . . we'd written him off."

"So had I." Their eyes met, quietly.

"He's all right? Tell him I've decided on a job for the

two of you—running Shiva Station. We'll turn the two of you into administrators . . . but flying ones."

Diego frowned at Lisa. "He's going to push for a Shiva colony? Really?"

She nodded and quickly told him about Reed's earlier comments.

"How come he knows so much about the space program?" Diego asked. "Knowles only knew enough not to trip over his tongue at a press conference."

She shrugged. *"A closet spacenik."*

"Yeah, now I remember. He was head of the appropriations committee for the Mars flights when he was in the Senate. But look, he's off his ass. It'll take ten years to get back out here, minimum."

"He'll realize that, once he calms down. But at least he's headed in the right direction."

"We'll see, won't we? With the jet tanks I think we'll have just enough air to last until Eddie Manx gets here. It's going to be close, though."

"Time to think about that flying desk job," Lisa smiled.

Diego snorted and made a face. He thumbed his mike into the transmission line. "Mister President, this is Colonel Calderon. Sir, I respectfully decline any permanent desk job, thank you very much." He looked at Lisa, who shrugged in agreement.

He looked out the port at the shrouded mass of Shiva. Vaporizing gases still poured from it, streaming yellow, blue, and orange behind it. Now it was just a big gaudy chunk of iron, and they would tame it.

Where the hell was Eddie Manx? They had things to do.